Ovation for Wesley Stace's

Misfortune

A *San Francisco Chronicle* bestseller

Selected by the *Washington Post* as one of the "best novels of the season"

A top 20 Book Sense pick

A Borders "Original Voices" selection

A selection of the Barnes & Noble "Discover Great New Writers" program

"I am in complete admiration, but will I give it a quote? Over. My. Dead. Body. *Misfortune* is remarkable, complex, delicate, sophisticated, highly unusual, and I am ashamed to have a novel published in the same year. There will be no public acknowledgment of my admiration except for this, which — if anybody sees — I will deny writing. I am now going to hide my galley of *Misfortune* in a place that no one will ever find it."
— Bret Easton Ellis

"A delicious tour de force studded with punning twists, turnarounds, and questions of identity. . . . Stace paints a London underbelly that's as poverty-stricken as any in Dickens but with an unflinching contemporary explicitness, a seaminess that the real Victorian would never have approached."
— Clea Simon, *Boston Phoenix*

"*Misfortune* breaks the postmodern bonds of self-consciously sparse prose and frees the reader to revel like Rose in a bountiful garden of delight: reading so rich and unbridled that the story grabs us. At last, an out-of-the-box, truly original storyteller promises to soar above the literary horizon, all because he wrote the kind of book he liked reading."

— Skye K. Moody, *Seattle Times*

"Readers starved for a good old-fashioned novel — with a hint of kink — will gleefully devour *Misfortune,* the ribald, rollicking tale of a boy raised as a girl. . . . Both in song and in print, Stace is a master of wordplay — nearly every page of *Misfortune* seems to contain some sly wink at the attentive reader. . . . A second read seems almost imperative to absorb all (or most) of the novel's nuances — the first time around you're busy just enjoying the ride."

— *New York Post*

"Impressive. . . . I read *Misfortune* with great excitement, astonished by its verve and sense of literary history."

— Rick Moody in the *Milwaukee Journal Sentinel*

"Stace uncorks a ripping transsexual romp set in Romantic-era England, and it reads like some inspired collaboration between Charles Dickens and Spanish filmmaker Pedro Almodovar: full of orphans, decadence, flouncy skirts, greed, deception, amnesia, incest, murder, religious and social intolerance, ballads, books, letters, wild farce, and all manner of meditation on sexual identity. It calls to mind another regal androgyne, Virginia Woolf's *Orlando,* though not as literary or as tiresome. Rose Old, a.k.a. Miss Fortune, is just the kind of narrator an old-fashioned yarn needs: one who makes you suspend disbelief not just willingly but with great enthusiasm."

— Rodney Welch, *Washington Post*

"Sparkling . . . loopily Dickensian . . . poignantly and mordantly funny. . . . Stace has written a very jolly picaresque. . . . *Misfortune* augurs a most auspicious debut."
— Alexis Soloski, *Village Voice*

"There is something musical, almost symphonic, about the sweep of Stace's novel, its single-minded pursuit of themes through sections strongly distinct in mood and approach."
— Colin Greenland, *Guardian*

"A gloriously funny, lovingly detailed debut novel. . . . *Misfortune* is also frequently dark and disturbing, full of nightmarish and breath-taking cinematic visions that sear into the memory. *Misfortune* is near perfect, a bold and memorable tale of buried secrets and haunting dreams, and a story that is never less than fantastically readable. Rose Old's triumph of self-discovery becomes the reader's own, and the novel is unquestionably a wondrous and creative achievement."
— Christopher Schobert, *Buffalo News*

"A rip-roaring, often hilarious, always original good yarn. *Misfortune* is a misnomer — for fans of great fiction, music's (temporary) loss is our great good luck."
— *Elle*

"Stace's writing is so casually virtuosic that it's breathtaking. . . . Writing like this is a guilty pleasure, but you never for one moment forget you are in a story being told by a stylist with a keen sense of the grotesque. Stace's pacing is dead-on."
— Monica Kendrick, *Chicago Reader*

"In its scope, ambition, and wealth of detail *Misfortune* is a remarkable debut from a promising new writer."
— *Daily Mail*

"Blend *Tristram Shandy* with *Hedwig and the Angry Inch* and you have something of the spirit of this spirited tale: a most promising debut."

— *Kirkus Reviews*

"A gloriously fat book. . . . One of those captivating period dramas that have huge resonances for the present day."

— Henry Sutton, *Daily Mirror*

"Ambitious, funny, and inventive. . . . If you've been waiting for one of those phonebook-size novels in which an English nobleman discovers an abandoned baby boy, raises it as a girl, and creates intrigues that lead to concealed identities, erotic high jinks, and endangered family fortunes, then your prayers are answered by *Misfortune.*"

— David Kirby, *Atlanta Journal-Constitution*

"Stace writes well, engineering some memorable set pieces and twists, and treading a careful line between whimsy and wry wit."

— Hephzibah Anderson, *Observer* (UK)

"It wasn't enough for Wesley Stace to be a successful musician and a devastatingly handsome guy; he had to go and write a novel as well. And it's not just any novel. Stace — aka folk singer John Wesley Harding — makes his fiction debut with a rollicking adventure told in classic bawdy-romance style."

— Becky Ohlsen, *Bookpage*

"For Stace, the question of Rose's gender is a starting point for a much larger coming-of-age story about society, wealth, class, and identity, with nods to Dickens and Thackeray."

— John Hogan, *Pages*

"A period page-turner."

— Laura C. Moser, *Newsday*

"Wesley Stace has reconciled his dual personae as soulful songwriter and bookish intellectual with a *Mansfield Park*–size novel. . . . Expertly constructed, with Dickensian plot twists and artful shifts in narrative voice, this ambitious work may see Wesley Stace eclipse John Wesley Harding."

— Edith Honan, *Tracks*

"A stunning novel."

— *Esquire* (UK)

"A delightfully diverting pastiche of a nineteenth-century melodrama . . . crinolinishly convoluted. Stace's attention to every detail is a delight, and he revels in the richly embroidered language of his period. . . . It's difficult not to skim along with it, even as you want to savor each linguistically filigreed contrivance."

— Helen Brown, *Daily Telegraph*

"This lengthy and involved tale makes for speedy reading. Best of all, Rose's original narrative voice is engaging from the get-go: smart, funny, observant, and even hip."

— *Publishers Weekly*

"I imagine Rose as Gwyneth Paltrow in *Shakespeare in Love,* rushing to meet her fiancé in a beautiful gown, still wearing her actor's mustache. . . . It's a lot of fun in a Gilbert & Sullivan way, and, yes, you will hear again of a boy, a baby, a ballad, and a dog."

— Susan Hall-Balduf, *Detroit Free Press*

"A whopping, whimsical romp involving cross-dressing, intrigue, incest, and murder. *Misfortune* presents a world as crazily Gothic as Gormenghast and as comedic as Thackeray's *The Rose and the Ring.*"

— Marianne Brace, *Independent on Sunday*

Misfortune

A Novel

Wesley Stace

BACK BAY BOOKS
Little, Brown and Company
New York Boston

Back Bay Books / Little, Brown and Company
Time Warner Book Group
1271 Avenue of the Americas, New York, NY 10020
Visit our Web site at www.twbookmark.com

Originally published in hardcover by Little, Brown and Company, April 2005
First Back Bay paperback edition, April 2006

The characters and events in this book are fictitious. Any similarity to real persons, living or dead, is coincidental and not intended by the author.

Library of Congress Cataloging-in-Publication Data
Stace, Wesley.
Misfortune : a novel / Wesley Stace. — 1st ed.
p. cm.
ISBN 0-316-83034-8 (hc) / 0-316-15448-2 (pb)
1. Eccentrics and eccentricities — Fiction. 2. Aristocracy (Social class) — Fiction. 3. Passing (Identity) — Fiction. 4. Gender identity — Fiction. 5. Sex role — Fiction. 6. Boys — Fiction. I. Title.

PR6119.T33M57 2004
823'.92 — dc22 2004002393

10 9 8 7 6 5 4 3 2 1

Q-MB

Book design by Marie Mundaca

Printed in the United States of America

For my mother and father

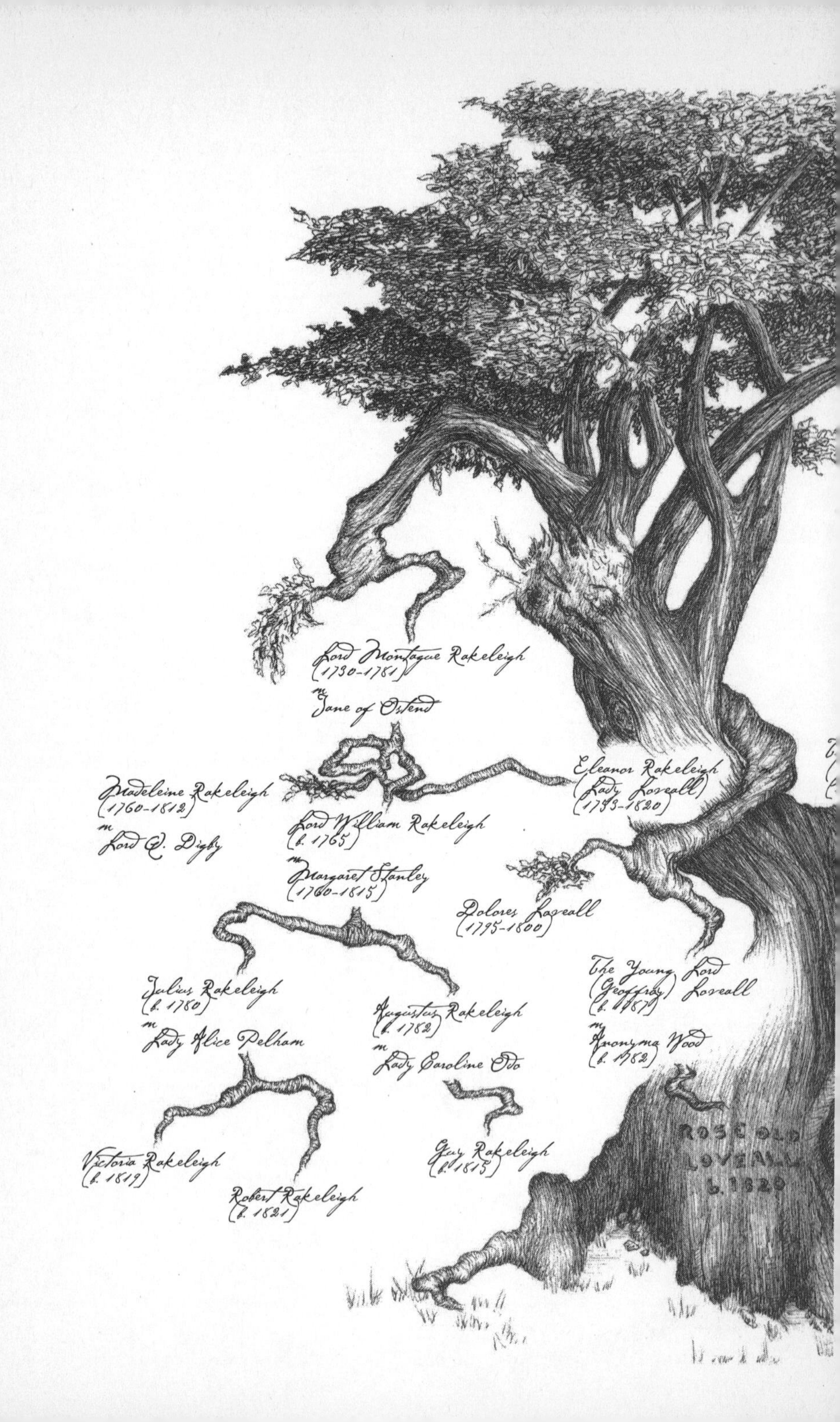
Lord Montague Rakeleigh
(1730-1781)
m
Jane of Ostend
Madeleine Rakeleigh
(1760-1812)
m
Lord C. Digby
Lord William Rakeleigh
(b. 1765)
m
Margaret Stanley
(1760-1815)
Eleanor Rakeleigh
(Lady Loveall)
(1753-1820)
Dolores Loveall
(1795-1800)
Julius Rakeleigh
(b. 1780)
m
Lady Alice Pelham
Augustus Rakeleigh
(b. 1782)
m
Lady Caroline Odo
The Young Lord
(Geoffroy) Loveall
(b. 1787)
m
Anonyma Wood
(b. 1782)
Victoria Rakeleigh
(b. 1819)
Robert Rakeleigh
(b. 1821)
Guy Rakeleigh
(b. 1815)
ROSE OLD
LOVEALL
b. 1820

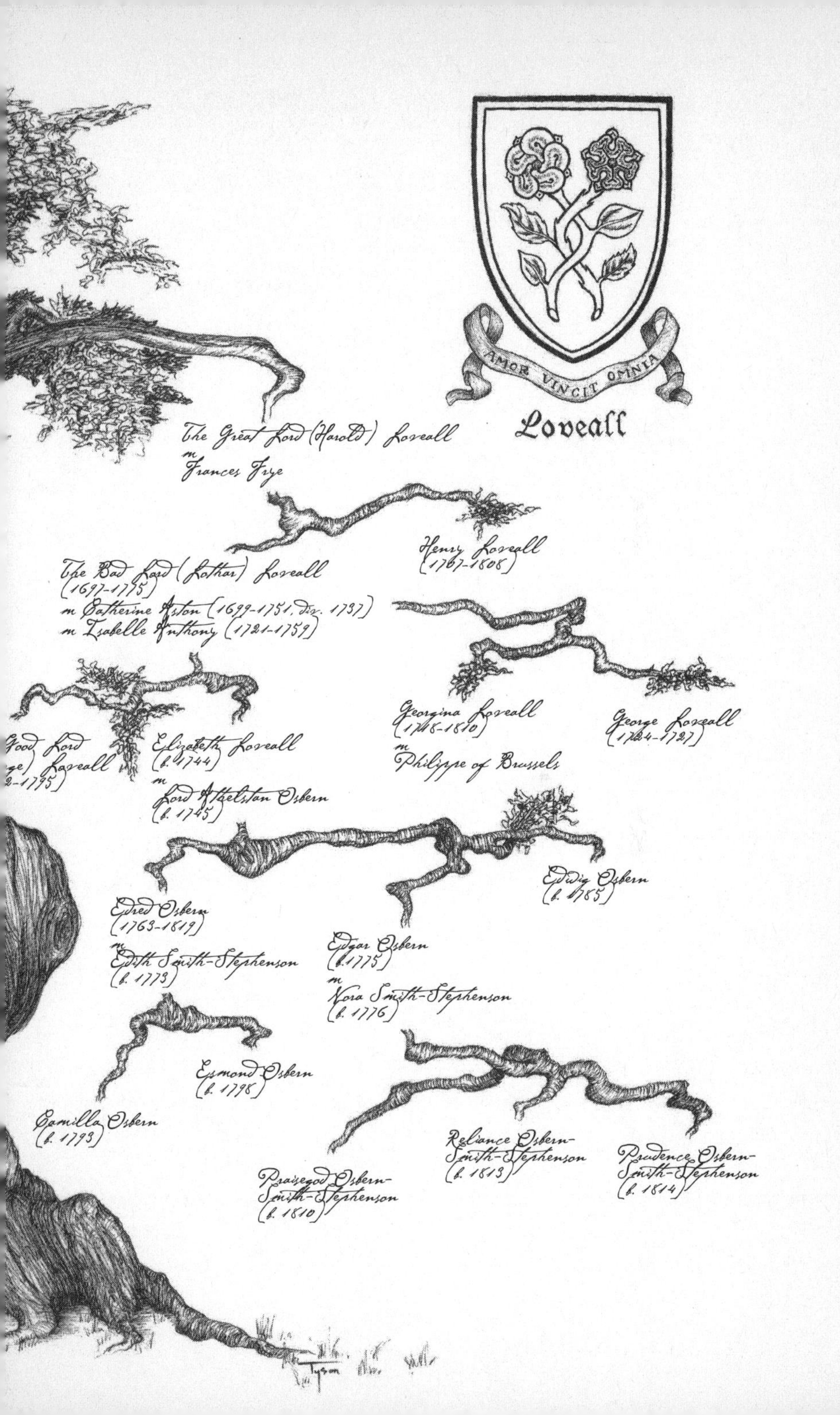
AMOR VINCIT OMNIA
Loveall
The Great Lord (Harold) Loveall
m
Frances Frye
Henry Loveall
(1767-1808)
The Bad Lord (Lothar) Loveall
(1697-1775)
m Catherine Aston (1699-1751, div. 1737)
m Isabelle Anthony (1721-1759)
Georgina Loveall
(1748-1810)
m
Philippe of Brussels
George Loveall
(1724-1727)
Elizabeth Loveall
(b. 1744)
m
Lord Athelstan Osbern
(b. 1745)
Edwig Osbern
(b. 1785)
Edred Osbern
(1763-1819)
m
Edith Smith-Stephenson
(b. 1773)
Edgar Osbern
(b. 1775)
m
Nora Smith-Stephenson
(b. 1776)
Esmond Osbern
(b. 1798)
Camilla Osbern
(b. 1793)
Reliance Osbern-Smith-Stephenson
(b. 1813)
Prudence Osbern-Smith-Stephenson
(b. 1814)
Praisegod Osbern-Smith-Stephenson
(b. 1810)
Tyson

I hope my Poeme is so lively writ,
That thou wilt turne halfe-mayd with reading it.

Beaumont: Paraphrase of Ovid's
"Salmacis and Hermaphroditus" (1602)

1

Anonymous

1

BY NOW, PHARAOH HAD REACHED his destination. A dirty young man of no more than fifteen years, he stood at the door of a crooked house in an alley, out of breath, gasping for air and wondering what to do. On one foot, he wore an oversized woman's boot he'd found while scavenging for nails at low tide. On the other was a tattered derby tied together with string that bit viciously into his instep, though he barely noticed. On his head flopped a ragged cloth, with little shape or apparent purpose, and in between his top and his toes, his costume comprised a patchwork of tears and mends in at least three materials from many more pieces of previously worn clothing.

Pharaoh was so relieved to have arrived in time that he had stopped his singing. Suddenly the world lost all clarity. His instructions: hear tip-off, run like lightning to Mother's, give the warning. . . . But the door was locked. The door was never locked, and he couldn't work out what to do. They hadn't told him. Pharaoh's concentration was a fragile thing and his mind was now too muddled to remember a tune. It was as though he'd never heard one before, and with no song to help him focus, all was lost. He stared down at the top edge of a silver twopenny bit that glinted in the mud, but couldn't even recognize it as something worth having.

Above him, out of his view, a woman was hanging a white dress on the railing of the balcony, from which hung a sign above the locked door: SHAVING AND BLEEDING AT A TOUCH. A placard for the adjacent NEW BAGNIO: MEN FOR SPORT swung close by, and from the bagnio's window a chubby female hand emerged to splash the contents of a chamber pot into the street.

For a moment, the laundress was unaware that there was anyone beneath. She began to sing as she worked, and this is what finally breathed life into Pharaoh again. It was one of the old songs, his favorite of the many she sang: the story of Lambkin the builder who tortures Lord Murray's family when his note is refused. The purity of Annie's voice contrasted starkly with the words of her song and the street below:

> *" 'Where is the heir of this house?' said Lambkin:*
> *'Asleep in his cradle,' the false nurse said to him.*
> *And he pricked that baby all over with a pin,*
> *While the nurse held a basin for the blood to run in."*

She had sung it so many times as a lullaby that the horror of the story was somehow soothing. Pharaoh joined in, slowly remembered what he was about, and began to bang on the front door with all his might. She looked below and her singing trailed off.

"Are you looking up my skirt, Pharaoh?" she called down. "Lucky I'm not in it!"

But his mind was too full to answer and he shouted up at her: "Where's Mother? Mother!" He kept up his frantic banging.

"Stop it, Pharaoh! You'll have that door down!"

"Where's Mother Maynard?" he pleaded, close to tears and barely able to get the words out of his mouth. "Mother!"

"Mother is otherwise engaged at the moment," Annie hissed from above, with a quick glance around to see who could hear. "She cannot see anyone, Pharaoh, not even you." Then something dawned on her, crossing her face like a black cloud over the sun. "You're early. What are you doing here now anyway?"

"They're coming! They're coming!" His frantic look over his shoulder told her everything. Annie dropped the dress, which floated down toward the street, opening up as it did and swaying from side to side before it completed its gentle descent. She disappeared inside and Pharaoh listened to her progress as she ran downstairs.

"Mother!" Annie was shouting. "They're coming! They're coming!" There was a scream from within and the door was flung open. Pharaoh fell inwards on top of her.

"Good boy," she said as she pinched his cheek. "How far away?"

"Now!" he yelped.

"How many?"

"Two police and another man. And they mean business, Sailor said."

"Stay," she commanded, as you order a dog that understands only five words. Annie bolted the front door and ran into a back room. Pharaoh tried to follow but was stopped at the door, which was closed decisively in his face. He tried to catch his breath as he rested his forehead upon the frame. A cat sniffed suspiciously at one of the dishes of what appeared to be red milk that lay at the door. Two buckets stood nearby as if to catch rain dripping from the ceiling. Flies buzzed around, and the atmosphere was as thick as glue and damp with sweat.

"Tell Mother!" Pharaoh pleaded to no one, and slumped down on the floor, expecting the front door to open (or be pushed down) at any moment. He had played his part, he thought, and now it felt that all the life had been sucked out of him, that it was his blood in the dishes and buckets, his sweat in the air, and his mess on his shoes. There was no song left in his head. Pharaoh had run as though his life depended on it because he owed that life to Mother, and his loyalty was all he could give in return. She was his "mother," as she was everyone's, and he had no other. Pharaoh occupied a place far down the hierarchy of her house, but he was a vital member, and during his tenure as the tipper there had been no trouble, because what trouble there might have been had been easily averted. Today was the first great crisis, and Sailor's warning had come woefully late. Pharaoh knew what Mother did, that she helped girls, that she bled them, at a touch, and he knew that some of the bleeding was illegal, but above all he knew this: no one else must see. Even he never ventured into the back room.

The interior door opened and a skeletal hand reached through as from the coffin of a child's toy money-box. The noise from beyond was fearful, just as the churchman described the sounds of hell: the endless howling of souls in torment, damned in the lake of fire. He looked over, too dulled to move. The hand grabbed the dishes, slopping blood on the floor and dousing the cat, which mewled and ran off. The bucket was next to disappear. The boy began to mop up the blood with a rag, not knowing why or if it was required.

The screaming suddenly stopped. Pharaoh stood at the door, not breathing, not thinking, not singing.

"They must be 'ere by now. They must be," he whispered as the door to the annex opened. This time he found himself pulled through. The room was teeming with people, but he saw Mother and, looking around, he gulped. Blood. He was sick in the back of his mouth and he swallowed it down. There was a bed that had a canopy with burn marks up its visible side, and on a central table, a girl in a grimy white nightgown, a dark stain around her thighs and belly. A Passover cake, coated with treacle to mire flies, dangled from the ceiling. Everybody ran around him, but he stood as still as he could and looked down at the ground. Suddenly Annie stopped in front of him and handed him a package wrapped in black tarp and rags.

"Pharaoh, you take this. Put it under your jacket. It's poisonous, mind, so don't you look at it. Walk for three hours and then throw it on the rubbish or toss it in the river. If someone asks you what it is, you tell them it's none of their business and then run away. But don't look at it or touch it, it's poison."

Pharaoh didn't ask questions, because he wanted so badly to leave. He knew to do exactly what she said and he knew where he'd take it. If someone asked, which nobody would, he'd say it was his lunch. That made him laugh, but he didn't dare look up. He stared at the little bundle and then shoved it up inside his clothes, but this, too, made him laugh. He looked like Annie when she was pregnant. He was so nervous that everything seemed funny.

Mother looked down at the girl with the stain and said grimly, "She's gone." Annie turned back to Mother and then, remembering Pharaoh, looked around at him.

"Go! Now!" He turned to leave by the front door, but she grabbed him by the collar. He'd never before heard her in such a fury. "No! The other door. Over there!"

And Annie showed him a door he'd never seen before just beyond the bloody girl. As he went toward it, he tried not to look around or notice the gurgling from her body like water spitting from a loose pipe. He opened the door ("Go, and we don't want to see you till night!" snarled after him), and the outside world shone in its brightness. He looked up at the sky and exhaled, biting his lower lip until it hurt. He breathed in as though he had been submerged for the past ten minutes, drowning in thick paste, and as he did, he heard the front door banging and the cry: "In the name of the law and His Majesty King George!"

Pharaoh closed the back door behind him. He was out in time. And off he sauntered, catching his breath, the little actor. He was invisible when he wanted to be. He was fascinated to have found this new door in a house he thought he knew so well, but he didn't want to use it ever again. They'd kept him out of the back room for his own sake, he saw that now. He looked back for one last time to see a small red stream running from the bottom of the door into the drain. No wonder he didn't know about it. It wasn't important. It's my lunch, thank you very much. He'd got there first and he'd done what he was told. This was his lunch. And he'd get his supper, too, back at Mother's later.

He was looking forward to supper. Tonight there would be something good, without doubt.

As he walked, Pharaoh sang, always, his life a long song cycle of his own devising. He didn't always know whether he was singing aloud or not, nor was he particularly aware that he was singing at all: each morning he awoke with a song in his head, and each night he sang himself to sleep. He sang for want of singing and fear of silence. Sometimes when he wasn't moving, there was no song. Then his gaping face drained of character and, tongue lolling out of his mouth, he looked like a tired dog desperate for water.

From time to time he would abruptly start a new song, and the previous one was entirely forgotten, sometimes gone forever. He made them up as he walked along, mumbling rhymes, words tumbling over one another, sometimes refining into sense, sometimes remaining nonsense. His eyes wrote on his behalf from the world in front of him, and he filled in whatever he couldn't see with stock phrases from older favorites. He made up most of the melodies, too.

Sometimes the less he thought about the outside world the better, for the more he tried to understand it, the less he did. But he knew his job well, and his songs kept him calm — the ones he made up and the old ones that he embellished. They kept the world at bay and stopped real thoughts and worries from entering his head, even now.

As he headed down the back street behind Mother's, Pharaoh stood on tiptoe for a moment to peer between the roofs of the houses and catch a glimpse of his favorite clock, above St. Cuthbert's at Marblegate. The dial was beneath a small stone statue of a man with wings, an angel possibly, Pharaoh thought. This fat little being wanted nothing to do with time and flapped his arms in defiance, as though he were trying to escape but couldn't drag himself away. His feet were attached to a motto: *Sic Transit Gloria Mundi.* Annie had told him what this meant, but hers had been a markedly different translation from the vicar's during one of his lengthy sermons, and Pharaoh hadn't known which one of them to believe.

The hands on the clock were equally hard to interpret, and though Pharaoh knew that he had to let the larger of the two hands do something before he was to stop and turn back, that wasn't why he looked at clocks. That was just one of the many things that he *knew* but didn't really understand.

People he loved and trusted told him things that he knew were true (if only because of the source), and he often said he understood something when he didn't, even though he could repeat it with confidence. No, he looked at clocks because church clocks turn up six an hour in the city, and he knew that meant he would have to see eighteen before he turned around and went back again. This was something that he understood because he'd worked it out himself. It very rarely let him down and he was never late for anything. It meant that he spent a lot of his life waiting for other people, but these were among the most peaceful times, sitting on a wall, making up a song or trying to improve the older ones when he could remember them. He couldn't read and he could barely write his name, so there wasn't much more he could be doing as he waited, apart from singing. Sailor had taught him to tell the time by the sun and the length of his own shadow, but that would be of no use to him on this trip. The shadows were off with the sun somewhere far from the city. Today everything was gray.

Their part of town was a maze and Pharaoh had learned to use this to his advantage. As a linkboy, he knew practically every way to get everywhere, and though he hadn't known exactly where he was headed when he left Mother's, he knew where to avoid: wherever he was known and might be approached. He steered clear of the Lane and, of course, the Coffee House, which were both on his normal route. There was always the crowd of chaunters, and they'd be looking for the opportunity of some work as the afternoon wore on. So, at Resurrection Gate, he had left the main thoroughfares and ducked into the alleys of Little Dublin, where he could travel secretly. The backs of the houses seemed particularly dismal today, and he had kept his eyes to his feet as he shuffled along through the mud. He passed the stocks at Ash Square, on which someone had daubed the words "Christ Is Good" in paint, with, it had been explained to him, one of the arm-holes as the extra *O* in *God*. He started to sing:

> *"Christ is God*
> *But where's his body*
> *Remov-ed from yonder grave*
> *Christ is God*
> *Let's drink a toddy*
> *Every man will too be saved."*

He wasn't happy with "Let's drink a toddy," but it didn't stop him from refining the six lines until it was the only survivor. That took three clocks.

He was two hours away from Mother's. He hadn't stopped to eat or drink. The urgency of Annie's voice had stayed with him, hurrying him along, and he was taking the task of depositing the bundle very seriously. Six clocks to go.

He kept the small bundle tight under his shirt, covered by his coat. He saw no one he knew until a ballad seller of his acquaintance, named Bellman, stopped him on his way.

"Pharaoh! Pharaoh!" Bellman called.

Pharaoh hadn't known whether to stop or continue on as though he hadn't noticed. But while he had been weighing these options he had been looking directly at Bellman, and he realized that it would be ridiculous to do anything other than walk toward him. Bellman had known him for years, ever since Pharaoh's father, an operator at one of the Covent Garden gaming shops where he worked the faro tables, had been murdered for feeding information to the law. Then the newly orphaned boy had begun to work for Mother, and after that he had always been known either as Mother's Boy, or simply Pharaoh, for his father's profession. Bellman couldn't recall the father having any music in him.

Pharaoh felt the bundle underneath his overcoat. It was his lunch.

"What have you got there?" said Bellman as he beckoned him over.

"It's my lunch."

"Rather a *late* lunch, isn't it?" said the ballad man, hopping from one foot to the other to keep the warmth circulating. He had a stick to one side of him, somewhat taller than he, and from the top hung a few long sheets of paper. He kept the bottoms from trailing on the ground, holding them like the train of a lady's dress. Each song was a yard long, but they were sold three abreast, and his usual cry was "Three yards of song! Three yards a penny!"

"It's my dinner," said Pharaoh, turning to leave.

"Pharaoh! Don't go. Have you got anything for me?" He referred to himself as a balladeer, but the police knew him as a pinner-up and a nuisance. "Have you got any songs? I'm off to the printer and p'raps I can suggest another one to him like the last time."

"I heard that one about Mary Arnold, the Female Monster," replied Pharaoh, who wasn't really thinking about the songs but was remembering the two pennies he'd been given the last time he'd sung to Bellman.

It had happened by chance: Bellman was drinking with him one night when Pharaoh had started to sing. The song, a ghost story, unrolled in almost perfect rhyme, as though it were already written by the time he sang it. Bellman, used to the boy's aimless singing, thought at first it was some sort of popular novelty that he might crib and started scribbling in shorthand. But it was unknown to everyone Bellman mentioned it to — and nicely poetical, to boot. Bellman kept Pharaoh's tune, changed the words around somewhat to improve upon the whole, and made himself a tidy profit, from which he had bought the very sheets he was now attempting to sell, bestowing the pennies on the boy from his own pocket. The sheets cost him one pence a dozen, and for taking down just that one song, Bellman had been able to buy enough stock for three or four months.

Pharaoh liked Bellman because Bellman liked songs. Pharaoh loved all songs, but most especially ballads: he adored a lamentation, when the "soon-to-be no more" reflected upon his own guilt and succumbed to the urge to detail most minutely the horrors of his crimes and the devilish instruments with which these crimes were committed. Pharaoh had stood beneath the gallows with Bellman and set up stall with "The Lamentation of Trilby the Highwayman" even as Trilby was being hanged above them. Seconds after the deathly hush, the bolt was drawn and the first copy had gone.

"Don't give me yer Mary Arnold. We know all about her! What were you singing when you came along here?" Bellman asked. "I seen you. Was it something you made up?"

"I can't remember. I was singing about what I was doing." Pharaoh kicked his feet out of awkwardness.

"What were you doing?"

"I was singing."

"Oh, go on. I've got no time for you today. But if you think up another song like that other one, then you come and tell Bellman first and he'll go to the printers, see. They're going to print up that first one on a piece of paper just like this." It was getting dark and the ballad man was ready to give up for the day. He had sold no songs at all.

"With a picture?" asked Pharaoh with growing interest.

"Just like this one," said Bellman with a laugh, showing him an engraving of a man strangling a prostrate woman with a large length of string. "A good picture that'll *illustriate* the story. Go on, Pharaoh, give us another. You've got the knack, and it's no small gift."

"I have to go now."

"What's your business down beyond?" asked Bellman as he folded up the sheets and shoved them somewhere deep inside the cavernous depths of his coat and then telescoped the pole into a stick that he leaned upon.

"To the clock seven after this one," said Pharaoh, and he walked away, leaving Bellman scratching his head for lice.

By the twelfth clock, Pharaoh was far outside his normal patch: everything was as unfamiliar and unreadable to him as the tunes on the sheets. The clocks were unusually far apart and he now found himself in a place where he no longer had to be mindful of avoiding people, where he would be grateful to see anyone to avoid. It was getting dark and he held the bundle tight, tucked down the front of his trousers now, and he sang to cheer himself up.

He passed a tavern called The World's End. He knew because of the sign: a globe with flames spouting from its core, burning right through the earth, exploding from the surface into the atmosphere.

"When forth in my ramble, intending to gamble
To an alehouse I ambled most freely
In The World's End far from town, I did spend near a pound
Until I became fuddled most really."

To his left there was a derelict church tower with a clock face that had no hands on it at all. A marsh stretched out to his right beyond a bleached graveyard.

As the houses and the pubs dwindled to rubble and the nature on the outskirts of town ate its way back into the city, Pharaoh realized that it was later than he thought, that he had walked much farther than he had intended, lost in his mind's song. The moon cast shadows around him, and to his right he saw a mountain towering above him. There seemed to be no way around it, and no alternative but to climb up for a better view.

It was the end of his journey, the end of the line, where the city oozed what it had no more use for and couldn't burn. All the avenues of excrement and urine made their way here and Pharaoh knew the stench was what came after the smell of life, after the sweat and the bodies, the rooms and their contents. It was what happened when things were left to die, when there was no more hope. It reminded him of the back room at Mother's. And he knew this was where he would turn around. It was time to complete his task, to go home again.

The foulness was magnificent, an acrid bilious smell of waste, the sweet rottenness of which worked its way to the back of his mouth and made him salivate. As he climbed, he could barely make out the bags and sacks around him that were his floor, walls, and, when he slipped, his ceiling. But he could hear the crunching underneath (eggshells and glass, bones and old china) and he could hear the seagulls above, cawing insolently. He fell onto his face and found his nose pressed against a sediment of muck, as though the earth were lying on her back bleeding toward him, purging her illness. And finally he gave up, lay on his back, and looked up through the early-evening sky at the stars, the bright stars so far away that he was rarely able to see above the chimneys of the city.

He felt for the bundle under his shirt and laid it beneath his head as a pillow. He stared up at the expanse of the night sky, and the eye of the silver moon returned his gaze. No one would ever find him here. Above him he saw the belt and the twins, the plows big and small, and he ceased to notice the stink just for a moment and sang a song, an apostrophe to the stars and the moon. It was a lullaby for himself, for the city at night and for the dead among the rubbish.

> *"Oh stars in the night sky*
> *Look down on the me."*

His body was at rest for the first time since he had spoken to Sailor. Just as he was on the point of sleep, he felt the stars reach down for him and kiss him, wet and sticky, breathing on his face to keep it warm. He woke with a start to find a large dog licking his cheek. The dog, on a nighttime scavenge among the leftovers, thought he had discovered food, but then identified his find, more correctly, as a playmate. Pharaoh, after the initial shock at his tumble from the heavens, pulled the dog toward him and laughed as they wrestled together, the dog sneezing with excitement, blowing out a drizzle of snot over the boy's chin.

There was a bone cruelly tied to her tail with a piece of string. Pharaoh undid the knot and put the bone in the dog's mouth. She immediately dropped it on Pharaoh's chest. She was crouching before him with her front paws extended, begging for the bone to be thrown, so Pharaoh hurled it as far as he could from his supine position and the dog ran off somewhere into the black. Pharaoh could hear nothing more than an excited scrabbling, until the dog suddenly bounded up to his right with the bone between her teeth as though having it thrown again would be the most novel thing in the world.

Each determined to tire the other out. Finally they crashed down in a heap as the boy tried to prize the bone from the dog's mouth one last time, and they started to slide down through the rubbish. The dog yelped and Pharaoh, laughing, reached out to catch her, cutting his arm on a shard as he did. They landed at the bottom of the rubbish slide in a mess of limbs. The dog shook herself with dignity and proceeded to lick Pharaoh, who was easily tickled. He sung the dog a song through his laughter.

> "*A dog there was, I'll have it be known*
> *A pile of dust the place she called home*
> *As happy as a Queen'll be*
> *If Pharaoh throws this bone for she.*"

Pharaoh could see the glow of streetlamps in the city in the distance, and he knew that it was past time to head back to Mother's. The baggage had been underneath his head, but he had lost any idea of its whereabouts when their game of catch had caused them to stray from the spot. But he wasn't worried. It was poison, to be got rid of, and now it was another piece of rubbish in a whole world of rubbish.

The dog watched him as he walked off, and it seemed to Pharaoh that she wanted to follow him away from the dustheap but couldn't allow herself to leave. Pharaoh said good-bye and heard the dog growl at him without anger.

"I'll take you with me," Pharaoh imagined himself saying, and the dog answering: "I can't come. I live here. I have work to do." Neither of them mentioned the little bundle of poison.

The journey home already seemed shorter, but he couldn't stop thinking about his new companion and, despite his hunger, turned back, thinking that he could persuade the dog to come, and, more unlikely, persuade Mother to take her in. He would at least finish his song about the dog that guarded the rubbish for a living.

To his surprise, he saw that the dog had made her way down the pile to the side of the road. She had somehow found the bundle, which she was licking with her long, slobbering tongue. Pharaoh watched with pleasure until a horrible thought struck him.

"Poison!"

His heart started to beat faster and things became obscure. He had to stop the dog, this he knew, but just as he was on the point of shouting and running over, a coach came up behind him and he ducked down. Lost in panic, he hadn't noticed until it was upon him, and he wondered at its incongruous splendor as it trundled by. The dog, which seemed none the worse for licking the bundle, also heard the carriage and picked up the parcel in her mouth protectively. The coach made its cautious way down the uneven road until it got to the dustheap, where it abruptly stopped. Pharaoh kept his head as low as he could.

The moon glinted on the shining side of the coach, and one of the two men in the driver's seat, after consultation with the passenger, finally dismounted. Pharaoh watched as the man, to the great curiosity of the driver, who got down and patted his horses, approached the dog. Conceivably it was their dog and they wanted her to come home? No — the man put out his hand and carefully exchanged the bundle for what was probably food, though Pharaoh couldn't quite see. He strained his neck as he tried to gain a firmer foothold in the subsiding matter beneath. The man lifted up the package, started to unwrap it, and, from what Pharaoh could make out and to his astonishment, slapped it. There was a cry. A cry? The dog? No, the dog growled, and in the boy's mind, everything started to happen very quickly.

A baby? A poisonous baby? This was bad. Should he let them know, or should he run? His first loyalty was always to Mother, but he soon ceased to be able to make sense of anything and closed his eyes to try and focus his thoughts. He started to sing,

> *"And into that carriage they handed the babe*
> *And may nobody call me a liar,"*

but it did him no good. There was shouting in incomprehensible accents, and Pharaoh, knowing only that he must not be seen, turned and slid down in the opposite direction as quietly as he could, determined to keep going even if he was spotted. This was nothing to do with him anymore.

As he left, he heard two quick flicks of the whip and the distant snort of horses before the carriage went on its way. Pharaoh started to sing something soothing, anything, but his mind kept trying to make sense of what he had seen. A baby? It could hardly matter. The bundle was gone. It was important only that he get as far away from the dustheap as he could. But what would Mother say? He knew too much, but what did he know? He didn't even want to know. A song would help him. Best not to tell her, all the same. Pharaoh sang quietly to himself, and before long, his heart beating slower and his feet dragging, he was once more lost in song.

He kept to the wider roads, but there were only a few people around and no one noticed him. There were men, the kind who come out only at night like cats, parading beneath the streetlights, spitting and sneezing in turn, bristling in silhouette; and women, moths gathering around the gaslight. They were interested only in each other. And there was the sound of the night around them, a steady quavering monotone. He missed his new friend.

As he got nearer home, he had the impression that someone was following him. Perhaps it was just his fancy, but he took a couple of odd turns when he found himself back in the refuge of the familiar maze. Here, he could lose anyone.

To his surprise, he ran into a man coming around a corner, a well-dressed gent in a dark brown cape who seemed, by his clothes and bearing, too rich for roaming the streets on his own at night. Pharaoh went one way to get past him and, by chance, the man did the same. Pharaoh moved again and the man anticipated him. They were at an odd stalemate, and Pharaoh's only option, his teeth chattering while he was not moving, was to wait for the man to make his move. Pharaoh held his patched clothes together with one hand as the man stared at him. The boy snapped at the man, but the man unexpectedly reached out his hand and put it on his shoulder: to detain him or to give him money. Pharaoh decided it was the former, turned around in an instant, and ran off, twisting out of his ragged jacket as he did so. In his hurry, it was left in the man's hand. He didn't turn around as he ran off back toward his patch. No one likes a busybody, and as Mother had told him many times: "Nobody wants to help."

2

FROM THE RELATIVE SAFETY of his carriage, Lord Loveall pulled the curtain aside and peered into the wilderness. He had no curiosity about his surroundings, but he knew to keep half an eye on the passing world to soothe the queasiness induced by the tottering of his carriage. Though this relieved one kind of nausea, it exacerbated another: it reminded him how far he was from home, and this very distance made the desolation around him more threatening, even from the opulent womb of the state chariot.

Despite his thirty-three years, Geoffroy Loveall looked like a small child peeking through the opening of a laundry basket during a game of hide-and-seek. He held a filter of lilac silk to his nose and mouth, and this hid a thin, perfectly elegant mustache. The kerchief was one small element in a complex and time-honored routine meant to improve, by tiny degrees, his infrequent trips to the city — the soft comfort of the silk on his lips, salts to revive him at a moment's notice, a flask of sherry strapped firmly in a recess beneath the window. His hand was poised constantly by the sash — one pull would get him the attention of his man above.

The vehicle was ideally suited for a gentle turn around the park on a Sunday afternoon, and it groaned reluctantly through the no-man's-land at the very edge of civilization. As it made its way back to the country seat of its owner, Loveall anticipated with delight his return to the warm reassurance of Love Hall.

"His lordship is invisible," his gentleman Hood had been known to inform the understaff: no one should notice him at all. Within the walls of Love Hall, Lord Loveall could command this kind of respect. But Hood could not stage-manage the rest of the country or direct its players in acceptable etiquette, so anybody was free to gaze upon his master (his odd dress, his otherworldly manners) as long and as insolently as he pleased. These rare excursions were almost too much for Loveall: the distance, the dark, the sporadic movement of the carriage as it lurched to and fro, the ominous cries of creatures unknown — all combined to terrify. The alternative, however, was a night away from home, and that was worse, far worse. How would Dolores manage without him?

The slough of despond spread out all around, unmanageable, unstoppable. Who knew where it ended? When did the houses begin again? Where were the people and their servants?

It was not the first time that Geoffroy had journeyed to the city in order to arrange his mother's papers before the final end was upon her. Lady Loveall's death had been monotonously close for the past three years, and as she was confined to her bed, her sole remaining pleasure seemed to be to keep her heir occupied with tedious tasks. Though dull in themselves, these tasks represented terrifying labors of love to her son, and she knew it. In her opinion, he wasn't yet fit for the world at large. She was trying to break him in gently before she died.

The master in chancery, in chambers bisected by shafts of light where the dust from the books played around him like tiny insects, had scratched his cheek beards continuously for two hours as he scrutinized the documents in question. Loveall sat in a corner, an orange-silk-gloved finger to his mouth in a perpetual gesture of surprise, communicating only through his man, Hood. It was agreed, yet again, that there was no cause for concern: Loveall had long since inherited and there was no doubt to whom the dowager was leaving her possessions. There were no rival claims. It was when his lordship himself died, if he died without issue — Merciful God preserve him for a long and happy life — that such problems would begin.

The carriage lurched suddenly to the right and Loveall coughed like a discomfited cat trying to rid itself of a hair ball. On a small traveling table in front of him, his man had laid out some morsels of food, which bobbed up and down with every seasickening heave. He picked at the cheddar, first smelling it and then taking but the smallest mouthfuls, biting only between his two front teeth.

Nausea overpowered him once more. He lifted the curtain again, to be confronted by a dirty tavern — he knew what it was but could barely bring himself to imagine what went on inside. Beyond, he was appalled to see a mountain of rubbish. The moon shone down on the mass of waste and broken glass, which glinted its reflection. At the foot of the heap, Loveall saw a stray dog pawing at something vigorously. She was holding a bundle between her jaws, and either it was a trick of the moonlight or her mouthful seemed to be . . . With unusual curiosity, Loveall looked closer.

"Hood!"

He pulled the sash and then, in case this wasn't quite sufficient, rapped a silver cane on the ceiling of the carriage. The curtain on the door whipped up with a twang of the drawstring.

"Yes, sir?" Hood had not expected this sudden summons but was at his master's side within seconds. He looked down at Loveall through the window, his jowls dripping like wax from a candle.

"Stop if you will," said Loveall, his soft murmur making it a legato sigh. "That dog . . . in its mouth?" And, as though it were an everyday occurrence, Hood issued an order and, when the carriage stopped, readied himself, dismounted, and approached the dog. She growled, but Hood, picking his way through the rubbish, had come prepared. He took a lamb chop from his pocket, a lamb chop flavored with rosemary that had been his treat for the cold journey home, and very carefully tried to exchange it for the package. It was a short and successful negotiation. The dog went for the chop, and Hood had the parcel in his hands.

He felt the dirty rags moving, but he was distracted by a rustling off in the distance as he began the careful business of unwrapping. He looked up but could see no one except his baffled coachman. Returning his attention to the task that he had continued unconsciously, he found the contents already on display, swaddled in soiled rags. Hood stood in a moment's astonished silence and then yelled over his shoulder:

"Water, Phillip! Get water . . . and blankets!"

With his right hand, he held the warm mess of blood, fluid, and saliva as a black oily stain started to spread across his pale yellow waistcoat, and with his left, not knowing what else to do and wondering whether the bundle was breathing, he smacked it. The baby started to cry.

Loveall opened the door to the carriage. It was the first time he had ever done this for himself.

The Young Lord had rarely known the elation he felt three hours later, coming over the crest of High Hill and looking down on Love Hall. He habitually felt great relief at the sight of his home, but for once this first glimpse was truly marvelous to its heir. The estate spread before him like a picnic, and the brook shone silver beneath the generous moon.

By day, this was not the house's finest aspect. The surprise view made a large crushed insect of Love Hall. The central house was the body with its armored exoskeleton of red brick. From this grew the head, the gray gravel courtyard between the front door and the mouth-shaped portico, with stables and chapel the beady eyes perfectly placed on each side. The driveway from the portico to the

Gatehouse Lodge, which marked the front edge of the estate, was lined with elms, each row a feeler sprouting from the insect's greedy chops. Behind the body, the Great Avenue was its long, once lethal, sting, and the pathways beaten through the garden were the bug's recently scurrying legs, contorted by the shoe that had just now killed it.

But in the semidarkness, it looked more like a dog nestled in a pillow, quietly and soundly asleep.

He looked down at the baby.

She was a tiny red ball, now wrapped in Hood's stained waistcoat for warmth (and to preclude any further messing of the interior of the carriage) and enthroned on the most comfortable of the cushions. Not for the first time on the journey, she started to cry. Loveall offered her the silk of the finger of his glove, but she continued and, in fact, improved her wail considerably. Loveall took off his glove and dangled it over the baby's face tentatively, but she would not be distracted. He had no idea what to do, so, carefully brushing any dust from the floor of the carriage, he got on his knees and considered the baby at eye level. He hushed her gingerly as though her toothless mouth might bite. The nearer he got, the less the baby cried, and when his face was almost resting upon hers, she was nearly quiet. Some fine powder of the kind that Loveall always wore had dusted the baby's cheek. Loveall saw it and, not wanting to soil his handkerchief, licked the powder off the baby, who immediately stopped crying and made an expression that Geoffroy interpreted as a smile. He licked again, more recreationally this time, and the baby started to gurgle.

"Naughty little angel!" said Loveall, as he had used to call Dolores. He scooped up the baby and held her in her bundle, their faces touching. Her face began to cloud over until Loveall touched the tip of her nose with his tongue and the sun shone through again. Loveall hugged the bundle to his face, lost in thought. Even the lights in the various windows of the Hall gave him a feeling of security, and as he thought of his mother, he did not shiver.

* * *

Love Hall, as it had been known for more than two centuries (in preference to the official name of Playfield House), had been in premourning for three long years. Lady Loveall had passed directly from mourning her husband (black for a year, gray for two, light grays for two more) to mourning her daughter, her estranged sister, and then finally, when she had run out of others, herself. In preparation for the demise of the great matriarch, and at her urging, the interior of the house had been draped in black. Loud noise was forbidden. All letters that emanated from the house were in black-edged envelopes, sealed with jet wax. Love Hall was a dark world of crepe and bombazine imported monthly from Holland. The whole house shone darkly and rustled autumnally.

And so it had for twelve long seasons as Lady Loveall lay abed, supposedly near death but surprising doctors and clergy alike with her dogged defiance. As a symbol of her daily struggle, two black terriers, Maxwell and Randal, were always at her bedside, hunched together like a Cerberus puppy, ready for Death's grim approach.

"I will not die," his mother had told Geoffroy repeatedly (and evidently this was a threat rather than a reassurance), "until I see an heir."

Visits from distant relatives had become suspiciously more regular during the premourning years. Once a year was only to be expected, but twice was more than coincidence, and three times clearly cause for concern. If Geoffroy died childless, the house and fortune would pass to the family of the Young Lord's aunt Elizabeth, the Osberns. His mother had spent years fighting against this eventuality, for though she hated all her late husband's family, she hated this woman most.

In her livelier days, when her body had allowed, Lady Loveall had created numerous liaisons for her son with young ladies of breeding. In quiet defiance of her wishes, Geoffroy adopted a policy of laissez-faire, demonstrating his lack of engagement either with polite disdain or by ignoring the young lady in question entirely, until even the greedy potential father-in-law was forced, on his daughter's behalf, to rethink his stratagem. This had been acceptable to Lady Loveall on only one occasion, when the unloved and greedy *distants* (her epithet of choice) had proffered their own granddaughter, the sallow Camilla. Geoffroy had left her marooned in the Entertainments Room for two and a half hours after he had gone "to get a doll." Some silently suspected that he might not be interested in women at all, that he was a bit of a Lady Skimmington. But the truth about Lord Loveall was a simpler complication: he had time for no one but his sister.

Geoffroy was the only member of the house in any way exempt from the masque of death, which had borne in him a need for color and gaiety, and although, in truth, his constitution was technically somewhat weaker than his dying mother's, he would almost certainly outlive her. As the years went by, he saw fewer people except the servants (who numbered around 250, including the denizens of the laundry, the location of which was unknown to him). His only allies were Hood, his manservant and constant companion, and Anonyma Wood, his sister's governess, who had lately been involved in the renovation of the Octagonal Library. He respected them both and talked intimately to neither.

Most of his time was spent in the library, happy in the presence of Anonyma without feeling the need to break their silence, and in the Doll's House, the nursery on the top floor of Love Hall, which was supposedly haunted. There he conferred with his own ghosts and ignored the sadness of his present existence. In the real world, it was he who was the ghost and his mother the medium, dispatching him to haunt her lawyer at will.

His mother's power over him was absolute, and he obeyed her without question. The reason for this, beyond the simple reflex of filial duty, was simple: his devotion to his sister.

Dolores had been born in 1795 when his current lordship was a typically feisty, noisy, and nosy seven-year-old. Their father, the Good

Lord George Loveall, died at the birth: he exclaimed with surprise at the means of her arrival into the world (as though he had previously known nothing about it), and immediately fell onto his back, choking. Geoffroy became the Young Lord Loveall.

His mother did not care for children, least of all her own. She didn't like to touch them under any circumstances, and both her issue had arrived prematurely, perhaps because she wanted them inside her body even less. Her considered opinion was that these unfinished creatures would grow into human beings eventually. To her, childhood was the tiresome stage of life after which conversation is possible (though, in truth, Lady Loveall did not need the companionship of a conversationalist as much as she needed a mute to admire her monologues).

Bereft of any parental influence, the small Lady Dolores Loveall became her brother's raison d'être. She was his favorite plaything and his preferred companion, he her sword, shield, and clown. He lavished his every waking second upon her and taught her everything he knew. This perfectly suited his mother, whose least favorite child was the one that was underfoot. While his protectors went about the business of mourning the Good Lord Loveall and managing the estate, the Young Lord fell in love with his sister.

By the time he was eleven he could imagine no other person sharing his life with him. All he wanted was his sister's happiness that she might thrive and grow in his care. He was still no more than a boy, but he alone knew what was best for her and he was ready to dedicate all his energy to chaperoning her through life. His parents' snobbery had determined that he had never been allowed to play with the local children, though he was used to seeing the servants' offspring disappearing messily around corners. Now he had no other interest than to play with his sister, whereas just a few years before he had been desperate to join in.

He was her guide around Love Hall, delighted to demonstrate the house's many tricks, its secret tunnels, trapdoors, and hiding holes. He ran with her through the Long Gallery, laughing and kicking a ball along the polished floors, then immediately initiated a game of hide-and-seek, for which a better house was scarcely imaginable. And when they tired of the interior, though you could get lost without a detailed map and a ball of string, they would explore the grounds of the estate. Their greatest love was to climb Old Rubberguts, the oldest and tallest tree on the land (it was said a king had once hidden there), and, lying back among the highest branches they could reach, look up at the clouds. Then they would go back to Dolores's playroom in the east tower and play with her dollhouse, a scale model of Love Hall made for the most recent female addition to the line by Hans Hemmen himself.

Geoffroy's protection of Dolores failed when she was five. He never knew what happened in the blur of seconds as she clutched at him momentarily, trying to wrest his attention from the shape-shifting clouds. He remembered only looking down at her lifeless body from the branch of the tree where she had just been sitting beside him. From the distance of his bird's-eye view, she seemed sprawled rather casually in her white dress; it was fortunate that he could see no closer. He was unable to move or turn his head away, and as he stared, eyes fixed, he waited for her to be transformed, to change away from death like one of the characters in the governess's Latin book *Metamorphoses*. At first, he expected her to become a bird, like Daedalion, whom Dolores always called Dandelion, but then he realized that it was too late, that this change would have already taken place, that she would have beaten the air beneath her new wings as she fell and, instead of landing, soared away, her short scream becoming her new caw. Then he thought she might possibly become a tree, to grow next to Old Rubberguts, like Dryope. Or a rock, some stone steps, a flower. He didn't stop staring, and waiting, but the time for change had gone. Nothing moved. She was dead. This was how they were found.

Geoffroy had spent the rest of his life recovering, unable to understand that he wasn't to blame. He rarely felt the urge to venture outside. The death of Dolores, the want of her hand to hold, sent him inside the house and further, inside himself. At his insistence, her possessions, including the now haunted dollhouse, remained untouched.

Now, old despite his thirty-three years, he still spoke to his sister in the dollhouse. When he needed her help — *assisterance,* he called it — he sat in front of the dollhouse and gently unclasped the front. He peered inside, worrying each time that she would no longer be there. Then she appeared. He realized that had she lived, their attachment would have faded, but with her death, and almost as fatally for him, the two of them could remain as close as the day she died. His feelings had been spent on his sister, so it mattered not to him whether his mother lived or died, only that she be happy with the way he attended upon her. One day she would depart and he could paint over the black, tear down the hangings, and let the house breathe again. His own lifelong mourning for Dolores was so personal that he would have considered it insulting if anybody else were to join in. It was his private passion and he found group mummery, of the kind to which Love Hall was in thrall, vulgar. His mourning was entire and perfect without display: the less others knew, the better. He would restore the house to the glory of colorful days past. It would be his final tribute to his sister. And now he had a way.

The carriage turned the final corner and Geoffroy looked out as they drove through the Gatehouse Lodge. A masterpiece of seventeenth-century granite, with two turrets above a crenellated parapet (from which the inhabitants could throw tar on imaginary invaders), the three-story lodge was built around the great iron gate, upon which was wrought the Loveall coat of arms: the rose and the briar entwined.

"How can the Loveall have a coat of *arms?*" Geoffroy's father, the Good Lord Loveall had quipped on many occasions. He was a man who enjoyed any opportunity to use the correct plural form of their family name. The official explanation for this anomaly was that the name had once been Lavelle, and in French, "the Lavelles" would always be said "les Lavelle." However, in less ancient history, *lovealls* had become city slang for ladies of easy virtue, and the family referred to themselves ever after in the more respectable collective singular.

Love Hall and estate stretched before its Young Lord. In the moonlight, he saw smoke curling from three chimneys. The lawns around him were filled with fir, oak, and cedar, and he breathed them all in as if for the first time. He disliked the morbid cries of the herons, but today, even in the murk, they seemed a happy greeting.

The house itself, still the length of the drive away, was a building of many periods, a glory of mellow red brick to which generations of the family had added. Civil wars and revolutions had come and gone, monasteries had been dissolved and inaugurated, yet the Hall itself remained and improved. The Loveall and their architects believed that nothing was as noble as the Gothic, which, in reverence, they spelled *Gothick*. The scourge of neoclassicism had not been allowed to afflict the house, and Geoffroy loved the dark medieval woodwork, the ornate knots in every door; he loved the oak hammer-beam roof of the Long Gallery, which looked like the inside of a boat, and the dark-stain staircases, with the rose and the briar carved upon every newel.

Loveall recalled a previous Lord Loveall and the song that bore his name, and he sang it softly to the baby. This ancestor had deferred his marriage for seven years while he went traveling. He returned after only twelve months, but as he rode home, he heard the church bells ringing, "for Nancy Bell who died for a discourteous squire." He died too of grief, as he gazed on her corpse lying in its coffin, and was buried next to her. From her heart grew a red rose and from his heart a briar:

> *"They grew and grew to the church steeple*
> *Till they could grow no higher*
> *And there entwined in a true lover's knot*
> *For true lovers to admire."*

No one in the family doubted that this was an ancestor, particularly because the Loveall coat of arms featured the very same motif. It was a strange, unheraldic emblem, despite the official description of the rose in the Lex Pantophilensis as "gules, barbed and seeded proper," but the Young Lord had always felt a deep spiritual attachment to the family insignia and used the entwined flowers, emblazoned on the very doors of the carriage in which he rode, as his signature. Others could keep their escutcheons of pretense, their water budgets and their compony counter-componies, he was happy with this simple sign and the motto beneath: *Amor Vincit Omnia*. In Loveall's life, it had.

His carriage drove between the elms of the Main Driveway, and Loveall lifted up the baby to show her the Mausoleum that sat elegantly on the hill to the left. One of his more classical ancestors — he couldn't remember which — had had it in mind to re-create the Seven Wonders of the Ancient World around the grounds, but had been able to realize the project only as far as the initial wonder, the Mausoleum of Halicarnassus. It was fortunate that he started there, since the Loveall sorely needed somewhere to house their remains. This copy of the original was effortlessly majestic, with its twelve columns and eight-step pyramid, all carved in Portland stone, beneath a statue of Lord Harold Loveall displaying an elegant leg. The Young Lord was very fond of the building, partly because of his profound emotional link to some of its contents and partly because the original Mausoleum had been built by Artemisia to honor the memory of her beloved dead husband, Mausolus. He was also her brother.

The stone of the Mausoleum glinted pale green, and within its cool interior Lovealls bad, good, great, and perfect lay together, beneath the phrase *Mortui Non Victi*. Geoffroy, too, would lie there one day among the dead, the dust, and Dolores. He had thought of preserving her in honey, like Alexander the Great, but had decided against it: she was incorrupt and would never decay. There was no need for saltpeter or formaldehyde, both were unworthy of her, but her triple-sealed marble casket would keep all water away, as the lead and zinc lining would protect her from the air. She would have as much assistance from him in the afterlife as she had had alive. No metamorphosis had happened before, and none should now be permitted.

Horses and deer grazed in the grass on either side of the driveway. Loveall placed the baby in the deep cushions on the opposite seat, banged on the roof of the carriage with his cane, and asked Hood to tell the driver, whose name he didn't know, to stop. Loveall told Hood to call Cyclamen, and his man whistled. A large white horse cantered over to the carriage, and Loveall reached out to greet his favorite. Though no equestrian, Loveall encouraged riding in others, particularly women and particularly upon Cyclamen, who looked like a unicorn. This effect was especially enhanced by the prosthetic horn attached to her head, which, for some reason, she bore quite willingly.

As Cyclamen came near the carriage, Geoffroy leaned outside and unclasped a silver chain that hung from her neck. He had placed identical chains on his three favorite horses, each bearing a silver heart that held a miniature engraving of Dolores. His mother had pooh-poohed this decorative whim ("an exceedingly unnatural despoiling of nature"), but Geoffroy had always suspected that she was more worried about theft of the silver. (The family plate was kept under constant surveillance, even overnight, when a boy was locked into the Plate Room, where he made his bed.) However, among the locals, there was no temptation, for Loveall was extremely popular. Despite his relative invisibility in the parish calendar, he could be relied upon to appear, with great aplomb, at the annual games in which the May queens and their attendants played at barleybreaks for the whole town. He looked forward each year to the ritual laying of his hands on the parish sick to keep away plague for yet another year, perhaps because, so far, it had proved successful.

Cyclamen trotted off into the fields again, shaking her long mane nonchalantly, the horn wobbling slightly on her head. Loveall tied the chain and miniature around the baby's neck. Then he lifted the newborn child an inch out of the window so her barely open eyes could take in the entirety of the house. As well as presenting the baby to the Hall, he was presenting Love Hall to the baby. At that very moment, as if in welcome — or equally, in warning — there was a four-gun salute in honor of Geoffroy's safe passage. Such a greeting always heralded the return of the lord of the house, the only exception being when he was in the company of someone even grander (a member of royalty or an archbishop) who merited an even greater waste of ammunition. The baby screamed as the first guns exploded, and Loveall quickly bundled her back in and shut the window of the carriage.

Loveall realized that he did not know who let off the four-gun salute, or where from, or precisely why, or how long it had been going on. When his mother died, he promptly decided, it would be stopped. He would replace it with a six-trumpet salute, a melody of his own devising — something pretty and feminine. It would be played by the six men who marched the passages, sounding time upon their horns. Why waste those trumpeters on time?

He bent down and touched his nose gently to the baby's.

Lady Eleanor Loveall sat up in bed and awaited the arrival of her son. Her useless body had been positioned this way (after much struggle and cursing) by Nurse Anstace Crouch, her hawkish help.

In the seated position, Lady Loveall did a good impression of someone in control of her every limb. Crouch had placed diamonds on the folds of her mistress's neck, but they fell awkwardly, as though the skin rejected them. The maid fussed around Lady Loveall, trying for a perfectly balanced effect as she choreographed the reluctant jewels. A dog nestled on either side of Lady Loveall, who was dressed entirely in black lace. Her fleshy face emerged from the tangle of weeds like a gnarled and chubby hand from a gentleman's sleeve.

The counterpane of the Great Bed, purple velvet edged with a delicate blue and yellow sarcenet, was heavily weighed down by the family arms embroidered upon it. Originally this bed had boasted four posts, but its occupant could not bear to have anything obscuring her view of the world beyond, however slightly, and the two at the foot had been removed. She lay beneath a flying tester of black satin in the Great Bed that had witnessed the conception of both of her children, the living and the dead. The cloying smell of patchouli, which fragrance had more than once caused the Young Lord to recoil as he turned the corner, enveloped her and permeated the farthest reaches of the bedroom.

This nighttime visit was extraordinary. Her son was allowed to see her in her bedroom (the one room she occupied) only by formal invitation. Upon a request of an interview by an interested party (son, housekeeper, visiting member of the nobility), the formal invitation was duly proffered for two hours later, or, in truly exceptional circumstances, half that. In this instance, the Young Lord had requested an immediate interview. Lady Loveall braced herself for his imminent visit with an interminable list of orders to the maid. Her only remaining physical capability was the exercise of her vocal cords, and in order to avoid atrophy, she took great pains to keep them in constant use. Her mind was always active, and her voice only slightly less so. She talked in her sleep more than some people in their waking hours.

Today she was unusually agitated. From an entirely different source, she awaited word of the execution of an unsavory piece of family business, news she had hoped to be delivered while her son was arranging her affairs in London. But word had not arrived and this unprecedented request from the Young Lord merely emphasized that she was still on tenterhooks, that she had been disobeyed on one front and ambushed on the other. What on earth hour was it anyway? And why did her son need to speak to her on such short notice? There was not even time for a visit from the resident hairdresser, and Lady

Loveall felt a sudden longing for the irritation that accompanied the white powder and pomatum on her forehead.

She noted signs of their unorthodox haste: a hairbrush awry on the ivory table, a bunched curtain where the sash would normally have been neatly tied, and telltale amounts of terrier hair on the black and white tiling that made a chessboard of the room. A half-finished decanter of orgeat stood on her bedside table, the stopper still spinning on the silver tray. It came to a stuttering rest.

Lady Loveall raised her eyebrows when she saw her son enter the room with such gusto. Now it seemed even more like a surprise attack. She would make him wait.

Lady Loveall had grown accustomed to her son's listlessness and had resigned herself to their one-sided encounters. She allowed him alone to wear color around the house because it was one of the few urges he seemed to have. At her behest, the servants had reported to her daily on his routine, but after years this had become a wearisomely short list of hours spent alone in the Doll's House and Anonyma's Library.

"Mourning, do you not understand," she had told him, "is for show alone. A few natural tears soon after the trying event, even tears cried alone, are quite acceptable. But to prolong the agony for so long, sir, is woeful." She had been most pleased with this little speech and had Crouch take it down in dictation before delivery. Most galling of all was the resigned and intensely private nature of his suffering. To show distress, whether you felt it or not, seemed acceptable — but to be distressed and not advertise it! The authenticity of his anguish baffled her.

Why was he like this? Where had she gone wrong?

She had wondered, in her quiet moments, whether there was possibly a taint in the Loveall blood. It was her greatest fear and she barely dared voice it to herself, although perhaps it should have been no shame in an age when royalty itself was growing ever more imbecile with each generation. Try to change him as she might, it was obvious that Geoffroy, this paragon of foppery standing in front of her, was one of the lesser Loveall, the less-than-normal Loveall. The ruthlessly attractive vigor of Sir Lothar Loveall, her father-in-law and the man to whom, as a very young woman, she had initially been attracted before she had even met his son, had clearly skipped two generations and would possibly die out altogether.

Lothar, the so-called Bad Lord, had been a force of nature up to the very day when, his black beard white with powder from kisses won (willingly or unwillingly, it was all the same to him) from every girl within lipshot — even his own daughter-in-law! — he had succumbed to a massive embolism. Of course, he had died happily, or, as was tactfully noted in *The Post Boy,* "in his sleep." Pretty Jennie Hoskins had been found pinned beneath his bulk, on top of the Austrian grand piano. The new Lord Loveall had been well disposed to her because, despite the painful awkwardness of her situation, she hadn't screamed, not wishing to bring attention to herself or her master. The new lord had found her only because she'd had the presence of mind to play a melody on the few keys available to her until somebody heard. She was lucky, and so were the Loveall — only the next lord ever noticed a piano being played.

Till his last gasp, Bad Sir Lothar had lived up to his name. Lady Loveall still referred to him as the Bad Lord (he had demanded it even during his lifetime), but memory had, if possible, improved him. Now he seemed worse than ever. How he would have despised Geoffroy!

Lothar was the great man whom she took as her inspiration in her battle to secure the Loveall line. He had gone so far as to divorce his beloved first wife, Catherine Aston, when her inability to produce a successful heir became apparent. Within a year of his remarrying, her replacement, Isabelle Anthony, a mouse-haired girl with wide hips and a toothy smile, named "the child bride" rather for her intellect than for her years, gave birth to the male whose arrival the family had begun to think impossible, a child who grew to be the Good Lord Loveall, Lady Loveall's now deceased husband. Only Catherine Aston, who remained Lothar's ever present companion, was allowed to take care of the baby, although she was neither his mother nor the current Lady Loveall. Isabelle had no idea how to fill her time except produce another baby, so she might have one to play with herself, and this endeavor produced the hateful Elizabeth Osbern, née Loveall, Lady Loveall's sister-in-law and nemesis.

This admirable Lothar had stopped at nothing until he was sure of success for his family. But Lothar had superior materials at his disposal, and he was himself active, relentlessly so, able to reinvent the world around him to suit his designs. All she had were her invalid frame, her weak son, her emaciated maid, and a mind already tormented by other family matters. Sometimes she wondered if it was all in vain. No! She would not give in gracefully until the dynasty was secure.

If she had seen the merest hint of the Bad in Geoffroy, she might have slipped away happily. But there was none. Her son was neither good nor bad. As far as she could see, he was and did very little. It seemed that he was prepared to float through life, borne on the wind like Count Zambeccari's hot air balloon. His resigned nature, his delicate sensibility, and his casual acceptance of his lot (all a cruel parody of his father, who, though a good man, had not been weak) meant that he did only the things he had no choice but to do. It was as though he were too dead even to die. He had once suggested a skull in every room as a memento mori, but his mother had observed that a memento vivere might be more the thing.

To see this indifferent Geoffroy standing at the end of her bed so full of himself, bursting with news, was almost too much for her. She decided to prolong the moment, if only to torture him. She waited until he was close to speaking and then stopped him with a firm word.

"Geoffroy!" she said, elongating the two syllables, singing them through clenched teeth. She pronounced it "Geoff Roy," as though it were two separate words. Her son remembered himself. There were rules of etiquette even at this extraordinary bedside session.

"I hope you are feeling well this evening, my lady," he said stiffly, anxious to give the lines their due, more anxious to continue.

"Feeling well? I am not *feeling* at all, sir. I am totally numb. Crouch! Anstace! Here!" Lady Loveall swiveled her eyes around as the maid hurried to her side. Whereas Lady Loveall was all useless flesh, Crouch's skin stretched drumlike over her bony skull. This thin casing was in such short supply that it seemed barely able to meet its owner's needs. In order for her short upper lip to hide any of her top teeth, she consciously had to force it to do so. This maneuver did not bring the beak itself any lower, so her nostrils appeared constantly stretched, two symmetrical red bullet holes in her face, and somehow bigger than her eyes.

"You see this poor creature, this bag of bones. She feels for me. She moves me. Crouch! My hand." The maid took her lady's right arm and lifted it in the air, the skin so coarse that it appeared wrapped in wet gauze.

"Look at my hand, sir. Look at it!"

Lord Loveall shuffled but kept his eyes fixed on the inanimate hand. This was not a new routine. He resigned himself to a wait.

"Anstace! Drop it!" and the maid did. The arm and its attached hand flopped to the bed, falling so deep into the upholstered counterpane that the bed let out a wheezing exhalation, relieved to receive the arm once more. To Lady Loveall, the effect was a pleasing one. "That, sir, is how I feel!" The arm lay there and twitched once. "That is my arm, sir, *my* arm, but it doesn't listen to me anymore. It is beyond my control."

"My lady, Mother, I want to tell you . . ." The admirable firmness with which he had begun the sentence faltered fatally when he realized, to his anxiety, that his mother had not finished speaking. She was just readying herself to read many more things into her limp arm. And he had interrupted her.

"Stop!"

She interjected the word so quickly and with such finality that Loveall expected a slight jolt as the world reconsidered its movement around its axis.

"I said: it doesn't listen to me anymore. It is *beyond my control*. I am making an observation!" She briskly changed the subject. "You were employed by me to consult the master in chancery about urgent family matters. You have returned. Your first order of business would be, I presume, to report to me upon the outcome. Am I correct?"

"Yes, ma'am," said Loveall, but declined to answer further.

"And?"

"All was well, my lady, all is always well," Loveall said testily. It was a tone that his mother had not heard from him before. She felt the nerve ends on her head tingle gently. She was faintly impressed by this decorous attempt at rebellion, though she would not let it show. Nurse Crouch caught her eye as she checked her mistress's reaction. Loveall had found heart. "Mother, there is nothing urgent to resolve. Your effects will be divided as you have specified. I come with news that will put this and many other affairs into perspective."

His mother pouted and her lower lip protruded grotesquely. She was as still as a gargoyle, and she eyed her son so fixedly that he was rooted to the spot.

"Is it war, sir?" It was not war. "Very well. This information that is so important, sir."

Loveall, who seemed to have spent his entire life waiting, now saw that there was no reason to wait any longer. After a deep breath and a glance over his shoulder, he bowed as gracefully as a man can and announced: "My lady, may I present the next Lady Loveall."

Through the door came the badger-legged Hood, pushing before him a baby carriage of astonishing splendor. Its beaten gold shone like sunlight and made the room seem brighter around it. The smooth suspension of this beautiful machine had lulled the Great Lord Loveall and all subsequent Loveall to sleep, and it rocked gently from side to side as if it were the most perfectly balanced hammock. Its progress across the floor was almost completely silent, merely the softest whistle of moving parts lovingly greased and combined in perfect harmony. Generations of governesses could sing its praises. Hood stopped the carriage and bowed to her ladyship. The silence waited nervously to be broken.

Loveall looked down at the baby, still a very red baby, far from the pink of health, and back at his mother. She had not been expecting to see the next Lady Loveall, much less see her delivered for view in a baby carriage. She felt powerless and moved her head what little she could to improve her view. The entire movement possible to her was no more than an inch from side to side, and she twitched maniacally as she strained to see, her eyes betraying her disquiet. She could hear a human gurgling but she could not yet see anything at all. Maxwell and Randal growled threateningly at the mechanical monster causing their owner's consternation. Lady Loveall had had enough of this game. Her son had tried her patience too long. He was useless to her and the entire family. She was now entirely clear about this.

"Sir, you cannot marry a baby!" she shouted. "I have attempted arrangements with many women for you, but all were of a marrying *age*. None were younger than twelve. Until females have attained a certain age, sir, one cannot tell whether they will be appropriate as the future bearer of the Loveall line." And, as an afterthought, "Crouch, clear the room. Get rid of them."

"Madam, you misunderstand. I shall not marry anyone." This time his confidence did not fail him, and he continued without fear of interruption, until he found himself talking in a raised voice, which almost immediately caused a tickling at his throat. "This is not the future Lady Loveall, my wife, but the future Lady Loveall who will inherit our name. She is my daughter."

Behind the baby carriage, Hood cleared his throat pointedly, but went unnoticed. It would have been an ill-chosen moment to speak. Geoffroy coughed to ease his discomfort and looked longingly at the decanter.

"How, sir?" Lady Loveall asked in her most piercing tone, as servants in the nearest quarters of the house stopped their work, lifting their fingers to ensure silence as they strained to hear. "Have you read this baby into being? Found it in the library? Did you bring it to life in your dollhouse? I cannot believe for a moment that you have created it in a natural way. I dare not think that it is the offspring, the happy bastard, of a liaison between you and one of the comely female servants I have purposefully placed like sirens around the house but whom you have pitifully and unmanfully failed to notice!"

"I found the baby, Mother. I saved her life. She was in a bundle of rags in the mouth of a stray dog just outside the city. Mother, I have needed to find something to which to dedicate my life, and now I have found this child. I shall bring her up as the next Loveall, as my own, as our own. My lady, meet your granddaughter, the savior of our family. The baby, Hood!"

A doubt had arisen in Hood's mind, which he tried to convey with a widening of his eyes. Loveall, however, was not paying attention and accepted the newborn into his hands to present to his mother.

"The new Lady Loveall." He held the baby up to the heavens and approached. The old Lady Loveall's mind was working harder than it had since the day she had taken to her bed. For the first time in many years, she was forced to improvise in a scene not of her making.

"Crouch, the baby. Bring the baby." She spoke with staccato brusqueness. "You have found this baby, sir?" Facts needed to be ascertained. Her heart pounded, and an unattractive vein bulged on the side of her neck as her face turned red.

"Yes," Loveall said, slapping away Nurse Crouch's greedy claws. "Anstace, carefully!"

"Hood, were you there?" She strove to put the pieces in order.

"Erm, I was there, madam," said Hood. "But I should say —"

"Silence!" She was thinking aloud as Crouch brought the child slowly toward her. "The baby is left for dead and you find her. She is now ours and no one will lay claim to her. The baby was left for dead, Hood?"

"Almost certainly, ma'am, but —"

"A birthmark. Any identifying mark. We must look. Does anyone know? Did anyone see? Are you sure?"

"No one, madam, I am sure," answered Hood. "But there is one matter —" Hood was trying his utmost to be heard within the strictest confines of decorum, but Lady Loveall overpowered him.

"Thank goodness for good sense. Get Hamilton's son. Immediately. She is ours. You will arrange a great marriage for her, Geoffroy. I shall be gone by then. My son, you have done well."

"Madam, she will marry only for love or not at all," Loveall answered finally. The praise was irrelevant to him. It made him feel nauseous even now as he watched his mother readying to infect the little innocent with her touch.

All eyes were on the handing over of the baby to her new grandmother. Lady Loveall received the baby near her and peered at it, brand-new, bruised, unhappy. Nurse Crouch lifted up her ladyship's hand and poked one of her mistress's useless fingers into the red face. Geoffroy blenched, but to his surprise, the baby did not immediately scream.

"Birthmark," his mother said. Crouch lifted the dress to see what lay beneath. Hood cleared his throat once more, with greater force.

Lady Loveall peered carefully, appraisingly, and then looked up at Geoffroy with surprise. Surprise turned to approbation, approbation to admiration, admiration to love.

"You are a clever young man, my son."

"My lady?" Loveall had nothing to say, unnerved by this new tone of conciliation.

"What was your plan? How long were you to keep this a secret?"

"I have brought the baby straight to you, Mother, as soon as she was dressed."

"Why the pantomime? Why do you persist?" She was half smiling, half questioning. Loveall was flummoxed. There was no humor and no answer. Hood coughed in a way that sought urgent attention. It was time to interrupt.

"Madam, I fear that the Young Lord may not yet know," he said with the utmost deference and a subtle bow in the direction of his master.

Lady Loveall was smiling broadly. The motions and expressions left to her had necessarily become quite absurd in their hyperbole, and Geoffroy had never seen her mouth open so wide. The effect was hideous.

"Geoffroy," said his mother with a horrible condescension. "You have sought to surprise me. Now it is time for *you* to be surprised, for *you* to meet someone. May I introduce you to the new *Lord* Loveall, Geoffroy? The baby you have found is a boy."

Loveall looked at Hood, who felt best advised to avoid his gaze, and then screamed. He stared at his mother, gasped, and yowled again like a cat whose tail has been caught in the door. The dogs on the bed, surrounding the grinning gorgon, howled too in celebration.

"It's a girl!" he pleaded. "It is my Dolores!"

"No, Geoffroy, it is better this way. You have done well," said his mother with relish. "Call the baby anything you will, but look at this, look! Proof, even to *you!*"

Crouch spotted her cue and lifted the baby upside down, holding him firmly by his legs, so his beautiful christening dress fell around his head. There hung the small but unmistakable pink twig.

Loveall threw his head back, screamed again in despair, and fled from the room, howling, "Dolores! Dolores!"

"It's a boy, Geoffroy!" his mother shouted after him. "A boy!"

She started to laugh hysterically as her maid righted the baby and laid him on the bed. Lady Loveall listened to the frantic progress of her son's retreat and screamed after him, "It's the new *Lord* Loveall! You wouldn't have brought it home if you'd known! Nothing you do ever works! Nothing! Nothing!"

His mother's voice echoed through rooms and down walls, bouncing like a ball through gallery and hall, but whether Geoffroy heard her is impossible to say. Her heart pounded victoriously until it could pound no faster, and Lady Loveall realized in an instant that all her prayers had been answered.

3

IF THE READER COULD NOW unclasp the front of Love Hall like a dollhouse, he would find a scene of surprising calm. No one ran this way, no one rushed that. The workings of the house, its structure and hierarchy, always prevailed.

The bedroom was the epicenter of all activity, and the relative importance of the members of the household could be seen by their distance from Lady Loveall's dead body. Crouch (bedside) was now the most important woman in the house as she fussed over Lady Loveall's diamonds and issued instructions to the hairdresser. She wanted the moment to last forever. Within feet of her, the manservant Hood and Hamilton, the house economist, stood by. Against their better judgment, they had just admitted the cantankerous and universally despised housekeeper, Mrs. Gregory, who immediately fell to her knees, crossing herself so often that she might have been conducting a small orchestra. Her one champion in the house finally gone, she had more reason than most to be distressed. Crouch eyed her with cold pleasure.

The household beyond the bedroom awaited confirmation of the presumed death. Talk on the other side of the door became rumor down the hall. Rumor hushed to murmur, then whisper, in the wings and petered into gossip and irrelevant conversation in the back sculleries, as servants asked how the potatoes were doing and where the lad who cleaned the cutlery was when you needed him. The groom of chambers (immediately outside the lady's bedroom) was superior to the house fiddler to the tune of seventy-two people. The head chef, wiping a stringy piece of tripe from his knife at the kitchen door, was twelve more important than the sous-confectioner, while the keeper of the beagles, who knew nothing about it, stood just outside the back door with a dog that circled a familiar patch in anticipation of a bedtime bowel movement. He had the hound to kick; though, to redress the balance, he also had to pick up its shit. Everyone, as soon as he heard, was concerned for himself and his future and was sure to demonstrate his indispensability by going about his given task with the minimum of fuss.

There were lamp and candle men and watchmen who called hours every hour throughout the night; there were men who ironed the newspapers before their second reading; there were men whose entire life was spent taking hot water from one end of the house to the other, and there were women who heated the water for these men to carry. There were even two Indians (father and son), who had been brought over by the Good Lord Loveall so that the Loveall would be sure to eat the best curries in the country. These men also cared for the tiger that had been sent over as a gift to Geoffroy by some unknown hunting acquaintance of his father's. (The tiger was seeing out its days in a cage behind the house, better fed than the people who fed him.)

Loveall didn't know who all these people were and, in fact, knew very few of them by sight, but he assumed there was a point to most, if not all, of them. He was no household economist — the Loveall had the family of Hamiltons specifically for that — and the expense mattered not at all to him: it was good that all these people earned a wage. But the servants knew they were expendable.

Within half an hour, only two people in all of Love Hall were not paying attention.

One was Geoffroy, who was upstairs, alone, crouched in a swimming blue light. The moon shone through the tiny windows of the Hemmen dollhouse in the Doll's House. The front was opened like a body on a surgeon's table, its organs on display. He stared into the dollhouse, waiting for his sister to materialize and then recommend a course of action, as she had so many times before.

The other was the house librarian, Anonyma Wood, who sat silently at a desk in her place of work. A dark-haired woman in her middle thirties, all her attention was upon a book called *The Divination and Prophecies of the Female Somnambule,* and she paused only to make occasional notes on a sheet of foolscap. Her hair was pulled tightly back from her freckled forehead, and her eyes were jet black, the carbon of each emphasized by a heavy brow and underlined by a deeply etched crease. She had heard the scream, just as, a little while before, she had heard the guns that signaled the return of her benefactor, but was so deeply involved in her reading that neither penetrated her conscious mind.

Geoffroy and Anonyma were untouchable gods in Love Hall. Just below them were their priests, the senior and trusted retainers, whose positions were also secure. The remainder of the household, the congregation, waited for the hymns to be called and said their prayers.

At the next servants' meal, it might have seemed to the unobservant eye that nothing had changed. The household sat exactly as it always had, but each retainer realized that Death's intrusion made change inevitable. Low whispers confirmed this anxiety.

Only two people in the house could lay down new laws affecting the servants' future. Lady Loveall was one of them, and she was dead. The other was Geoffroy. Their gravest fear was that the Young Lord, though essentially a good man, lacked the necessary character, that he would be at the mercy of malign forces that did not respect the smooth running of a household, that wanted change to profit themselves rather than Love Hall.

The queen was dead. Long live the king.

It might not be as bad as they imagined, if only they could survive the changing of the guard. Geoffroy would not bark orders like his mother, and the presence of an employer who might be occasionally glimpsed, rather than only heard, would be a novelty. Few of the servants had come into contact with Lady Loveall, but they had all seen her son wafting in and out of corridors like a delicate mist. They had each been told at various times that he was to be ignored, that he was invisible, and they had all laughed at his odd whims. But the retinue took their orders not from these deities but from their own ranking seniors. What if these seniors were enemies of the new lord's man, Hood? Lady Loveall had not lived forever, and those, like Mrs. Gregory, who had used their position in the secure knowledge that she was immortal would rue the day.

Only very few could be assured of their place in the new household. Hood was indispensable, the only channel through which his lordship could communicate. Anonyma was in charge of the library and, as Dolores's ex-tutor, was Geoffroy's one living link with his sister. These two were vital not only to the house but to the very survival of its new master. Then there was the Hamilton family, who had been too important, too loyal to the Loveall throughout history: as with all his ancestors, this particular Hamilton's position was secured by the fact that he knew too much. The only other likely survivor was Anstace Crouch: it was assumed, certainly by her, that she would replace the outgoing housekeeper, Mrs. Gregory. Beneath this quadrumvirate, all was uncertainty.

As far as the rest of the village and the world beyond were concerned, it would be the Young Lord who ruled; but inside Love Hall, it was common knowledge that they would be under the sway of a coalition — Hood, Anonyma, Hamilton, Anstace. Quickly the word spread around the tables, originating with Thomas the under-butler (who felt free to say anything he liked because he knew his days were numbered), that they were now ruled by the HaHa. And who wanted to be a laughingstock?

* * *

While the rest of the household grappled with news of his mother's death, Geoffroy's powers of concentration focused on the interior of the Hemmen House as he waited for Dolores. The Hemmen was not strictly a dollhouse at all, but a walnut cabinet on legs, decorated with exquisite tortoiseshell marquetry and engraved pewter, with glass doors through which the interior could be admired. It was meant not for a child, but rather for an adult who had no children of her own.

Geoffroy had unlocked the doors and was staring in at the Irish stitch on the walls of the Tapestry Room, a full-size version of which no longer existed in the real Love Hall. Everything else was an exceptional facsimile, down to the minute encaustic tiles with the family motto inside the front door; if the actual hall ever fell into neglect and disrepair but the Hemmen House survived, then the contents and the spirit of its arrangement would be easily recalled. Even the kitchen iron, a quarter of an inch in size, was made of real brass. In relief behind the middle hall, there was the fountain in the formal garden, spouting real water. Geoffroy had replaced anything that was imperfect. If the painters of the real artworks in the house had still been alive, then Hemmen had tried to ensure that it was they who provided the miniatures on the walls of Dolores's house; and if they weren't, he painted the copies himself.

Geoffroy loved Love Hall itself. Notwithstanding its enormousness, the house was surprisingly well designed for comfortable living. The lower floor was for noise, dirt, and business, and the most useful rooms were there: a breakfast room, a small dining room and a dinner room, a room for afternoon entertainments, and another for "quidnuncing," all branching from the massive Baron's Hall. It seemed potentially the windiest, least livable house in the whole country, but legend had it that a candle would not flare in the Long Gallery at night.

On the first floor were the principal formal rooms, recently carpeted with Axminster and hand-knitted Donegal with the family crest woven into each corner. Here, the curtains were lined with Spittalfields silk. These rooms were reserved for pomp and parade. Unavoidably, this floor was rather more modern. The Reception Room in particular was profoundly uncomfortable and clearly intended for just the shortest of receptions: furniture was produced only as it was required. Most of the life was below, the kitchens and the bustling servants, and most of the memories above, where Geoffroy whiled away his days. These he spent in the library and in the Doll's House on the fourth floor, which might as well have been a million miles away from the bedridden mother. That was where he felt safest.

Loveall was lost in dreams, wishing he could shrink to the appropriate size, climb inside the dollhouse, and close the doors from within. After his sister's death, he had commissioned a tiny miniature of the Hemmen dollhouse and placed it in the top floor of the dollhouse itself — a house within a house within a house. As the dollhouse had been Dolores's favorite toy, so he had arranged that she would be able to play with it in the afterlife, and it was there that she usually appeared. He couldn't find her now, but that didn't worry him. She had proved as willful in death as in life, and he loved her now as he had loved her then. He would find her elsewhere, by other means.

He idly worked his way through a large box of dolls, where the whole history of the family was written. The Loveall had been great doll lovers over the years, and Geoffroy sifted through the collection of ivory and wood, clay and beaded buckskin. Some had been brought to their home by visiting guests in homage to the family, either as mementos of their grand tours or simple boasts of their adventures, while some had been sent from abroad by traveling relatives who wanted to curry favor. Others were premature love tokens for Dolores to inaugurate an extended courtship that the giver, or his parents, hoped would find its ultimate expression in marriage. There were also the remnants of the doll collection of their grandmother, Isabelle, the child bride. Hers were pretty dolls, like wax babies, whose faces had no more character than their owner's, their once magnificent clothes now dirty rags.

Geoffroy was looking for something in particular, searching carefully where normally he might have stopped and loitered, seduced by memory. Then he found what he was looking for: an ancient doll, made of bone, called Mark, a name scratched into the back of the left leg by a previous owner. He dragged it out by its leg. Mark had a flat head and a permanently furrowed brow with two elaborate symmetrical curls on either side. His big eyes were sideways teardrops, and his expression suggested that he had just seen something frightening. The doll was unquestionably male to Loveall, a boy warrior, but on his chest were two pinched, pointed breasts that projected almost perpendicularly. It was Dolores who had pointed out that the doll was actually not Mark at all, but Mary.

Dolores and her elder brother had played games with all the dolls, assigning them roles, having them talk in languages that no one else understood. Even the two ventriloquists did not understand some of the words, but the dolls made sense of them all. Loveall's patience with Dolores was infinite. He talked any garbled language that would amuse her and let her toy with him in any way she pleased. He was one of her dolls: she could brush his hair, untie his shoes, topple off his cap, and he bore it all without complaint. Between the two of them was this unspoken understanding: he was on earth to please her. Whether it was Squeak Piggy Squeak or All Fours (her favorite), Dolores would be whichever part she chose. If she didn't want to seek, she always hid. And if the game was designed for more than two players, then the dolls were drafted as participants. They had no one else to play with, nor did they want anyone.

In this room the two of them sat for hours with a book called *Nuts to Crack,* which had been brought to the house by Edred Osbern, the least likable of all their relatives, who had only this book to his credit. *Nuts to Crack* contained two hundred "hieroglyphics, enigmas, conundra, crinkum-crankums and other ingenious devices" and came complete with a book of answers called *The Nutcrackers, a Key or Enigmatical Repository,* which Loveall had hidden from Dolores and she had subsequently found and hidden from him. She was a serious young lady, and when she sat with *Nuts to Crack* in front of her, she would jot on a piece of paper in a magnificent dumb show of mental labor. Once, she had filled in a word puzzle for over an hour, and when Loveall had looked at the page after she had gone to bed, he discovered, to his wonder, the page filled in, *solved,* with complete gibberish.

When Dolores pored over *Nuts to Crack,* she became so deeply involved in the pictures, strange arrangements of letters that were supposed to mean something entirely different, that it was sometimes impossible for Geoffroy to get her attention. The most wonderful puzzle was an engraving that looked distorted and ghostly on the page, a spill of ink stretching away from the eye. The "Conundrum Comments" beneath explained that when viewed from one particular perspective, the picture would not only be "perfect in all respects" but would also, and most marvelously, stand out from the page in three dimensions. To their huge disappointment, they could not make the ink anything but a nonsensical blot. Perhaps it was a town, or a figure, or a word with distorted outlined letters: it was agony not to know. They looked at the page every way they could imagine, at eye level, in mirrors, at strange angles, twisted and bent, but still it would not yield its mystery. The answer would, of course, be found in *The Nutcrackers,* but Dolores would never say where she had hidden it. Her brother wondered if she even remembered, because it was evident that she wanted the solution as much as he did, but she was stubborn in every way. The picture defied them and remained a mess on the page.

Today, Geoffroy had *Nuts to Crack* and still had no answer. Perhaps it would soon be time to find out. *The Nutcrackers* was bound to be somewhere in the house, and perhaps in the answer to that picture, he would feel closer to his sister. She would soon be with him, beneath the same moon that had shone on the two of them together. All the shadows were distorted as Loveall lay there on his back. The trembling shadow of a branch fell across him and he felt the cool of the floor beneath. On this floor, in this room, in the dollhouse, he felt her more strongly than anywhere else.

He seemed to see something move on the top floor of the Hemmen House. It was then that he heard the voice of Dolores whisper to him: "Build a new house, Joe. Anonyma will help you."

Anonyma would help him.

Anonyma Wood had come to Love Hall when Dolores was four. Lady Loveall, still in the relatively time-consuming work of mourning her husband, her clothes imperceptibly changing elegantly from dark to light gray, had decided to employ a governess for her daughter.

At first Geoffroy was against the idea: what could Dolores need that he could not provide? But Hood (who, twenty-five years older than his Young Lord, had been his companion and caretaker since the age of four and to whom his lordship always deferred in matters of the world) explained that there were certain things that Dolores would need to know, which neither he nor his young lordship nor indeed any *man* could teach her. Further, these things, though unknowable to men, were necessary to Dolores's very survival in the world. Survival! Only then did Geoffroy accept that a governess would be a sensible addition to Love Hall. When he was told that the governess would also teach embroidery, crewel, and needlepoint and that he (already known privately, but affectionately, among certain of the servants as "Miss Molly") would be allowed to attend these classes with his sister, there was no longer any question.

The governess would be required, he overheard his mother say — and when she was overheard to say something, there was always a reason — to undertake the education of the "humane mind" of the girl entirely. The successful applicant would have perfect health, equanimity of temper, and cheerfulness of disposition; be of prepossessing appearance, refined manners, and excellent education; be fluent in all the important languages, with a working knowledge of German; and be a flawless musician. She would be expected to produce two introductions from families whose name was known to the Loveall, and on no account should either of these be foreign. She would dress in black and earn twenty guineas a year.

Even at the age of twelve, Loveall was wise to his mother and he dutifully told his sister what was expected of the governess so that Dolores was prepared for the best and the worst.

It was all rather a shock to Dolly, and the governess-to-be's list of attainments was baffling to her and Geoffroy. How could anyone on earth know that much, be that good and healthy, speak all those languages? Did this paragon even exist? So they invented their own governess while they waited for the real one. At first she lived only in their minds, but then they started to construct her as an automaton with parts pilfered from the toy box. This miniature governess was perfect in every way — she never tired, knew all the languages in the world (including ones yet to be invented), and was extremely beautiful, except for a few loose springs. She didn't move an inch, but despite this drawback, she was so perfect in their minds that the real governess would never be able to live up to this ideal. Though Dolly was gradually warming to the idea, Geoffroy wondered about the wisdom of exciting her expectations. He hated the thought of her disappointment when a plain woman with a French accent worse than Dolly's took off her coat to reveal a sad black dress.

On December 31, 1799, there came into Love Hall something even better than the miniature governess, something infinitely more real and beautiful and brilliant: Anonyma Wood.

The reason for Anonyma's timely arrival on the marketplace was well known to her prospective employer. Her last ward, the Right Honorable Lady Makem's daughter, Mo, had been kidnapped by her father and conveyed to Italy. Lady Makem had originally retained Anonyma because of a certain directness of gaze (not for herself, but in the interests of her husband). Anonyma was shy by nature, but her eyes showed none of this reserve and she had realized, to her surprise, that they could get her whatever she wanted. She hadn't meant, or asked, to have such secret weapons in her artillery, but she used them whenever necessary. Sadly for Lady Makem, there was no need to provide a spur for her husband's libido, which was neither dead nor dormant, but, on the contrary, spry, straining, and pointed in another direction entirely. Anonyma's obsidian eyes were not noticed by his lordship, who would shortly, rather than spend time at His Majesty's pleasure, be taking a protracted trip to Italy in the company of the Earl of Elthemere's son, Cocky, and his newly abducted daughter, Mo.

The Makems were a moneyed family racked with scandal, but society had generously declared that this shame should fall on those carrying the family name rather than their employees. Anonyma came, therefore, with flawless recommendations from a reliable source: exactly what was required. Lady Loveall's only initial objections were her comparative youth — heaven *forbid* that she should form an attachment — and her name, which sounded Continental and if not entirely native, then tinged with the alien. But chasing a crumb of scone across her china plate with some determination (more than was in her voice), Anonyma explained that her parents, both deceased, had not been able to agree upon a name for her and had celebrated that fact with the name upon which they finally compromised. Her name meant rather "the unnamed" than "without a name." When Anonyma mentioned that she was called simply Ann by her previous employers, Lady Loveall found all doubts vanish.

Ann Wood was a very fitting name for a governess: dull, English, and short. Terms explained, with hair length to be further discussed, Anonyma was handed over to an excessively unwelcoming and taciturn housekeeper, who, as they walked away, gestured at rooms and sights of interest, without once opening her mouth to explain anything about them. The new governess was shown to a small but neat room in a far-flung outpost of the top floor and left there, without instruction.

The bed had oppressive purple velvet curtains: she had never seen such absurd magnificence in such an unlikely location. She placed her three cases on the bed and started to unpack them, fretting immediately over the lack of bookshelves. The first case she opened without undue attention and took from it clothes, dresses, skirts, which she arranged in the closet. She took much greater care over the others. From the second, she took books, books upon books, which she placed gently on the desk: some were in sets of eight or nine quarto volumes, some were larger folios more foreboding than those friendly families, and others had indistinguishable diagrams and incomprehensible typefaces, possibly foreign languages, on the spines and covers. She blew sharply across each cover and, with one firm stroke of a cloth, removed any dust; then she examined each surface at eye level like a luthier inspecting the neck of his new violin. She set aside one specific volume, an old edition of poetry, her father's best copy: no book would be set on top of this one. By the time the case was empty, the entire surface area of the desk was covered.

From the third case, she took yet more books, but these were the traveling books that she had brought for her new ward: they were at once sterner and more reassuring than the others. She cared for these, too — they were books after all, and she would sooner have her own spine broken than manhandle a book — but not with the same devotion, and they were placed in a neat pile on the floor.

She sighed and sat down on the large monk's bench by the window. Beneath her to her right, there was a complex formal lawn, symmetrically cut with a walled rose garden. In the middle, a fountain constantly spouted water straight up into the air, arcing it into the large lily-covered pond beneath. Looking beyond the Terra-cotta Bridge, which crossed the river that snaked along the bottom of the parterre, her eyes fell upon the Northern Avenue. Lined by dozens of elms, the avenue stretched far away from the house, a bold boast of the size of Love Hall's local empire. She gazed north, where she had been born. At the very end of the avenue, in the distant mist of the horizon, she could see the ruin of an ancient tower.

That evening Anonyma spent New Year's Eve on her own for the first time, not knowing where to go for food, nor being asked to accompany anyone. But she did not feel alone as she sat on the bench with her back to the night, memorizing passages from one of her most precious books, the one she had set aside, *Letter of Ptolemy to Flora* by Mary Day. Elsewhere, rumor of her arrival had reached the children.

On the auspicious morning of New Year's Day 1800, Anonyma, still without guidance, walked up the grand staircase toward the Doll's House. As she ascended, the portraits went back in time and she felt scrutinized by years of Loveall history and splendor, wondering if she would have to journey all the way back to Adam and Eve before she reached the top; however, the last two portraits of two children, a rather girlish-looking boy and a boyish-looking girl, were more modern. The boy held in his hand an apple, which he offered to the spectator. Behind him a house burned on a distant hill. In the next painting, the girl wore a tomboy's defiance in her eyes and nursed an ever-so-slightly bloody knee. Someone called Eugenius had painted both the portraits in the same fashionable allegorical style, and his elaborate signature filled the bottom left-hand corner of each. Lady Loveall had told him exactly what to paint.

Anonyma looked around the top floor and found the boy from the portrait sitting in a central chair, in the same light blue costume. Could it possibly be what he wore around the house? A pair of eyes peered out from behind him. Anonyma stood at the top of the stairs with her head bowed, presenting herself to the children, her youngers, her superiors. The boy, behaving as though he were the father of the young girl, whispered something quite sharply to her as his eyes narrowed. It was her cue. The girl crawled out from behind the chair and, getting up, smoothed out a long pink dress. Her blond hair fell down around her shoulders, and coming up to Anonyma, she curtsied.

"Comment allez-vous, madame?" she said, and scraped the ground a little less gracefully than she had intended. Behind her, the elder boy mouthed every word with his sister, his pupil, and nodded, gratified by the finished result.

"Très bien, merci beaucoup," answered Anonyma, and curtsied back. *"Et monsieur?"*

She looked up at the Young Lord, who had stopped gazing at his sister. His eyes caught hers for a moment and she saw a startlingly beautiful boy. He wasn't used to being questioned in any language, certainly not by strangers. It was as though he felt above the world, invisible: the master pulling the puppet strings above the curtain. But there he sat, in plain view. He had concentrated all his efforts into providing Dolores with the most magnificent of entrances, and now he was trying not to blunder himself. She inferred from his silence that she had strayed outside the boundaries of propriety, but with considerable effort and at length, he answered:

"Nous sommes enchantés de vous faire la connaîssance, madame," and then, getting up and performing the slightest possible bow, he switched to English. "We are told that your name is Ann Wood."

She looked at her feet again, acutely aware of her plain boots, and noticed the books that were lying around the floor, the sun shining onto them through the delicate blue stained glass. She answered, wondering whether she should, "My full name is Anonyma."

Dolores laughed and her brother looked at her. "Then we shall call you Anonyma. Dolores?" The girl stood like a tiny prizefighter in a loose dress as she considered the complications of what he had just said.

"Amonyma," murmured Dolores to herself.

"Anonyma," said Anonyma. "But if you would prefer Ann . . ."

"I like Anomyna," said Dolores.

"Then we will call you Anonyma," said Loveall.

"Anomaly," said Anonyma, eyes down.

"Anemone!" said Dolores, and giggled.

Anonyma looked at him. She felt that she would be here for some time.

"And what, sir, may I call you?" She looked him in the eyes, but he didn't answer.

"I am Dolly," said the girl as quickly as she could. "And this is Joe." She was the one person in the world who had ever called him Joe and the only person who would ever be allowed to. Even his mother habitually called him "sir." Loveall let free a mousy squeak. It was laughter.

"Indeed, Dolly does call me Joe, but perhaps you should call me 'sir' for the time being." He said it with such kindness, so there might be considered no chastisement whatsoever either of his sister or of the new governess, that Anonyma saw that if Dolores liked her, then Loveall would like her. A fly buzzed around the room and landed on top of an absurdly large and ridiculously ornate dollhouse in the corner of the room. Anonyma looked at the house more carefully and realized that it was Love Hall. She could even see her own room, which included a strange and inappropriate metal figure with one leg sticking out at right angles from the body as though in a bizarre ballet position.

Dolores interjected: "Before you came, we were drawing in a book." And she turned around to get the book to bring back to Anonyma, thinking it would impress her. She held it out in offering.

The book was an ancient illuminated Latin bestiary. Acquired by the Quiet Lord many years before, it had lain undisturbed in the Octagonal Library until Geoffroy had pulled it out on one of his rare sorties to that distant region of Love Hall, thinking it might be of interest to his sister, if only in pieces. Dolly held it open to a picture of a saintly-looking wild-beast tamer astride a fire-breathing dragon. The monster was eating, feet first, a bewildered but otherwise unconcerned frog. On the next page was a parrot. Around the parrot were some pencil lines, presumably the ones in which Dolores had been engaged prior to the dress rehearsal for Anonyma's arrival. The governess looked at the charcoal lines in the book, and tears welled in her eyes. Unable to stop herself, she snatched it from the hands of the young girl, closed it, and exclaimed: "No!"

Anonyma clutched the book to her like a baby, safe from Dolores; it was as if she could feel each individual hit of the hammer that had rounded the spine. There was a thin layer of gold finish on the cover, stamped in a symmetrical curlicue and on the painted edge of the book, a picture of a man — perhaps the author. She assessed all this and much more in a matter of seconds, just as she had been taught to appraise and appreciate a book.

"Madam!" shouted an angry Loveall as he came toward her. She had grabbed the book that her new ward had shown her in love, and only the child's dignity and pride had kept Dolores from tears. Anonyma felt the position of governess slip away from her, but she could not control herself. Instead of the abject apology that Loveall was expecting, he saw defiance in her eyes. It was an emotion that he had experienced only in, and thought was unique to, his mother.

"Sir, are you not old enough to know that this book is not for writing in?" Her speech was measured but firm. "There is enough writing in this book already."

"Miss Wood . . . ," he said, but was interrupted. Another first.

"I am sorry I took the book by force and, Dolores, to you most particularly I apologize. But this book must not be written in. This is an ancient book. It should be safely in a library, and I cannot bear to see how it has been abused." She was firm and unmovable. Dolores looked up at her with wide eyes, feeling none of the blame. Her brother considered his position and chose his words most carefully.

"Miss Wood, I see no reason to be so stern over a mere book."

"But, sir, there *is* a reason. There are many reasons. The privileges of your family have bequeathed you this book that should be safe under lock and key. Just because there has not been anyone here to tell you how to look after it does not mean that common sense would not have dictated to you that it is not a plaything." Still she clutched the book to her in protection.

"Mustn't I draw in the book?" Dolores asked with disarming honesty.

Anonyma looked down at her and laughed, almost, as Dolores blurred before her. "No, you mustn't. I'm sure you have a better book for your pictures."

"But why not? The parrot is so pretty," said Dolores. Loveall watched the two of them and saw that Dolly's moment of unhappiness had passed. He decided to let them continue, but he eyed the developments with suspicion, ready to defend his sister if necessary. Anonyma took the book and laid it carefully on the floor, inviting Dolly down next to her.

"Look," she said. "And I'll show you." She opened the book to the picture of the saint and the parrot. "Do you know what animal this is?"

"A parrot and a dragon."

"Yes, that's a parrot and that's a dragon, but look where my finger is pointing." She was pointing at a blank space on the page.

"That's a parrot and that's a dragon, but that's a page," confirmed Dolores.

"This is a calf," said Anonyma, and laughed, remembering her father telling her the same thing in a smaller house with a less valuable book. Loveall was not prepared for his sister to be insulted and then lied to, and he readied to interrupt by clearing his throat. But Dolly laughed with Anonyma.

"A little cow? Why?" asked Dolores, who was sufficiently interested in the problem at hand to ignore her brother's influence. It was beginning to seem more appealing, a nut to crack.

"The pictures are of a parrot and a dragon, yes, but when I asked you, I pointed at the page, didn't I?"

"The page is paper," said Dolores confidently as her brother nodded his approval.

"If it were made today, yes, the page would be paper. But this book is very old and was made before paper existed. Do you know what people wrote on before paper?"

Dolly shook her head, and Anonyma continued.

"There was a plant called papyrus that grew on the banks of a river in Africa, just like the tall reeds that grow beside the river in your garden. The stems were beaten and dried and then used for writing. That was what the books were made of in Egypt. They were made of big rushes."

"Rushes?" Dolly was lost in the mysteries that Anonyma was outlining for her, enigmas she and her brother had never heard or imagined. Perhaps the governess did know everything.

"But once upon a time, just before Jesus was born, there was a king called Eumenes and he had a wonderful library of papyrus scrolls."

"Made of reeds from the garden?"

"Yes. But another king, whose name was Ptolemy, owned all the papyrus from which the books were made. He had an even better library and he feared that Eumenes' collection might grow to be bigger than his own, so he refused to sell his rival any papyrus. Eumenes had to invent a new kind of book, and he did this by finding a way of preparing animal skins so they could be written on, and the name of his kingdom, Pergamum, gave its name to the next kind of paper: parchment."

"Is this parchment?" Dolores was all concentration.

"Yes, but feel it . . . gently. . . . It is the most special kind of parchment, called vellum, made from the skin of a baby cow. They'd wash the skin and remove the hairs, scrape it, and then stretch it tight so they could make it as smooth as possible for writing." Anonyma acted out every gesture for Dolores. "And then they'd dust it with chalk and rub it with pumice so that they could write on both sides."

"This is a calf?" Dolly was trying to keep up and mostly succeeding, but some of the more far-fetched elements required reassurance.

"Yes, like your shoes in a way, but much thinner. One single copy of the big Bible that Gutenberg printed used one hundred and seventy calfskins."

"How many copies were printed, Miss Wood?' interjected Loveall.

"My father told me thirty, sir." Anonyma looked up at him, as surprised at his interest as he was.

"That's a lot of calves for thirty copies of the Bible."

"Perhaps the Gutenbergs ate a lot of veal, sir," said Anonyma.

"What's a veal?" Dolores asked, and Anonyma hastily brought her back to the page.

"And this book would have been written by one man in a monastery and then passed on to another man who would do all the paintings. And look at the colors. . . ."

With Dolores's full attention, Anonyma told her that the monks made the black ink by boiling tree bark and iron filings but that sometimes they had to make do with water added to soot scraped from the bottom of the pots and pans in the monastery kitchen. (They could possibly try the same to see if it worked.) The yellow in the rider's collar and belt was from the dyer's rocket plant, and on the bright breast of the bird, you could almost see the scales of the insect whose skin was crushed and used for crimson.

"In this book, just in the colors alone, there is animal, vegetable, and mineral. There is a whole world of life, a world of long ago, on this one page."

Suddenly Dolly had never seen anything so beautiful.

"We mustn't write in this book, Joe," she said from the floor, shaking her head and frowning seriously, but her brother had left while she was too engrossed to notice. During this impromptu first lesson, he had walked down the stairs, not secretly but without fanfare, to the gallery and an appointed interview with his mother. He found her in the main dining room on the ground floor and presented himself to her with the expected decorum. His mother looked at him imperiously.

"I expect we shall have to send her back where we found her, sir?"

"On the contrary, ma'am, she must stay. Dolores likes her."

"Good. You may go. Your own tutor awaits you."

It was decided. Anonyma Wood stayed. Dolly's lessons continued.

Closing his eyes as he lay on the floor, Geoffroy remembered building a house of cards in this room, many years before, to test the legend about the lack of draft in the house. Dolores placed the cards flat along the tops of the props that he made. The first row made a sturdy base for the second, and even when one of his small bridges collapsed onto the cards beneath, there was no sign of impending disaster. It was, they agreed, the firmest house of cards that had ever been built, and it rose and rose until they hardly dared talk in case the extra noise made the cards shudder. Further packs were requisitioned: Mother's piquet cards and an old set of tarot belonging to Anonyma. As the house grew, so it became more remarkable to them and also funnier, and they started to laugh, sporadically at first, until they were laughing all the time, laughing at the very laughter. They knew that it was the worst thing they could do, so they turned their heads away and covered their mouths. Then they would glimpse each other through sly eyes and start another round.

A breeze made one of the highest cards shiver in its extremity. Geoffroy got up to check that the window was fully closed. As he turned back, the carpet slid beneath his foot and he fell hard to the ground, his knee hitting the floor with a painful thump. The house of cards seemed to jump slightly and land in exactly the same place. They stared at it in amazement but this time they didn't laugh, because they realized that nothing could bring the house down. Constructed of four packs of cards, it was magnificent, stronger even than Love Hall itself. They rested a marble at the apex so that if it ever fell, they would hear the marble drop, even in their beds in the middle of the night. Otherwise, they would have to stay in the room to know exactly how long it stood, and at the moment, that seemed like pitching a tent on Salisbury Plain to keep watch on Stonehenge, just in case.

The next morning they crept upstairs together, with no thought of breakfast. Opening the door gently, they found the card castle still standing. Not one card had moved, not a joker, nor a chevalier de coupe. They edged toward it, crawling along the ground, not talking.

Dolores stood up and said in her most serious voice: "It will never fall."

With a look of pride, she approached the castle and removed one card, the farthest right on the bottom story. She whipped it away with as deft a savagery as when the master of the hunt knifes the fox's brush from its body.

The marvel did not move. It was as stubborn as she was. Or perhaps it simply didn't dare defy her.

She removed the lowest card on the left with the same movement. Solid. Then she started to take cards from elsewhere in the structure. After each one she would consider briefly where the next dismemberment would occur, and then strike. Within five minutes, it was an impossible shape, a conundrum, wider in the middle than it was at either the top or the bottom.

"That was fun," said Dolores at last, pleased with herself and the world around her. "Let's climb the tree as high as we can so we can see into the window."

Afterwards, he had found the house of cards lying flat on the ground, too, as if felled by her scream.

After the Fall of Dolores, Anonyma became the Young Lord's only living connection to his sister and, thus, to life. It was not, however, considered appropriate for her to take over his tutoring. In this respect, a Dr. Ormerod continued to exert a successful grip over Lady Loveall's imagination, and she thought that he could do no wrong. And she was correct, for he very rarely did anything at all.

Loveall was happier in the company of Anonyma than with Ormerod. As a preference, this was hardly more impressive than preferring something that existed to nothing at all, but in fact he liked

Anonyma. Because of their shared grief, he found himself content only with her, and he alone used her full name. Although there was no longer any need for her at Love Hall — she couldn't govern a memory — Geoffroy knew that he did not dare let her leave, for either his or his sister's sake. He had to find a reason for Anonyma to stay.

Accordingly, and to his mother's undisguised surprise, Loveall expressed a wish. Hood had helped him with it. This wish was that he might start a grand library in the Octagonal Tower and that the governess would become the house librarian. There had been a working library there many years prior, but the room was otherwise unused, except for the housing of the few books that had survived destruction or neglect, and was now almost entirely ignored. The only person who had ventured there recently was Anonyma, who had been heard to complain about the shameful state of the room, particularly considering the value of its contents (at which even Lady Loveall pricked up her ears).

It was such a relief that her son wanted anything, since he had barely taken sustenance since the fall, that Lady Loveall granted him this trifle on the conditions that it be called the Octagonal Library rather than the Dolores Library and that the major focus of the collection not be sisters, death, or trees. The newly thirteen-year-old proclaimed, having no better or more immediate idea and thinking mostly of Anonyma's preferred subject, that the library would be filled with books about libraries and books and that there was therefore only one person with the qualifications to take care of the collection. Anonyma's bibliophilia and her natural proclivity toward ordering and collecting were well known by now and her credentials as a librarian beyond dispute.

Lady Loveall immediately agreed. Despite the fact that she did not care for books, she had heard that libraries were becoming centers of sociability in certain good houses. Things had certainly changed since her youth when, to her knowledge, the library of her family seat had boasted seven books in toto: two of these were Bibles, and the remaining five a Ready Reckoner and four technical manuals. The only form of literary product that her family considered of any import was the sermon, and they owned none. She couldn't herself see the appeal of a roomful of books, but conceivably it was a good investment both in the future of the house and its heir. Her final word on the subject was straightforward:

"I don't like to read, sir. I always feel that I am doing something beneath me."

"It depends where you hold the book, ma'am," her son replied with a rare smile.

"Yes, well, have your library. And your librarian."

And there was an end to it.

Anonyma thus retained a position at Love Hall. She would have accepted the post under almost any conditions — it was her dream to surround herself with books, and here she would have almost unlimited funds to buy any book she wanted for the good of the Loveall Collection — but she had a particular reason for her happiness, and in the interests of honesty, particularly toward one who had showed so much trust and kindness to her, there was a final question she had for Loveall. She asked it at the next opportunity.

"Sir, although the focus of the library will be libraries, might I also be able to keep a small section on my own interests?" She was looking at the floor, so desperate was she for him to answer yes of his own free will.

"Anonyma, the choice of all the books is yours, and no one will question your decisions," said the Young Lord, and turned on his way up to the Doll's House. She would not have to persuade him; the choice was hers.

She called after him. "Sir, there are some books in the library by a writer named Mary Day. They are unique to Love Hall and I would like the chance to —"

"Anonyma, the choice is yours," Loveall said as he turned beyond the first banister. He was only a few feet away, but already his quiet voice had drifted into the distance.

The choice was hers. The library was hers. It had taken every ounce of her resolve. She went to her bedroom, so overcome that she cried. The tears were for her father, her own happiness, and for Dolores.

Love Hall had not always had a library. The collection had begun when the king's men had first looted and destroyed monasteries and then ransacked the universities. The Quiet Lord had hidden his books in the Octagonal Tower to keep them safe from plundering hands. When they were finally liberated, the Quiet Lord, flushed with success in his new role as Defensor Librorum, decided that more books should be added to the collection, but he was not a man who could do anything by half measures, and an acquisitive impulse to ownership modified the idea of *more* books to *all* books. The task became impossible long before he realized it, for he had severely underestimated quite how many books there were. As more arrived by the barge- and cartload, he quickly ran out of room. It was a disaster.

The idea of the perfect library had been a source of embarrassment to his heirs, and after the Quiet Lord's death, most of the books not used as kindling were given away. Some treasures had nevertheless remained (for example, the Great Bible of 1541 — noted in early Hamilton accounts as having been bartered for a prize wolfhound). A few of these had escaped the rotten Octagonal and were kept behind glass elsewhere in the house, where they were used to impress visitors but were never otherwise considered. The black hole known as the Octagonal Tower now stored what was left of the original library in no particular order, the remnants of an esoteric collection that no one cared to see: no one except Anonyma, whose official title was now librarian of the Octagonal Library at Love Hall. Her first task was to save the books.

Straightaway, she diagnosed that the room was unnaturally dark.

No wonder the books were in such pain. Even with the lights burning their brightest, there seemed to be no light at all. Her first instruction was that all the remaining books be taken out and put in dry places around the house (to the annoyance of the servants, who had to learn to dust around these little outgrowths of odorous leather). She then proposed that an oval window be created for ventilation, and a portion of the ceiling replaced with glass so that the books could possibly be seen in their shelves. Loveall immediately agreed to Anonyma's changes. Building (and the pursuant financial expense) gave the project an air of importance, and he listened to her with admiration as she described how the bookshelves would be modeled on the first and most distinguished in the country at the Bodleian Library in Oxford. In her library, the books would not be stacked barbarically in piles, as was still common, but with their spines facing outward and vertical. Here, they would not be chained to bars in the center of the room, a medieval torture still practiced in some church libraries: the books of Love Hall would be free to move about, although no one should be allowed to remove them from the library, except his lordship. She recalled the Bible — its presence long overdue. It would be the centerpiece. "It's only a book, the Bible," her father had told her, "but a very good one."

She even suggested that the Young Lord might like to design his own bookplate for the family library. Geoffroy idly sketched a tree with a tear falling from the bough. It was a moving picture of his own obsession and therefore immediately vetoed by his mother, who demanded that the plate be a copper engraving of the family coat of arms, complete with motto.

While structural work continued within, Anonyma began to catalog the books outside the library. As she waited for the arrival of the Bodleian shelves, she readied herself to replace the books in a proper and logical order. Under her protection, these books (and their new brothers and sisters) would be easily found by anyone who cared to seek; they would be kept in perfect condition, and the room would be free of bookworms of all varieties, thysanura and psocoptera alike. There would be triple desks, revolving lecterns, and metamorphic rosewood chairs that opened up to form small steps. Anonyma's budget was unlimited, and the very first acquisition, which took the catalog number J.i, was a dictionary that had recently been published and, coming in two volumes, folio, cost four pounds and fifteen shillings in boards.

Although it was now fashionable for families to use their libraries as informal drawing rooms, Anonyma emphasized that this would not be that room. She thought it best to nip any such idea in the bud, and the Young Lord supported her fully, mindful of the benefits of any space that was outside Lady Loveall's jurisdiction. He suggested that the south drawing room downstairs, with its wide bay window and wonderful view of the Castello d'Acqua, could easily be transformed into a drawing room. There, Anonyma said, the books upon the shelves could be dummies, while the real collection was secure.

Anonyma had a grand vision for the Octagonal Library. She told Loveall of the great libraries and his mind was transported from its grief as she filled it with stories of the first libraries, of Khufu and Khafra in Heliopolis and the great collection of Osymandyas — stories her father had told her many years before. Geoffroy had to close his eyes when he thought how much Dolly would have enjoyed hearing them. And Anonyma told him of the great private collectors: Plato; Charles II the Bald in medieval times; Dick Whittington's library at Grey Friars; Augustine's in Canterbury; John Bell's famous library in London with its eight thousand volumes; and Harley's at Wimpole, which had been bought for the nation. To this list would be added the name of Geoffroy Loveall: his library, the library of libraries. She told him of the 700,000 volumes of the Alexandrine Library founded by Ptolemy and the first five librarians of this, the greatest early library. Above its portal was written the simple phrase "Medicine for the Soul."

At the opening of the Octagonal Library, Loveall reduced Anonyma to tears by revealing an astonishing piece of masonry about which he had been suspiciously secretive. It can still be seen. Above the door of the new library were written the names of Ptolemy's five librarians, with an added sixth:

Zenodotus
Callimachus
Eratosthenes
Apollonius
Aristophanes
Anonyma

Now, twenty years after the great collection had begun, Lady Loveall lay dead and Anonyma sat in her kingdom, her library, communing with a copy of the anonymous *The Divination and Prophecies of the Female Somnambule,* poring over some marginalia. Geoffroy was in the Doll's House, eyes closed, meditating on the advice his sister had given him: "Build a new house." Neither the Young Lord nor the librarian knew anything of the death or the changes that were already taking place around them.

Geoffroy heard footsteps climbing the stairs. Hood coughed and knocked on the door. Without waiting for permission, he entered and, after a brief bow, said to his master: "Lord Loveall, sir, I regret to tell you that Lady Loveall has died."

Geoffroy looked up urgently from his prone position and asked, "Where is Lady Loveall?"

"In her bed, sir," said Hood as compassionately as his position allowed him.

"No. The *new* Lady Loveall," insisted Loveall.

"Sir?"

"My baby girl."

Me.

2

I Am Reborn

1

E. YOU KNOW WHO I AM.

I remember the first time I returned to Love Hall after our exile, now many years ago. The house hadn't long been deserted, but it felt haunted. There was a coat of greasy dust upon everything, as if the house had laid a winding-sheet over its contents. I ran my finger along the banister. If I took it away, it felt as though the whole covering would lift like skin from milk.

When I spoke, though I spoke quietly, the noise was so incongruous that it woke the echoes — "Hello?" they answered with a sleepy question. They were otherwise unbothered, grown lazy through lack of exercise, and so I hummed instead, which induced in them an odd pleasant quiver. In the Entertainments Room, a piece of china, for no apparent reason other than surprise, fell from a coffee table as though it had been waiting for the tiniest vibration to send it on its way. It cracked and the sound smacked from wall to wall like a ball in a fives court. The dust slept on. I sifted the evidence.

The house had the appearance of a museum that had shut down but, expectant of a new owner, had never stored its exhibits: the artifacts would remain where they were until the reopening under new management. The attendants, however, had been removed and not replaced. And the owner was finally arriving only now.

How quickly dust settles and the past seems further removed. Where were all the cooks? All the ghosts of all the cooks? Take away the people from a house and you may as well take away the house, too. Ruin seizes upon the lack of movement. I had never experienced such emptiness, and yet the house had been empty for so short a time. I would fill it again.

There was a friendly mouse in the kitchen, doing her bit to fight the general inertia by scurrying around a loaf of bread, which was encrusted with the family arms. She looked at me in surprise and then started to nibble the last letter of the motto. And that loaf of bread — everything, a name and a face. The local miller and baker had designed it especially for the occasion of my first viewing by the village, and everyone was too polite and happy to ask whether or not it should be eaten. This impressive piece of edible masonry had been down in the kitchen all that time, on display; and there it sat, most of it, amid the damp salt boxes and the empty pickling tubs, a culinary wonder. Uneasy at my presence, the mouse was dragging much of the letter *I* away with her, tumbling along with it anxiously.

I saw the empty egg basket and pictured the hard-boiled eggs nesting there, each with a date penciled in Roman numerals. I heard the clank of spit, skewer, meat hook, and knife where there was only silence, as they dangled lifeless like hanged men. And then I imagined I could smell the yeast and the sherry, the currants and the caraway seeds of Sarah's sugar cake. And I was home.

You know who I am. But perhaps you don't know my name: Rose Old. I was unwanted at birth and thrown away, evidence best disposed of. If you consider that, bloodily new to the world, I was bound for a dusty grave and that I was saved only by a distracted boy and a stray dog, it's a miracle that I lived an hour, let alone as long as I have.

Who'd have imagined I'd live to tell the tale, as it were? Fortune patted me on the head at an early age, but it wasn't all walks and treats. We had a complicated relationship.

What else do you know? Well, you know I'm alive now, unless I'm telling this story from beyond the grave. I'm Old but I'm not that old and I am not going to die in my story (unless I do it with the last full stop — that would be acceptable; after all, I haven't finished yet and I can't see the future any more clearly than you can).

Rose Old, alive.

I should apologize for not revealing myself in the first volume, which I chose not to tell in my own voice. "Why," you may ask, "when you are so very first person now?" The answer is simple: There was no I. And if there was an I, that little baby passed from hand to paw, there wasn't enough of an I with which to speak, or see. I didn't think my own voice would be persuasive enough, so I opted for the old-fashioned narrator, the All-Seeing One — or let's call him God.

No one knows how God knows everything He knows — after all, it's bound to be a man (and He blithely assumes that you are also male) — but He says He knows and we all believe Him. He speaks with knowledge and the force of history on His side. He says: "By now, Pharaoh had reached his destination," and Pharaoh has reached his destination after an unspecified amount of time. It was I who made up the first line of this confession, but when I read it to myself in His voice (deep, echoing), even I believed it. Print, too, is very persuasive — it has saved my life on more than one occasion.

I have an entirely different style from God. I deal only in the truth, that is, the truth as I witnessed it. If I had written the foregoing part in my own voice, I would have been covering, waiting for what I knew and making up the rest: there would have been a few arias but also whole scenes of recitative and a good deal of rhubarb. This would have been rendered less persuasive by a preponderance of the seasickening word *probably,* not to mention the cowardly limitations of *slightly* — a *slightly* irritating word. I would have induced in you the queasy feeling that I was backpedaling away from definitive statement. I would have excited your apprehensions with periphrasis such as "It might have been at about this time that . . . ," or I would have spoken too knowledgeably and later been caught in a lie. People can play fast and loose with the facts — sometimes they have to — but no one likes or trusts a history book that begins: "Julius Caesar hummed to himself as he walked through the sun-bedecked Forum in his purple-edged toga on that bright July morning as he considered the invasion of Britain." It is inappropriate. My intention was to convey you to this point with the minimum of fuss, to have you trust in what you were reading. I needed God, so I put Him to work for me.

Of course, I also spoke with my own voice — for even God, however neutral He pretends to be, must commit a little of Himself. Mine was the obsession with Ovid's *Metamorphoses,* which my mother read to me over so many nights and I have since read to others. There are also other inconsistencies that will have been, or will be, spotted by the caring reader. The truth works its way out in the end, like a splinter.

From now on, I am alive. I can write from fact.

I am born. I have memories. I am surrounded by evidence. Many years have passed since the events of "Anonymous," and that time has afforded us perspective — things have changed. My world has changed. The world has changed. Novels have changed. Spelling has been mostly standardised, or standardized. There have even been improvements in punctuation, although these are balanced by disastrous deteriorations in the world of fashion. Man is no longer sure of his position in the world — you may have known this. Or perhaps you weren't sure.

God, however, is dead. What I write from now on, I know for myself. And what I didn't witness myself, I know is true. There are newspapers, diaries, and libraries full of books. Of the previous part of the story, what I didn't know from my parents, I found out through my own personal inquiries. The rest I concocted: a detail here, a name there — I have always had a terrible penchant for good names and silly puns (blame my father), but they'll be no Allworthys or Fanny Prices and certainly no Hargrave Pollexfens. Conceivably, I shall have to call upon God again, to have Him come answer my prayers. That is my prerogative. But I have declared Him dead, so best to do without Him if possible.

The remainder of this must count, I suppose, as autobiography.

God narrated my beginning, my birth. Here is my second beginning, my rebirth, told by me.

Like any member of a noble family, I have an official birthday and a real birthday. It's a wild child that knows her own father, and I was rescued from the dustheap by mine, the richest man in the country (including, they said, the ruling monarch).

It was a strange beginning, of course. I started with nothing, less than nothing, and then within a few hours I had everything. I was to inherit the Loveall legacy: that's why they called me Miss Fortune.

The Official Version

After the death of my grandmother (whom I met only once, briefly, just as God told you), my father asked my mother to marry him. She said yes.

Stories of an affair had been whispered outside the house for many years, ever since my father had attained his majority, but rarely had been spoken with certainty and more recently had all but been forgotten. The servants knew there to be no such attachment, that the Young Lord was entirely celibate, but so fierce was their loyalty to the family that they would not even stoop to dignify the imputation with a denial. The town's tongues, whose appetite for gossip about Love Hall was rarely satisfied with tasty detail, drew their own conclusions as to why it had taken the midnight-eyed governess so long to catalog some old books. Surely this kind of work could be done in a week or less. What possible reason did she have to remain at the house? Open that door and the story told itself.

Though there were no outward signs of intimacy between the two, a secret liaison stood to reason. They had lived together under the same roof for years, while Geoffroy grew into an attractive, if self-absorbed, man. Yet he showed no inclination whatsoever to leave the house for any length of time: what kept him there, if not Anonyma? By all accounts, they spent long hours in each other's company in the library. She was the only woman he spoke to, apart from his mother. And though both were enslaved to the bedridden widow, they were next in command: my father by birth, my mother by his choice. Put two and two together and you get a couple. Wasn't Love Hall made for them? It was all circumstantial, to be sure, but damning enough.

Eventually, however, the rumor ran its natural course. Nothing happened. Nothing kept happening for years. Perhaps "Miss Molly" was quite as uninterested in women as he appeared.

But the death of Lady Loveall and my father's subsequent (and immediate) engagement to the librarian — the two pieces of information arrived hand in hand — proved that the gossips, some of whom were dead themselves by now, had been right all along. Cries of "We told us so!" were said to have been heard from the village churchyard. Not only had the couple been having an affair, but this affair had somehow been managed in secrecy beneath Lady Loveall's very nose. This revelation was greeted with no surprise whatsoever. The surprise was that nobody had previously been able to confirm it.

The only plausible alternative was that their bond had been unspoken, and even unacknowledged, for the past fifteen years, out of deference to the powers that were. In his mother's shadow, their love had been unable to bloom, but now that she was herself a shade, the sun shone on them. It was all very rambling rose and briar — classic Loveall family business, except that they hadn't had to wait till death to entwine.

However, this touching theory was rendered impossible by the next revelation: my mother was with child, and the blessed event was close at hand. Lady Loveall's death had merely been good timing for the lovers. My father's stock rose with each new development.

My mother was then moved into the library, where, with doctor and midwife in attendance, she gave birth to me a few months later. It was thought that this union and its fruit could never have been recognized during the life of my grandmother. Her son with a servant, a *pregnant* servant: they might as well have buried Lady Loveall facedown, to save her the bother of turning.

No one could bring herself to imagine what might have happened if Lady Loveall hadn't died. When things turn out well, we tend to take it for granted that this was the only possible outcome, to deceive ourselves that we deserve it, and neglect to consider the disasters that might otherwise have been. (God would have enjoyed that last thought. He would have used it as the centerpiece of an entire *digressive essay* before He got back to the plot. I tried a few of these, but they didn't suit my style. However, I did feel Him move within me as I gave my humble opinion about mankind and its mores in that casually omniscient way — you'll be glad to know that the urge to moralize is weak within me.)

With my grandmother dead, the one bar to their happiness had vanished and my parents were free to live as man and wife. They ignored or never mentioned the scandal (though they freely admitted that my birth was "premature"), and within a few months Love Hall housed a family once more.

That is the story of the marriage of my mother and father and my birth, what people were led, and led themselves, to believe. It's a very satisfactory truth that when you want to disseminate a lie, you can release a certain amount of information, markers along the line, and depend upon the popular need for a good plot to finish the job.

Now there remains no need for untruths or secrecy. Anyway, I have never much been one for secrets. I prefer the daylight to the darkness.

How many people will read this book? It is a matter for conjecture. The only thing I can say with certainty is that you are now; so, between the two of us:

The Unofficial Version

My father realized that the baby needed two parents if he was to make her his heir. ("Her?" "Me?" A bit of both, I think. Hermia? Pronouns are problematic, so we'll leave the word *him* aside for the time being. My father was certainly unaware of it.) The relatives would not tolerate a mere foundling suddenly placed in front of them in the waiting list, and in this, the law would be entirely on their side. Therefore, I would have to be someone's — that is, the offspring of my father and someone else: my father needed a wife; his baby needed a mother.

It was Dolores who first made the suggestion. Anonyma would be the woman. My father liked Anonyma, even admired her, having particular respect for her quiet erudition and determined dominion of the library. What is more, she had the sole perfect qualification: she had cared for Dolores, who loved her. Anonyma was the only grown woman with whom he felt at ease — this would be important to the masquerade — and he wasn't related to her. There was no other female in the world with these credentials. But Father had no idea how to manage the situation. He therefore asked Dolores again, and she told him what he should have already known: Ask Hood.

When Hood returned to the Doll's House with me in his arms, he agreed that there was only one course of action — I should be reared as legitimate — and that Anonyma was the suitable candidate for the office in question. Hood's means to this end was simplicity itself. My father would ask her to marry him. It was that straightforward.

Hood's reasoning, however, was more complex than anything my father, a sweet man incapable of a scheme, could have dreamed. The probable success of the plan rested upon my mother's age and diminishing prospects. Scarcely any longer of a marriageable age — this being in the days when women of thirty-seven were considered spinsters — she had few alternatives. She loved the library and would want to perform her daily devotions there for the rest of her life, and this marriage would ensure that she could. Her station in the world would rise in such startling measure that no one would doubt it an absurd marriage of love, especially those who knew my father's quixotic nature. Hood did not give voice to his assumption that any reluctance upon Anonyma's part could be quickly eliminated by curt reference to her library. Success was assured.

Within an hour, as my father showed my baby eyes the interior of the Hemmen House, his man had conceived the most practical parts of the plan. The whole house must believe that I was legitimate, and those who knew otherwise, those who knew that Anonyma had not been pregnant (though it was amazing how little people did notice, when all their lives they had been encouraged to ignore anything worth noticing), would have their silence bought, either to be kept in the house as preferred servants or pensioned off to one of the family's other houses on a distant isle. In a mansion the size of Love Hall, there were many people who never saw one another and perhaps half of the staff could be kept. Of the rest, many would understand that no questions were to be asked and nothing to be told.

It was a good plan, but there was only one man in the house who could effect it: Samuel Hamilton, the current in the line of Loveall household economists.

Like all his ancestors, Hamilton had the most meticulous handwriting, a precise knowledge of codes and ciphers, and a supernaturally good memory. With these weapons, recording everything in encoded ledgers, Hamilton fought to defend the Loveall. His family's loyalty had been unimpeachable and necessarily so, for in those accounts were hidden the Loveall secrets, so deeply encrypted that no one Hamilton could comprehend all of them. Only he and his revered predecessors in any way understood the fiscal calendar of Love Hall and the financial arrangements of its occupants.

His father, Jacob, had died a few months previous, leaving Samuel in sole charge of the management of Loveall affairs. Jacob's death, though unexpected, had ultimately been a blessing, since by the end of his reign he had become unpredictable, handling secretive affairs of such byzantine complexity that his son could not hope to grasp them, when a comprehensive understanding of family business was the only key to success. There was knowledge that would die with him, and Jacob had said as much, as though prepared for the final reckoning. However contrary Jacob had become, his grip on the job never wavered, and Lady Loveall's dependence on him never diminished. Samuel Hamilton was, and always had been, in awe of his father, so he preferred to remember him in his days of great power rather than during the autocratic decline of these last years. Hamilton would manage the situation before him as he had seen his father manage so many other crises in his heyday, with speed, stealth, and single-mindedness. He was summoned.

In the Doll's House, Samuel was a minute king, dwarfed by a wooden throne so high that his feet barely skimmed the rug, his crown a prematurely bald head, the sides and back of which were skirted by two inches of straight brown hair. He was a prim little man with a tidy wife, Angelica, who had recently given birth to their second child, a son to accompany their daughter. When I think of the father and mother now, it seems inconceivable that these plain, nondescript people could have produced two such gorgeous children. Perhaps beauty skips a generation. To his children's good fortune, resourcefulness and ingenuity do not: for within the dull, sweet frame of their father lurked a genius of criminal proportions.

Hamilton listened to Hood's plan without a flicker of emotion. From time to time he nodded in reassurance as he took notes in the code that had been passed to him according to the Lex Pantophilensis.

Such plans as this, such disruptions to the norm, were his family's very raison d'être. It was certainly not the strangest story that a Hamilton had heard from a Loveall, and he treated it as carefully as the planning of a military exercise. This is what his family had taught him. It was his tribute to the memory of the great man, his father.

After a thoughtful pause he said that there was no difficulty, and he and Hood talked in the company of my father for the next hour. Father pretended to listen but was lost in nervousness, sweating anxiously at the thought of the imminent proposal. Around his panic, which eased itself (as it would for the rest of his life) in fussing over me, the plan for the deception fell naturally into place. He forgot to pay attention, and when he was reminded, everything was already arranged.

Word would be put out that the librarian was pregnant and that she and my father would be married. The librarian (who would be expected to be expecting) would be hidden in the house, it would be thought, out of shame. I would be secreted for as short a time as possible: three months was considered ample. Like most babies during this period of their prelives, I would be close to my mother but, unlike most babies, I'd be beside her rather than within. Neither of us would be seen. Then we would emerge magnificent into a new story: radiant mother, the new Lady Loveall, and a somewhat large baby. There would be only family employees present at "the birth," and no one would be any the wiser. Hood and Hamilton were in control of the whole situation. In their minds, the crisis was over. As far as my father was concerned, it was just beginning.

"Hood . . . why would she want to marry me when the baby isn't hers?" my father asked.

"With all due respect, sir, the baby isn't yours, either," said Hood without looking up. They had not spoken about anything in this vein, let alone mentioned my sex. Hamilton, meanwhile, was only for the first time entertaining the idea of addressing my father at all. He was to this Loveall, it occurred to him, what his great-grandfather had been to the Great Lord Loveall himself. Pride prickled inside him.

"Sir," he said, and cleared his throat. "This plan is doomed to failure unless you approach Miss Wood as soon as possible."

My father stood up, sat down, then stood up again as though he'd landed on a pin. Hamilton, who very rarely looked at his lordship, blushed, as the saying had it, like a black dog.

"Do you have any last wishes, sir?" asked Hood, which was the only joke he ever made to my father in his many years of service. My father left the room knowing that what he had to do was the best thing he would ever do for his family. Hood — with me in his arms — and Hamilton followed close behind. The short procession had a funereal air. On his way to the library, my father noticed things he had never had time to see before: a scratch on one of the stairs in the shape of a flower, a small portrait of a dead relative hidden between one of the banisters and the wall. Servants stopped at the bottom of the stairs and bowed their heads, raising their eyes to see if they could catch a sly glimpse of the delegation. Perhaps my father made a wager with himself: if I can turn around now and see the eyes on the face of that portrait from this angle, then everything will come off according to plan. He turned, he could, and he felt some relief. Or he couldn't, because from that angle a forest of banisters obscured the view. That's what I would have done, and I inherited my superstitions from him. It was only later in my life I realized that it can sometimes be a relief to lose that kind of wager: then you can throw luck out of the window and step boldly forth to meet your destiny with nothing but your native intelligence.

Now they were at Anonyma's Library. My father advanced into the room alone.

He knelt on one knee in front of his librarian. Anonyma had been busy cataloging and cleaning, and was still, at this moment, lost in consideration of *The Female Somnambule,* fretting over a problem posed by the marginalia. She was therefore only half paying attention when

he came in, until suddenly she became aware that he w
His stiff manner was extraordinary. Perhaps he was gu
offenses, she thought, but the look in his eyes said otherwise: it apologized, it pleaded forgiveness, it begged silence. Undoubtedly, she thought, it was bad news about her library. It was the only possible explanation. She wanted to cry.

"Miss Wood . . . Anonyma . . . Will you marry me?"

What had he said? Marry him? What was he talking about? Why was he teasing her? Perhaps she was missing his metaphor. Yes. Perhaps he had said something before while she had been deep in study. Marriage? She tried to read his face. Loveall looked up at her through the eyes of failure. He had never been more comic or earnest.

Anonyma opened her mouth. Out popped "Ha!"

It was a laugh that sounded for the world like mocking rejection. She did not, could not, answer; she was dumbfounded, gagged by her own astonishment. There was hush among the stacks. Inside her head, however, there was no silence but a deafening scream. As she looked down at him, she was suddenly struck by the truth, that he honestly wanted to marry her. Why did he? She could immediately understand some of the motives behind his proposal — the need for an heir, his solitude — but what of Lady Loveall? Her mind raced. It might have been his mother's idea. No. No. Anonyma was nothing to her. The librarian was practical enough to know that she would never receive a preferable offer, that there might not actually be a preferable offer anywhere in the world. Outside Love Hall, there was no one waiting to grant her a title or a library, no one about to present her with everything she wanted. And here, on one knee, someone was, someone she knew well, whom she had watched grow day by day, haunted by a tragedy they shared. She was squeezing the life out of the book she had entirely forgotten she was holding, her knuckles white with the pressure.

She relaxed her hand, and the book dropped. Loveall caught it before it landed. The spell was broken.

"Yes, my lord," she said. "I will."

She expected him to stand up, take her hand and kiss her, perhaps even smile, but he had rarely done anything she expected ever since that first day when he had presented poor Dolores to her. Instead, in the same formal, faltering way, he inquired if she would be the mother of his child. She was about to answer when Hood appeared with me at the door. I was wrapped in fresh white swaddling, and my face poked out like a strawberry. (Her words, in her diary.) Hamilton followed close behind.

"This is the baby to which his lordship is referring, ma'am," said Hood, presenting me for approval. "I take it that the blessed union is to occur, my lady?" he asked, putting the tip of his finger into my mouth to stop my gurgling — my mother remembered this most specifically. And it looked comical to her, these dignified men handling a baby. Loveall looked anxiously at my mother like a schoolboy requesting a second slice of cake. She nodded.

"Should I declare my intentions to your father?" asked my father.

"Dead, sir," she replied.

"Ah." He could not recall if he had ever known that her father was dead. "Your legal guardian, perhaps?"

"You are he, sir," said Hood.

"Ah," sighed my father, and retreated a small distance.

"And what is Lady Loveall's opinion of the matter?" she remembered to ask. Forebodings of the old woman had been casting shadows over her sudden happiness. She had managed to banish these thoughts to the very back of her mind, but now that she remembered her, Lady Loveall loomed even larger than life: the one person who could ruin everything.

"Is also dead, ma'am. Died," said Hood, finally.

A proposal of marriage, a baby, Lady Loveall dead. Oh.

Her face burned and she fell backward into the nearest chair. Hamilton was over her immediately, fanning her with the nearest thing to hand, the manuscript of Mary Day's *The Houses of Dead*. Despite her swoon, Anonyma had the presence of mind to tell him to replace it on the table *gently*. He tried to cool her with his notebook, which was so thick that it produced barely any current at all.

"I am well, tolerably well. Lady Loveall is . . . ?" Anonyma was impatient to know more.

"You weren't aware, ma'am. These three hours," said Hamilton, who administered. Hood had been left with me, holding the baby. My father bit his top lip and looked out of the window, which offered a view of the avenue that he had never quite noticed before: it seemed best to fix his gaze in this direction for as long as possible.

"I should like to know something of this . . . ," said my mother, but Hood interrupted her.

"Of course, my lady." She had never been addressed so decorously before and had experienced such deference only directed at others, often by herself. Hood bowed with the baby in his arms. Anonyma beckoned him and took me gently from him, worrying that Hood, though capable in so many other ways, had exhausted his child-care repertoire. She looked down at me and smiled. She didn't yet understand where I had come from or what exactly I meant to her, but she knew instantly that, whatever I turned out to be, I was the nearest she would ever have to her own child. Parts of my father's face creased into the smallest smile. He dabbed nervously at his brow with a silk.

"Miss . . . my dear." The words fell quite unnaturally from his lips. "This is Rose Loveall, the heir of Love Hall."

"My lord," Hood interrupted smartly, returning to his former self now that he was newly liberated of the baby. "Your exertions today have been considerable. Might I suggest that you take a moment to yourself and that you and her ladyship reconvene at dinner?"

"An excellent idea," said Loveall, pleased with the outcome of events, quietly proud of his sangfroid, and in a desperate hurry to leave the room. As he left, those remaining heard him hum the air of "Nancy Bell" to himself.

Anonyma assumed that the dream would leave with him, that Hood and Hamilton would excuse his lordship's derangement (possibly with an offer of money) and arrange that her things be packed and delivered to the servants' entrance before morning. Instead, as soon as they'd watched him float away, Hood and Hamilton turned to the new Lady Loveall and bent into their most stately bows, hands almost scraping the floor in front of her.

"Ma'am," said Hood. "If we can be of any assistance, we are now entirely your servants."

"Felicitations, my lady," said Hamilton, as if to his shoes.

Anonyma surveyed the library, the baby in her arms, the men in front of her. Everything had changed beyond recognition in so short a time.

"I think, sir . . . Should I call you Hood?" He bowed. "I think you should tell me from which Rose this little petal came."

Hood assured her that I was not stolen, that it was on account of a commendable act of charity on the part of his lordship that I was alive and breathing. He told her everything, the discovery of a baby lying neglected in savage conditions, Lord Loveall's decision that this baby would be his heir, Lady Loveall's overexcitement and extinction, and finally Loveall's realization that his heir would need a mother — at which point (Hood emphasized) it was his lordship's idea, because of his extreme admiration and affection for her, that the mother and new lady of the house should be Miss Wood. He then explained that it had been an idea of Hamilton's and his own to move the two of us, mother and child, into the library for a certain time to give weight to the story of the pregnancy.

The telling lasted twenty minutes. My mother listened with incredulity and pleasure, in equal parts. She might have agreed to the marriage under any circumstances, but none could have been more unexpected than these. Infrequently, she would ask a question of Hood, and without taking his eyes from hers, he would answer. She knew that she was being told the truth. When Hood was finished, she asked if there was anything else he had passed over — a truth omitted, even with the best of intentions, could be fatal to them all. She could see nothing wrong with what they were doing, but she wanted to be in full possession of the facts so that those who thought the marriage a scandal could never know more than she.

"There is one thing, my lady, one small thing," said Hood, and he approached us. "As Lady Loveall discovered before she died . . . ," and his words dwindled to a stutter as he unwrapped my swaddling to show my mother *the netherlands*. She looked down and back at Hood.

"His lordship knows, of course?"

There was silence.

"Does his lordship know?"

"That," opined Hamilton, "is an extremely vexed question."

"Lord Loveall doesn't know?"

"He has been *aware* of it, but he either does not understand, has purposefully put it out of his mind, or does not believe it. We have not mentioned this aspect of the child between us, madam. There is no doubt that he believes or wants others to believe that this child is a girl."

"What should we do?" asked Anonyma, lost in wonder.

"We should not mention it, ma'am." Hood looked at Hamilton, who nodded his head once in approval. "Not yet. I fear that the consequences would be grave. The death of his mother, the new responsibilities that this entails, his proposal to you — his lordship's nerves are severely weakened. He is, of course, to be your husband and we defer to you, but I" — and he indicated Samuel Hamilton, who was once more taking notes in his ledger — "*we* would very much recommend that it remain our secret."

"For how long?" My mother looked at me in disbelief.

"For the time being."

"It is a good while before a boy need be breeched, ma'am," added Hamilton. "There is surely no harm in keeping one in skirts for a short while, and there would be nothing unusual in it. Our new boy, Stephen, will be in skirts, too."

"This is what we think best, until the appropriate moment," Hood continued. "His lordship will doubtless be able to receive this intelligence with more equanimity in the near future. Time is the great healer, ma'am."

My mother agreed that this was, for the *time being,* the right course of action, for his lordship and his peace of mind, for her and her beloved library, and for the house and family who had been so good to her. But as Hamilton and Hood turned back to the ledger, she drew me closer to her bosom with a private smile, indicative of a deeper satisfaction. This smile was meant for no one other than the two of us, because, though she would tell no one, she believed above all that this was the right course of action for me, for the baby she held in her arms.

My mother had a secret of her own. And since the time for secrets is gone, and since God didn't tell you — though He *knows* everything, He doesn't have to tell *you* — I shall. She had one reason and one reason alone for this private smile, and it was the very same reason she had wanted the position of governess at Love Hall in the first place: a poet, *her* poet, Mary Day.

Mary Day. The name is more familiar today, but at the time, little was known of her. Whatever was certain my mother's father knew by heart. Jeremy Wood had been a bookbinder with a side business in printing, specializing in trade cards and the odd broadside, and my mother grew up with inky fingers. His business crumbled after an unsuccessful foray into publishing, taking his press with it, and he turned antiquary. Then it was dust, not ink, under my mother's nails.

His life's passion was the printed works of Mary Day. During the torturously slow death of his beloved wife, Jeremy introduced his eleven-year-old daughter to these works to distract her from the stagnation of gloom that overwhelmed their house. He enthusiastically impressed upon her the wonder and novelty of the radical printing techniques used in the creation of the books, which were full of complex diagrams. Day and her printer seemed to like the ink and the page as much as the words, and her father revered their designs, as though the words were somehow secondary, but it was those words that caught his daughter's attention.

On initial acquaintance, in fact, far from distracting her from the miseries at hand, the poems brought my mother closer to her own. Mary Day taught her to return Death's stare:

> *Though bodies pass — alas! —*
> *Their expiration may our inspiration be.*
> *Look upon her where she lies*
> *And know the light of embers in her eyes*
> *Will burn again eternally.*

After her father's death, my mother suffered a bitter disappointment in love. She never spoke openly about this event, which made up her mind to become a governess. Though it left a scar across her heart, things might have taken a much darker turn without what she called "the Day light." For a second time, the poet came to her assistance, speaking to her, as if directly, of a greater love that transcended the "febrile flutterings of a sentimental soul." It was a love that seemed attainable through the poems of Mary Day.

It was as if Day tried to cut to the very heart of human origins and destiny. As she read, my mother felt lulled into a deeply contemplative state, yet alert to the rhythm and meanings of the words. Day's work inspired great fervor in her disciples (or Daysciples, as one of our more boorish literary critics has called them), and the unavailability of her writings engendered a powerful sense of possessiveness in the hearts of her admirers. Unaware of one another, each enjoyed a special individual relationship with the poet: my mother was one such. She took her father's passion and made it her own. Before he died, leaving my mother to make her way in the world at sixteen, their closest moments were spent in shared study and reading.

It had been her hope to one day complete an edition of the poet's works, continuing her father's lonely, pioneering study, and she applied for the position of governess with this purpose in mind, for here, somewhere in Love Hall, was the chance to discover more about Mary Day, the writer who spoke to her as no other poet, and no other human.

Not long before her father's death, a shady colleague of his, who went by the assumed name of Albion Mills, reported that on a recent visit to Love Hall to appraise a collection of tapestries, he happened to find himself in the library, a room in a most lamentable state of disrepair. Here he saw, in a forlorn crate, some editions of the poetry of Mary Day, together with, he thought, fragments of her own handwriting. He had not been able to examine them quite as carefully as he would have liked, owing to a premature disturbance, but he was sure that this was either a collection of her works and ephemera or books owned by the poet. One stray piece of paper had happened, *unfortunately,* to become separated from the others, somehow attaching itself to the inside of Albion's customarily baggy jacket, and knowing of Jeremy's interest, he had kept it for him. Albion tossed it over with the shrug of shoulders that might normally accompany throwing a dog a scrap of meat. The Woods read it with awe, breathing it in, basking in it as though light sprang from the paper.

It was a letter, recto and verso, from Mary Day's printer to the author, addressed simply as M, outlining certain changes he was bound to make to the text of "Sophia of Light" to enable him to include the designs she had requested. Day had written her own responses on it, presumably before transcribing them into a fair copy. It was the first time these Daysciples had seen her handwriting.

Albion Mills was not interested in the poetess (or "the Female Poet," as Jeremy preferred); besides, an owed favor was a valuable commodity in the world of the antiquarian. The Loveall had not seemed interested in Mary Day, either, Albion told them, and the valuation of the tapestries had exceeded all expectations.

My mother had decided there and then that, if possible, she would try to explore this cache of material. Upon the death of her father, her determination became an obsession. When she heard of the opportunity at Love Hall, she did all she could to persuade a distraught Lady Makem to write her the strongest letter of recommendation. It all seemed so auspicious.

On the night of her arrival at Love Hall, as she sat gazing the length of the Northern Avenue, she tried to imagine what might possibly be waiting for her in the library, wherever that library might be. Manuscripts? Marginalia? Editions of the poems? She had no specific plan but knew that she wanted to touch them, to read the books read by Mary Day in the very editions that the poet had used, to indulge herself in them. Perhaps the box wasn't there anymore — but if it was . . . What wouldn't she do to see them?

A week after her arrival, she dedicated her first solo expedition in Love Hall to discovering if the unscrupulous Mills had been telling the truth, if any of these books were in the library. They were. Amid all the crumbling paper and leather, they were easy to find, too — they still had yet to be properly unpacked since their arrival and were now wedged up against the inside of the door, so that she had to squeeze through the available space. "Imagine being kept *out* of a library by Mary Day," she thought.

The stale air smelled so badly of mildew and clammy paper that, on first entrance, it almost brought tears to her eyes, partly for the books and partly for herself. She opened the top of the most accessible of the four small boxes in the crate to see notebooks and an ornate copy of *Pistis Sophia* — of which she knew the existence only because Mary Day had quoted from it, had quoted perhaps from this very book. Immediately underneath, a crisp copy of *Become Passers-By,* Day's simplest book of poetry that began with "Assembly of the Holy Ones, The Shadowless Lights," one of the many sonnets that my mother knew by heart. She caught her breath and suppressed her urge to ransack the boxes in a frenzy. There would be time for everything, she told herself. She exhaled, puffing out her cheeks, and looked up at the ceiling to remind herself that she wasn't dreaming. My mother knew that her moment with these books was yet to come, and so consoled herself with stealing the volumes away one at a time to read in her room. It was not difficult to do so unnoticed and she soon realized that it was unlikely anyone would have cared: no one ever mentioned the library.

Although events — her own shyness and the subsequent death of her ward — initially conspired against her openly asking for permission to put the Mary Day books into any proper kind of order, my mother suddenly found herself, quite unexpectedly, offered the post of librarian by Loveall. She had mentioned Mary Day at that moment and he had put everything entirely in her hands. The library was hers. Mary Day was hers.

She could continue her father's work surrounded by key primary materials that he had not lived to see. She would be able to refute, once and forever, the tedious imputation of a certain critic that Mary Day had been the nom de plume of a male poet and that only the blindness of the cult of Mariolatry kept this fact from the world. Though this charge was beneath contempt, a well-researched biography had to start somewhere. She owed it to her father, to the poet, and to the world.

She relished her new position and set about the task of getting the library in proper working order. This she managed with methodical efficiency. Her own part of the library, on the other hand, she oversaw with a more profound, more private enthusiasm. It was here that she kept the complete works of Mary Day and Day's copies of gnostic texts, scrupulously cataloged. She purchased an edition of Tertullian's *De praescriptione haereticorum,* brought under lock and key from Paris. As she had learned from Mary's own notebooks, the only proper collection of gnostic writings would almost entirely comprise anti-gnostic treatises that contained fragments of the very texts they attacked. Justin, Hippolytus, Irenaeus — all polemicized against the heretics, quoting them at length. All would therefore be in her library. And this was poetic justice.

My mother came to Love Hall for Mary Day and found her. Now she could repay the great house by using all she had learned from Mary in my upbringing. First, Loveall had given her the library, then his hand in marriage, and now . . . the baby in her arms. She was a practical woman in matters of the world, yet in agreeing to bring me up as a girl, she was becoming engaged in what others would have thought an absurd deception. Why? Once again, the reason was Mary Day.

My mother believed that every human being is part male and part female and that the truly poetic mind should harness both these forces. In Mary Day's notebooks, which my mother had been engaged in transcribing and was shortly to have printed in a private edition, she had read: "God created man male and female. Adam, the only parturient male, was created both man and woman. Until we deny any distinction, we shall not feel the pure poetry of the eternal fill our lungs with its breath." And in "The Houses of Dead":

When the two become the one
And the inside outside, the outside in
So that the male be not male nor the female female
Then will you see me.

Day also referred to the ancient legends of other cultures that told of an androgynous divine who created the world and was then split in two, spawning male and female, who were thus destined to pursue each other to re-create the idyllic innocence of their original androgyny. This was a good story, but my mother had no expectation, or even desire, that the quest might end in success. She did feel, however, that it was vital for the two halves of the soul to be respected.

To Day, the separation of the two sexes represented a deterioration from the original perfection and fruitfulness of the imagined undivided sexuality. In Christian terms, sin had caused this division —

and certain of the church fathers said that, at his resurrection, Christ was neither male nor female. For Mary Day, this suggested a time after life and beyond death, a golden age, a place where men and women would exist in equality. She called it Feminisia.

My mother thought of all this in much more practical terms: no person was either completely masculine or completely feminine. When men were too manly, they were as inept as women who were too feminine. Perhaps this is why she was drawn to my father — the clothes he wore were sometimes fabulously effeminate. This was many years ago now, at a time when gender roles were closer together, particularly with regard to fashion. Nowadays, everything is defined, the lines more divisively drawn. Then, men wore their hair curly and luxuriously flowing; a graceful leg and an elegant wrist were considered symbols of virility — witness the Great Lord Harold on top of the Mausoleum: he looks as though he's showing off a new garter.

My mother cared less for the pure poetic breath of the eternal than she did the air that she breathed every day: a Daysciple, yes, but a discerning one. It seemed obvious to her, however, that the idea of the androgyne had practical and useful applications for the potential of humanity here on earth.

And with me, little Rose — or RoseMary, as she sometimes called me — she had literally in her hands, in her arms, a chance to test her theories. A baby's inner sense of itself was neither male nor female, until society taught it which role it was to assume. (Has this been entirely discredited yet? If not, it will be.) Boys and girls were therefore made and not born, and I would be made. I would without a doubt be the most adorable and original child ever born, and an even more successful adult. Perhaps I would be the most perfect person in the world, a symbolic challenge to every assumption on heaven or earth. My mother was giving me the greatest gift that she could offer.

It hadn't been her idea to bring me up in dresses. This was presented to her as a fait accompli. I was male? Yes. I would be brought up as a girl? Yes. She imagined that this phase would probably last only a year or two: then, undoubtedly, and with the approval of my father, once he had overcome his current agitations, everything would be stabilized. It was simply a matter of deferral till he could accept the idea of a son. She wasn't to know that my father could never accept this, could never even discuss the facts.

As she held me in her arms, her mind was suddenly brimming with thoughts of Day and "The Houses of Dead," which told how God, having no sex, provided the mind with no sex at birth. And what was I but her tabula rasa?

That was why, as she drew me closer to her bosom, she smiled.

It was an eccentric proposal and an eccentric marriage, but my father and mother were very happy. They never once argued and they never once made love. They kept separate rooms, as I well know, but they brought me up together.

Both the official version and the unofficial version of my beginning had the same ending: my parents were married, without great ceremony, and I was born.

The Announcement

In the best national newspapers, without date, carefully worded by Hamilton so as to be entirely true:

"Sir Geoffroy, the Young Lord Loveall and his wife, Lady Anonyma Loveall, rejoice at the birth of a child, Rose."

The Celebration

LONG LIVE THE LOVEALL, proclaimed the banner outside The Monkey's Head for weeks on either side of the local holiday that celebrated the arrival of the new heir. The local population was happy and relieved not only for the family but also for themselves. For as the house stood (and still stands) above them, so its master stood above them, too, owner of all the land in view. And though they might have wanted a more active landowner than my father, they could never have wanted a more caring one. They knew that the Alternative Lord Lovealls would not have been so considerate. The future of the Loveall was the future of every single drinker standing, or slumped, at the bar. The village depended on our well-being.

On the official night of my birth, the landlord raised his pewter pint-pot in the direction of the house and proposed a toast to the assembled company: "Let no one call this child a bastard. She is a blessing for all of us. Long live the Loveall!" And the people in the public house cheered and lifted their glasses toward Love Hall, pints brimming with the local brew poured free of charge for the entire weekend at the behest of the Loveall. They were in no mood to disagree.

And being born, I had to be viewed. It was the time of the year when the townsfolk came to pay their respects to the family and my father was called upon to lay his (gloved) hand upon them. Doubtless, part of the excitement was that it was the only time they found themselves in physical contact with the richest man in the country. And this year there was a fascinating bonus: the presentation of the new baby. The locals brought me gifts of cake, corn dolls, and trinkets. As I was perambulated, we were showered with petals, herbs, and confetti. I was held up to them on the balcony by Hood under the anxious eye of my parents, and as his arms reached their highest extent, there was a deafening cheer of relief. I would always remind them of free beer. I looked like their future and the future of the great Hall directly behind me as they shaded their eyes against the sun.

Oh, it was a day of grand celebration. The locals milled around the grounds all afternoon, drinking and eating whatever they were offered. They wandered between entertainments, in and out of the huge marquees that my father had erected so that the aged could keep out of the sun, and the drunken out of his sight. Even the Mausoleum had been tastefully separated from the revelry, half hidden behind fences of twisting vines and summer flowers. One might have been forgiven for thinking my father had forgotten about Dolores altogether.

The local poet, a friend of Hamilton's, declaimed a long ode from a first-floor window to universal approval. He had brought a professional ballad scholar from the University at Oxford who instructed the villagers in the correct singing of the songs that they knew better than he. To the delight of the locals, syllabubs were delivered on ice all the way from the city's Lactarium. Tug-of-warriors took the strain and heaved, some looking as though they would fly off into the air, so puny were their bodies and so tight their grip on the rope, while others appeared rooted like trees to the ground, never to be moved. Children from town and gentry alike lined up for unicorn rides while races — sack, three-legged, and wheelbarrow — were fiercely contested, won, and lost. Eggs fell from spoons and broke their yolks on the ground, which was so hot that they almost fried where they landed. And some of the revelers, falling victim to the heat and the beer, fried where they landed, only to wake later with one side of their face overdone by a vicious sun.

And still nothing ran out. There seemed to be an inexhaustible fountain of barley water and porter for all. The trays of pickled cucumbers went initially untouched, along with the large ornamental loaf, but the appearance of Toby the Learned Pig caused great astonishment and the swine was given the cucumbers as remuneration.

My mother showed some local children bookbinding techniques. They watched her for hours, entranced not by the books or the arcane pleasures of spine sewing but by her, for they had never before been so close to a female member of the nobility. They tried to smell her, she remembered, like little dogs. The jousting exhibition passed "without grave incident," the dances of the local children "pleased young and old alike," as did the singing of the Sunday school (the same children), and "even in a happy crowd of over 400, there were no arrests." In the evening, when the sun finally went down, there was a fireworks display from the Terra-cotta Bridge. The colored lights reflected in the big pond to the oohs and aahs of all. And just after the very last firework fell, a shooting star flew across the sky. There was a breathless silence and everybody left, happy, thinking of the new star of Love Hall.

The gates of the great house had been thrown open: a symbol of the changes within. And on that particular day, they had been open to everyone from Playfield, the farmers and their wives, their children and their animals. It was my father's greatest day.

The newspaper, which I have in front of me, reported it all under the headline ROSE OF ENGLAND and pronounced my birth a new lease on life for Love Hall.

And there lived the Loveall: Lord and Lady Loveall, with their beautiful daughter, Rose — a daughter who would marry well and save the Loveall line. It had not been expected that my father would successfully produce progeny. He had certainly married beneath his station, but he had married. He had fathered a child, not perhaps in the desired way, but he had fathered a child, and in a rakish style reminiscent of his much-missed grandfather.

Love Hall itself started to change for the better, too. Gone were the black coverings on the windows, a solemn correction to every smile; gone the mourning that shrouded the entire household; gone those two beastly dogs my father so hated, now kenneled elsewhere on the premises. (He had briefly considered killing them and burying them with their owner, but the senior of the curry chefs had looked with such tenderness on the unsympathetic grimace of one of the little brutes that the Young Lord had been moved to spare them, provided they were never heard of again. They never were.)

Instead of the perpetual gloom and growl, there were colors and brightness, sunshine, my mother and I. My full name — Rose Old Loveall. Above all, a new Loveall and a new Love Hall.

This was a lifetime ago. Since then, I have traveled around the world. I have kissed the eyelids of a sailor from Greece. I have taken shillings and torn tickets. I have lost loved ones in war. I have finally been persuaded to stop using the phrase "cast a sheep's eye at" when I mean "direct a romantic glance toward": however, I think the language is worse off for the absence of this phrase (and that it will have a resurgence). I have read every book in Anonyma's Library.

People used to come to Love Hall only rarely, but now attendance is up. Today I live with my family, my friends, and my library of dying memories. After all, and despite everything, I am me. I used to read, and now I am read to. I used to write, and now I dictate. Full stop.

2

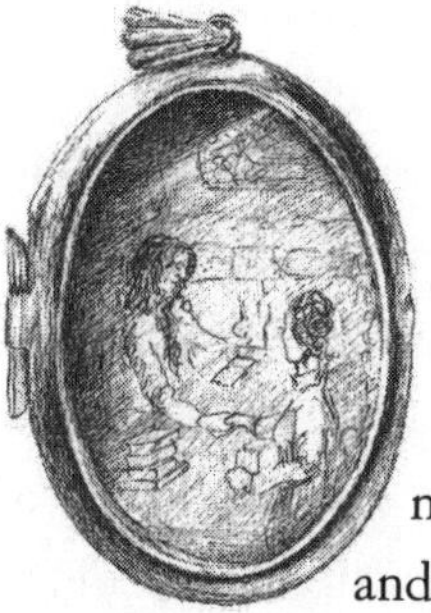

OF ANY CHANGES AROUND me, I was blissfully unaware. I gurgled. I mewled. Perhaps I puked. After some time, I said a word or two: "mama," my mother recorded in a red diary that is a minute and repetitive record of my infancy. I grew up slightly. And I did it in both my parents' company, while my father, as best he could, made sure that everything was perfect. He was always with us and often one step ahead, monitoring my progress, watching out for potential hazards, making sure that any fall was comfortably cushioned. Hamilton greased the wheel, and my father, with the help of Hood, made sure it took me wherever I wanted. My mother, with my happiness overseen by others, made my education her concern. We lived in my room, the Doll's House, and the library.

My first memory proper finds me sitting in the library on a rose-patterned mat, a small white fence around me. I am at my mother's feet while she reads. She sings to herself, soft songs, and her shoes, black and hard with no heel, tap gently on the floor, much the same as my own feet are doing now in imitation. I can hear the hushed rustle of paper and breathe in the volumes that are stacked on the floor, rising like Babel above me.

I was surrounded by roses even as a baby, and their smell predates my first memories. There was even a rose named after me, which is fitting since I was named for the rose itself, Sappho's queen of flowers. Petals were scattered on my crib as I went to sleep.

I remember my father crying as he spoke to me. I clearly remember because the tears from his worried, loving, questioning eyes fell on me. I don't know how old I was. Everything was entirely happy. This was life and I was new to it.

By the time I uttered my first sentence, Love Hall had been thoroughly aired. Rugs were held out of windows, either to be beaten or simply dropped and then distributed among the cottages at the edge of the estate. Some of the servants were found too set in the silent and respectful ways of perpetual mourning and, unable to adapt to the new détente, were among the first victims of the spring cleaning.

Love Hall needed a different ambience to accompany its new arrival. This meant a leaner, more efficient household upon the European model. Hamilton had been working on just such a blueprint in the privacy of his own chamber for some time, purely for his own amusement. It had, however, remained in the realm of platonic speculation, and the deeper realm of secrecy, for his father, Jacob, was much opposed to rearrangement of any kind — and Samuel would fight with Jacob over nothing. Now he outlined his conclusions to Hood and my father.

Precisely one half of the salaried positions at Love Hall were unjustified. Like automata, all parts were in perfect working order and the whole unarguably beautiful, but to what purpose? These situations were relics of days past, hollow symbols of privilege: a waste of space. However, since the intention was not to save money, those who found themselves out of a job would part with a generous pension, and many would continue to live in their cottages around the estate without the burden of rent. The unpleasant news of their redundancy would be tempered by the revelation that they could live exactly the same lives without the labor, the front rooms of their cottages dwarfed by incongruously glorious pieces of furniture discarded by the big house. They would depart on friendly terms and, where necessary, in debt to the Loveall. Our family needed no enemies.

Around the country, other families were tightening belts to make houses more viable financially, but my father's motive was entirely different: the weight of tradition that had stifled him would not fall on me. I would not be allowed to choke on the stale air of a museum. I would have all of the pleasures but none of the handicaps. So, with my father's encouragement, Hamilton's process of modernization began in earnest.

All the water carriers were immediately cut off (with pension). Half the footmen were auctioned to a distant country house, with much success due to their legendary deportment — those remaining were thereafter called the Six-Inch Men. The HaHa were no laughing matter, and they showed the kitchen staff no mercy: the sous-chefs were chopped and the sauce makers reduced. On the next Sunday, the great flag was raised and lowered twice for the last time — did the world at large really need to know whether the Young Lord was at home and well? Wasn't it possibly better that they didn't know at all? Even if this constant semaphore were necessary, did Love Hall need someone whose entire life consisted of raising and lowering the flag? Hamilton had calculated that this job could be combined with sixteen others to create a single position. And this man would still have time to light the candles on the first floor at dusk.

Though he had ordered the process begun, my father watched some of these changes with bemusement. He felt odd pangs of sadness over unexpected things. The dispersal of the orchestra around the country, and the return of the kapellmeister to the court at Prague whence he had come, gave my father pause. Hamilton had decided to keep only a more portable harmoniemusik — a wind band consisting of four pairs of instruments. My father thought this a mistake, but when the newly slimmed unit accompanied him on a picnic and played arrangements from the Opera as I learned to totter before his very eyes, his misgivings vanished.

He knew he had to have the strength to see this vision through. Instead of a house dedicated to Dolores's memory, there would be a house designed around my life. Memorials to Dolores were removed without ceremony. Only the Doll's House and a few specific portraits were left untouched: items that would be helpful to my own upbringing. My father considered himself the past. I was today and tomorrow. He would not fail in his protection of me: from harm, from those who meant harm, even from those who meant no harm at all. I would be shielded entirely, the whole house arranged for my comfort and safe passage through life. This purpose bred in him an energy that no one had known.

I was just a baby, safe in my mother's arms, but he was drawing plans all around me. He put his proposals for my education before my mother for her approval. At such-and-such an age, she would commence my musical instruction; he would tutor me in etiquette and deportment a year later. Languages and literature would, of course, be left entirely to my mother, with the understanding that at the age of sixteen I should set out on a Grand Tour of Europe, in her company. No, no, he would not go. His constitution would never stand for it. My world should not be allowed to contract to the size of the grounds of Love Hall as had his, nor would I have need to paint what lay beyond as any more of a paradise than it was. The grass would always be greener within the gates, but I would come to understand that for myself as they brought the greater world to me. And at such a time as he was sure that I was ready, I would be allowed to go out and meet it.

My mother shared his enthusiasms for this smaller household and noticed that it breathed new life not just into the old house but also into the Young Lord. Both seemed to be getting younger. Love Hall, and everything within, was improving.

But there were also those who didn't like the changes and didn't want to work anymore. Hamilton knew exactly who they were, and Hood was pleased to show them the door. Nobody would be allowed to poison the new atmosphere. Almost nobody.

Nurse Anstace Crouch was the most obvious canker on our bloom and, at that time, one of the very few malign influences. Although she had the respect of most of the household, she was universally disliked. Anstace had never wanted a life in the theater, to end up as dresser to a decrepit old actress, so she was glad when her tormentor died. She had watched her mistress's dying face turn bright red until it looked just like the wrinkled baby, and though she had briefly considered trying to help, she decided against it, partly out of respect and partly out of pleasure.

Yet the grande dame had bequeathed her some of her worst habits: most particularly, the need to be heard and obeyed. It was an addiction that Crouch started to satisfy toward the end, when it was almost as though it were she who was able to wield all the power at that old woman's disposal, purely by virtue of being so necessary. After the death, this craving became infinitely more acute.

By Anstace's reckoning, it was now time for her to climb the ladder. She had one unique qualification. Like the nurse in the story of Iphis in my *Metamorphoses,* she knew the secret of my sex. More than this, she knew that I was not the real offspring of my supposed parents. She could keep her mouth shut quite as well as anyone, couldn't she? Didn't the Loveall owe her a living? Events, she thought, had proved her eligible for any post she wanted, but there was one she truly desired: housekeeper.

The unpopular Mrs. Gregory had been dismissed within days of Lady Loveall's death. The position of housekeeper had long been the apex of Anstace's dreams, so she put herself through the rigmarole of an official application, assuming her accession was a foregone conclusion.

The vigilant Hood and Hamilton, with the assent of my parents, had decided that it would be prudent to retain Anstace, at a generous salary, in whichever situation she felt most comfortable: she was a greedy woman and this would doubtless appease her. However, they also thought it of paramount importance to keep their own ranks as closely knit as possible, and the decision had already been made that Hamilton's wife, Angelica, would become housekeeper. Furthermore, they worried that Anstace, part of the old regime, would be anathema to the new atmosphere they hoped to foster. Under no circumstances could her application be successful. She was informed.

Anstace had been utterly unprepared for failure. Hamilton apologized, politely explaining over her unseemly accusations that there was no alternative: long before Lady Loveall's death, my father had requested that Angelica become housekeeper. He assured Anstace that her financial needs would be met, her every demand for time away approved. The Threat of Untimely Revelations lingered, but Hamilton felt sure that money would mollify the unsuccessful candidate. And, slowly at first, it seemed to: a change came over her until she became a silent mystery, stubborn in her new wilderness, unmoved by tempting offers of relocation elsewhere within the Loveall family. She elected to stay at Love Hall.

And so Anstace was allowed to sit at the head of the servants' table, a figurehead, a sphinx watching over us, biding her time. Belowstairs had predicted that she would help define the HaHa, but she had not been given the chance. The *A* that was originally hers now stood for Angelica, and everyone was grateful: Hood, Anonyma, Hamilton, Angelica. Anstace's position at Love Hall was now purely honorary, borne out of necessity.

To this day, the servants still call whichever cabal rules the household the HaHa. Some have thought it insolent, but I like it. There's something saucy about an acronym. It shows an affectionate lack of respect.

* * *

It wasn't only Anstace. Even then, the world was encroaching. Hamilton, Hood, and my father had one guiding principle: Beware the family.

The relatives. Three sets of them.

(I hope this volume includes a family tree. I tried one, but it's surprisingly difficult and I find I always run out of space to the left. I know Hamilton drew one up. Perhaps it's at the front of this book; I wonder if I shall ever know.)

I see them all staring into my crib, clouding every inch of available sunlight: nothing but faces and powder as they fight for a better vantage, clambering toward me, suffocating me. But the truth is that they would never have been invited at the same time. The Osberns and the two sides of the Rakeleigh family could plot against Love Hall if they so desired, but they would never have been allowed to collaborate under its very roof.

The distants could not be kept away from me, or from Love Hall, forever. But it was in our interests that they saw me only as Love Hall wished to present me, in the best possible light. The family had congregated for Lady Loveall's funeral, but since my mother was supposedly pregnant at the time, and I within, we were kept from view. Hood and Hamilton dealt with their scandalized reactions to the reading of the banns at the memorial service, while my father glided through the throng as though his veil made him invisible.

It was only through the newspapers that the family was able to enjoy the celebration of my birth. Months afterwards, when they were finally invited inside Love Hall, what they saw was in marked contrast to their previous experience. The house transformed, its future became more than ever the focus of their intense interest.

Geoffroy's marriage, though inappropriate, was perfectly legal and its offspring, though saved from bastardy only by hasty nuptials, an actual living, breathing thing merely a nasty accident away from inheriting the entire Loveall fortune. It was I, this sole legatee, who would be the focus of their finagling from now on. Every morsel of the energy they had spent on Lady Loveall, hoping that she would disinherit her useless son or that he would simply dwindle away without issue, would be redoubled and concentrated on my father and me. Now they were left to coo over my cot — watching for the first sign of the dementia inevitable in any child of my father's or, failing that, counting the days until they could begin proposing matches.

It is no surprise that of all the family it was the Osberns who arrived at our house first to survey the new landscape. They were the family of my father's aunt, the Good Lord Loveall's sister, Elizabeth. My grandmother had always despised this high-and-mighty fool, not to mention her husband, Athelstan, the idiotic old booby who had squandered their entire fortune. My mother, as a servant of the household, had never had the opportunity to observe this side of the family at such close quarters, though she had sat in her library and worked to the distant accompaniment of their bickering during the annual visit. Now that she was the lady of the house, she saw them in all their brutal splendor, as her journal entry shows.

> The first relatives arrived today en masse. A strange selection. An entire list of the dramatis personae follows:
>
> *Athelstan and Elizabeth Osbern*
> *Edwig Osbern,* their youngest son (unmarried)
> *Edith Osbern,* the widow of their eldest, and her two children: *Camilla and Esmond Osbern*
> *Edgar Osbern and Nora Osbern-Smith-Stephenson* and their children: *Praisegod, Reliance, and Prudence.*
>
> I thought it most unfortunate that the seating was arranged as though we were meeting for battle. We presented them the tableau "Loving Parents and Child":

Geoffroy sat to my right, with Rose, resplendent in white christening dress, between us in the Whiting Crib. This was an odd reverse of the nativity — I am a little like Mary, I suppose (not you, Mary, but the original!), and Geoffroy is as innocent as Joseph. But these were no wise men or shepherds: the gifts these travelers brought to the manger were jealousy, greed, and hatred. The members of the family approached and, variously, peered at, scrutinized, prodded, drooled upon, and poked Rose, as Geoffroy looked on anxiously. Hood discouraged them from lifting her and finally politely barred them from all contact.

The elders, Athelstan and his wife, Elizabeth, both in their seventies and surprisingly full of bile, could barely bring themselves to talk to me but planted themselves opposite and within spitting distance. He looked like a red potato, knotted, oval, and ugly; she, a stick of rhubarb in bearing and complexion, her thin head stiffly arching back. Their behavior was quite proper, I am sure, and perfectly rude.

Geoffroy did not allow his great suspicion of them to undermine the courtesy their status as family allows, but conversation is oftentimes beyond him, particularly under awkward circumstances such as these. He made a valiant effort, however, and with the help of Hood and myself (when I was heard and, less often, listened to), he played the host well. The role of doting father, on the other hand, needs no such pretense and he is so very proud of Rose.

If only I could remember all they said.

"Oh!" Elizabeth observed to her husband, among the general hubbub: "An eight-piece orchestra! Only eight pieces! And I hate wind! Where on earth are the violins?"

"We used to have a whole orchestra," came the bitter reply.

"We did, when we could afford it, and he could afford it now. There's simply no excuse." She surveyed us imperiously as she spoke, squinting, though I am sure she sees perfectly. Geoffroy made a good show of not hearing her as he entertained Rose. I thought his head would entirely disappear into the crib, where it could remain hidden for much of the afternoon.

"We couldn't afford a bloody secondhand fiddle now," said Athelstan, swiping at a child's passing foot with his stick, "unless he gave us one."

Of his children, only two of the three are living: Edwig and Edgar, both present. Edwig, the youngest, is a debauched and comical man of about thirty-five, though he looks much older and is evidently a martyr to gout. He continually leered at me. The other, Edgar, is an intolerably boring (but apparently sincere) divine who is married to the female devil, Nora — we shall leave her till last — and has three of the most loathsome children imaginable: Praisegod, Reliance, and Prudence (known to Geoffroy as Idolater, Selfishness, and Impudence). These terrors ran around the house, breaking things and shouting, until the youngest finally placed a piece of paper on Rose's face *in her crib* while the middle child diverted my husband's attention. When he noticed, Geoffroy let out a scream of horror at an astonishingly high pitch and Hood quickly intervened. The girl, a beautiful child of seven with quick, proud eyes (she tried to outstare me and failed) said she had only wanted to "see the paper rising and falling"! "It was so pretty," said Prudence wistfully, after she realized that none of the family was asking her to apologize. Rose was removed immediately.

There was a nameless and apparently unintroducible woman, in widow's weeds, who had been married to the missing third son, Edred. Sisters had married brothers and this Edith, Nora's sister, seemed as empty as if the harpy had stolen her character entirely to put it to use for herself. She spoke once, certainly no more than twice, and only to the clergyman.

She had two children of her own, both present: a limp handshake of a girl, a good few years younger than I, called Camilla, who could not bring herself to look at Geoffroy and did not know what else to do. She sat meekly at her mother's side, as perhaps she expects to for the rest of her life. The other child was a sneering, ill-mannered yet handsome young man of little more than twenty, called Esmond. He stood at a remove, as though he were the only member of the family who saw this for the charade that it was. Despite his age, he looked around at everyone with the air of someone who knew more than they did, determined to give the impression that he was here against his will.

In case this makes him sympathetic, for it *was* a charade, he was not. At one moment, I caught his eye — if you are worried that someone is looking at you, it is almost impossible not to check. He held my gaze for a little too long and then, in perhaps a completely coincidental gesture, raised his chin and traced a line along his throat, looking casually away as he did so. I swallowed but found my throat had grown very dry.

And now to the best. It was of Nora, the vicar's grotesque wife, that my husband bade me beware only this very morning, and her eyebrows — dark, angry clouds hovering over her face — were sufficient reminder. (If it be true, as I read, that the mode of the day calls for the thickening of these with *mouse skins,* then I only hope the vermin are certainly dead: her brows were so fashionably full, I feared one would take us all by surprise and scurry across her forehead.) Whereas barely anybody else addressed me, talking mostly among themselves and only occasionally troubling Geoffroy's attention, this woman, perhaps ten years my senior, could not restrain herself. She gave me her opinion of my clothes ("acceptable"), my accent ("North British?"), my looks ("eyes pretty but nose ignoble"), my library ("if it's necessary to have books, I suppose you must hide them somewhere"), and my marriage ("a surprise of the *other* sort"). As proud as Lucifer, she said it all with a gracious smile as though she had just told me I was beautiful, clever, and a valuable addition to the family. Hood kept steering her back to her side of the room, but she was not to be diverted from her assault. When the offensive could no longer be sustained, she set her children upon me, and finally (as a last resort) the old inebriate Edwig, who, although without doubt a lecher, seemed relatively benign. His face looked like a blood orange exploded from the inside out and bespoke a life spent in the service of immoderation and immodesty. I caught him observing me, yet whereas most men will assume a mask of indifference upon discovery, he was disarmingly honest. Instead of apology, he merely raised his glass to me and smiled, remarking loudly to the widow: "Girl's recovered her shape remarkably quickly, and quite a shape, too. Let's hope the little blighter gets her looks from the librarian. She's got some form on her. Magnificent teeth." This, all in all, was the kindest thing any one of them said to me.

The widow was not listening. She anxiously watched her nephew Praisegod toying with a curtain sash before he tied it in a noose around the neck of a small doll, which he left hanging in midair. She was the only one who took any interest in the children, and no one paid any attention to her.

There was so much to watch and hear that it was almost impossible, as if one had gone to see *The Comedy of Errors* and the *Tragedy of Macbeth* playing on the same stage

> at the same time with the same cast. Elizabeth and Athelstan finally lost interest when the new heir was spirited away, and Geoffroy professed himself fatigued, a wise and well-timed move which signaled the end of the afternoon's entertainment.
>
> When they left they seemed rather smaller than when they had arrived, dwindling away in decidedly shabby coaches, bickering among themselves. We seemed to hear Nora's voice, shrill as a barrel organ, until her coach was at the very end of the driveway and beyond.
>
> Geoffroy — I have called him Geoffroy so comparatively short a time, though I am learning — breathed a sigh of relief and presented himself to me with his charming courtly bow.
>
> "My dear," he said. "Congratulations. The worst is over."
>
> Poor Geoffroy! I was lucky to be excused these people before.

This first meeting, though my mother didn't know it at the time, was haunted thoroughly by the widow's departed husband: Edred Osbern. His presence would have been tangible, for even in death he had a greater influence than his brothers, Edgar and Edwig.

Edred was the only one among the Osberns that my grandmother had admired: she knew he could have overcome us all single-handed. Having joined the army at the age of twenty, he had found the financial arrangements not to his liking and determined to fight for anyone who would grant him an income that better reflected his worth. He watched his country's empire disintegrate with enthusiasm, mindful of the increased business opportunities this might afford him.

Between employments, he made a mercenary marriage. His father, Athelstan, in a desperate attempt to recoup some of the Osberns' wasted fortune, arranged two unions in tandem: Edred's with Edith

Smith-Stephenson, and Edgar's with her sister, Nora. The pairings, based on age, were a disaster. Edith was terrified by Edred's brutality of manner, whereas Nora found his power magnetic; Nora despised Edgar's piety and general lack of vigor, whereas Edith, wrung out by fear and harsh usage, came to view him as her only salvation.

Edred and Nora's alliance was inevitable. His shame at his family's failure and his hatred for his wife, his children, and his brother drove him to father two more children by his sister-in-law: Reliance and Prudence. All Osberns revered him, even the innocent victim of this cuckoo strategem, Edgar, who was ignorant of the fact that of his three children, only Praisegod was his own.

Edith, his widow, was now left with two children, the pallid Camilla and Esmond, her husband reborn, who was quite beyond her control. Her sole remaining pleasure was religious discussion with Edgar. This necessitated contact with her dreaded sister, but she could bear even this to hear Edgar's inspiring homilies. She thought him the best of men, kindly, gentle, and truly God-fearing. If either of them had had the wherewithal, they might already have found happiness together, and cruel jokes were made to this end at their expense. They bore these barbs with a Christian charity and offered no rejoinder, dulled victims of an evil power.

Nora was victim only of her own malevolence, which ate away at her ever more viciously since Edred's death the previous year. Her own husband would never be Edred, she realized, but any of the children might be pushed toward that perfect pattern. Edred remained her moving light. Together, they had dedicated their lives to one glorious end: the restoration of the Osbern family to the great place in history that it had once occupied. She would continue this work into eternity. In the short term, however, Nora was engaged in a quest about which Edred could not have been so enthusiastic: to discover whether his son Esmond had inherited any of his finer qualities. She ached at the very thought.

My mother's diary ends defiantly after that first visit: "Now, Loveall distants, leave us alone! You'll get nothing from us this time!"

But the HaHa knew it wouldn't be long before their next visit, by which time the family would have had time to think, to plot.

I learned to crawl among the stacks, tearing out the knees of innumerable dresses in the process. My mother was happiest surrounded by her books and assumed that I would be, too. It was from books that she got her best ideas, and in a sense, she believed that I was one of these — that she had read me into being, the word made flesh, just as my father believed he had thought me into being: the reborn Dolores. Rose.

Everything I needed was in Love Hall. It was my whole world, and everything within the house and its grounds was beautifully, blissfully normal. From my earliest years, dresses seemed completely ordinary. I knew no different. What does a child know? All that he (or she) is told. And as I toddled into childhood, I was told that everything was perfect — and so it was.

My pleasures were many and chief among them were the two Hamilton children. These two were my greatest friends and had, in their way, as great a role in my upbringing as my parents. They were there from as far back as I can remember, and their influence over me, and my love for them, never waned. I will miss them as long as I am alive. Memories surround me as I write — pictures, the dressing-up box, even the smell of his tobacco still in the old armchair. Dear old boy, he was.

But I mustn't rush ahead. I must try to think of them as I first knew them. Then they were simply Stephen and Sarah Hamilton, my first beau and my first belle, my schoolmates and my constant companions. Even before that, I had seen them at chapel with their parents. We'd exchanged furtive glances between pews, eyes barely able to see above the row in front, but I wasn't precisely sure where they went for the rest of the day. The next thing I remember, as we shared our first days together at my mother's play school, is that I had known them all my life. We sat in the Doll's House, making prints of a rose from a potato carved with a blunt knife. Sarah, slightly older than I, showed me how, as though the world held no mysteries for her.

"Stephen's not old enough yet," she said confidentially, just as my mother had said a few minutes before. So her brother painted, though he seemed put out when any of his medium made it to the page; his preferred canvas was his hands, face, and clothes.

Those relatives who witnessed us together commented disparagingly on the unsuitability of my friendship with the offspring of an employee: such was the old Loveall way. My father had grown up too alone, too divorced from other people, so that it was too late for him to feel at his ease with anyone else by the time he lost Dolly. This was his parents' fault: he would not make the same mistake with me.

The Hamiltons had been looking after our family for many years, and this next generation would continue the tradition. In this ring of the family tree, it looked likely to be the girl who would do the sums and the boy who took care of the labor. It was clear the moment you met them.

Sarah was two years older than her brother and had inherited her father's sharp mind and her mother's practicality. We wore the same dresses, but whereas mine were always in my father's favorite colors (lilac, soft pinks, light greens), Sarah's parents dressed her always in white, as if to emphasize her virtues. Her blond hair was fine and curly, her skin snow and milk, her appropriately plump cheeks suffused with a delicate red, and her mouth a rosebud that was beginning to bloom: the effect was of an angel in thriving health. Her hair became darker as she grew, but her skin never lost the soft perfection of her youth: she was the essence of the English countryside. Even when she was a little girl, however, her eyes told the fuller story: she could see through the most careful lie. I could never fool her. I regarded her as an elder sister and was encouraged in this both by her parents and by my own. Very often she reciprocated, sitting on my back on the bed for hours, braiding my hair or sewing clothes with me that required no sewing at all.

Sarah was a natural organizer. She could plan anyone into doing anything: a doll's tea party or, a few years later, an actual tea party. To her, life was something to be prearranged, something that she would make sure to untangle, like my hair. She never changed, that beautiful girl. She may have been bossy in her own way, but as a child I never noticed, perhaps because I was ready to be told what to do. My father never ordered me to do anything, earnestly entreating me with silent eyes as he bent down to my level to discern whether, deep within my soul, I truly wanted to do whatever it was he had in mind. My mother and Sarah were the ones who instructed me. And I listened because I was their Rose.

Stephen, on the other hand, was a rapscallion of almost exactly my age. We were the same height and had the same brown hair, but though mine hung long around my neck, his was cut very short. It had to be so, because of his propensity for putting his head where it was not meant to be and getting things caught in his hair that then had to be cut out: cropped hair was thought preferable to tufts of varying heights. His parents would never have dreamed of dressing him in white. His lifestyle was set against the color.

Stephen was a hobbledehoy. Often in trouble, never bad trouble, he climbed trees when he shouldn't, then sloped home with new clothes torn from bramble patches or soaked from an accidental dip, unintentionally tramping mud over the best rugs, while I looked on in horror, envy, and admiration. He was invariably forgiven, and there was one particular reason for this: he was entertaining me. He was my clumsy court jester, and the breakages he left in his wake were the necessary casualties of our recreation.

Sarah and Stephen: my angel and my devil, my good conscience and my bad. Sarah whispered in one ear, "Don't do that, Rose!" and then scolded her brother, "Stephen, you mustn't make her . . . ," and Stephen whispered in my other: "You know you want to. There may never be another chance!" And I, a fair and just child, tried to distribute my decisions between them equally, never doing what Stephen dared me more often than I agreed with Sarah that it would be better not to. More than anything else, however, I yearned for the rough-and-tumble. And there we were, three peas in a pod, I in pastel, Sarah in white, and Stephen in darker colors. Sarah didn't like a mess, so it was my hems that always looked the muddiest.

As we grew, Stephen urged me on to gymnastic feats of bravery, which were most often discouraged by his sister, who knew what was best for me. Life around him was a constant drama of fantasy and imagination. He could never resist one more act of courage, one last heroic flourish. He was the pirate; his sister (who would ignore him totally because she didn't share this imaginative energy), the damsel in distress. Without a hint of her participation, Stephen acted out the whole scena around her. Sarah, like a sleeping dog who ignores her ear being flicked, was barely aware that the drama was taking place at all, let alone that she was a protagonist.

Soon I graduated from observer to participant. First, I was the changeling that needed to be rescued (by Stephen) from the clutches of the evil but sleepy witch (Sarah), and then I became the good-looking pirate lad. Finally it was Him Against Me for Her, or Him Fighting the Female Highwayman. Something would invariably be broken, and Stephen would scuttle off to the relevant party to report the calamity. Single-handedly, it seemed, he tore apart and redesigned the interior of the house. The taller he grew, the larger his gestures and the greater the wreckage. Of course, I wouldn't want to give you the impression that there were no tears, but they were rarely mine. We grazed our knees and we squabbled. We were even carefully reprimanded — or, at least, I saw others being reprimanded. This was all the correction I required.

Mother taught us, all three. That was her job and her pleasure. My father could never have let me go away to school and he felt that Love Hall, carefully managed, could be world enough. So he welcomed Stephen and Sarah into my schooling.

The Doll's House became the Doll's School. Our three desks stood next to one another in a row. Sarah, sitting perfectly upright, willing me to the correct answer, was to my right and Stephen, messy and rather befuddled, to my left. Sarah was, of course, the best student, her books the neatest, her pencil the sharpest, and her writing the most legible. She had a firm grip on facts the moment they were told her, because she was listening hard, whereas I, though never outwardly disobedient, was paying slightly less attention and Stephen the least of all. From my left came the sound of scuffling. Out of the corner of my eye, I could always see a blur of hands hiding something, mending something, or poking a pair of compasses into the bottom half of the desk, scratching a name, his own name, which he hadn't realized might incriminate him at a later date. To my right, however, there was serene calm and order.

And that was how we spent our days: at school with my mother (with many visits from my father, who enjoyed the spectacle of my learning) and at play, just the three of us, occasionally bumping into someone, literally, and being told not to rush down corridors or run around corners. I was a bit of a tomboy, as you might imagine, though I was heavily discouraged from eating mud, throwing crab apples, and picking at scabs. My father was especially strict about climbing trees. Educated by my mother, cared for by my father, entertained by the children of the employees, I was the shining star of Love Hall.

The days were full of school and play, but the nights were different. The Hamiltons went back to their house, the Gatehouse Lodge, the lovely cottage where I now write. It had always been their home and seemed so cozy to me as a child that I wanted to stay here, though I used to worry how they all managed to move around at the same time in such a confined space. Now I can't imagine how anyone could fill Love Hall.

When they were gone for the night, everything was very quiet, lacking Stephen. And at night it was just the Loveall.

Many years later, when I was sixteen, my father became seriously ill. So grave was his condition that I was not allowed to see him and, tormented by the fear that he might interpret my absence as a lack of caring, I addressed an endless paper chase of letters to his bedside. I have them still, tied with a pink ribbon, preserved by my mother. For a long time I could not bring myself to break her wax seal, fearing that the letters would bring back unhappy memories of this enforced separation. When I finally did, the letter that most affected me recalled a Loveall evening at the time of these early school days. Memories had grown fainter year by year, until it seemed as though someone else might have lived this part of my life. To read it set down so precisely touched me a great deal — though it is impossible to say how much I, as the writer of the letter, was remembering perfectly and how much I exaggerated, trying to please my father, to soothe him into recovery.

When you were sixteen, perhaps you *are* sixteen; how much could you remember of when you were five, and how much of what you could remember was accurate? And how much can you remember now? How much more difficult it was for me in Love Hall, where dates were flexible within their seasons and where there were no school terms around which to fix events? But I remember all of this now, or, at the very least, I remember remembering it. I could even calculate the exact date, because this was the evening that my father told me, to the day, how old I was.

We spent many of our evenings in the downstairs library, where my parents sat across from each other at the partners desk of pale amboyna wood. In reference to a joke they shared at their first meeting, my father had many pieces made of amboyna in Mama's honor. I am writing at that very desk now; at each corner their interlaced initials are inlaid in the woodwork, entwined like the rose and the briar:

A variation on this theme, which spells out their mutal happiness, can be found elsewhere in the house:

Partly these monograms were a sign of my parents' equality, and partly, we always laughed, a talisman to ward off the evil spirits of the rest of the family.

In the downstairs library, the desk sat next to a vitrine called the Museum, full of those family mementos that were valuable to my father: my first tooth, which my mother said he handled as though it were a sacred relic; the cameo broach that bears my mother's profile; the locket containing my miniature drawing of them at the desk. And all around the room, such color on the upholstery: every surface bright and cheerful, enriched with pattern and decorated with the symbols of our family. Even the firedogs had our crest carved on their chests.

Books covered the entire room. It wasn't until I was older that I realized these were merely the dummy spines of books, decoys painted to look real, with a few proper volumes I couldn't reach placed among them. And it wasn't until much later I realized that if I had looked closer, I could have seen that their very names were jokes: *Neither a Borrower nor a Lender Be* (a set of three, comprising only volumes one, three, and six), *The Spine And Its Anatomy,* and *The Way To The World* (just by the handle of the door that is cut into one of the bookshelves). These were my father's jokes par excellence. With the curtains drawn and the fire roaring, the three of us were as snug as we ever were.

From my low perch at the miniature desk, I watched the two of them facing each other, their legs next to each other's in the kneehole. Their fingers, like their initials, entwined.

My mother was reading — I cannot remember what, although I think we can assume the general topic — and Father was involved in his Rhodopaedia, the idea for which he had from a comic novel that Mother had persuaded him to read: except that in *Tristram Shandy,* the father is never able to finish his Tristrapaedia because his son grows up too fast. My father was not about to let the same thing happen with me, and he seemed to spend his every waking moment upon the plans for my continuing education.

I was copying out a recipe. Sarah had wanted to try to make some gingerbread, but Cook wouldn't show her, so my mother had secretly found a recipe for me in one of the old family books: the only problem was that this recipe was for gyngerbrede and almost incomprehensible because of bad spelling — "take quart of hony, and sethe it, and skeme it clene; take safroun, pouder Pepir, and throw ther-on." My mother explained that it wasn't bad but olde, and read it aloud to me in translation, suggesting that I write out a nice copy for Sarah. It took all my concentration. Almost every other word appeared wrong to me, so I had to keep asking her which word was which.

And there we sat in silence, punctuated by my questions.

"What is *clowys,* Mama?"

"Didn't I tell you, Rose?"

"I can't remember."

"*Clowys* are cloves."

Silence.

"What are cloves?"

Father laughed while my mother pointed me the way of my dictionary. The only other disturbances were the turning of pages, the crackling of the log fire, the odd introspective murmur of reader appreciation, and my parents' occasional questions to each other, which I only rarely understood, so never paid attention to.

It was my father, the least likely person, who broke the silence.

"I had quite quite forgotten!" he said in surprise.

"What, my dear?" said my mother.

"I had quite . . . *forgotten,*" he said again in wonder, lost for words. He looked up at the ceiling, shaking his head and smoothing his mustache with his thumb and index finger.

"Geoffroy?"

"I'm sorry. The date today. A day of celebration. We shall have Portugal cakes; they were a great favorite. Today is a very important day in Rose's life, after which no harm can come to her."

This seemed delightful to me, and I remember looking up from my recipe. Everyone was so happy.

"Today, Rose, you are five years and one hundred and thirteen days old."

"Ah," said my mother, and smiled. "Tell Rose."

The happiness left his face for a moment.

"No, my dear, I don't . . . You, Anonyma, you. Rose will sit here."

My father beckoned me and lifted me with ease, my legs dangling in front of me. He pulled his chair back slightly and we both looked at my mother as she placed her book on the table.

Then she told me the story of Dolores.

It wasn't the first time, of course, but it was the first time I heard about her whole life. I knew about the miniature governess and the marbles, but I had not heard about the house of cards before. Dolly had never had an ending. And now she did: five years and 113 days after her birth. At first, Father wore a faint smile. As her story went on, however, his eyes moved away from Mama toward the portrait above the fire: Dolly's defiant eyes, her bloody knee. And as I realized the story was reaching its conclusion, he leaned forward from his chair and laid his head in my lap, his brown curls falling over my white skirt. I stroked his hair and he cried. I looked at Mama, who had finished, and she widened her eyes as if to say: Say something.

"There, there, Father," I said. "Dolores is safe and I'm safe. I'm your Dolly now." He reached his arms around me and hugged me.

The next morning we picnicked outside the Mausoleum: just my father, Mama, and I, Hood, the harmoniemusik, and attendants. When I asked for an almond on the way, my father said: "Rose, you can't start a picnic the moment you leave the front door — you're just like her," and laughed. And on the rug in the long grass, as the musicians played "Süsse Traüme, Liebling," my mother explained the family motto and father told me about the Latin above the Mausoleum: *Mortui Non Victi*. And, just as it seemed our picnic could be no more idyllic, Sarah came running with gyngerbrede, still warm from the oven.

After that evening, we never spoke of Dolores like that again. I heard her name pass by; I saw her in his eyes, on the wall, but we didn't need to mention her.

I had not yet worried myself about any differences between Sarah and me. I don't know if I even noticed that there were any, *if* there were any. Looking the same, wearing the same clothes, we felt the same. We were the way we were, and we were neither vain nor anxious. On the much-awaited day Stephen was finally trousered, we laughed and burst into spontaneous applause as he proudly entered the Doll's School in his new black knee breeches. It confirmed what we already knew — that we were girls and Stephen was a boy; and we knew that this was normal. Everything was normal.

My mother taught us together, so as we grew, what we learned, we learned as one. But I was receiving extra tuition after school to which Stephen and Sarah were not privy and I remember feeling even then that the rules were more complicated for me. I attributed this to my higher station in life: my society would require a knowledge of genteel *ladylike* behavior that would not be useful for Sarah, and certainly not for Stephen. Love Hall, after all, would be mine.

It was in the privacy of my bedroom that Mother taught me my own code of personal conduct, not as laws to be obeyed or truths to be wondered at, but merely as common sense. As I got older, I didn't think to change (or even question) any of these excellent habits.

"Never disrobe in front of others, Rose," she said as she combed my hair at my dressing table, where I had washstand, bowl, and ewer.

"Never disrobe in front of others," I repeated.

"Why?"

"It isn't proper, Mama."

"And?" She looked at me with a tutorial eye, amused but not convinced.

"We must always keep our bodies as well covered as possible."

"Why?"

I couldn't quite remember, so I hazarded a guess.

"It isn't proper?"

"No, to protect . . . to protect our delicate . . ."

"To protect our delicate skin from the rays of the sun!" I said triumphantly.

"Good girl."

"And never perform any of one's toilet in front of others," I continued, flushed with success and ready for a bedtime story. She could hear that I thought I deserved a reward, but she hadn't quite finished.

"Why should we never preen in public?"

"Because there are no advantages to public displays of vanity." It was perfectly acceptable to groom in private, and mother and I often beautified together, but it was vulgar to talk of such things, let alone allow others to see. The lesson over, it was finally time for a story.

There was a certain kind of book we called "a lying-down": a book with no pictures, which meant that I had no need to peer over my mother's shoulder or have the book on my lap while she read it out loud. She stroked my head with her other hand as she read, pausing only to turn the pages. And slowly, slowly, lulled by my mother's voice, I fell asleep, feeling a silly need to pretend that I was still awake, as though going to sleep were shameful, as though it might make her think that her reading went in some way unappreciated.

There was a thick blue plank of a book called *The Gallery of Heroick*

Women, which was meant to be inspirational to me. The stories told of the contributions of great women to history, most particularly, war — Boadicea, Artemisia, who had built the Mausoleum, and Joan of Arc. My mother softly sang me "The Ballad of La Pucelle" as I sucked my thumb.

Often she stopped reading from the book altogether, lost in her own telling of a fairy story. The next morning, I would remember a wonderful moment and look in the book, but I would find nothing approaching it. For her, the books were only a point of departure, so many of the stories I loved were never written down. I am trying to write some of them down here in order that they not be forgotten.

My mother wanted to breathe life into everything around me: Love Hall should never be a relic museum. She wanted to make the world of art as real as the world it decorated, so she gave every picture in the house a history. I don't know how much of it was true, but each picture told me something new when my mother explained it to me.

In the Long Gallery, there was one particularly large bucolic painting of a beautiful pool of water. Stage left, dwarfed by the countryside and the pool itself, was a young woman so fat that she seemed to have two bottoms, the second perched cheekily on top of the first. She gazed after a man who seemed about to exit through the frame on the far side of the painting as he fled. He had just been bathing in the pool, and either he was embarrassed to be seen naked — as well he might be, for he had broken at least *two* of Mother's key rules, possibly three — or he was afraid of her. But I had never paid the picture itself any mind, besides giggling with Stephen at the lady's remarkable bottoms, and I had no idea who these two people were. Nor did I care. And if it weren't for my mother, I might never have known.

She wanted to tell me how the painting was made, with which kind of paint, pigments, and brushes, but, more important, she wanted to explain the moment in the longer story that the painting depicted. What other children were told, I am sure, as merely diverting tales of the unlikely, I was told as provable fact. In this particular instance, the most seductive detail to my young mind was that the spring actually existed. On a map, she was able to show me almost its exact location, near Halicarnassus, home of that heroick Artemisia, in a far off place called Turkey ("proud Turkey," as one of the songs we knew called it) — and this was before she had even told me the story. By the time she began, it was as though she were telling me something she had actually witnessed.

From the notebook in front of her, an unpublished Mary Day translation of the relevant part of *Metamorphoses,* and from her own memory of other translations of Ovid, not to mention her own embellishment, she told me that the woman in the picture, the one with the dual bottoms, was a girl called Salmacis. She and her sisters protected the pools and springs.

One day she found Hermaphroditus, the son of Hermes and Aphrodite, bathing in the spring that was named for her. Hermaphroditus begged her forgiveness, and the moment Salmacis saw his face, she fell in love with him. Hermaphroditus was scared and ran away, but she chased him and pulled him back into the water, begging the heavens that the two of them would never be apart. And somehow, in the splashing water and the thrashing limbs, they became a single body. This new body had one pair of arms, one set of legs, one head, and one face. They would be together forever.

Hermaphroditus cursed the pool for joining a man and a woman in the same body. To this day, Mother told me, men will not drink or bathe in water taken from the fountain of Salmacis for fear that a similar fate should befall them. It was the perfect "lying-down" story: romantic, mythical, even a little frightening.

By this stage of any story, my mother hoped I was asleep. Sometimes I fought hard against the weight dragging my eyelids down just to keep awake. But sometimes she told a story with such drama that sleep was forgotten. And the first time I heard this story, I wouldn't go to sleep until she told it again. When I woke up the next morning, there in the Long Gallery was a picture of the event, a picture I saw with new eyes.

When I was old enough, I read to myself, which I did in a very specific manner. I lay flat on the bed on my stomach, with my eyes just peering down off the side of the mattress. My body was mostly covered but my feet were always exposed. I placed the book on the floor beneath me, which means that I have never been able to sleep in beds that are too high, certainly none higher than an arm's length from the ground, which is also, coincidentally, as far as I am (or used to be) comfortably able to see — both of those things (the arm for page turning, the eye for reading) vital to my technique.

The book lay on the floor, and if its covers were tightly bound, it was hard to keep open. (Newspapers and journals are therefore ideal for this kind of reading, though I was more interested in books.) If it wasn't too cold, I held the book open, watching the blood flow down to my hand till the veins on my arm stood out like branches. My other hand was underneath my body in the warmest place available. But when it was cold, too cold to have anything outside the covers at all (even my feet), I balanced something gently on the side of the book and thrust both my hands beneath me, letting them back into the elements only to turn the page and rebalance the paperweight with the smartest of movements. And then it was back into the warmth of my bed as I tried to see how long I could eke out the next page before I had to turn over. I knew my mother would not have approved of the books on the floor, held open by whatever was handy (a heavy ring, the weight from the end of the sash cord, another book), so I tended to rest them on a cushion, bringing them a little closer as they lay in purple state.

I read as far as I could and then I let myself fall asleep, as if I were falling between the covers of the book itself, deliciously, slowly, continuing to read the same sentence until the words, words the, swam around around around before my eyes on the page and then swam into my head and my eyelids drew together irresistibly. And in that same position I slept, always waking under the covers a few minutes later, the book open to the same place, sometimes only two pages after my starting point. My eyes were only briefly open and they dragged heavily closed again as I burrowed backward to the middle of the bed. And slept.

3

LIFE WAS A DREAM.

When I was that happy little girl, I slept in satin sheets. There was nothing more beautiful than slipping between them, parting them with my body; yet there was also a playful streak of asceticism in me. In the middle of winter, particularly, I slept under only one cover until I woke at first light or before, freezing. Then I stole under the blankets into the waiting cocoon that I had warmed throughout the night while so cold above. I could just bear the iciness, and have always been a deep sleeper, but it was the sure knowledge of the warmth I would later enjoy that made the cold actually desirable, its own pleasure. With the inevitable cozy conclusion, lying in that glow and looking up at the inside of the canopy, which had been painted with roses and decorated with heroes of mythology, I was in heaven, on Olympus.

I woke up every morning with a sense of the day's potential and my own. And this was fitting: every day, though I didn't know it, I was reinventing the world. I was my mother's idea and my father's idée fixe. Simply lying in bed after I woke made me squirm with happiness. Even the rain was beautiful. I felt that it wouldn't have dared rain if I hadn't thought it so beautiful, that I could turn down the wind with a flick of my wrist.

I don't remember ever once having that feeling, the feeling I so often had afterwards, that empty moment of waking up and dreading the day, of being a stranger, an impostor inside my own skin, scared of my surroundings, sad that I had woken up. One morning, one long, gradual morning, I started to wake up without the covers on me, cold, breathing too quickly. That morning lasted four years.

Some days you wake up but there is more sleep in you and you can let yourself drift, wake again, then sleep, picking the moment to open your eyes properly for the first time. You swim against the day, kicking your legs to push away until you are ready to feel it pull you in. Other mornings the more you concentrate on sleep, the less you will. The sheets are too hot, the bed too cold, and the curtains never perfectly closed.

These days, I wake each morning with surprise.

When I was perhaps five (these were the dream years, when the sun and the moon were on their own seesaw), a troupe of jugglers and tumblers was brought to Love Hall. The jugglers were amusing, but the Hamiltons and I watched in wonder as the tumblers cartwheeled into action and produced a seesaw. One acrobat stood on one end — it's all common-enough stuff now, I know — and another leapt off a comrade's shoulders and, landing on the other end, catapulted the first one backward onto a fourth man. They were juggling *one another,* and this was the most incredible thing we had ever seen. I can remember little else of that day.

A seesaw, therefore, became our one desire. Although my father thought it far too dangerous, he was (after considerable entreaty by my mother) finally persuaded on the condition that I not sit on either end of the seesaw but ride only in the middle. Tumbling was out of the question.

A handmade model, in pieces on the back of a carriage (rather to our disappointment), arrived all the way from the city. We watched from my bedroom as two workmen erected it. It seemed huge and it took forever. We cursed their every pause for refreshment.

Finally, after a frustratingly protracted lunch, we were able to climb aboard: Stephen on one end, Sarah on the other, and I, sitting in state, strapped to a small throne in the middle. I must have looked like the umpire on his high chair at a tennis match. Doubtless we were observed from a window and the Hamiltons were under strict instructions not to have me sit on either end, so I was not invited. Stephen made sure his end landed as hard as possible so that Sarah's bottom rose off her seat at the highest point and then came down again with a thud. The louder she squealed, "Ow!" the more we laughed as we rocked from side to side. I looked out at the gardens beyond and heard the slow, persuasive creak of the wood beneath me, not feeling that I was missing out on any of the fun.

"Seeeeeeee-saw!" we shouted as we rocked up and down, making up rhymes.

"We should get a swing," said Stephen.

"I'm not sure," said Sarah. "Ow!"

"A roundabout!" said Stephen.

"I'll sit in the middle!" I said. And they rocked up and down on either side of me, Stephen astride the seesaw, his legs able to give him tremendous lift when he landed, and Sarah, sidesaddle, pushing back as best she could.

"I have to piddle!" she suddenly announced. Stephen did, too, victim of the same excitement. They ran behind two different bushes and I sat in my chair, feeling a little dizzy. From my vantage point, I saw Sarah duck down behind a tree so she could squat and lift her skirt in privacy. Stephen, on the other side of a small statue of Cupid, stood up and sprayed a generous arc (which I couldn't see but wished I could), singing loudly.

We have a choice, I thought. *Interesting.* I had always been encouraged to sit down — more ladylike — but there was something intriguing in the way Stephen swung his body from side to side and sang with such happiness. It made me curious if it would be more fun to stand and sprinkle, and I didn't see why I couldn't find out.

"Oh, do be quiet, stupid! Stop singing!" said Sarah. She had to concentrate so hard on what she was doing. It seemed too polite, and I saw new freedom in Stephen's technique. It made me tingle. It seemed to me that all girls would want to copy the boys at some point — why didn't Sarah? I would look into it.

If I wondered anything other than this, I couldn't yet articulate it. But that was when I began my slow subconscious investigation, like the obsessive detective who tries to work out the solution before there is even a mystery, purely because he finds a clue. I had no worries, no inkling of anything, but I had a question. It all started with a seesaw and piss.

The Osberns always came en masse, a swarm of flies plaguing the estate, but the other side of the family visited more fitfully, a bit here and a bit there. Unlike the Osberns, the Rakeleighs, my grandmother's side of the family, had squandered nothing. Their union with the Loveall had raised the family as far as it would ever climb, and their fortune, though small, was intact. A family of scholars and lawyers, occupations that had slowly begun to yield larger dividends, theirs had been a perennially rising trajectory.

On a rather overcast afternoon in the longest autumn of my childhood, Lord William Rakeleigh, Eleanor Loveall's younger brother and therefore my father's elderly uncle, was brought to Love Hall on an excursion from his university. He was a lifelong scholar whose classical bent had led him to call his two sons Augustus and Julius. Of the two, Julius was the more dutiful — the two brothers never spoke to each other — and it was he and his family who accompanied his father.

Of all the distants, these Rakeleighs (pronounced "Ray Kellys") were the most normal: in dress, in manner, in ambition. They paid us exactly the right amount and the right sort of attention, without design or scheme. To Julius, such a visit was nothing more than the chance for a nice family jaunt for his revered father. Their trips were fairly regular, but I remember quite clearly the first time I met them properly.

This outing was a major undertaking for a man as weakened as Lord William. Although only in his sixties, he appeared as decayed as our Gothick Tower, with which he seemed to identify. Ruin had seized him years before, at the death of his beloved wife. His religion was the classics, and he thought Juvenal the most contemporary of all poets. He relished his infrequent trips to Love Hall, for he had identified a kindred spirit in my mother. As this relic entered the room, he leaned heavily on a stick to his left side and, to his right, on Julius, who was happy in his dual role as crutch and occasional translator.

Julius and my father immediately entered into a rather stuttering but well-intentioned conversation, the very best that my father could manage. Husband and wife bore a remarkable resemblance to each other, as though from the same nest. Both were tall, thin, beaky, and beady, but they had kindly faces nevertheless. They perched awkwardly on their chairs, particularly Julius, whose heron legs tangled around each other in a knot. His wife was less interested in the conversation and she monitored the behavior of her chicks. She would have no problems with them today, however. They would be too occupied with me, and I with them.

"Ah! Where *is* the young ancient?" the old man cried with a rather frightening grin, peeking around the room to find me. One of his teeth always managed to avoid the cover of his mouth and hung down over his lower lip. And it was always a different tooth — the top lip simply could not cope with all of them at once. I walked up and curtsied in front of him, as my father had instructed me. He afforded Uncle William the most generous treatment of all the relatives, for his was the world of books, not legacy hunting.

"Maxima debetur puero reverentia!" The old man seemed to become

more nimble when he saw me, as though he would do a jig if only he could cast away stick and son. My father applauded softly behind me, where he stood, making sure my curtsy went off perfectly.

"The greatest reverence is due to children," translated Julius as his own brushed past him to observe me. My mother laughed politely.

Her diary captures this gathering better than my own blurred memories could.

> June 6, 1826. There sat the old man in front of us, installed safely in the best chair.
>
> "Juvenal," Julius confirmed for me. It was his job to try to draw his father into all local conversation. "The quotation about the children."
>
> "Juvenalia," I replied. This piqued his father's attention.
>
> "Juvenalia! You have studied the Scorpion of Aquino, madam?" he said, his voice younger than his body.
>
> "Yes, sir. In the house library, we have some very early editions in which I have taken great pleasure. Perhaps you would like to see them." Geoffroy rested his hand sweetly upon mine.
>
> "I should be most delighted," said the old man, among mutual smiles.
>
> "If you are interested, we also have some fine editions of the work of Mary Day," I added: it was rare to meet someone who might recognize the name.
>
> "The lunatic poetess?" he exclaimed in enthusiasm. "I should be charmed!" His little feet kicked on the floor in glee, and so I decided not to correct him, though I do hate "poetess."
>
> He asked me which satire I liked the best, claiming with a smile that his favorite was satire six, which he knew that I knew was *against women*.
>
> "Number eight, Lord William. What good is your family tree?" He looked at me with a younger man's eyes.

"*Stemmata quid faciunt?* Indeed!" he said, making sure he caught Julius's eye. "So true, my dear, so true!" Then he set off on a lengthy quotation, which I decided to understand quietly to myself rather than have Julius translate for everybody else, though I understood none of it. The old man rather tired himself out with this, I think.

The children — their two are bright-eyed and curious — went upstairs to play, and Julius questioned my husband concerning Rose's upbringing, whether she could become the Great Lady of the Land by virtue of her name alone, without any assistance from the world outside. His caution was genuine, but it agitated Geoffroy, who is bound rarely to let Rose out of his sight and is becoming, as she grows, even more wary (if possible) of outside influence. Rose's absence at that moment would have added to this nervousness. He was, as so often happens in public, at a loss for words, and he looked to me for inspiration, perhaps another piece of Latin.

"Well," said Julius, in all innocence. "It is lucky that you have a large family, including my brother Augustus and me, and our children, at your disposal, cousin. Not to mention all the other Loveall. I'm sure that any among us would be most happy to entertain Rose for a season, if you felt that the child would benefit from a wider exposure to the world."

His wife smiled at him, and the dear old scholar muttered something epigrammatic and Roman, but Geoffroy was aghast at the prospect and froze, squeezing my hand in an icy grip. His foot began to tap on the floor with an increasingly quick rhythm and I wondered whether I wouldn't have to still it with my own. Julius was mortified that he might have caused offense, but his father, perhaps understanding some of Geoffroy's feelings, said, in measured speech:

"Ah . . . *Sed quis custodiet ipsos custodes?*"

"But who will guard the guards? Your uncle quotes Juvenal again," I said, turning to my husband, stroking his hand as soothingly as I might. He squeezed out a smile and nodded gravely.

"One of my father's favorites," said Julius, relieved that he hadn't unwittingly caused any displeasure, as his wife clucked agreement.

"Anonyma knows them all!" said the old man with delight.

Apparently, no one had kept him so entertained since his wife died. I'd met Julius and Alice before and found them most proper — I remember that on the first occasion, Lady Alice immediately complimented me on my dress. It was a tremendous relief! But it was this meeting with the old scholar and his family that will do our small family the most good, I think. We may rely on these people. And I like their children, too. I have extended them all a permanent invitation to our library.

While the conversation whirred and stammered around us, and tea appeared and vanished, we children turned our attention to one another, coming face-to-face over the flapjacks. It was natural that I should talk to them, and Mother had encouraged me to do so, but I could barely take them both in at once. They were smartly dressed in matching green, edged with the same tartan: Victoria, a year older than me; Robert, a year younger. We curtsied and bowed in imitation of our grown-ups, and then we moved to the window, where we could be less observed and more natural.

They walked around me in scrutiny. I couldn't help but compare them with Stephen and Sarah. Whereas Stephen was scruffy, Robert was perfectly neat in his shiny many-buttoned tunic, the trousers of which rose almost to his chin. Whereas Sarah was girlishly guileless, Victoria was businesslike, a bit of a tomboy: her pantalettes protruded below her skirt and looked almost like her brother's trousers. The two children looked at me: what did they see? A tall young girl in a home-made dress, hair carefully parted à la Madonna with ringlets on either side of the forehead.

I wondered what they thought of my pink Lyons silk, the dress I had partly made myself. I was so proud of it, particularly the white lace around the neck, which Sarah and I had stitched together. Surely, Victoria must envy me! (I had no inkling that my clothes were probably rather unfashionable, particularly compared with their matching outfits. My mother always believed in the one-piece, and this is what I knew.) I was tall for my age, but not unusually so and no beanpole, merely taller than most and certainly taller than they. Everyone said that I was always smiling, but though I was a happy child, this smile was no more than the natural shape of my lips. Even then I had a small cleft in my chin, the stem of the goblet.

I had always been rather shy of strangers, and these two immediately began to throw questions at me. I had never had to field so many before, not even at school. And there was no Sarah to answer for me.

"What shall we call you?" hooted Robert loudly, his voice an owlish legato.

"Rose."

"Shouldn't we call you Lady Lovely, or something or other?"

I didn't have the opportunity to answer.

"You have lovely eyes," said Victoria.

"Thank you. They're green," I said. "Like my grandfather's."

"Do you know how eyes work? I do," said Robert.

"You're very tall, aren't you?" asked Victoria, with a tone of absolute awe, as though I were the biggest marvel in the traveling show. A gentleman had once visited the house to exhibit a collection of marbles, including *The Fish Boy of Naples*. As Victoria held her brother's hand and they walked around me, I began to feel like the original of that statue.

"I don't know. I'm not as tall as Stephen."

"Who's Stephen?" asked Robert at the same moment as his sister asked me how old I was.

"I'm five. He's my friend." I should have been nervous, but as they looked at me, I found that I liked them. They were asking questions because everything interested them.

"Where is he?" asked Robert.

"He's here. His family works here. We play together."

"Oh," said Victoria. "Can we play, too?"

And we were friends.

I curtsied and asked rather formally (to the cooing delight of the Rakeleighs) if we could go and play upstairs. I saw doubt in my father's raised eyebrows, but this was ignored in the general enthusiasm. My mother quietly reminded me on my way from the room that I was representing the whole of the family and the house itself and that I should be the perfect hostess. I knew that she was trying to communicate something unspoken, but I wasn't quite sure what. I had the idea that I shouldn't overpower them with Stephen and tie them up like pirate hostages, that this wasn't what a perfect hostess did, so instead I took them up to the Doll's School. I showed them some building bricks and some of our beautiful toys, but before long the dolls had yielded all the fun they could — Victoria was only somewhat interested, and Robert merely tested any movable joints to check that they were in working order. These two seemed most happy asking more questions and exploring on their own. They were fascinated by the history around us and asked me what things were, what they meant, and why we had them.

Though I liked them, they were a little stiff and formal compared with Stephen and Sarah. I realized that they were behaving exactly the way one should behave as a guest in someone else's home and I made a note to do the same, should the situation arise — though I couldn't quite imagine how it would.

Robert tried to unhinge the dollhouse's front, assuring me that he could slightly improve the ease of its opening. The appearance of my mother, who came to monitor us, put an end to any further tinkering. When she had gone, satisfied at our progress as friends, Robert tried to adjust the pendulum on the grandfather clock: he couldn't help himself. His sister, on the other hand, stared through the windows, asking what we could see in the distance (about which I knew very little). The dolls hadn't held her attention at all, and she didn't seem the type to make up any games of the kind that Stephen and I played. I tried to explain our games.

"Why do you do that?" asked Victoria.

"Do you have an awl?" asked Robert.

They were certainly the two most questioning people I had ever met in my life, and I answered as best I could. When was the house built? Once upon a time. Why was the tower that Grandfather likes falling down, and why didn't we get it mended? It was built that way by Father. Why? I didn't know. Would I prefer to have a brother or a sister? I had both in Stephen and Sarah, I said. What did I want to be when I grew up? Robert wanted to be a Royal Engineer, and Victoria an explorer. I wanted to be me, I answered. Had I met our cousin Guy? No. He's horrible, they warned.

After we had spent an appropriate amount of time upstairs, I walked them back. I tried, in what was, I'm sure, a comical impression of my mother, to tell them about the paintings on the way. Thinking of Stephen, I showed them the nymph Salmacis's four buttocks, but this didn't seem to amuse them quite as much as I had expected.

"What does it mean?" said Victoria, who was now sitting halfway up the stairs, her green dress floating up behind her so that her drawers were on display. Robert sat down, too, and with his hands crouched under him and his legs unseen behind, he looked even more like an owl. It was the one question that they had asked me that I felt truly qualified to answer. So I told them the story.

"She's a girl and he's a boy, but she drags him down into the water and they become one person. . . ." The moment I said it, I realized that I hadn't fully understood it. It had sounded so convincing coming from my mother, but when I said it, it sounded flimsy.

"What?" asked Robert.

"One body."

Victoria couldn't believe it. "With two heads?"

"No. One head, silly." I laughed at her foolishness. This was something beautiful, not a monster. They seemed put out by the whole story, as if it defied common sense, and I felt myself starting to agree with them. For the first time in my life, I had a feeling that I was to know very well in the future: of trying unsuccessfully to persuade someone of something she couldn't understand.

"Then, how can you tell?" asked Robert, who was only mildly diverted by what seemed to me the key amusement in the house, when he had evinced such great interest in the smooth movement of the dumbwaiter. But this was a good question.

"Boy or girl head?" asked Victoria.

"I don't know. Both in one. How can you tell?"

"There *is* a difference, you know," said Victoria.

I was a girl, of course, and of that there was no doubt. Victoria was a girl, too. We were similar, our hair long, our clothes roughly the same, certainly distinct from Robert's, whose tall tunic trousers were molded so much tighter to the shape of his body. Our skirts billowed. But of our faces: was there a difference? Robert was a little rounder, but Stephen wasn't. I looked at the painting again and wondered. There was the piddling issue, too. Stephen and Robert versus Sarah and Victoria: boys against girls. I bit the inside of my left cheek and decided to inquire.

"Can you piddle standing up?" I asked Victoria.

"No, since you ask." She seemed awfully sure.

"Have you ever tried?"

"No," she said firmly.

"How can a person be a man and a woman?" asked Robert. How indeed? It wasn't as if there was much to separate us to begin with, so how would you know? I would have to research further.

Victoria had come over very quiet, lost in her own thoughts. She had a memorable smile on her face. I can see it now. It's still the way I think a face should look almost anytime that genitalia are considered.

"I know how," she giggled, and then added as if it would clarify everything, "like in the tub." She would go no further, and Robert and I had no idea what she was talking about. Perplexed, we left the confusion of the painting behind and walked back toward the Entertainments Room.

"Why has that horse got a horn?" asked Robert, pointing out of a window. I was getting tired of not knowing the right answers to all their questions, and I decided to answer them with greater confidence.

"It isn't a horse, it's a unicorn."

"There are unicorns?"

"It flew from Africa."

"How did it fly here, if it hasn't got any wings?" asked Victoria.

"It was so happy here that they slowly disappeared because the unicorn knew that she wouldn't need to fly anymore." I was thinking on my feet, and it felt good. It became a habit I could never break.

"What is its name?"

"Dolores" was the first that came into my head.

My father received us as though we had been missing for days. Julius asked how we had spent our time.

Robert answered: "I took apart the dollhouse and we saw Dolores. We talked about piddling."

Suddenly it felt as though the afternoon was drawing to a close. To the senior Rakeleighs, this was further evidence of their children's inquisitive nature, to which they were quite accustomed and about which they were beyond embarrassment, but Robert had caused my father some disquiet. After swiftly excusing himself, their host was not then seen until the visitors had left.

My mother and I saw them off. Victoria, Robert, and I promised to write.

"I do hope Lord Loveall will be soon recovered," said Uncle Julius as they left. "And I hope Robert didn't damage the dollhouse. He so loves to know how things work."

The old scholar had barely been paying attention to any of this. He was, however, highly impressed with my mother, whom he had inadvertently started to call Margaret, the name of his much-mourned wife. As the Rakeleighs departed, he turned and said something in code to my mother. Julius looked at her to see if she understood. She nodded and we curtsied.

In her diary, she wrote that he had called her "a classicist's dream," noting that it was the first time a man had made love to her in fifteen years.

"Were you the perfect hostess?" asked my mother as Victoria waved gaily from their carriage.

"I was the perfect female host," I said, thinking it might be a trick.

Within a week of this delightful meeting, we received a visit from the other side of the Rakeleigh clan. These other Rakeleighs were the very worst of our relatives. Incredible, when you think of the competition, but they were. Augustus Rakeleigh began to plague us with letters soon after I was born, but somehow the HaHa had contrived to keep him at bay, and I had yet to lay eyes on the man. He was a thoroughly different proposition from his brother, with whom he had nothing in common except parents, and my father detested him, refusing to speak his name and putting his visits off whenever possible: the longer the deferral, however, the more disastrous the final appearance.

On this occasion, Augustus simply appeared at the house, unannounced. I was hurried from the room, conscious that something exciting was happening, something that I wasn't meant to be aware of. I tried to decipher the mumblings and mutterings of discontent through the wall but could make nothing out. I refused even to play with Stephen, as if I knew that a new and malevolent force had arrived in my life, a force upon which I would have to keep a watchful eye over the coming years. But on this occasion, I still wasn't able to get a good look at Augustus. Hood got rid of him, claiming that my father was not well enough to receive visitors and that my mother was at his bedside. A "briefing" appointment was made for him in one week's time. I was to be on display.

On this second trip he was accompanied by a Mr. Thrips. Augustus Rakeleigh, it transpired, rarely went anywhere without this Thrips, whom he referred to as his "doer." They made a sinister duo. Augustus was a huge, frightening man, his face wide, leathern, and badly scarred by the pox. He hid, or rather highlighted, the pockmarks with little pieces of taffeta, and the unfortunate effect was as if Stephen had chewed up wads of paper and used Augustus's face for target practice. He loomed over me as I performed my signature curtsy, and one of the ribbons fluttered to the ground. I gulped, transfixed by the crater it revealed. I had no idea that humans came this size and, wherever I went, I could not escape from his shadow. His voice, in stark contrast, slithered like a snake, worming its way as it went.

Thrips was the first person I ever met whom I could not imagine touching. He was a mean presence, reptilian, his frame more suited to Augustus's voice, and he stooped as if imprisoned by clothes that were two sizes too small. His sleeves frilled from his tiny jacket, his cuffs covered in ink. According to our natural-history book, snakes' skins were dry, but Thrips seemed to ooze even on the coldest day. He spoke in a bureaucratic monotone, with the wide-open eyes and barely moving lips of a poor ventriloquist practicing for the arrival of his dummy. Inseparable from a ledger that he consulted frequently, he seemed a monstrous parody of our own Hamilton.

August, as he preferred to be called, and Thrips, who was addressed as infrequently as possible by anyone other than his employer, were received in the Reception Room. Hood stood by my father, and Hamilton manned the door: they attended every meeting between the two parties. Though our family was seated, chairs did not immediately appear for the intruders. "August" seemed to be waiting rather impatiently to be offered one, but then surprised everyone by declaring that he wouldn't detain my parents. My father's sigh of relief at the promise of a brief interview, however, was premature.

"And this is the lucky lady!" Augustus said, looking at both Mother and me at the same time. "Cousin, I can't tell you how happy I am. My revered father, though I so rarely see him, wrote to tell me how delightful she is and I realize that I have been remiss in not making a better acquaintance. Sometimes I am almost of the opinion that circumstances have kept us apart. I would be so honored if I could bring my own wife, the dear Lady Caroline, and young Guy, to meet her." He clapped his hands. "Thank you, yes, I would! Thrips, when shall we come?"

Without consulting his ledger, Thrips said that the following Saturday was a good day for everyone involved.

"Next Saturday it is!" said Augustus conclusively as my father felt the avenging spirit of his mother renewed in this man with every passing moment — she had never liked this brother, perhaps because they were rather similar. "We shall anticipate the meeting with great pleasure, cousin, and look forward with particular relish to seeing where in this magnificent hall you have displayed the portrait of our family, which was sent you as a wedding present. Tea, was it, Thrips?"

"Tea, sir," Thrips confirmed.

"Thrips will take care of the details with your lackey!"

And Augustus bowed curtly, turned, and left, winking at Hood as he did so. They walked down the stairs to the front door, Thrips (taking care of no details) trailing two feet behind his master. None of my family had said a word for the duration of the visit and there was silence in the Reception Room, until the front door slammed.

No one knew quite what to say at all. Something extraordinary had happened in front of our very eyes. My father looked at Hood in disbelief.

"I'm afraid, sir, that we've been bamboozled," Hood said.

"Did we invite them?" My father was lost.

"No, my dear," said my mother. "They invited themselves. They knew we should not invite them. They will have to come."

"Should I hang the painting, sir?" asked Hood dolefully.

My mother interrupted: "No, Hood, but find the painting for me. I shall personally attend to its exhibition. Next time we shall entertain them in the Entertainments Room."

Eyes, master's and servants' alike, turned in horror but she was prepared.

"We shall surprise them. They have not yet won."

Hood and Hamilton closed the double doors of the Reception Room behind them. The moment the doors met, there was an explosion of furious whispers from the other side as the two men considered who was more to blame for this grand failure. My father looked at both of us, cocking an eyebrow, and we began to laugh.

At teatime the following Saturday came Augustus; his wife, Lady Caroline Odo; and their son, Guy. Thrips followed with his ubiquitous ledger. My mother had determined to show them every consideration. Augustus and Caroline seemed pleasantly surprised by their welcome but made it clear that they were used to such treatment wherever they went and considered it no less than their worth.

On his first visit, Augustus's pox silks had been somber black, but he wore gaudier colors depending upon the occasion, and today his face was stippled with all the hues of autumn. Caroline was a squat, manly woman of Swiss descent, her accent thick with pantomime. His son was two years older than I, but Augustus had him sit at their feet like a little dog, where he obligingly begged for food. For the most part, he was ignored. He was dressed entirely in black, which made his red hair seem more livid, his pasty freckled skin more measled.

As they sat, these Rakeleighs appeared like a three-headed monster. One head looked at me while the others diverted my parents' attention with conversation. The dogboy sniffed at me suspiciously from the other side of the room as though he had caught my scent on the air. I determined to look at him as little as possible. The toady Thrips stood by Hood at the door, consulting his ledger regularly.

"We are so happy you were able to accept our invitation," said my mother. "We had a most delightful time with your brother's family. Very pleasant children."

"Very pleasant people, very rarely seen," said Augustus, forced by his height to look down his nose as though he were lining us up in his sights. His wife's head barely reached his shoulder, and he generally addressed his remarks to the bun of hair atop her head.

"Very grarely zeen," repeated his wife, whose nationality precluded her from pronouncing the letter *r* with comfort.

"The children ask so many questions," Augustus continued. "That's what I recall. Guy never asks questions." Guy said nothing but stared rather aimlessly around him as he scratched himself behind the ear. "Is my father still in his right mind? Does he have his health?"

"Mens sana in corpore sano," said my mother, and smiled. Augustus ignored her and instead turned his attention to his wife's knot.

"My dear, you had some questions for Lady Loveall."

Caroline had been in the middle of appraising the contents of the room, her eyes traveling ruthlessly along the dado so her inventory was complete; this process seemed linked to Thrips's ledger consultation. Interrupted in this pursuit, she turned her attention to us: her every look seemed to calculate, specifically, how much we were worth. As she began, the boy edged toward me. In the middle of her first word, she grabbed his collar and pulled him back, with a brief "Stay, Guy!" (She pronounced it "ghee.") Then she posed my mother some pointed questions about household management, as if she were planning to move in herself. When she inquired if her bizarre name was by any chance Greek — another single-word tongue twister for her — it was my mother who interrupted.

"Perhaps Guy, Ghee, would like to go and play with Rose." She said his name both ways to placate the two parents, who pronounced it differently from each other.

I didn't think it was a good idea. What was I going to do? Throw a ball for him? Watch him bury a bone? To my surprise, everyone agreed, even my father. The only two people who didn't approve were Guy and myself.

"No. Not with girls" were his first words. His speech was monosyllabic, as though he only barked orders at servants.

His father cuffed him sharply on the back of the head.

"This isn't a girl, Guy. This is the future Lady Loveall and you will play with her if we tell you to." He flicked his son's skull on each of the last five syllables. Guy growled.

"Hamilton," said my mother. "Would you be so good as to fetch your son? He might be a more appropriate playmate for Guy, and perhaps then the three of them can play together. We all know boys like to be with boys."

"Is that quite appropriate?" asked Augustus, looking at Hamilton disdainfully.

"Oh, I think so, wouldn't you say so, my lord? Stephen has practically grown up with Rose. They play the most marvelous games together. You never know what they'll get up to next."

Thank goodness for Stephen. And Mother. She did know best after all. When Stephen appeared, in clothes so strikingly clean and crisp that they looked pressed directly onto his body, I began to form the notion that this had all been scripted. Augustus offered a harsh admonishment to his son to play fairly. As the three of us left the room, I heard him change the subject: "Now, concerning the portrait. We would so like . . ."

Guy was a complete enigma to us. He had been brought up to believe that he was superior to everyone except his parents, to whom he was vastly inferior: his parents, himself, then the rest. This last category included women, servants, working people, and anyone else similarly degraded. He straightaway began to play the Lord, presuming that Stephen would feel lucky to be hobnobbing with the aristocracy. His bad manners aside, it was immediately obvious that there was no fun in the dogboy. As we arrived in the schoolroom, I was delighted to have Stephen as a shield, not for the last time in my life.

"What does *he* do?" was Guy's opening question to me. Stephen moved in front of me protectively so Guy couldn't get any closer. However, Guy was more interested in the house, as though he was under instructions from his family to see as much of it as possible. Perhaps he wanted to mark some territory for himself.

"This is a very bad room," he concluded. "Where are your toys?" The quality of the room had never occurred to me. I wondered whether he was unable to be more specific. He had still used only the very simplest of words.

Stephen said that we had dolls. Guy wasn't interested and asked us what games we played. Stephen said we made them up.

"That's bad. I won't know them. Do you know hide-and-seek?"

I caught Stephen's eye. He had once hidden in the grandfather clock in the Baron's Hall for three hours while Sarah and I looked everywhere for him. He was discovered only when his father was informed that the clock had not struck four, and doubtless he would have stayed there all evening, missing supper in order not to be found. Another time we found him fast asleep behind the dog in its kennel in the back courtyard. Hide-and-seek was the unofficial house amusement, and Stephen was the undisputed master. Guy had picked the wrong game.

He first had to tell us exactly how to play properly (as though we didn't know!), what was fair game and what was foul, and how we would know exactly why he had won when the game reached its end. Then he pointed at Stephen: "You! Seek first."

I hid underneath the piano in the Music Room, a familiar hiding place, and Stephen found me straightaway. I wanted to be found, preferring to spend my time with Stephen, looking for Dogboy. Unfortunately, we found him easily behind the hot water pipes in the very room where Stephen had counted. The game had taken three minutes, one of which Stephen had spent counting to one hundred.

Next it was my turn to seek. I stayed and counted in the Doll's School with my eyes closed. I didn't actually count. To my relief, I found Stephen first, his shoe peeking out from the top of the canopy above the Great Bed.

"Good lass. I knew you'd find us. Where's he, then?" asked Stephen. I hadn't even thought about it.

"I know where he'll be." I followed Stephen to the stairs and he whispered to me: "Behind the armor. Go and get him."

Guy was furious, as though his hiding place had been the most perfect place in the world.

"He told you! You told her!" he shouted in accusation. "She couldn't find me on her own. She's a girl."

Stephen stood his ground behind me, lying blatant in my defense, saying that I was capable of doing anything a boy could. But Guy was beside himself.

"I won that game," he ranted as we returned to the Doll's School. "That was the best place. Now it's my turn to seek. I'll count twice, to give you a chance of finding a good place, but I'll still find you quicker than you found me."

We were determined to make this game the longest yet, possibly ever. The moment Guy put his hands over his eyes, Stephen called out, "No looking!" and then grabbed my hand and we ran away.

"He'll start looking before he even gets to fifty!"

I suggested we hide together. I didn't want to be alone with Guy for a second, and the idea that he might find me first filled me with dread.

"Under your bed!" he said. We even left the door open to give Guy a chance. Stephen slid under the bed and pulled me behind him. There was the scurrying of our limbs and anxious giggling and then we fell into a deep, purposeful silence.

The dusty floor smelled oily. Beneath my right hand, I felt a book, possibly the one I'd been looking for. I tried to pick it up from my rather awkward position, but Stephen stopped me. He pulled me toward him and put his hand over my mouth. I felt safe with his warm breath tickling the back of my neck. I started to giggle, but he shushed me again.

"Rose . . . ," he whispered right in my ear. "Hush. He'll find us." It was a horrible thought.

We heard footsteps come toward us, stop, then start, and then stop again as Guy looked in doorways. Finally he was at ours. We could see his shoes. We didn't breathe. He turned and went away. I exhaled and Stephen let go his grip on my mouth.

"Well done," said Stephen, barely speaking the words as he mouthed them. He let go of me. By Love Hall rules, our work was done. The unwritten goal was not to be found the first time, because this meant an arduous and dispiriting trek around the house for the seeker before the seeker returned. We were therefore victorious and had only to stay there for the duration of Guy's fruitless mission. Then he would find us, and that would be that. However, there was no question of giving any extra hints today, so we stayed under the bed, whispering.

Finally, we heard his footsteps again and saw his shoes at the door. We heard the floorboards creak and felt them shift beneath us. Guy stood by my dresser and started toying with the things upon it — my hairbrush, my necklace. I heard him sniffing something. Unexpectedly, he said:

"I know where you are, girl. And I'm coming to get you."

The tone in his voice was metallic. If I had been on my own, I would have screamed. Stephen held me to him and put his hand over my mouth again. He pulled me into his body. I was aware for the first time that I might be a bit bigger than he.

"You can't hide anymore, ugly little girl. I know where you are. I know where the farm boy is, too . . . and I've locked him in a cupboard and I won't tell you where until you come out. He'll die otherwise, because no one will ever find him. I'm not going to get you. You have to come out. I'll tell you a little rhyme."

A moment passed. We didn't breathe.

Guy snarled:

> *"You never can tell from where you stand*
> *Where the girl in the tree is going to land."*

Stephen had heard enough. Guy had been prowling around the bed, and Stephen thrust out his hand, gripped Guy's ankle, and yanked it. Guy yowled as his body crumpled and he collapsed on the floor. We got out from under the bed to find Guy looking up with disgust.

"You were hiding together. That's unfair. Cheats! That's not how you play properly."

Stephen wasn't interested and he sat on Guy's stomach, one knee dug deep into each of his shoulders, pinning him to the floor. I stood back and watched with pride. Stephen was younger than Guy but much stronger.

"You say sorry to her now!" Stephen put his hand under Guy's jaw to try to force Guy to look him in the eye.

"No. Get off me, boy."

"Apologize!"

Guy shook his head.

"Right," Stephen said, and told me to get the curtain sashes. He tied Guy to the bedframe with astonishing ease, then told me to come with him. We heard Guy's futile attempts at escape, followed by whimpering and a plea of "Don't tell my parents." I assumed we were going back to the Entertainments Room, but Stephen wasn't leading me in that direction and I didn't dare ask him what he had in mind. I knew I had to go along with whatever it was, so I put my hand in his as we went down the stairs.

We had hidden and not been found the first time. We had won in every way. Now it was up to Stephen to crown our glorious achievement. I didn't think for a second that he'd let us down. Together, we headed toward the kennels.

This took us past the Entertainments Room, and we couldn't resist looking in through the window to spy on the adults. We were just in time to see the unexpected appearance of Nurse Anstace Crouch at the door. As she planted an aggressive foot inside, I had a horrible premonition that she had found Guy tied to the bed, that we were in terrible trouble. But it was nothing of the sort.

"The noise!" she shrieked, a fury unbound by ceremony. "The noise is unbearable! I am at my prayers!" She must have been complaining about the noise we had made during our game of hide-and-seek. The house was otherwise quiet. Had we been that loud? I looked at Stephen, who was as puzzled as I was. We couldn't tear ourselves away from this bizarre scene.

"Crouch, what on earth . . . ?" exclaimed my mother as Hood blocked Anstace's further entry.

"Hamilton!" he called. "Housekeeper!"

The Rakeleighs were amused by this proof of the unsavory conditions at Love Hall, where a servant could rule her master. My father looked away and raised his eyebrows in embarrassment, pursing his lips. Clearly, Anstace had gone quite mad, but she would be heard. I pressed my face to the cold glass so I could catch every nuance.

"The hubbub! It is too much for a Christian woman to bear! Control your children, sirs!" She beat her bony hands against Hood's chest in protest.

"Control your servants, more like," observed Thrips without attempting assistance.

"Those *boys!*" she yelled. "There's bound to be trouble with all those *boys!*"

"Madam! *Leave!*" said Hood through his teeth. "This is a matter for the housekeeper in her office, not the Entertainments Room." With this, he lifted her bodily from the room, an easy accomplishment. As she left, the words "And, as for the housekeeper . . ." escaped before her mouth was smothered, but she had done the damage she intended. The room was left in awkward silence.

"I am so sorry," said my mother. We strained to hear.

"Yes," my father agreed.

"Crouch has never been the same since the death of Lady Loveall."

"No," my father agreed, again.

Hood returned to the room, closing the door on the problem.

"Gravest apologies, sir, madam."

"Eef I voz you, I vould be grid of her immediately," said Caroline.

"A relique of my mother's," said my father in excuse, but the Rakeleighs were unmoved.

"Meddlesome old bird, that one, ain't she?" said Augustus with a laugh, ever easy at the discomfort of others. "Always was. Obviously lost her wits now."

"We shall be rid of her tomorrow," said my mother firmly, to close the conversation. "I'm sorry, Geoffroy, I'm sorry, but Augustus is right. We must."

"So be it," my father said with a sigh, perhaps wondering why she thought he would object.

We could risk being caught at the window no longer; besides, we had bigger fish to fry, so off we went on our business. At the time, however, Nurse Crouch's scene confused me. Looking back now, her motives are obvious: she had chosen this visit to demonstrate both her dissatisfaction and her ability, should she choose, to bring our idyll to a crashing end. What did she care what people thought of her? She would be as mad as they liked, but she would make her point, and she would remind us whenever she pleased. Her timing was perfect: she was leaving the next day on her travels and it would give the HaHa time to stew. Ever after, whenever she asked Hamilton for money, it was given without question. Hamilton summarized the situation, whenever my mother inquired, with three unencouraging words: "it is manageable."

In the Entertainments Room, something had to be done to change the mood with the Rakeleighs. My mother had an entertainment planned that would prove the perfect antidote.

"The portrait?" she suggested. Her diary conveys her pleasure in what followed.

> An astonishing afternoon! The vile brother and his odious wife, a fat Swiss truffle, visited with their son as they had threatened.
>
> To begin with, they had inveigled their way into Geoffroy's house — *our* house! — on the pretense of wanting to view their own portrait. I could barely remember what this painting looked like, and when Hood finally found it, I remembered that there had been no question of our ever hanging the wretched thing. It was ghastlier than we previously thought, painted by someone with no sense of proportion at all, for he looked wider than she did. And it was so flattering to both of them that the artist, a Mr. Kettle, must have been very well reimbursed for his time and trouble. I knew exactly what to do with it.
>
> When the time came for the viewing, I made sure that the children were off playing. I suggested that Stephen accompany our pride and joy and their horrid son. I hoped that Stephen would take as great an exception to him as we had. It turned out much better than I could ever have imagined.
>
> I had placed the portrait in what I felt was the most fitting place, and Geoffroy agreed, though he was a good deal more nervous about the whole endeavor than I. We walked in great solemnity, led by Hood, with the dour "doer" Thrips behind us, and Hamilton behind him. When we got to the corner around which the portrait could be seen, I called the procession to a halt and advertised that the canvas was just steps away and that this position would afford them the perfect view, the light being just right at this hour.
>
> It was with some pride that they turned the corner, and, indeed, I had not lied, for the portrait itself could not

have been displayed in a more advantageous position. However, it was the context of the painting that was the ultimate triumph.

Previously this wall had been covered with paintings of local prize livestock, a tradition started by, I believe, the Bad Lord Loveall. The large portrait of a hairy shire horse had been almost exactly the same size as the portrait of the Rakeleighs, and replacing one with the other was easy. The rearrangement of the paintings around it had been somewhat more diverting. But when I decided that the small Henderson oil of the virile bull, in all its parodic black masculinity, should be put to the left of the portrait next to the handsome figure that vaguely resembled Augustus and that a most comical painting by a local rustic artist of a contented pig should be placed next to his wife, then the other pictures — sheep, cows, dull-looking racehorses, and even a strange painting of a monkey that I found in the attic — found their place in the design quite naturally. The effect was tremendous. There they were, in all their glory, among their equals — and I apologize to the barnyard.

Above all, however, the painting was on display and magnificently, complete with small marble plaque into which were carved their names, the date of the arrival, and an annotation that it had been a wedding gift. They could do little but thank us for the honor we did them, but there was a cold distaste on Augustus's lips and the atmosphere turned icy upon extended viewing. I could hardly bear to leave the spot, despite the various notes of finality so loudly sounded by the Rakeleighs: "Well, perhaps we should return . . . ," and "A last cup of tea's the ticket. . . ." About their humiliation, they could say nothing at all. It would have been to admit defeat.

But a greater defeat was to follow and at a most unexpected hand. We had returned to the Entertainments

Room, where we were attempting further conversation, steering a course as far from the portrait as possible, while we waited for the children to return. They had been gone so long that I began to fear that things had not gone off well. Geoffroy was positively giddy after our success. If I did not know better, I would have thought him gloating when he went so far as to offer them a portrait of our family in return.

At this moment, we witnessed one of the great coups de théâtres of my experience. The first I was aware of it was when I heard Stephen come down the corridor, running in that ungainly way of his. When he came into view, he was alone. I took this to be an ominous sign, but his arrival was merely the overture to the grand spectacle.

It was such a gorgeous sight and reminded me of the games that Stephen plays with Rose. There was high drama about the masque and I don't doubt that Hamilton *fils* was the mastermind. I coughed pointedly and Geoffroy turned around in the direction in which I was looking. I smiled at him to divert attention, but the gruesome duo had not missed my cue and turned in horror to see what Geoffroy and I were already witnessing.

Their son was on all fours, wearing a muzzle, being led down the hall on a leash by Rose. She looked beautiful in her new green pinafore dress and affected a courtly regality, coupled with knightly pride, as though she had tamed a most ferocious dragon and saved the kingdom. The hall was long and she took her entrance at an exquisitely slow pace.

Geoffroy, in deep appreciation, applauded loudly. Whether he thought that all three children were collaborating in the venture, I know not — but his applause was ill judged. Augustus rose from his chair and started spluttering with rage.

"Get up, Guy! Now!" he thundered. Rose seemed rather disappointed, but I could tell that Stephen, just out of view, was frantically directing her to let go of the dog's lead. Guy struggled to his feet, but when asked "the meaning of this," he couldn't answer because of the muzzle, which Thrips stooped to remove. The mother remained silent while Augustus raged for both of them.

His anger was not because he thought Guy might have deserved this treatment — this he would have applauded — but because the boy had let himself be so compromised. He grabbed Guy by the collar, tugged him back to the chair, and apologized to us. I even felt sorry for the boy when he told his father they had done it because they thought it fun. He was so thoroughly in defeat that he was speaking lines that Stephen had written for him.

They left within minutes, the fat woman, her heinous husband who had wormed his way unwelcomed into our house, and, of course, Guy, his tail between his legs.

"Give me the muzzle," said Augustus ominously, before he left, though I demurred. I thought Rose might like this as a symbol of her first triumph.

What I remember most clearly of the day is that later in the evening, all Hamiltons, Loveall, and Hood sat down to a marvelous meal that had been prepared in case the guests stayed. Although Nurse Anstace Crouch had not been invited, she sent a note saying that she declined to come: she was leaving the next day on a lengthy carriage tour of the Continent, fulfilling the ambition of a lifetime. Of course, Stephen and I knew another reason, though we couldn't mention it. Without her, we made a large and extremely happy family.

Though it is no longer on display, the Kettle portrait is still listed in the Love Hall inventory and cross-referenced to the Livestock Collection, where it sits comfortably between a Hobbins and a Mullery.

3

Metamorphoses

1

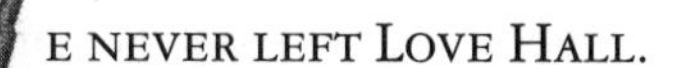

WE NEVER LEFT LOVE HALL.

That's not entirely true. I remember a trip to the seaside, where the birds sounded nothing like our birds at home and my dress was too hot.

It was the first time that I had ever seen the sea — except in my dreams and in paintings. The original was disappointing, neither blue nor brimful of sea-horse waves. It smelled awful and I could taste its salt stinging my lips as it tried to worm its way within me. The counterfeits on our walls were far more vibrant than this lifeless pretender.

I don't remember anybody else there, except our party: my mother, Hamilton, and his children. Where were the people? Either I didn't notice them or they had been removed.

As seagulls mocked the scene from above, Stephen skimmed a stone that bounced five times on the gray surface before it finally disappeared. I tried to copy him but, hampered by my skirt, I couldn't get the required speed or distance. I complained about my disadvantage.

"It's not your skirt," said Stephen. "You throw like Sarah, like a girl." But I felt then that my skirt *was* the reason, that I could throw farther, faster.

* * *

When I was at home, the sun always shone. Those were the days when life's red carpet unrolled before us. My father had delegated all his responsibilities to Hood, Hamilton, and my mother so that he might spend as much time in admiration of me as possible. Ours was a beautiful love: I was dressed in the most gorgeous clothes and given everything my heart desired, though my needs were few. He wanted only to look at me, to wonder at my growth, to commend me on my bearing and improve it if he could. I tried, in return, to provide him with as much to admire as possible. I would sit in the downstairs library and read to him. He did nothing but watch, listen, smile, and write the odd note, which he then gave to my mother, who would deftly insert it into our next lesson. He could scarcely bear to correct me himself, but occasionally he did. With a simple "Perhaps you mean vouch*safed,* rather than *vous-shaft,*" he would steer me straight, before adding: "But *vous-shaft* is so elegant, Rose."

The world, when we allowed it, came to Love Hall. Entertainments were brought expressly for our amusement and music played at our leisure. We clicked our fingers and magic happened.

At my eighth-birthday party, a strange little man from Italy, his face caked with makeup, made Stephen vanish. The conjurer brought his act to a sensational conclusion when he rolled Stephen out of a length of carpet, my troublemaker's dizzy and dazed expression changing to delight when he found that a substantial amount of money had appeared in his pocket. I hadn't had a lot of experience with money, but it was plain to see that it made people happy. The first time I held coins, apart from the old Roman coins we used to play shop, was in Paris years later. Then, for many years and until recently, I handled money every day, and grubby stuff it is, too. But Stephen was as pleased as Punch.

"What happened?" we asked, wide-eyed, hoping we too could make him vanish at will.

"I won't say," he said, jingling his bribe.

As I grew, the tenor of the entertainments changed. My mother was the moving spirit behind this. Writers materialized, wild-haired and sincere, to address us with all the florid rhetoric at their disposal on the glories of art and the beauties of literature. After their lectures, my mother would pose a leading question about Mary Day and, with the least excuse, take them firmly by the arm and escort them to the library.

One day, one memorable day in my ninth year, a troupe of strolling players arrived. The substance of the drama is long forgotten, but the actors are not. It rained that day, so the scenery and the gadgets, which aided the rudimentary dramatic effects (a saltbox and a rolling pin for the thunder: I think it was the story of Noah! At least, there was thunder. . . .) — all was moved within, where we had a closer view of the actors than we could ever have imagined. They were people like us, but such extraordinary caricatures with their beauty spots and their overabundant lips painted crimson far beyond the line of their own. The smell of the slap and burnt cork on their faces and the garlic on their breath mingled with the burning tallow to make the atmosphere quite foreign. I can still hear the deep, toasted voice of one of the females, more like a man's, emerging from somewhere deep in her large frame. I had never heard such loud whisperings, dramatic pauses, or uproarious laughter — and that was before the play even began. Ah! From that day on, I have always loved a curtain that is about to be raised.

The entertainment enjoyed universal approval until one of the male actors appeared as a woman, possibly Noah's wife. This Mrs. Manly — his stage name — did not make an attractive female, nor was he meant to, with his bosom absurdly inflated, his cheeks daubed with bright red circles, and his wig a bird's nest of blond curls. Even I, at my age and with my weak grasp of the facts, likened it to Stephen wearing Sarah's clothes: very silly. His entrance was met with gales of laughter from most of the assembled audience, but not from my father, who unexpectedly muttered to himself and summoned Hood.

Hood halted the presentation, while we moaned at the unexpected interval, and asked the actors for a private interview. The comedian in question attempted to offer an apology, but after a moment of awkwardness and a pointed conversation with the stage manager, the "usurper of the skirt" was ushered behind the scenery, to be replaced by the attractive young lady who had earlier played the flirtatious daughter. She gallantly improvised her lines but found greater success mouthing along as Manly spoke them from backstage. During this farce, my father's attention wandered, and shortly after, he left the room with a sigh. When the play ended, the actors took their bow, all except Mrs. Manly.

The play planted ideas in us, some deeper than others. Shortly afterwards, Stephen proclaimed one day that he and I should dress up as pirates and kidnap Sarah. He whispered it with the utmost confidentiality: it had the potential to be our most daring escapade. Sarah was too engrossed in finishing a sampler for her mother's birthday to notice as we stole catlike from the room. Stephen brought me some pirate clothes, and when I emerged from my room with curved cardboard scimitar, black pants, striped shirt, and eye patch, he yo-ho-ho'ed and laughed aloud.

As we were making our final plans, my parents turned the corner on their way from the library. My father was the very picture of the "parfit gentil knight" of Mother's diaries, with his hand resting on hers in midair in courtly fashion and she laughing appreciatively at one of his bons mots. Deep in discussion, they hardly seemed to notice us at first, but when my mother looked closer, they stopped in their tracks. She eyed him with nervous concern and put a hand on his shoulder. He stood stone still, as if petrified, one hand suspended in mid-gesture. Mother prompted him with a reassuringly dismissive laugh.

"Children will play at dress-up. Rose, you look adorable! Doesn't she, Geoffroy?"

Father's mood changed instantly, as though his mechanism had suddenly fallen into place.

"Yes. A lovely boy. She makes a lovely boy. A handsome boy!"

What went through his mind in that moment before he spoke, I wonder? Was he burying memories in order to find the appropriate paternal response? Or was something clawing its way from the grave, something forgotten and glimpsed only in jarring moments like this?

I was pleased. It all seemed most natural to me at the time. I did make a good boy. Stephen and I were about the same height and roughly the same build. There were more similarities between us than between Sarah and me, and we shared many of the same interests, to boot. Of course I made a lovely boy! My father clapped his hands together, and as they disappeared down the corridor, we heard him say: "So droll! Such a good little boy she makes. Lord Ose! That's what she'll be called: Little Lord Ose!"

"You do make a good boy," said Stephen as we went about our evil business of abduction. "Better than I'd make a girl."

How old was I exactly on the day I fell into the river? I can't remember dates very well or the precise order of events. Perhaps other people remember their childhood more clearly than I because at a specific time they lived at this address, went to that school, or had their hair in this style or that, but I have few of those chronological markers: only *before* and *after*. I depend on my mother's journal to place things, but as her loving experiment became a necessary deception for my father's well-being, she began to write more of her literary endeavors than she did of life within Love Hall. The turning point is an abrupt entry on October 12, 1828, which reads in its entirety: "Poor Geoffroy is innocent. The artifice is now entirely mine." After this, there was much more of Mary than of me.

Seasons passed and games were invented. Summer's glade became the winter's icy path. We never strayed from the Hall. I never went to school. I never went to stay with family friends at Great Yarmouth, because we had no family friends. Our relatives demanded our hospitality occasionally, but never those I wanted to see. After their father had relocated his practice nearer to their grandfather's university, Victoria and Robert were sent away to be schooled, a brutal concept I could barely understand. We wrote often but rarely saw each other.

Esmond Osbern and his cousin Reliance appeared regularly. Whomever my father favored, they imagined, would be the successful suitor, the savior of the Osberns, the victor sharing his spoils to the mutual advantage of all. Reliance was much younger than Esmond, but they both seemed ancient to me and I found their attentions disquieting, nor could I be bought with misjudged gift of abacus or carved Hottentot weapon, though Esmond once gave me a calico bonnet that I gave to Sarah (not wishing to enjoy it myself). Though I was kept at a distance from them, they appraised me with their every look. Reliance's cold eyes gave nothing away — he was either yet to become someone or was already a vacuum — but Esmond was simply unbearable. He spat out words as if consonants tasted foul, tapping out rote compliments like Morse code. I paraded before them briefly and then excused myself, laughing in relief as I ran away.

Augustus and Lady Caroline came only extremely rarely, never again accompanied by their son, Dogboy. The family portrait, however, remained on the wall as a happy memory of their visit.

The river. I was allowed bathing only with my mother when the two of us were alone — this I took to be a safety issue — though I often sat on the banks of the river, in the willow's shade, and enviously watched Stephen and Sarah. When schooling was done, the rest of the days were long and peaceful — although it was a fragile tranquillity easily shattered by a Stephen Hamilton cannonball from the bridge. I longed to be part of the pandemonium, but I knew that it was wrong to participate.

On that day, I had been egging Stephen on to some misdeed when in retaliation he made a pantomime of pushing me into the river. Seeing he was off balance, I pushed him instead. He clutched at me and, to my joy and surprise, took me with him. I heard Sarah scream,

"No!" but nothing could stop our momentum, not even our conscience. After a moment's exhilaration, we were lying in the cold water and my clothes were soaked. Sarah was soon helping us out, though Stephen and I couldn't stop laughing.

"Stephen? How could you?" scolded the good angel.

"It wasn't me!"

"It was my fault," I said.

"We mustn't let anyone see you," said Sarah, ever pragmatic, though unconvinced of my guilt.

"I'll say I lost my footing. I won't get the blame." I had everything worked out already. I wanted to take off my clothes, but I knew that I must not, that I was condemned to a cold, heavy trudge. So brother and sister helped me, shivering, to the house.

"You pushed her," Sarah kept muttering all the way back. But I wanted the blame: I was proud of my crime.

"I pushed *him*" was my final statement.

Upstairs, I remembered not to remove my clothes in front of Sarah, and I stood in a puddle of cold river until Angelica arrived with water and Mother poured me a hot bath. Once alone, she scolded me for monkeying around by the riverbank when I should have been reading, but I could tell she was gratified that when it came to the most important things — our rules — I did as I was told.

Everybody, particularly my father, treated me as the epitome of a perfect, beautiful young girl. Even with my heavier eyebrows, my aquiline nose, the depression in my chin (which in a girl might well have been called a dimple, but was clearly a cleft), and my long-legged gait, I felt entirely feminine. I excelled at the handicrafts that Sarah enjoyed but I also wanted to play in the dirt. I saw muddy boys outside, mucking out the pigs and throwing clumps at each other — Sarah would point and stick her tongue out in disgust, but I was only angry that I couldn't join in: my body longed to.

My skirts were the sole reason, I was sure, that I was never quite as quick as Stephen. I knew I could have beaten him and looked over my shoulder, laughing, if I'd been wearing the same kind of trousers as he; but lost in a tangle of slips and hoops, I never had a chance.

So my first practical experiments began. I remember the sadness and anger in my mother's eyes as she looked at the pool of piddle I had mistakenly sprayed on the floor around the bowl in my attempt to imitate Stephen. I had even sung a merry tune as I did it. Her look told me that it was a habit best avoided. She gently advised that if one sits down, one never misses. And this is good advice, which I still practice.

Soon after, our pirate play took more concrete form and we invented an entirely male character for me. Our games had always grown with us, reflecting new interests, but this latest idea of Stephen's showed a subconscious genius for improvisation. This male persona needed a permanent name and in honor of my father, Lord Ose it was. Stephen always played the daredevil, and his characters were many — Captain Stephen, Pirate Stephen (his face dyed brown with a broth of walnut leaves and twigs for which Mother gave us a recipe), Stephen the Jolly Little Middy (redbrick dust applied with a rabbit's foot) — whereas I was always the good Lord Ose, the upright hero who was never quite as charming as the villain. It was I who would always rescue Sarah. I have entire original scripts, every line ending with an exclamation:

Ose: Valet! [Presumably, "Varlet."] Unhand her!
Sarabelle: Save Me!
Pirate Stephen: Never, I tell thee, never, 'pon my life. My cutless, coxcomb!
Ose: Your Cutless meets my steel!
Pirate Stephen: You flashing blade!
Sarabelle: Have a care, Ose. He's a swine.

They fight. Stephen vanquished.

Sarabelle: My hero!

These scenarios often ended with my carrying Sarah off to my bedroom, where, still in character and as dictated not only by our scripts but by romance itself, I claimed her with a victorious kiss. The first time we kissed, my lips felt awkward, obstacles that were not properly attached to my mouth. What I was doing was undoubtedly incorrect, for I was doing nothing. Lord Ose would never have kissed his heroine so passively and ineptly. Longing for a role model, I turned away, frustrated with myself, my gaucheness. Sarah, to my surprise, put one hand on either side of my face, drew me back to her, and kissed me again, my mouth still shut but less defiantly so.

"Lord Ose wins the lady!" Stephen shouted, appearing at the door to announce the end of the game. Then as an afterthought, he said: "Sarah, will you dress up as a pirate? I want to be Ose for a change."

"Rose does make a very good lord," Sarah said with breathless enthusiasm. I tingled with pride. He may have been Stephen's idea, but I had made Lord Ose flesh: it was a role I was born to play. Lord Ose always wore exactly what I was wearing, with the addition of a handsome brown tunic tied on by a large belt, the buckle of which dug into Sarah's midriff. I tried always to do what I thought Ose would do, and this enabled me to save the heroine, and then kiss her, on a number of occasions. The kissing became less self-conscious and my technique was immeasurably improved by practice and adventurous maneuver. For Sarah, it grew into quite a habit. The rush to victory always preceded the meeting of lips: the climax of the game.

On other occasions, we acted out the stories of the ballads. I was the female sailor forced to dress in man's array — this is where that quaint word came from — and go to sea to seek her beloved, who, pressed into service, was dying on the shores of Barbaree. This time, it was Stephen I saved. The loving kiss was less natural to him, until I took off the topmost layer of my disguise, the easily removed brown tunic, to reveal — ta-da! — my dress beneath! That it was I, his love, sweet Janie of the Green Willow rescuing her darling Willie! We had seen the pictures, read the ballads, and tried to sing the melodies, but we left these guidelines behind to create infinitely more contrived amusements.

By this time, Sarah had been moved to the Hall with us as my companion. She had her own bedroom, much to the envy of Stephen, who thought he might well be missing out on some larks. He was, but not whatever he was imagining. Sometimes at night, often after such triumphant kisses, I tiptoed to her bedroom. She would hush me as I opened the door and then pat the bed beside her, where we'd lie next to each other on our backs in the dark and giggle. We would talk for hours about what to do the next day and the next day and the day after that, as though nothing would ever change. I always associate the warmth of her body through her nightdress with the secret to the perfect Barnet sugar cake.

This couldn't last all night. I didn't know precisely which rules we were breaking, but we had the thrilling feeling of doing wrong. I would finally, unwillingly, make my way back to my own room. Sometimes, though, we would fall asleep. More than once I woke with a start and had to scurry back to my own room to slip between my cold sheets. Sarah would visit me, too, but rarely: only I could afford to be caught walking the corridors at night.

Stephen encouraged me in other things: my sportsmanship, for example. The pinnacle of my career was a cricket match between the children of the house and the village, in imitation of the inaugural annual game between the workers at Love Hall and the Playfield team, to welcome summer. Hamilton had arranged this unprecedented event as a way of cementing new alliances, and our short game was to be played between their two innings. After much deliberation, I was allowed to play for the Hall children, who were short on numbers, on the understanding that I was not to be terrorized at the crease by any young villager with a quick delivery. The tomboy in me was thrilled, and though we all knew that mine could be little more than a celebrity appearance, it was something to be taken very seriously in a life as circumscribed as mine. Stephen, therefore, with my father's reluctant consent, arranged practice sessions in the back garden.

The moment my bat first made contact with the ball, it sent a shuddering jolt up my left arm. I immediately lost my grip, squealing and shaking out my arm as if scalded. My father, previously unnoticed but now an unmissable quiver of pink agitation against the ivy, nearly toppled from the window. He would have been happy to end the practice there and then, and with it, my entire cricketing career, but at Stephen's hissed prompt, I picked up my bat and waved, smiling through clenched teeth.

"Watch the ball," Stephen said. "Don't look where you're going to hit it. Look at the ball."

But still my frustrations continued. The ball, not moving very fast, either, missed my bat on all sides, and I got tired of replacing the sticks behind me, so I stopped. On the few occasions that I managed to make contact, it went nowhere near where I had intended. With his arms around my waist, Stephen showed me how to hold the bat properly, standing in the correct position. He worked it firmly into my hands and then stood in front of me.

"Eyes forward. Shift your left foot round. Yes. Watch the ball." He held it up so I knew precisely what I was meant to be watching. This wisdom came quite naturally to boys, I assumed, so I tried to put all his knowledge to use on the next delivery.

It wasn't so much my hitting the ball as the beautiful sound that this made and the pleasurable feeling that I got from hitting it. It was as though I had transferred all the energy of the ball coming toward me back into it, sending it away with even greater velocity than it had arrived. There was no shudder, no shock. The ball left my bat and cut along the ground at terrific speed into a thick bed of nettles over by the tomato shed. Stephen watched it go — there was no pressing reason to run after it — and looked back at me, his hands on his hips.

"Cor! Rose! Do that again!"

And I did.

The day of the game finally arrived. Stephen had originally thought of me as an ornament to the team, but he now realized I might be better employed as secret weapon than figurehead. Unfortunately, all my practice had been with Stephen, and subsequently Sarah, who had been pressed unwillingly into the Hall team, along with the curry chef's son, who used an Indian overarm bowling technique of questionable legality. I had no real notion how anyone else played the game. Our rehearsal — for so I called it, much to Stephen's annoyance — had been done wearing a specific slim skirt, which allowed me to face up to the bowler well and didn't interfere with my wielding the bat. However, the skirt was not tailored for running. I was more than likely to hit the ball, but unless it reached the boundary and I didn't have to run, I wouldn't be able to make the other end without falling over. I felt like ripping it off above the knees.

We watched the gentlemen's teams go at each other first. Balls came down at a dignified pace from portly middle-aged men, whose compatriots could not bend down quite far enough to stop daisy cutters running through their legs. There were stately calls of "Umpire!" and "Played, Playfield!" and before an hour or two had passed, everyone was delighted to be back in the pavilion, eating wafer-thin sandwiches. In fact, the game during the interval was, because of my appearance, quite as eagerly awaited as any of the day's entertainment. We even took precedence over tea itself.

Our team was to bat first, and I would not be required to field. I was therefore placed relatively early in the order and I arrived at the crease to great applause and shouts of "Long Live Rose and all at Love Hall." My mother and father, who had become increasingly agitated about my participation and repeatedly pleaded with me to give up my wicket on purpose if I felt scared, watched from beneath a grand canopy, with the village vicar. Stephen, as planned, was my batting partner. I surveyed the scruffy children of the village, dressed up in the smartest whites they could muster. They looked at me, in my perfect cream dress, with my brand-new cricket bat, a generous gift from the village to their benefactors, with open mouths and wonder. If they envied me, they envied me the bat most of all, and they gazed on it with awe. Best look while they could, they imagined, since this would be a brief glimpse before I began my ceremonial and much-applauded walk back to the pavilion.

I dispatched the first ball, a decidedly generous slow delivery from a freckled boy on his best behavior, toward the shortened boundary. It skipped over the rope with its final gasp. The reaction was astounding, as hats were hurled, landing topsy-turvy on different heads. Next ball, I improved the shot; it went over without so much as a single bounce, accompanied by an even greater roar of approval. I had never felt such pride, to be universally applauded for something that came so naturally to me, something that made me as heroick as the women in my book, as bold as Stephen, as graceful as Sarah. I could barely hide my happiness. Even the fielders of the opposing team seemed delighted.

By the end of the first over, however, their mood had perceptibly changed. I was quite clearly too good, much better than they had expected. The balls they were floating toward me, gently, underarm, were so much more straightforward than the tweakers and yorkers of practice. The village immediately had to adjust to an awkward problem: how to keep my score down without bowling too aggressively. The umpires had a short meeting. About me, I presumed.

Stephen was lapping it up. We were on top, and our partnership could not be dislodged. My first fifty, in my first game of cricket, came up after sixteen balls, and I began to feel guilty, as though I were imposing my superior strength on these other children, bullying them.

"Rose!" Stephen whispered to me as we met halfway up the wicket between overs in imitation of our elders. "We'll win. Retire. Pretend you've hurt yourself."

And so I did. Before the next ball, I lifted my bat, feeling an imaginary twinge in my back, before I walked off to great cheering. Hood scampered onto the field to see if I was in any pain, but I told him that Stephen had advised me to retire early, which news Father received with delight. Our team amassed an unassailable score, Stephen and Bannerjee skittled the village out for twenty-two and I earned the nickname "Maiden Century."

It was a memorable debut, but something in it saddened my father. After the game, he drifted back into the house with Hood, while everyone else stayed to enjoy the revelry. I felt freer than I had under his scrutiny, and some of the town children struck up a conversation with me through Stephen. One particularly bold young child of my own age asked if he might kiss me. I could have considered it, but he was immediately shooed away by his guardian with a smart clip around the ear.

"You terror! The nerve!" she scolded. "You can't kiss a lady!"

"Why does she talk so low?" he asked as she dragged him away.

"She doesn't talk low. She 'as a lovely voice. She's perfect. And she's better at cricket than you, too."

"I only asked if I could kiss 'er. That's what you ask girls."

And he had asked so nicely.

The cricket game whetted the local appetite to know more of the strange gangling young lady with the majestic off drive. Sealed letters were left tied to the gates for me. The locals tried to catch a glimpse whenever they could. They must have thought me a curious child, of course, and privately they wondered whether I might be a little "amphibious." My voice earned me the affectionate nickname Froggy, which one or two people still call me to this day. This was explained to me by my mother with reference to the actress in the play — the real woman, not Mrs. Manly: "You heard her voice, didn't you, darling? Everyone sounds a little different. It's quite normal to be different, Rose."

I read in my mother's diary that a joke circulated even then that I had been born a male but that my parents had so hoped to have a girl. And those villagers were a superstitious lot, no strangers to dressing a son in a girl's nightgown to protect him from harm and hide him from bad fairies: old wives told that such a boy would grow up to fascinate all the girls. And it was common knowledge that girls don't grow feminine till their mother's milk is out of them, so perhaps they wondered whether I was still at the teat. But people will talk, and it was all dismissed as unkind. It is astounding what effect the confidence of wealth can have upon the general consensus. No one stood up and declared that I had no clothes — perhaps they had barely noticed — so I was the best-dressed young lady in the kingdom.

It was after the cricket match that my father took seriously ill for the first time. He recovered, but never entirely. It is possible that my mother knew such would be the case, and it made her decide that the date of revelation, which had already been deferred so much longer than she had imagined, would now have to be pushed back further still. Perhaps until after he died, lest it kill him. But he didn't die: Dolores saw to that.

Stephen and I continued cricket rehearsal. There were no matches to "rehearse" for, but there was always next year's game. One afternoon a particularly high shot, which had left my bat somewhere away from the middle, saw the ball lodge up in the tree that we should never climb, Rubberguts. We could see the ball nestled in the crook of two sturdy branches. We threw sticks at it, to no avail.

"Blow!" Stephen said. "I'm going up. Keep watch."

I saw him crawl along the limb and thump the branch until the ball, none the worse for wear, plopped down next to me. He started to back down the branch, since it was too high for him to swing and drop off. When he was out of view, I heard him shout: “Hey! I’ve found something.”

“What?”

“I’ll bring it down.”

It was a box containing a damp little book, very old, with the pages stuck together; somehow it had become embedded, or had been carefully placed, in a little hole in the trunk. Much of it was unreadable, but it seemed to be a book of answers to riddles and questions. We showed it to my mother, without telling her where we had found it, and she knew immediately what it was: *The Nutcrackers*.

To our surprise, this damp, smelly artifact, a combination of mush and paper, assumed a great importance to the older inhabitants of Love Hall. Should they tell my father? When should they tell him? How did we find it? We admitted that Stephen had climbed Rubberguts to reclaim our ball. They weren’t as angry as we thought they would be.

No wonder *The Nutcrackers* had never been found. It had accompanied Dolly up a tree that no one had been allowed to climb since her death, and there it had remained ever since. But what could they tell my father of the manner of the book’s retrieval? It was decided, to our amusement, that Hamilton had climbed the tree to fetch our ball and that he had found the book, and this was the story, forever.

“Why can’t we tell him the truth?” I asked.

“Your father doesn’t want the truth, my darling,” said my mother. “He needs a beautiful story. He is very agitated and we are all doing our best for him. This book will make him so happy.”

And it did. Finally, he managed to solve the enigma of the drawing that he and Dolores had studied together all those years before. If the page was folded in two certain ways down the middle and the two sides pushed together, and if this was then viewed from an oblique angle to the right or left, the “answer” could be seen without too much difficulty. *The Nutcrackers* cheered him, and we saw him outside his bedroom again.

I am looking at it now. After all his waiting, it could have been a sad disappointment — it only barely resembles what it's meant to — but my father would not have been disappointed under any circumstances, for he could read something into anything connected with Dolly's death, and in this case, it was easy.

It was a tree.

If only they had solved it at the time, if only she hadn't stubbornly hid *The Nutcrackers,* my father told my mother, they would have had good warning. They would have known not to climb Rubberguts.

She would not have died.

I would not have lived.

2

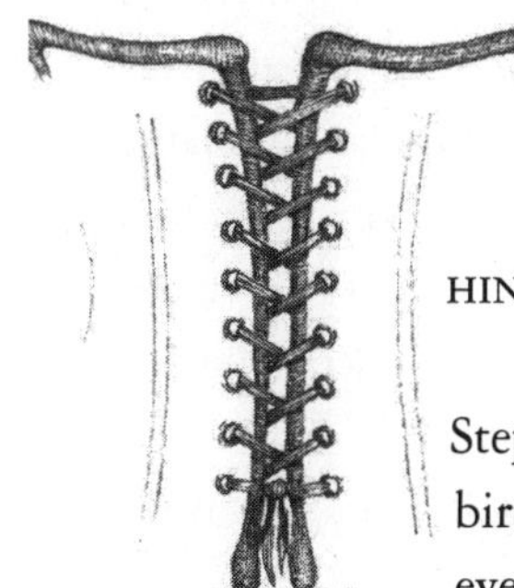

HINGS GOT WORSE the year I learned to shave.

Stephen received a cutthroat razor for his twelfth birthday. It was the most impressive thing we had ever seen, too real, too terrifying to use even as a prop. His father showed him how to rub up a lather in the wooden bowl of fossilized soap and then daub it on his face with the smart little brush. Ill-advisedly, Stephen was then left to his own devices. With its scant blond down, his upper lip was barely ready for such close attention and he made a meal of it. He emerged smiling through gritted teeth, his chin speckled with red. I sympathized, though I felt I could have done a little better for myself. I was, if anything, more in need of the razor — but I knew that girls didn't shave.

There was much that I accepted at face value, but there were also things that mystified me, things I longed to understand about myself. I kept these curiosities and confusions from everyone, even my mother, for I knew that I should keep up the appearance of a happy girl to please everyone and that it was doubtless my fault if I felt any differently. If only I'd listened harder, I told myself, I wouldn't feel so muddled. I didn't even like to think about my physique, so I tried never to touch or look below. Sometimes it brought attention to itself in humiliating ways, but panic overwhelmed me when I tried to reach any conclusion about what was happening, and I became an adept at concealment. Mother had impressed upon me that it was a topic for neither conversation nor consideration; it was certainly far too embarrassing to mention to Sarah, even if it was a secret that we both shared. She, being more sensible, had never needed to bring it up, and neither should I.

No, it would have to be my mother or nothing. Those were the rules, but I was too embarrassed. I feared that there was something wrong with me and that Father would hate me. Could I tell anyone? Would I one day *have* to tell everyone? How great would be my shame then? Just the thought of it sent me into a spiral of gloom. And so I tried not to think about it at all. One day I would need to solve the mystery, but for now I had to bury it, to forget about it, to make it more secret.

One more thing made it difficult to talk to Sarah: why, when we were so close, were we becoming so different?

I wasn't growing as quickly as she was, and I envied her. If we wore the same clothes, they hung differently. Her easy bearing had always made me feel angular and bony, but her body had now developed an elegance far removed from my straight, simple lines. Her skin had taken on a warm olive hue whereas mine, which never saw the sun, was still pale. We had the same wavy, soft hair, but mine grew elsewhere and was coarser on my arms. Underneath her dress, up a loose sleeve, down a neckline, I saw how she was.

She let me lace up her stays as tightly as I could. I breathed in the scent of her hair, slipping my hand beneath, between her chemise and her skin, and feeling the curve of her waist. I had worked out how to tighten the stays halfway and then, using my forefinger, pull from top to bottom to make them tighter still, before finally eliciting a small yelp of surprise with a sharp climactic tug. As when Stephen and I tumbled into the river, I was falling, falling.

Loosening them was an even greater pleasure, altogether less scientific. I released her bit by bit and felt the tug of her body pull the laces apart as it relaxed. The ribbon slid through the brass eyes as I took my hands away, the natural movement of her body doing my work for me. She groaned in deep appreciation and I felt her pleasure.

While I grew straight up — I was a few inches taller than she now — she was growing all around. Of course, I was almost two years younger, but could this account for all the discrepancies? Perhaps I was paying for my own failings: perhaps my tomboy yearnings had adapted my body into its more boyish shape. I spent as much time with Sarah as possible and tried to imitate her.

Some of my greatest discoveries were made on the lucky nights when we were on our own, with the noise and distraction shut far away in the Gatehouse Cottage till morning. Lying in the drowsy half-sense of sleepy conversation, our bodies barely touched. She lay in the crook of my shoulder, I with my arm around her. These clandestine nights were perfectly childish until once when, on an inspired whim, I lowered my voice.

"I, Ose, hope milady was not harmed during today's rescue," I whispered into her hair in the darkness.

Sarah feigned a swoon and giggled with pleasure, wiggling her toes in approval.

"No, my lord," she replied through a smile she was trying to suppress. "I am unharmed, and disarmed by your knightly courtesy."

"I am gratified. I assure you I am unarmed, milady."

"So much the better, milord, but shall we speak of armor?"

"Rather, amour."

There was silence. She was facing away from me and I kissed her, just as Ose would have done. My lips felt the down on the back of her neck. She did nothing to stop me. The bed shifted beneath us as we angled our bodies toward each other. Slowly, I worked my way around to her mouth and our lips touched, without any movement, until they became quite dry. It was as if we had forgotten all we had learned during the victory kisses, as though we couldn't cope with being horizontal. With an embarrassed laugh, she moistened her mouth to prevent our adhesion. Only our lips touched, but I could feel the aura of her body beckoning me, pulling me in. I dared not touch her more. With a "shh!" I hurried to my own bed, where I lived it all again and imagined yielding to her warmth.

These were thrilling nights, which quickly became ritual: secret, warm, exciting — our moves a constant exchange of imaginary hostages, the climax never more than the union of our lips. What incredible fictions lay beyond? It was something to speculate upon as I fell asleep.

But the worries returned with the sun.

"We all are what we are," my mother said, "and we are all beautiful. . . ." Then she added, "But no one is as beautiful as your cousin Prudence!"

Once when the Osberns visited, we were treated to the nauseating sight of Prudence's preening at the hands of her mother, while her father, the man of God, looked on, muttering wistful words of apology for their *vanitas*. Nora recited a litany of clichés to the girl — she was the most beautiful who had ever lived, her hair the softest and richest, her eyes the most lucid, her skin the most blemish-free: how proud her uncle Edred would have been of her! The unease and embarrassment of the cuckold divine was evident, and he was moved to gloss for our benefit: "Excepting present company," and "Your ladyships permitting." Nora continued regardless until her daughter asked: "Am I more beautiful than Rose?" Her mother was just about to answer (in the affirmative) when Edgar raised his hand as if to heaven and shouted, "No!" He then recovered himself and said firmly: "I absolutely forbid you to answer that question."

No more was said. The truth, however, was that Nora would have had to lie not to say yes. Prudence *was* beautiful and, at seventeen, her body, with its enviable languor of movement, boasted a more advanced version of the shape that Sarah's was inching toward and in which my own seemed not to be bound. Her entirety would be as smooth as her arms, and this was indescribably beautiful to me, as I bristled under my clothes, yearning for such softness. Prudence's movements complemented her body and she swayed from side to side. Later, I did an impression for Sarah and she was immediately able to adapt her own walk to the sway, as if she'd thought of it. When I tried, I thought I looked like a monkey, and Stephen, without my prompting, confirmed this.

Sex, the big dictionary confirmed, was "the property by which any animal is male or female." This was followed by a citation from Milton: "Under his forming hands a Creature grew / Manlike, but different sex." So it was either. The second definition was "womankind, by way of emphasis." So it was women. The encyclopedia defined it as "that which *separates* male and female." So it was something else entirely. I had been taught to trust these texts unreservedly, but they were as confused as I was about this gray area, and no wonder. If sex was what separated boys and girls, the matter was very unclear, for there was little that separated Stephen and me. We were different, of course, but not very: for example, the sound of our voices, both of which were becoming scratchier. If anything, mine was a little higher. It was a slight effort to keep it that way, but it more resembled the way Sarah spoke — and I wanted to be like her. Stephen's voice deepened until it settled on a dulcet tenor; mine went through a strange period of alternating between rasping treble and yodeling alto. I hoped it would pick one or the other, purely because the effect was more comic than I would have wished. Finally, by my thirteenth birthday, it plumped for the alto, and after some practice, I was able to pitch it higher without such concentration.

For the first time in my life, I noticed a look of something other than love in my father's eyes. I took it to be embarrassment and shame of me — perhaps he knew as much about my unthinkable muddle as

I, perhaps he knew my secret, whatever it was. I caught his eye once across the dinner table, and the look I saw was distaste. He knew that he had communicated more than he had meant to, though I do not remember the look in his eyes so much as the side of his head as he turned. I can summon this moment exactly, and it is the only way that I do not like to remember him. I couldn't understand it, and it upset me. I asked my mother about it later that evening, and she told me, of course, that it was nothing, that all children worry about their father's love as they grow. But I knew this wasn't all. I now know from an unimpeachable source, myself, that fathers can feel flickerings of unease when their daughters bloom into womanhood: it summons conflicting feelings within them. Not my father. He shunned me when I didn't bloom at all.

Meanwhile, the hair above my upper lip and around my cheeks had grown thicker and less babyish. Gone were the gentle wisps. Sarah had a hint of these in the smiling corners above her mouth. On Stephen and me, this region had now been appropriated by a cruder growth, and now I truly needed the razor more than he. My mother, to my surprise, agreed.

Out came my own cutthroat razor and bowl of hard soap.

"All children worry about whether they are *right* or not, darling, and the truth is that you are *all* right," she said as she nevertheless worked on my rightness, showing me new ways to take care of myself, to look more beautiful. First tweezers, then razor. She showed me how to take the blade to the hair above my lip and then cover it with the powder, which made me sneeze. Our toilet took longer and methods became complex, ever more elaborate combinations of face powder, mascara, and rouge. Girls shaved after all.

At first, I enjoyed the novelty, though it was painful when I caught a piece of skin and cut myself. My mother bought me some perfume that stung deeply, though the sweet fragrance somewhat dimmed the agony. Attargul was the first, then Eglantine, which I liked even more, and lastly Floris's Lily of the Valley, which I have worn ever since. The powder, a noxious combination of lead plate, vinegar, and perfume, prepared (to my horror) in horse manure, suffocated and chafed my skin, so every night I rubbed my face with Mother's fard of sweet almond oil, melted with spermaceti and honey, which soothed me until the next morning's onslaught.

Soon I began to wonder what the point of all this shaving was. I had only once seen a woman with a beard, it was true — she had come with the circus — but she hadn't looked so very terrible. In fact, I thought her rather elegant, in every way preferable to the strong man, who was overly swollen and stretched from end to end, yet admired by all. Shaving was a painful, boring, and time-consuming occupation. So why didn't women just grow beards? I could even see the faint dark hairs at the corners of my mother's mouth. I tried to picture her with a mustache as she brushed my hair, and the image that came to me in the mirror was dashing.

I looked rather grown-up with more makeup, and Sarah thought it most attractive, though her skin was so much more naturally lovely than mine and it was clear that she had no truck with the razor. Unfortunately, the razor's ministration seemed to encourage a quicker growth, so I had to endure this procedure more often as days went by.

Worried conferences became an increasingly regular occurrence. I had the impression that I was being hurried through rooms ever more quickly, as though something that I shouldn't see was happening just out of sight. I felt left out, as though a secret was being kept from me, and this was mirrored by my own growing unease with myself. For the first time, I knew self-consciousness and I began to monitor my behavior more closely, to doubt my impulses, to think twice before speaking.

Mother finally revealed that my father was very ill. His nerves had collapsed and he was suffering from a serious fever. His only hope lay in rest, and we were to pray for him. I feared that my ignorance was somehow exacerbating the crisis, but the truth was much worse.

One evening Anstace Crouch appeared at the library door, her restless period of quiet at an end. My mother was working there alone. She looked up from her work, astonished to see Anstace so far from her room, and asked her business. Anstace approached with as much dignity as her rickety frame allowed. It was as if she were walking on stilts. She stood over the desk in silence, looking down her nose, her nostrils so taut that they appeared translucent.

Again my mother asked her business. Anstace calmly informed her that she had written two letters, one addressed to Julius Rakeleigh, the other to Athelstan Osbern. The matter was twofold: I was not a girl. Moreover and worse, I was a foundling, not the natural child of my father and mother. Phillip, the coachman, who had found me with Hood and my father and was now employed on a distant estate, would corroborate her story. She would destroy the letters on only one condition: that I be put in her charge.

"I shall call Hood and Hamilton," said my mother with great sangfroid, reaching for the bellpull in astonishment.

"Do not," said Anstace, raising a cadaverous arm. "I want to speak only to the Young Lord, and out of respect, in this one instance, I am prepared to do this through you."

"Since my husband is ill, the HaHa will need to —"

"The HaHa — ha! Enough of this charade! It must end, and I can do it. If you do not tell the Young Lord, I shall go to him myself or I shall find justice elsewhere. Rose likes a good story, too, doesn't he?"

My mother stood, spilling a well of ink in her anger. The black ink spread across the desk toward her working papers. It was far too much for the polite piece of blotting paper that she had to hand. Anstace looked on as my mother stopped the flow with the nearest thing available, which was her skirt.

"Shall I mop up, Anonyma?" she asked with no intention of giving any assistance. "Or shall I call the *housekeeper?* I know what is best for Rose. I know what Lady Loveall would have thought best. Didn't I implement her every wish when she was alive? And I shall now. I will send the letters, unless Rose is given to my charge."

"You are not Lady Loveall, Anstace. Lady Loveall is dead. *I* am Lady Loveall."

"You are an inky-fingered librarian with ideas above your station, but my feelings for you and your strange philosophies are irrelevant. I have said my piece."

"Do not dare to communicate with my husband or my child."

"Your *husband?* Your *child?*"

"Do not dare!" shouted my mother. Anstace became more serene as my mother's anger reached its height. My mother clasped an inky hand to her mouth to silence herself. Then she looked up. "Would you kill him?"

Anstace was unmoved, her silence an acknowledgment that she had planned it so. Eventually she spoke.

"You think me evil." Anstace smiled. "But it is you, not I, who are criminal and murderer."

"Murderer! I?"

"The murderer of that poor boy. And for what? So Geoff *Roy* could live in his world of childish fancies." With every passing moment, she sounded more like her late mistress. Refused her wish to become housekeeper, Anstace's imagination had taken her straight to the top. "I do not wish his death, but it might be a mercy. If the letters are delivered, he would certainly be declared insane. And you! You'd fall the same way for your connivance. Then how could such an ill-gotten wretch inherit one of the largest fortunes and the oldest family names? It is the answer to all the Osberns' prayers, the spur they need to wrest control of Love Hall. The name Loveall would be no more."

"That is the last thing your employer would have wanted."

"*This* is the last thing she would have wanted." Anstace surveyed the library as though it were to blame. "I know what is best, Anonyma. Time and nature are on my side. Certain key proofs will soon become clear to the rest of the world, whether I send the letters or no. Now you have a choice. Soon you will not. That is all."

She turned to the door, leaving my mother wiping her hands on her skirts, then clutching up the papers around her. With Anstace out of sight, she was finally able to call for Hood and Hamilton.

They saw the situation with horrible clarity: they were completely dependent on Crouch. My father's life was in her hands. The HaHa had known that at least one of the two truths must emerge, but they were terrified that it would out before they were ready. They had hoped that it was enough for Anstace to grow old in luxury, knowing she held a high trump that guaranteed both living and pension, but they had hoped in vain. Hers was blackmail of a different color: she'd had all the money she wanted and traveled in luxury wherever she desired. She didn't want a large house far elsewhere with servants of her own. She had no one to provide for and nothing to enjoy except the vestiges of her power at Love Hall. What she now demanded was completely out of the question: the restoration of her old power. In short, she wanted to become her dead employer.

Angelica reminded her husband that the present situation was the direct result of denying Anstace preferment. Perhaps the position of housekeeper was their way back into her good graces. They should inquire whether the job still held its appeal. Anything to buy themselves more time. Hamilton blamed himself, and his thoughts took a darker turn as he considered other options. Perhaps a new kind of household economy was called for. His father would have been ashamed at the alternatives that flashed across his mind, he knew. There had always been rumors of vendettas settled swiftly and violently, but Samuel did not know who, how managed, and why. He was on his own now, so he tried to summon up all the acumen of his revered father in his heyday.

Until now, Hood and Hamilton had been able to deal with Anstace's threats, but this was too vital not to be conveyed to my father. At opportune moments, Hood made discreet references to the growing danger. It was the first my father had heard of Anstace's threat. He had long wondered what this querulous old woman was still doing around the house. Now he understood, although the full scope of her threat was kept from him: Hood did not feel the need to mention the revelation of my sex, about which he felt my father did not need to be reminded, if indeed he remembered. It was disconcerting to know that one of the household would trade family secrets to the highest bidder or that a family as great as the Loveall had to buy their own privacy, but it had happened before in the best of families and doubtless would again. Hood described the situation to his master as unpleasant but not hopeless. No matter how much she raved about my being an orphan, he said, the world would think her insane. Right was on their side. There was nothing to worry about: it had merely been their duty to inform him. In his moments of lucidity, my father was calm. Money meant nothing to him. He would happily pay Crouch. Hamilton and Hood would doubtless be able to arrange it to the satisfaction of all, and surely that would put an end to the matter. But he did not understand that the time for bribery was past.

All he had planned for me was happiness and, with the help of my mother, he thought he had provided it. Now one of the few remnants of his mother's world was coming to haunt him. What did Crouch have against our happiness and the future of Love Hall? He grew weaker with worry each day. It should have been kept from him altogether, for it set other wheels in motion, carriage wheels clattering back in time to the dustheap.

In her threats, my father heard another more distant voice — the truth. I had been growing up in front of him, reminding him every day. It was I, not Anstace, who would finally exhaust him. She was the messenger, but no more. He had lived so much of his life in denial about me that the consequences of being reminded now, of breaking down that old locked door, were far too great. He started to waste away, waiting for good news that wasn't coming.

It was therefore of paramount importance that Anstace be kept away from him. Not to mention from me. No one knew what poison would next spit from her venomous mouth. This malign woman of uncertain occupation had recently passed us in the hallway and whispered something through her teeth.

"What did she say?" said Sarah.

"Did she call me 'master'?" I asked.

"That wasn't it. It was more like 'barster,'" said Stephen. We had no idea why she would say anything.

"Perhaps she has a cold," I suggested.

"Poor woman!" said Sarah. "She certainly doesn't look very well, does she?" It was true. Her skin was unnaturally wrinkled and brown. My mother unexpectedly asked if Crouch had been bothering us at all, and I was pleased to be able to report this incident. I heard no more about it.

Hood and Hamilton kept an increasingly close watch on Anstace. Deprived of all authority, not allowed anywhere near me, let *alone* as a nurse, Anstace gave them the impression of being always coiled. Her trips became less frequent, and her behavior suggested that her time drew nigh: her air at dinner was superior and she was eating more. Odd letters arrived for her from beyond the village. She started to encourage people to call her by her first name, as Angelica did. More often than before, I would see her at the end of a long corridor, casting a skeletal shadow down the hall, keeping an eye on her investment. But she made no more dramatic entrances, preferring to loom in the wings.

Father's situation became graver and Mother's diary for this period makes pitiful reading. He lay in bed, pale with sweat, talking to himself for hours, sleep a distant dream. My mother moved her work to his bedside so she could nurse him.

Mother cared only about his health. She had made a correct diagnosis and refused to pay Crouch any mind at all, though Anstace was often glimpsed or heard in the corridor outside the bedroom. The blackmailer was soon banned from the floor entirely and exiled to the distant reaches, so far away that even the echo of her heels could not carry. But time was running out.

Left rather more to ourselves as this threat swelled, our dramas took an even freer rein. I had often worn a penciled-in mustache as the gallant Ose, but now that a noticeable shadow had crept along my top lip, we saw new opportunities. Stephen liked it and suggested that I forgo shaving, so I did. With the addition of some charcoal, my "beard" looked very realistic. Sarah was less enthusiastic, saying that when it didn't tickle, it scratched her. My mother chose to ignore this little piece of individualism, possibly because she was occupied by more pressing matters, probably in the hope that the novelty would naturally wear off.

One day, as I passed his open door, I caught sight of my father in bed. I couldn't help but stop. He was sitting up, frail against a wall of pillows. He sipped at spoonfuls of broth while my mother dabbed at his chin with a napkin. I was in full Ose regalia, stubble and charcoaled mustache. I looked rather fine and, feeling very pleased with myself, thought it might cheer him. As I called out his name, the pitch of my voice let me down, plummeting into its lower register. He stopped, looked up, and immediately fainted away as if he had seen a ghost. The door between us was shut at once, and I was left staring at the grain of the wood where my beloved father had been. Why couldn't I help him? My eyes filled with tears as I pictured him prostrate, soup trickling from the side of his mouth. My stomach ached and I had no thought of moving. We had seen a ghost in each other.

Eventually my mother came out. I hid my tears and she hurried me off to play, calling down the corridor after me: "Wipe that silly nonsense off, darling!" I immediately did. Not shaving was a luxury I would have to forgo.

I never saw him anymore. I hated our separation, but others clearly thought it best. Having little experience of illness, I accepted that this was how the sick were treated, as when Stephen contracted the measles and was put in quarantine for ten days — ten of the most peaceful days of my life. I wrote Father letters to his bedside, which I addressed to "Lord Loveall, His Bed, the Great Bedroom, Love Hall." My mother read these to him (or most of them — certain parts, it strikes me now, would have felled him with one blow). In the letters, I detailed how Stephen and Sarah and I filled our days in his absence and how very much I missed him. These were, I am sure, some of the most sentimental letters ever written. I knew he was ill, and I knew that illness led to death and that he had given me life. (I am now reminded of a Greek tragedy — he gave me life and I killed him.) I owed him everything, but I had no way to show him except in writing, which is all that is left to me still. I made sure that letters arrived at his door in a constant flow, and my mother told me how he treasured them.

While Mother was busy tending to my father, the blackboard in the schoolroom nightly became filled with incomprehensible chalk marks. First there appeared a stick figure in a crudely drawn skirt shaped like an equilateral triangle, then a stick figure with a little bob of hair, x-ed out, so one could see precisely where the chalk had broken with the force of the striking out. At first I thought it was funny, but then I intuited that something was being communicated. I didn't know what, I didn't know to whom, and I didn't want to know.

The only person who would do such a thing was Stephen, but he swore blindly, and persuasively, that he was innocent. He was as surprised and puzzled as we were. Who else in the house could it be? The only reasonable choices were Stephen or I, and I hadn't done it, had I? I buried my worries deeper.

I started to sleepwalk, the female somnambule. One night my mother found me lifting a certain painting from the wall — only human backs were on display — to see what might be on the other side. I remembered nothing about it when I awoke the next morning.

Another night I awoke — or thought I awoke — alone, looking at the painting of Salmacis and Hermaphroditus. My finger was touching the surface of the oil and I felt as if I could crawl into it, or pull something from it. I saw an unhappy man in a rumpled suit on the canvas. He lay at the side of the spring, and his hand hung limply, sadly, into the water. Could I help him? Could he help me? He looked finished, exhausted, relieved. I let myself fall into the crystal pool of the painting, but it was far too viscose to be water and started to suck me in like quicksand. I awoke in bed, sweating, gasping for breath. I ran down the stairs, but there was no sign that I had been there, no man in the painting.

On some specific date during this uncertain and increasingly miserable time, the Osberns had been granted permission to descend because of the death of Lady Elizabeth Osbern, Athelstan's wife and my grandmother's archenemy. Hood, however, recommended that, things being as they were, we should not have to suffer the added strain of unsympathetic scrutiny and, furthermore, that it would be foolish to tempt Anstace to expression. My mother had written a letter of excuse and apology to Athelstan, suggesting a postponement for exactly three months, by which time my father would surely be improved. Doubtless they received news of this illness with even more delight than they would have received confirmation of their arrival.

News of the postponement had not reached Edwig Osbern, who lived most of the year at his club in town, where, by design, only a very small percentage of his messages were delivered. Edwig was not of the Osberns' world. He concerned himself only with the pursuit of pleasure, and his was a lifetime in the service of immodesty and immoderation.

On his visits over the years, he often stared in great wonder at my mother, whom he thought remarkably beautiful. He was wont to enthuse throatily about her to the family at large: "My God, that young bookworm, I'd like to take her over my knee. . . ." and "She might just be a librarian, but she's a Venus when she smiles. . . ." When eyebrows were raised at his crudeness, he excused himself, claiming that as an admirer of great beauty, he was helpless in her thrall. Mother assured me that this was how Edwig behaved toward all women and that one day he would stare so at me.

The other Osberns ignored Edwig as far as possible, embarrassed by the incorrigible old sot. They never apologized for him, either, and I didn't mind. He was a breath of fresh air among that gaggle of hypocrites.

Once, a few years before, he had hoisted me off the ground and dropped me on his knee. There, in his alcoholic daze, he had thoughtlessly trapped me. I thought he might have taken me for the cat and I didn't see any reason to be scared. He stroked my back and I noticed he smelled like the towels that the cooks wring out into the gutters when they finish in the kitchens. There was a large piece of pickled herring clinging to the front of his jacket with which I urgently tried not to come into contact. Perhaps he thought that as the cat, I'd be glad of it. As he stroked me, he listed his family one by one. Whether he knew that he was speaking aloud or not, I don't know, but he was certainly not sober enough to care:

"Edgar . . . pious arse . . . Nora . . . cold bitch . . . Praisegod . . . little prig . . . Reliance . . . no discernible character whatsoever . . . Prudence . . . she'll come to something, little whore . . ." At this, he cackled through crackling phlegm, before he continued. "Esmond . . . military arse . . . Camilla . . . can't remember which one she is, oh, slip of a girl, the *tight* one . . . Edith . . . I'd rather bloody die . . . Geoffroy . . . bonkers . . . the librarian . . . saucy little bluestocking . . . Mother and Father . . ."

And at that point he started to snore. I dismounted from Uncle Edwig and went inside to find paper and pen to write all I remembered. I recited this litany to my mother later on that evening. She was somewhat sterner with me about the event than I might have imagined but seemed to approve of my initiative in recording the details for posterity.

Having missed the letter of postponement, the old goat (as my mother called him) arrived at our house exactly three months early. Word reached my mother during her vigil and she decided that he couldn't very well be sent away. She therefore scribbled a short note for me to present to him, since, Stephen and Sarah being away for the day with their family, I was involved in nothing more than writing to father.

"Rose," she said. "If he drinks all he wants, he'll look after himself, so let him. I'll be with you soon and we'll get rid of him, but until then keep him occupied. Let Hood pour."

Edwig's drinking was legendary. His first drink was invariably "medicinal." The second helped him regain the equilibrium that deserted him after the first, and by the third, he was back to normal — drunk. He took snuff on average once every two sentences, and veins exploded in excitement all over his face as he inhaled. When he laughed, which he did often and at great volume, a wave of crimson rolled from his chin to his forehead, where it pulsated in large ridges on his temples.

I went to the downstairs library, where Hood was waiting with Edwig, who had come directly from an all-night party at the Hey-Go-Mad Club.

"Hello, child," he said with a yawn, toppling forward but somehow regaining his balance. "Where's your mama?" He was disappointed to see me.

"Sir, she asked me to give you this." I presented him with the letter as I curtsied. Hood invited him to sit down, but Edwig preferred to stand, leaning heavily on a bust of the Quiet Lord Loveall, the pedestal of which groaned in warning.

"Would you take something, sir?" I asked. I loved to play the host.

"I rather think I *would* take something."

He skimmed the letter absent-mindedly, far more interested in the vista offered by the decanters on the buffet. Hood motioned toward one or two of the bottles, which caused Edwig to emit small but telling noises of discontent. Finally Hood reached for the whiskey and Edwig exhaled with enthusiasm. He brandished my mother's note at various distances from his eyes and then looked over at me as he reeled from his first gulp of the alcohol.

"What's it say?"

I politely told him everything and mentioned that my mother would be with us directly.

"No librarian? Oh. The thing is . . . the garden . . . outside . . ." He splashed whiskey on the carpet as he gesticulated out the window. I assumed that he had been nauseated by the carriage ride. Clearly, it was fresh air that he needed.

"Would you care to take a turn around the Rose Garden, Uncle Edwig?"

I offered my arm, letting Hood know that I would take him on a revivifying stroll. Edwig's smell came back to me pungently, a reminder of the last time I had been so close to him. We walked through the French windows toward the Rose Garden. Edwig leaned on me heavily but seemed to regain a little of his own vigor as we progressed.

"A turn round Rose's garden . . . how delightful . . . Now, my dear, how is your mother? A most delectable woman, in the *blue* way, you understand."

I was expending a lot of energy in helping him, and the strain was taking its toll. He had recovered his voice, and conversation came more easily to him as the drink smoothed his passage back to normality, but his movement was still unreliable. When he stumbled, every few steps, he became intolerably heavy.

"She is attending my father, sir."

"And how is your father?"

"He is very poorly."

"Oh *dear.*"

We were still short of the Rose Garden but had arrived at a stone bench, where he slumped awkwardly. His glass was now empty, spilled rather than drunk. Delving deep within his clothes, his hand reemerged with a silver flask. His initials ERO were engraved upon it, at the end of which was scratched a small S. He poured himself a tumbler and we sat quietly while he composed himself. After a few minutes, much recovered, he leaned toward me and tried to stare at me. His eyes took a short time to focus, but when they locked upon me, I had to look away in embarrassment.

"A shame about your mother. Lovely woman . . . You have a little of her. Ah, *yes*. You will make someone very happy. Walk for me. Parade."

It seemed a harmless-enough exercise, so I took a turn in front of him, emphasizing my thin hips in the way that I thought that Prudence Osbern would have done, the way that came so naturally to Sarah. He conducted me idly with his hands, as though I were an orchestra, and as he did, he sang to himself.

"Oh, yes. Look at you, so tall and elegant." He spoke with a deep and moist appreciation of my feminine form. I was delighted. "I am reminded of the dog rose: the pretty libertine of the hedges. Ah! But they prick so! Lovely. Walk away, my dear . . . ," and I did. I was wearing an old dress that my father had brought back for me on his last trip to the city, and Edwig was most fulsome in his compliments about my figure. "Rose, I do believe that you are the handsomest of all the family. It's a wonder I haven't paid you more attention. . . ." He spoke with true regret.

He beckoned me and I approached. His glass was empty again, so, remembering my mother's advice, I took the flask from the seat where it lay and poured for him once more.

"Come and sit next to your dear uncle Edwig." He had a look in his eye that I had never seen before, but it was not unattractive. "It's getting just a little cold. Perhaps you could keep me warm." He patted the seat next to him.

Still trying to be the perfect host, I sat down next to him, aware of some kind of mischief in the air. I could tell from his breathing that he was expectant, but of what I could barely imagine. There was something extraordinarily intimate about the look in his eye, coupled with a buried ferocity that began to unsettle me, but not quite enough to leave. He took my hand and massaged it.

"My dear, I'm sure you know . . ." His voice was much calmer and more relaxed, though his breathing was still abrupt. "You've put me in a devilish position. I'm sure you know that a man has needs. . . ."

His breathing was getting shorter and shorter. He edged my hand across his chest until he rested it in his lap. He seemed pleased with his progress. And I was pleased with mine. I was keeping him occupied.

"Good girl. We shan't call you *prim* Rose, shall we? Leave your hand there, my dear."

I could feel what was happening in his lap and, of course, I recognized it from some of my own fumbling self-explorations. Everybody must know this private feeling, I thought, but nobody spoke of it. Since I could not even mention it to my mother, I had talked of it to no one. When Sarah and I were in bed together, in each other's arms, I was most careful not to let this area of my body anywhere near her, arching my back away in case of this specific eventuality. She had no trouble concealing herself in this way, and I knew that it was certainly the best thing to do — for I followed her lead in almost everything. It was supposed to be kept secret, and I was ashamed of it, so now I actually felt a modicum of relief that Uncle Edwig was bringing it into the public forum. Perhaps it was an issue for discussion after all, something that could be aired, rather than an embarrassment to be shut away and denied. This gave me a sensation of warmth, and feeling a little of my own shame evaporate, I squeezed him appreciatively. I shall also admit that, incredible though it seems, I was enjoying our collusion and I knew that this might soon become clear to him. Whether it was despite myself or despite Edwig, I could feel myself springing toward him.

This aside, his breathing over me — and his bearing in general — was becoming less pleasant by the second. When I squeezed him, he gasped for a moment, as if suspended in midair, and then stopped breathing altogether, his head falling backward. The power of the moment was such that he had even forgotten his drink, which sat neglected on the armrest of the bench. His hand came to rest on top of mine, which he encouraged to rub at him in a way that I could imagine would be pleasurable. But his attention . . . his *attentions* were aimed elsewhere. The path of his hand toward the hem of my skirt, which he was soon pulling up in great wafts of material, was bearable, but it meant that his entire body was angled toward me — and this was more than I could stand. At that moment, I realized that he wanted to return the favor I was doing him, which seemed fair exchange but quite unnecessary. I was keeping him occupied, which was all that was required: I didn't need to be kept occupied myself. His smell, the alcohol mixed with that stale air of leftovers, that seemed to emanate from his every pore, the sight of his skin so close, its purple pumice finish and the hairs sprouting forth from his nostrils crusted with dustings of snuff, his bushy whiskers, the flecks of dead skin that were sprinkled over his shoulders, and the little eruptions of lava from the tiny volcanoes on his chin added up to a most horrific effect. I took my hand from him, but this merely gave him room to angle his body even farther over me, until I was trapped. I was totally unprepared for the animal nature of this advance, which came from a different person, a much livelier beast deep within him.

"Touch me, my darling girl," he commanded brusquely, kissing my neck as I tried to push him from me. He was rubbing himself up against the side of my leg, his entire weight falling on me now. His hand skillfully worked its way under my dress (through years of practice, no doubt, on those less fortunate than myself), and though it was nothing more than I had done for him, he was deriving a great deal more pleasure from it than I had.

"Let me at you, Rose. Niece! Let me touch you at the very moment that I —" he cried. I could feel his lump frotting against the side of my leg as his hand came within inches of my own. "Ah! Let me inside you, Rose. Let me inside."

Inside? Inside?

What? That tiny hole? No, no! This was a rude awakening. Nothing could go in there. Was that what this was all about? Or the other one? The back hole? I could hardly believe that, either.

And then he cried, "*Yes!*" at the top of his voice, and scrabbling around desperately between my legs, he seemed to be trying to look for something that had been misplaced, as though the candle had just blown out in the bedroom. Helpfully, I pushed him in the right direction, and finally, finally, he grabbed hold of me, groaned, stiffened, choked — it could have been pleasure, it could have been pain — and then stopped.

Everything stopped. All movement, rubbing, resistance, breathing, and groaning. It was most unexpected.

I knew that I was witnessing powerful new emotions, but I had no idea what to do. I lay there in the silence which followed that unleashing, wondering, twitching, and looking to see if there was anyone to offer assistance. After some deliberation, and realizing that all blood was cut off to my left leg, I pushed Edwig from me. His eyes were rolled back in their sockets. He seemed to me a big fat double bass that would never be played again. It was as if I had tried to tune him and his pitch had risen higher and higher, and he had tightened and tightened, till his neck could stand it no longer and suddenly snapped. I pushed him, as best I could, up and back into a sitting position on the bench. Like me, he was now limp. He sat in his own mess.

Edwig was broken forever. I'd never seen death before, at any distance, but if I knew what it was, this was it. It was unsatisfying. I tried to imagine him turning into a small animal, scuttling away out of his flesh into the undergrowth, a bird swooping into the sky, a bee going to buzz around the flowers, or even a tiny earwig — so often people become the thing their name fates them to be — but nothing. His body was slumped, expired, out of life. He was becoming nothing at all but more dead.

He looked pathetic, exposed in the way that he was, so I tucked him back in as best I could, trying, failing, not to come into contact with any of his spew. I then walked back through the garden toward the French windows. My mother and I entered the library at the same moment. She asked me how Edwig was.

"Dead," I said as I walked past her, wiping my hands on the back of my skirts. When I had left the room, I ran up the stairs and burst out crying. Mother would know my guilt.

The funeral took place two weeks later, which meant that the Osberns' trip was rather less delayed than the HaHa had hoped. Edwig had died on Loveall soil, and despite his family's lack of interest in him, they claimed the ancient right that he be buried there. Not all the Osberns managed to attend — Prudence and Praisegod were absent, although Edgar presided over the ceremony. My mother and I completed the congregation. I was delighted to be wearing a veil, so the others could not stare at me. My father was too ill.

I wore too much fragrance. It mingled with the various perfumes of the Osberns, and our collective odor required that the doors of the chapel be kept open. Crouch hovered ominously that day. She bore an ever increasing resemblance to a gargoyle that should rather be carved upon the outside of a church than standing inside, and she sang unnaturally loudly in the quavering voice of a proud old lady.

The funeral was a solemn affair and everyone was much pleased to see Edwig's body trundled off to the Mausoleum, where he would lie forever. The Osberns didn't care one way or the other, but I could have told them that he died happy. They were curiously withdrawn on this particular day, though much concerned about the state of my father's health.

Esmond had clearly been advised to spend as much time with me as possible. His eyes betrayed that his mind was working hard all the time and, even through the defenses of my veil, they caught mine, repeatedly, at the reception.

"Cousin," he said to me, and smiled as he bowed. His smile told me, for a second, that he knew about Edwig, that he knew about everything, that he knew things he couldn't possibly have known unless he had communed with Edwig's spirit, and, finally, that he knew things even I didn't know. I had to remind myself that this was simply his modus operandi. Like any compulsive seducer, he made himself appear more interesting and mysterious than he actually was, to speak more intimately, to suggest an unimagined secret bond between himself and his listener. He had a charmless charm about him and yet, physically, he was undeniably attractive. I blinked nervously as I turned away, preferring also to banish other imaginings of my own, in which I replaced the uncle with his nephew. Truly, one should be most afraid of oneself.

Esmond's protracted attentions provoked an interesting response from his aunt Nora. The proprietorial look in her eye immediately told me that he played Ose to her Sarah. Even as he spoke to me, some of the conversation seemed intended for her.

From the safety of my veil, I watched the Osberns leave in a good facsimile of a mournful procession. Esmond took Nora's hand and they walked in intimate conference at the rear.

The least important, most ignored member of their family had died. In all probability, I had killed him, though no one knew. As a murderer, or a manslaughterer, I was not feeling quite as much guilt as I felt that I should. The actual death meant little to me. I had greater pangs about the fact that I couldn't bring myself to tell anyone about it. But these were secrets I had to keep, secrets I knew people would use against me.

My mother had taken Edwig's death seriously, and I had thought from her manner that I would have to explain myself. To my surprise, I hadn't. Instead, we had engaged upon some unexpectedly imprecise philosophical conversations about growing up and "the change of seasons." This was handled decorously, though I understood that the matters in discussion had more in common with sweat and toil. And the death of Edwig.

"These things I speak of are of the earth," she concluded as she took me by the arm so I knew she was serious. "But you, my darling, can have eternity. It is your choice." She read me a Mary Day poem called "Limpid Skies of the Infinite — Rejoice!" which went over my head, though the language was appealingly seductive. Neither Mary nor Mother was being specific. My mother, frank in so many ways, could only be coy about this. She had to be, for she had decided to defer anything more definitive until a later time, until the next, nearer, inevitable death.

3

DURING THAT LONG YEAR of my father's illness, Mother was the only parent I knew. When she could do nothing for him, we would sit together in the library, where I assumed the role of her assistant. Years before, I had lain at her feet, surrounded by roses, but now I was at her side, following her every instruction, trying to help in any way that I could. I would perch on top of the moving ladder to fetch down some or other tangential volume. I explored the farthest spines with my fingers and then delivered the correct volume to her desk, where she would lose herself in its investigation. While Father lay still, slowly dying in his bedroom, we kept our thoughts in constant motion. It was a relief from my own anxiety, too, which was turned toward the dark chasm of ignorance within me, an investigation with no hope of success.

We never left the library in our work on Mary Day, and for the most part had our noses buried in musty pages, but this research was my door to the world and I found myself looking further afield than ever before. A theory took wing, and our conversations soared high beyond the vale of Playfield. When my mother made a new connection, even if she thoughtlessly spoke aloud to herself as she worked, the succession of her ideas would inevitably lead to new avenues of analysis and flights of fancy.

She had access to materials unimaginable to her father and could not bear to leave any alley unexplored, however dark or out of the way. Inspiration might come from anywhere. The truth was not found in a straight line but, as Mary Day said, in the uncharted winding road — the "circuit" — the paths of which branch off in different directions, all unknown. To the mystic, the truth is entangled among these choices and alternatives, hidden in the glimpse of perfection in the distance. The obvious answer is a lie.

The Mary Day mysteries were many, including the texts themselves: how the books had ended up in Love Hall was the most perplexing. Perhaps one of our ancestors, despite all evidence to the contrary, had been an ardent collector of obscure literature — but in this case, why had the books lain in such lamentable neglect? Perhaps Mary Day had been an acquaintance of a Loveall and therefore a visitor — hardly! It was scarcely creditable. Mother's mind played tricks on her and she would imagine that such-and-such was a reference to something it couldn't possibly be concerned with. At such moments she would shake her head and laugh at herself, exclaiming, "Oh, Mary! Stop it at once!" But read in Love Hall, this dark house of secrets, trapdoors, and hiding holes, the poems assumed a deeper meaning. No wonder I, too, felt the force of them as though they spoke directly to us.

We began to keep a collection of notes written on tiny cards for ease of reference. The cards stacked up against us, mocking our attempt to tie together the many loose ends that my mother had unearthed: Foreign Words, for example, a long list of oddly inflected phrases and bizarre word endings, either a function of Mary's erratic spelling (caused by her lack of education) or conscious choices demonstrative of a great eccentricity. These cards became so many that they needed their own system of cross-reference: *madness, mesmerism, Paracelsus, Pistis, printing.*

From time to time, even after the exposure of so many years, Mother would sit back and exclaim: "Rose, the manuscript!"

This was my most sacred mission. Though she had long ago transcribed everything from the manuscript, that there might be no reason to touch and further harm the original, sometimes the copies simply would not do. She had to touch what Mary had touched, more deeply to feel her presence. She would put her arms around me, trace the words with her finger above the pages, and then: "Away! Good-bye."

I would return the document to the holdings, and my mother would look at the clock, mindful of her other duties, before hurrying away to see how Father did. She would leave me with instructions for further research, the spadework that would make her job easier. I was happy to do it. It was good to be lost in something.

The atmosphere grew more somber through a slow and difficult winter. Unexpected physicians tramped snow across the floor as Sarah and I, the rarely glimpsed wildlife, watched from behind the banisters of the upstairs landing. The snow hadn't yet melted by the time they left with kind words of consolation, refraining from making future appointments. Another year crawled by. I felt useless and excluded. Even our games were too hollow for me now.

One day we heard a servant mention *occurrences* in a suspiciously hushed tone. Any deviation from my sad routine was of vital interest, so further investigation was necessary. Sarah somehow wrung it from her mother that there had indeed been occurrences, which had been downplayed because of my father's illness. Their precise nature remained uncertain, but rumor whispered that my pewter christening cup had been found hurled across the dining room. I went to see for myself and concluded that either the original had been replaced by an identical christening cup in exactly the same place on the mantelpiece or nothing at all had happened. The tattle showed how uneasy we all had become.

As if occurrences in themselves weren't enough, the next month brought rumor of *further* occurrences. These could not be ignored. According to Stephen, strange messages had been left around the house, cryptic hieroglyphs that seemed to have urgent information to communicate, possibly from the dead to the living. I thought of the drawings on the blackboard.

I was predisposed to disbelieve anything of this nature coming from Stephen. And yet there was a definitive sense of unease for which I couldn't account. The head of the house was dangerously ill, and this fact alone required a certain decorum of bearing, but I could see from the servants' sideways glances and their cautious surveys of newly entered rooms that something was awry. I was impatient to witness one of these further occurrences myself.

One winter morning my mother opened the curtains of my father's bedroom window. He loved to sit in his old bath chair at this window, known as the Widow's Watch, and look out upon as much of the world as did not make him nervous. From there he could see Rubberguts, now empty of leaves, and the drive heading out to the country beyond, a country almost as foreign to him as it was to me. He loved to see the dew on the lawns in the morning, and this the gardeners sometimes shaped in an artistic process known only at Love Hall. The dew sculpture faded away before his eyes as he sipped his morning cup of tea.

On this morning, as Mother pulled the curtains, she took a look outside and then drew them immediately, excusing herself. She left my father sitting in the semidarkness and went to find Hood. I was standing in the Long Gallery, talking with Sarah, when my mother walked by us with great purpose: "Sarah, take Rose upstairs to the back room. Thank you. Now."

There was an urgency around the moment that was uncommon in our house, and Mother marched away down the corridor.

"Hood. If you please! Hood!" She rang bellpulls randomly. "Hood! The driveway. Now. Now!"

We ran upstairs as soon as we could and made straight for the schoolroom, rather than the back room as we had been directed. From the window we saw, to our surprise — our delight, in fact, because it was such an odd sight — one simple word carved into the dirt by displacement of the stones:

BOY.

Our first thought was equally simple: Stephen.

He was such a fool! Why write BOY, when he was the only boy in the house? He was bound to be caught, just as he had been when he cut his name into the school desk. What a ninny.

And there, suddenly, was the culprit below us. Perplexingly, however, he did not seem to be in disgrace. Stephen was working in perfect harmony with his father and one of the gardeners, overseen by Hood, raking out the driveway until it was smooth once more. As soon as we had truly grasped what they were about, the word had been erased almost entirely, except the very top right-hand corner of the letter *Y,* which Bailey the gardener was at that moment ironing out. Then the driveway was perfect again and its restorers vanished, as though we had dreamed the whole scenario, and we were left staring from the window to wonder at this apparition and disappearance. Stephen had time to come upstairs while we were still making hopeless deductions in the Strange Case of the Word in the Gravel. He was breathless.

"Did you see it?" he panted.

"Was it you?" we both asked, pleased — surprised! — that he had got away with it.

"No." He was adamant. He lied often, but it was easy to know when he was telling the truth. "They didn't even *ask* me if I did."

This was all the proof we needed that something very strange had happened. The obvious suspect hadn't even been questioned. Like the driveway, the event was smoothed over, unmentioned, but it didn't go away.

We were supposed to have seen nothing, so it was in our interests to keep quiet, but still we wondered. All the day long, we heard servants gossiping around corners until they heard us coming. At those moments, silence fell like a hammer, accompanied by coughs of embarrassment, raised eyebrows, and furtive downward glances.

That afternoon the three of us went up to the library to find my mother. To our astonishment, that same word was crudely chiseled into the stone below my mother's name in the list of librarians above the door.

BOY.

We stood gawping until my mother appeared in the doorway with a handful of books to read to my father. She stood underneath the very thing that had us mesmerized, and the light shone from behind her so that we were barely able to make out her features. I looked at her, then above her; I imagine we all did the same. We were dumbfounded: the christening cup, the messages, the driveway, and now this. She came toward us with great calm and turned around. She looked above the door, sighed, and said very carefully, "Children, to the Doll's School."

"Lady Loveall, why does it say BOY?" Sarah asked, but my mother had no answer and repeated her request with greater insistence. We went. As we turned the corner, she called after us:

"Stephen Hamilton, fetch your father and tell him to bring Mr. Hood."

It had been one of the strangest days in living memory at Love Hall, but little did we know that the worst evil was yet to come.

That night, nothing further revealed and nothing resolved, I crept to Sarah's room at the accustomed time. We lay in bed together, whispering. This felt so natural to us that we had developed a comfortable routine. We hadn't come anywhere near to being caught, but I knew that we would be, that we had to be, that we were doing something wrong. My body was telling me that things would soon change, that the game was up. The *further occurrences* seemed to presage our exposure, as did my own increasing feelings of bewilderment, which I foolishly hoped to ignore. I was the child who closes her eyes and thinks no one can see her anymore.

We theorized about the mystery until all avenues of investigation and imagination were closed. I tried to employ the Mary Day approach — anything but the obvious answer — but it seemed to have no practical application to the Strange Case of the Word in the Gravel. Sarah lost faith in finding a solution and started to talk about the future, imagining a time when my father was better: she and I would travel to a distant land. This blossomed into a lazy romance about the adventures that would befall us upon our arrival, how the king would act (mercifully), how the people would behave (foreignly), how the prince would look (handsome). He would fall in love with both of us. These were all stock elements from the games, but they sounded even better when she recounted it just for the two of us.

As she spoke, I kissed the back of her neck and moved my hand around to the front of her body. A different country. Sarah's bosom was soft and round. I had none at all. I knew this was merely the luck of the shuffle — she was bigger than I there, and I was bigger than she elsewhere — but how I envied her. As deftly as I could, I edged my hand between her breasts and opened out my palm so that her left breast was resting there. I felt its weight shifting in my hand, but she continued to talk, ignoring me. I touched her more forcefully so that I was actually *touching* her rather than grazing against her or brushing her by mistake — this was a big difference. I could feel a layer of gristle just beneath the smooth skin. Sarah seemed not to notice. I was barely listening to the story anymore. All I could hear was the dreamy tone in her voice, and that she was not telling me to stop. Her breasts were fascinating, like nothing I could imagine would ever belong to me. As she lay on her side, gravity pulled them both toward the bed. I stopped for a second. I touched her nipple. It was literally one hundred times the size of mine. I was in awe. I stopped again and rested, listening.

"And Clement the Prince raises his arm above the lists, where the two knights are about to joust for our favors. Don't stop. But he knows, secretly, that it is he who should be fighting for us, and this awful knowledge shows in the trembling of his hand. He drops the handkerchief — the fight begins. Rose. The white and the black knight gallop toward each other as we watch from the mirador: your interest is only in the white knight, and mine only in the prince. We hold hands — our fates hang in the balance. What if the black knight prevails?"

In light of her continued lack of complaint, I moved my hand farther south as she kept talking. In a spirit of adventure, of venturing into uncharted territory in honor of Mary, I had forsaken her breasts for what lay beyond. She was in a daze of words and I was a great explorer, a character from one of our stories, Lord Ose himself.

I wasn't sure that her tale meant anything in particular to her anymore. The dreamlike monotone had gradually become a low narrative moan punctuated by the odd murmur. The story was now stripped to its essentials, single-image thoughts separated by increasingly long pauses: "Dark eyes . . . the sun shining brightly . . . my prince . . . a pigeon flying from the castle wall carrying a message . . ." In the lulls she moved into my hand. Previously she had been motionless in response to my touch, but now there was a constant to-and-fro, an undulation, toward me and away from me, which I interpreted as enthusiasm and reticence. As my hand moved down farther, past her naval (similar to mine), I reached a place where her stomach puffed out slightly. She froze. She had stopped speaking. My fingers were at the uppermost edge of her hair, which grew, I was glad to feel, in the same place as mine but was so much less, less coarse, less plentiful. Her body trembled softly, not from fear but pleasure. It was a shiver that I had felt before only in Uncle Edwig. At least this time with my lovely Sarah, I was better prepared. I wouldn't push her so far. I would be much more careful.

Everything was suspended. She was silent, barely breathing. I was breathing very heavily (when I remembered to breathe at all): in out, in out. I felt giddy. Blood pumped through my body and suddenly our silence became extreme, the evidence of our intent. I was going to push my hips toward her so that we were touching from head to toe, but something made me stop.

I knew what I was going to come into contact with next, as her skin and hair slowly passed beneath my fingers and I was thrilled. It was momentous. Here it would be.

But where? My southward progress continued and I thought, *I'd have a handful of myself by now!* I had noticed from Edwig that they weren't all the same size, but where was hers?

In fact, where *was* hers?

And then my hand was between her legs. Nothing.

Nothing!

My mind started to race. Sarah seemed to be telling me that I had found somewhere good, somewhere we both would be happy, but I was horrified.

There was nothing, only damp, warm absence.

I could feel the flesh of her thighs on either side of my hand. She moved them together, as if she wanted me to stay there, to trap me, but I whipped my hand away as quickly as I could. What was happening? What had happened to her? That poor girl. All the time I had expected her to be the one to stop the progress (and I was waiting for, almost willing, that inevitable final moment), but I had done it myself.

Then I thought: *Oh, my God. Is this what happens?*

Edwig, me, Stephen.

Sarah.

Had she lost hers?

Worse. Had it been *removed?*

Suddenly I was revolted by her, by her want, her deficiency. I was nothing like her. I was more complete.

My mouth parched and I held my breath. Was this what I hadn't understood?

It must be, but what did it mean? Help.

I was clearly destined to end up like Sarah because I was a girl, but it hadn't happened yet. I hadn't understood — all this time — that my nasty thoughts, though I had tried to suppress them, would inevitably lead, must lead, to *this:* either my complete withering away or, no, the forcible removal of the apparatus. I had entertained lewd desires, I knew it, and Sarah must have done the same — her softness, her beauty, her shape, yes — but this, *this* was the price! Witness her punishment. And here we had arrived in our bed of mutual shame. My heart was beating uncontrollably, and whatever it was between my legs throbbed obnoxiously, either with horror or fear at its immediate prospects. My blood coursed through me.

What were men, like Stephen and Edwig?

What were women, like Sarah and me?

We were not good enough to be men, who are destined to wear the mark of their superiority proudly. I had not yet started my metamorphosis, and suddenly I understood that I would never be able to grow like Sarah, to have her beautiful soft hair, her gentle curves, until I did. Was it a punishment or a reward?

Punishment, clearly. How could there not be pain? Did we all start as men, and it was only those who fell in their thoughts who succumbed to temptation, who became women? It must be punishment. Or perhaps it was not punishment but simply the destiny of some, a metamorphosis before death.

Becoming as beautiful as Sarah, as Prudence, that necessary rite, must hurt: but when would it happen? When? Why was it happening so much later for me? I was repelled and fascinated by the idea. If nature wouldn't help me, I would have to do it myself.

And now, now, I saw. Finally, with clarity. I saw myself alone, in the woods. With a knife. No, no, I wouldn't — I couldn't — but how I longed for what I feared! To be done. I would welcome it. I wanted to be rid, so I could become what I was meant to be. I was a disappointment to everyone the way I was. I had seen it when my father turned his head. Why hadn't I realized? It was up to me.

Sarah had replaced my hand with her own, not noticing that I paid her no attention. Then she tried to pull me back toward her absence, her hole.

It was more than I could bear. I shrieked and leapt from her bed, gathering my nightdress around me. Sarah was as shocked and horrified as I was. I fled, unable even to look at her.

"Rose," she called out as I ran away. "Don't worry. It's fine. Come back!" I heard a groan of frustration from somewhere deep within her body, but I was already running as fast as I could. I thought about what had just happened and tried to make sense of it in my mind, to shed light on the darkness. I screamed at the top of my voice. It echoed down the long corridor, which had recently known only silence, and the report was doubly terrifying.

A light came on behind me and I heard scurrying, urgent voices. There was the swish of satin and the whip of slippered feet. My scream seemed to have mobilized an entire household already on alert.

I made it back to my room, relieved to be alone. I hadn't thought what I was going to tell anyone. I was thinking only about myself. I slammed the door behind me. Candles were lit, though I certainly hadn't left them burning. A window was open and a night wind gusted through, flapping the curtains haphazardly, making the room unfamiliar, unwelcoming. With the freezing cold that was blowing through me, nothing seemed right. And then I saw. On my bed, written across the bedspread — which had not yet been slept in — the word

BOY

in blood. Or something that looked like blood, not yet congealed.

Immediately there was a banging on the door behind me, and I moved aside as Hood tumbled in, my mother just behind him. They both stopped still and looked at the bedspread. Hood immediately surveyed the room, the possible entrances and exits, the likelihood of the wrongdoer still being present, and calculated the extent of the damage.

At that moment, I was almost thankful for this bizarre reappearance. The Strange Case had been the last thing on my mind and operated as a useful excuse for my own behavior. Mother came toward me with all the love in the world and bent my head down to her bosom. I rested there, pleased for the sympathy, regardless of the motivation. I knew I was wild-eyed and strange. Something terrible was beginning to dawn upon me.

"Oh, my poor darling. All will be well," she said, and stroked my hair. "Don't worry." It was what Sarah had said. They all knew.

Hood removed the offending bedspread, bundling it under his arm with all the dignity he could muster. With a brief acknowledgment to my mother that they should resume their discussion in the morning, he secured the windows and disappeared. My mother suggested that I might like to sleep in Sarah's room if I didn't want to be alone.

"No!" I said too quickly, and then caught myself, adding, "No. Thank you."

Did I want to sleep in her bed tonight? No, tonight, that seemed even worse. I just wanted to be alone. I persuaded my mother that I was calm, not able to believe it myself.

"You are so brave, my RoseMary. There are events hard upon us, I know, with which you are going to need all our help. We all love you. If you need anything, I shall always be here." She tucked me into bed on her own, behaving as if nothing had changed, but as I looked up at her, I wondered whether she even saw the same person. If she had any sense that it was odd that the bed had not been slept in, she betrayed nothing. She kissed me on the forehead and left.

I lay there alone in the night. The candles threw ghastly shadows on the ceiling. They flickered thoughtlessly on the inside of my eyelids. The word on the bedspread. The word in the gravel. The word outside the library — these were all one thing. But what about Sarah? What was she doing now? Was she doing anything?

I gasped.

She was dead.

I had heard her quick breathing, just like Edwig's. And the groan. Had I killed again? Stop me, stop me. My mind wouldn't work in straight lines. What if she were dead in the morning? But Sarah couldn't be dead. The tuning had barely begun. I had spared her.

I couldn't sleep. I couldn't read. I lay there alone, waiting like a murderer for the first light of morning to creep accusingly in the window on the day of her execution. I said my prayers, but no one answered; I felt as alone as I had ever felt. I was alienated from the very sheets but, outside them, the air was damp like the hands of a ghost upon me. What had she and I shared? What did I now know? My mind raced uselessly around and around, like a weather vane in a storm.

The night grew blacker and the candlelight more erratic as the wicks burned lower and lower. When would I change? When had Sarah changed? Years ago. But had she changed at all? I sighed. It was then that something new, some even darker thought from the back of my mind, started to announce itself, to elbow its way forward — it was the truth, which lay in the unimagined alternatives, the choices with which I hadn't dared present myself. I didn't try to recognize it and I couldn't face it. I pushed it away from me, but its approach was inevitable. Then, as I lay there, now sweaty and burning, I felt its cold upon me.

Uncle Edwig. Sarah. Stephen.

BOY on the gravel drive.

I crawled blindly toward the understanding of something that had been too horrific even to contemplate.

BOY above the library door.

Could it be true?

BOY on my bed.

I needed no more information. It was unthinkable, and yet I felt calm: it was the calm of decisive thought. I had decided to allow the truth to speak to me. It could be deferred no longer. My life had changed forever. I understood. I understood the difference: women had everything hidden inside their bodies, folded inward, whereas men were exposed. What separated me from Stephen and Edwig? Nothing. What separated me and Sarah? She was hidden and I was exposed. I was exposed. Women had babies. Where did the babies come from? Inside the fold.

BOY on my bed.

BOY in my bed.

BOY.

I had kept myself from knowing it. I had been waiting for someone to tell me, when I had only to tell myself, to let myself listen to what my body shouted. It had known all along. I had known. One thing was certain: this would kill my father.

I lay shrouded in the damp winding-sheets. What would I do? Was it a secret that I was keeping from others, or one that others were keeping from me? Who knew about me? Whose secret was I? I knew at that moment that I was doomed to abandonment and isolation. What was I now? I felt different. Would I have to invent myself in defiance of everything natural? The more I had grown, the more lost, the madder I had become. Now everything made sense, but I was foreign to myself. My body lay limp and useless, but my mind was working too hard, too fast, to no effect at all. Now I knew. I thrashed around, sleep no longer a possibility. The sheets were damper than the air.

I could stay in my bed, in my bedroom, no longer.

Glad of the bracing air on my skin, I walked around the house, not knowing what I did or where I went. My eyesight was blurred. I found myself at Sarah's door. Why listen? She might not be breathing. If she was alive, if I hadn't killed her, we would be dead to each other. I needed to anchor myself in something firm to stop myself from floating away into the night forever. The portraits looked down at me with pity. I was lost. My fingers were dusty white. I couldn't even find the nymph Salmacis. I didn't know where I was in my own house. Worse, I was not even my self! What did I call myself? What would my name be? From now on, I could refer to myself only in the third person — was there even an "I" to speak from? What had happened? He wandered, a stranger in a foreign country, not understanding the signs or the language, not knowing where to find help. He tried to gulp down the tears, but they conquered him, me, again and again. Stephen? No. Sarah? No. My mother? No. They would all hate me now, if they even recognized me as their own Rose, their own girl. I was drowning, gulping, breathing in water, dying.

I went up to the library, where I lit as many candles as I could to keep the phantasms at bay. Then I started to take books from the shelves. I had a sense of purpose now. I pored over the books; it was as if I had never read them before. I recognized the truth about my body, how I was, in every plate, in every sentence of every novel. Everything I read about girls applied to my outer layers only: my clothing, my upbringing, my surface. I was perfect on the outside, but beneath I was a different person, a grotesque. I sat on the floor in agony, crying. I was a failure, a secret kept even from myself. What could I tell them? I had spent my whole life trying to forget something that I didn't even know, driving it under. I trusted nothing, least of all my own thoughts, and yet I felt a certainty I had never known.

Beneath the desk, I saw the trapdoor where the old family paintings were kept in storage. Why had I never been invited to open it before? And why had I never tried? I lifted it, propped the door against the leg of the table, and stepped down a small ladder to the landing below. I made two trips so I could take the books with me. I saw framed canvases stacked one in front of another — a collection of figure paintings that had been removed from the walls. The answers were there before my eyes. I hadn't known and I hadn't wanted to know. I hadn't dared try to articulate any recognition of not being a girl, for fear of . . . what exactly? Perhaps this? No. I had feared so much *less* than this. Could I save myself somehow? Could I keep my secret? If I didn't tell anyone I knew, if I got rid of it myself, could I fool them that I was still their Rose? I would try to make them happy, try to be more like the lady they wished I were. This would keep my father alive. I was killing him, too. Why had they done this to me?

I stripped and lay on the floor, looking at the ceiling. Through the open trapdoor, I could see up to the roof of the library. I should have closed the door and lay here forever. They would never have found me. This room might lead to one of the hiding holes, and I would be able to disappear in the warren of tunnels forever, lost, alone.

I looked at my own body, and even he mocked me. I clawed at myself, crying, bleeding. I kneaded where my breasts should have been and scratched at the abomination between my legs. I hid it all behind me and put my knees together. At least there, it couldn't be seen, but it grew in defiance until my stomach knotted with pain. I wasn't a woman, but I wasn't yet a man. I had looked at the pictures of men. I had none of their muscles on my scrawny frame. Perhaps I was my father's child — somehow, this thought soothed me. I would be a gentle man like my father. I knew everything. I hated knowing it. I hated everything. I hated myself.

I was there until morning, surrounded by paintings and books. I had lain them around me in a circle, my barricade in the hope that their magical power could keep the real world at bay. But it was too late. Magic was dead. I lay in the center of the room, on my back, my arms out on either side of me. I didn't even realize that day had come until I heard the handle on the door turn.

My mother looked down. I was sniveling and naked. My immediate reaction was to cover myself. I put both hands over my groin and drew my knees up tight around me. I didn't know what she would do. She stepped down and took me in her arms.

"Who am I?" I heard my voice ask.

"My darling." My stomach throbbed with emptiness, and I slumped into her as she held me.

"Does Father hate me?

"He loves you."

Silence, as I lay in her arms.

"Who am I?"

"You're a miracle, Rose."

She took me back to my bedroom and I howled like a wolf. I couldn't even picture the normal world anymore and I found that it was a memory, that it could never be normal again. I couldn't imagine playing with Stephen and Sarah or seeing my father. I would be obnoxious to him. How he would loathe me when he found out. He would turn his head away, walk out of my play.

Mother lay with me on the bed and stroked my hair. It was hours. Days. She told me that I was beautiful and that I was loved. Beyond that, nothing was said. Inside it was a strange dream that hadn't yet stopped, like the dream you have in which you wake up and you're still asleep and then you wake up again. My whole life wasn't real. Wake me up.

Over the next days, weeks, months, I lay in bed. My mother nursed me. During this illness, she answered my one question — the only three words I could think to mouth: "Who am I?" She told me the story. Found. Male. A loving adopted father and mother. How beautiful she was. How they loved her, the heir to their wonderful fortune. She told the story to while away the time, as though I couldn't hear, but it was all I cared about and it kept me alive. The tale did my breathing for me, yet I feared its every development, for I knew the end. I could listen with interest, provided I didn't identify with the child; but the moment I caught myself and realized that this happy little girl would one day become me, experience *this,* bile rose in the back of my mouth. I could communicate this only with my eyes, since my throat produced nothing more than a dry rattle.

My sickness began to reveal itself. I developed black spots all over my body, which itched and then burned. I clawed at them at night, and the sheets became flecked with spots of pus and blood. The black spots became dark purple lesions and I had to be sedated. I remember little of this, though I still bear some of the scars, one along the inside of the top of my right thigh. Now it is lost in the folds of age, but I remember where it is and I can touch the spot and take myself back to that bed, where I underwent this metamorphosis from my old self to my new self, from butterfly into grub.

As I lay there, I fantasized that it was my unconscious mind that had taken control of my body and, unbeknownst to me, written and chiseled and painted the telltale signs inside and outside the house — but of this, I was innocent. These acts of terrorism had been Anstace's.

Mother told me that on the night of my discovery, our nemesis had gone so far as to chalk BOY around the house, on the canvases of paintings, on as many available surfaces as she could reach, though no one could understand how this elderly woman had reached some of the more inaccessible spots. I knew. They were my fingers that were white with chalk dust that night. What did it matter now anyway? Perhaps Mother knew. She told me that I could still be, still was, the perfect human being. I felt mocked, as far away from perfection as I had ever been, lost and alone.

Confined to my sickbed, time was evident to me only in the way the light changed, dragging a shadow all the way across my face. I had learned everything about myself that I have since written down: my discovery and the deception. I had been everyone's victim: my father's replacement for Dolores, my mother's experiment, Mary's theory made flesh, Anstace's means for advancement, a pawn in the HaHa's fight for survival. But what would I have been if I had been left abandoned? Nothing. Dead. Worse than nothing.

Once, in the middle of the night, I woke to find myself lying in a pool of blood, which seeped from my midriff. Emerging from sleep (one of the few times I could even differentiate between sleep and dream), I experienced a brief moment of relief at the onset of my monthlies. I remembered when the stomachache that caused the bleeding had first upset Sarah, and the ensuing pride we shared at the approach of her adulthood. And now here was my moment of glory. But in the next second, I remembered everything and I looked down in horror to see where my nails had clawed at my flesh. I fainted and woke to find my fingernails wrapped in bandages, which I would have to find the strength to remove if I were to attempt this kind of self-mutilation again. Angelica leaned over me. She said, without malice, but not with the kindness for which she was known: "You've got it, and it isn't going away."

Another night I dreamed of Sarah and Stephen. My mother had just mentioned Sarah to me that day as I swam in and out of consciousness, to tell me how much she missed me. I don't even remember feeling relief that she was alive, but I kidnapped her into my dream. She and her brother were swimming in the river while I, as always, was sitting on the bank. It was a beautiful warm day and the birds chirped their happiness. Sarah and Stephen emerged from the water and I realized that they were both naked. Sarah's breasts were first revealed. They were so perfect, so real. And then as they both waded from the deepest part of the river with graceful ease, I saw their complete nakedness. I had never witnessed anything more divine. At least, that's how I remember feeling in the dream: what this beauty actually looked like, I cannot say, for it was represented by a kind of light and an absence of detail. As they came toward me, they stopped and beckoned me into the water. I got up, worrying rather about my mother and the rules; but hiking up my skirts, I went to meet them. They lifted my dress over my head and embraced me. I could feel myself getting hard like Edwig, like a man, and worried that Sarah might take offense, but I could feel Stephen, too, and I knew that everything was forgiven. They started to drag me down into the water. The feeling as I was taken below almost made me collapse. It was a result of both the rush of the water around my thighs and legs and their soft skin on me. Stephen rubbed himself against me and I reached down and felt him. He was sinewy, straining to meet my hand in gratitude. And as I surfaced from my dream, I felt my hands on myself in the same way and I swooned. I closed my eyes and tried never to wake. Again I found myself in a mess, but not blood.

Sarah and Stephen were staying with their mother's brother. Of course, they'd tell me that Sarah was away if she were dead, I remember thinking, but then I faintly recollected that they had planned to visit their uncle sometime in the autumn. Could it be autumn already?

I wanted to see my father but I wasn't allowed out of my room. My mother divided her hours between her two patients. When she wasn't with me, Angelica was as attentive as my mother would have been. News from the house trickled through when I heard them talking. Perhaps they were talking to me, perhaps to each other, but these half-heard conversations told me how desperate the situation was, where both the head of the house and his heir were so gravely ill.

It had been thought wise to either bring Crouch back into the fold or subdue her, as quickly as possible. Report of the molestation of the paintings had found its way to my father, and the knowledge had sent him toward the precipice. My mother thought Anstace dangerous to both our lives: she had to go, come what may. Hood and Hamilton, however, had insisted that she stay, for they could not allow a willful hastening of the crisis. After a summit meeting at which Anstace, to all intents and purposes, threatened double murder by means of an immediate alliance with the Osberns, Love Hall suddenly found itself with two housekeepers. Angelica, outgoing, was to advise through the period of transition. This gave the HaHa time: what more could Anstace ask for than all she had ever wanted?

I felt almost ready to talk myself, but I was too scared to imagine what kind of voice I would use. It raised too many horrible questions.

One morning my mother sat me up in bed and started to cut my hair. I was still groggy, having slept a deep sleep. I had dreamed again of Sarah and the final night we spent together.

Then out with the razor, and as I came fully back to consciousness, I felt my mother combing my hair and powdering my face. Before I knew it, I was out of bed and clothed in a long purple dress that reminded me of the sheets covered in blood. It was only then, when I was nearly ready, that I comprehended what she had been saying to me while she was dressing me.

"We are going to see your father. This may be the last time, and you must look as beautiful as you can."

On the walk to my father's room, I focused my mind with an effort almost beyond me. I had wanted to see him for so long, and now, I understood, there would be no more chances. Perhaps I was going to die. My mother walked on one side of me, with Hood on the other, supporting me, but I could feel a little of my strength return just from being outside in the unreal world. I had been in my bed, in my bedroom, for so long: fed, shaved, and washed. Love Hall seemed to return to me a fraction of my former strength. The house was exactly the same. Nothing had changed at all. But how would my father have changed? I wondered if I would find him as transformed as he would now find me.

We knocked on the door, and Hamilton bowed as we entered. My father was propped up in bed against a mountain of pillows, just as I had last seen him, but now his head lolled to one side like a rag doll. He was now entirely a ghost, a faded memory of himself. It was not I who was dying.

He was unshaven and drawn, his skin pellucid, mottled with a polite version of my own disease. His face had sucked itself in around his cheekbones and he was murmuring softly. The room smelled stagnant, far worse than my own, through which biting fresh air was continuously circulated. On his left next to the huge bed was the Hemmen House, placed so that the small replica dollhouse within was at eye level. His head was turned toward it. Most of his conversation these days, even when he was speaking to someone else, took place as he peered into the dollhouse. Occasionally, he would smile as though Dolores had just arrived to talk to him. He was unaware of our presence, but my mother walked in front of me and bade me keep up with her by holding my hand. The sight of him sobered me to the point that I almost felt myself. I'd seen death before, but it had been sudden. This was a gradual waste, a withering, the eviration I had feared for myself.

"My dear, I have brought Rose here to see you," she said somberly, and without expecting an answer, or even recognition, she moved to one side as I walked toward the bed. I sat on the side away from the dollhouse, where he was looking. He stretched his hand out to me with two fingers extended, like a priest.

"Shh . . . ," and he continued to look into the dollhouse for an unbearably long time. I looked back at my mother and she smiled, to let me know that she understood, that this behavior was typical. Then, desperately slowly, he turned around to face me.

"Dolores," he said, and smiled, laying his hand on top of mine. "No surprise." His smile amounted to nothing more than a twitch at the corners of his mouth, but I could tell that his soul was overflowing with happiness. It was time to talk, to try to sound like myself.

"Father, it is Dolores. Though you have also called me Rose."

The moment I said my name, my father stopped and tears welled up in his eyes. He clasped his other hand around mine as tightly as he could. His grip was feeble, but the effort that it cost him was clear from the minute tensions and relaxations of the muscles around his mouth and cheeks.

"I am sorry" was all that he said.

"Thank you, Father, for giving me life. I was the luckiest, happiest child in the world. Your love for me was infinite. Every day for the rest of my life, I will pass that generous love on to others."

I didn't know how I managed to be so controlled, so normal. It startled me, when my body felt so hopeless and alien. Somewhere deep inside me, in the soul within my soul, there was something that I recognized, something that was real and essential to me, and it was from this tiny kernel that the rest of my life would have to grow. I looked at him as he blurred faintly through my tears. He began to speak his last. He held my hand throughout.

"My Rose. I am a fool, but I love you. Blame only me. I loved you so." His speech was getting slower, the carriage creaking to its final standstill. "You were everything to me. I have lost a daughter but found a son . . . just in time, Lord Loveall . . . just in time."

And with that, he sat bolt upright in bed, as though a puppeteer had jerked suddenly on his invisible strings. The sheets fell down around him, revealing a pink nightdress, with intricate lace designs down the sides. The body beneath was emaciated, bruised with hunger. As he stiffened for the final time, he stared at me and said, "Dolores!" as he saw her tumble for the last time. He was shouting at the top of his voice, but no louder than the mewl of a tired cat. As he slumped back into his pillows, his hand, which he had tried to guide toward the dollhouse, caught the side of the tiny house inside and knocked it out of its home. It fell to the floor, setting off the music box that I had never known was within. It played our favorite lullaby, "Süsse Traüme, Liebling." I was still sitting on the bed, holding his other hand. I felt all the muscles relax. I remembered that there were other people in the room.

My mother was softly crying, her eyes cast to the ground. She came forward to the bed and kissed my father's forehead, cradling his head in her hands, just as she had cradled mine when I was dying in my own bed. Hood picked up the dollhouse. Hamilton stood, a guard, by the door, but I could see his Adam's apple tremble. Unexpectedly, he too started to cry.

"He loved you so, Rose," my mother said. She took my fingers, leaned over to him, and drew his eyelids closed with them. "Dolores was the last thing he saw, and we should try to keep that beautiful vision with him forever. It is a mercy for all of us."

She took her hand away from my fingers and I looked down at him — in the sharp jolt of an instant, I imagined that I felt his soul leave his body and move into mine. When I took my fingers away, my father was completely lifeless, his mansion empty.

"We shall live up to his love," I said. A new script had been given me, though I didn't know where it was from, and the words came from deep inside me. Hood muttered his commiserations and bowed deeply. At first, this seemed a bow of sympathy, but he said, "Your lordship," and I realized that it was not only compassion.

I was his new master, the new Lord Loveall. Now it was my mother and I, alone together, in the house. My father was dead. I didn't know who I was. Stephen and Sarah were gone. I didn't know where to begin.

We went back to my room, where my mother undressed me again and helped me into bed. We didn't speak. We were both crying softly. Someone came into the room, saw us together, and left.

Over the next few weeks, my mother and I spent all our time together: to whom else could we turn but each other? My health gradually returned while I tried to make sense of the past. As I did, the terrible blind fear that had preceded my discovery was replaced by a hardened resolve. The truth was unpleasant, but it was based on fact, not ignorance. This mingled with a child's pain at the loss of her father: I saw him in everything, heard his voice around a corner he would never again turn, and smelled his gentle perfume lingering around the dark patch where his pomade had stained the headrest of his favorite chair. We had been so distant during the last years of his life. It was obvious why, but when I thought of him I thought only of the great love he had given me, the life he had given me. I blamed him for nothing. What would I have been without him? Dog food, eyes pecked away by the scavengers. He had saved me from hell and tried to give me heaven. Without him, life seemed impossible, but I knew that I owed it to him to survive. More than ever, I felt that he was part of me. He had died that we would live.

From the moment the black flag was raised, letters started to arrive from the distants. At first these were mournful and regretful, but they soon began to adopt a tone of high dudgeon, particularly in response to the death notices that my mother sent. These noted simply that the funeral would be private.

On this day of great mourning, however, and unbeknownst to our relations, the villagers were invited to file past the coffin, which was laid in state for an afternoon in a tent erected at the bottom of the driveway. It was reported that my grief was too great for me to attend, and my mother stood in my place. The locals shuffled past and gave their sincere condolences. And how was I coping? they inquired. As well as could be expected, my mother told them.

I sat at the Widow's Watch in his bedroom and observed the ceremony from my father's old bath chair. In resignation, and because I knew that the change would have to come shortly, I was wearing a drab men's mourning suit that I found among Stephen's remaining possessions. It was stiff and cold upon me. I was a stranger in my clothes and, beneath them, in my own body. I watched the line of locals through the leaves of Old Rubberguts. I looked down at my legs, spindly in the unforgiving confines of my colorless trousers. There was nothing left to imagine. There I was, alone, dressed in someone else's clothes: all angles, elbows, and kneecaps.

The tent was to the left and the Mausoleum to the right. With one look, I was able to take in my father's entire life, and my own.

4

Y MOTHER AND I were entirely decided on one thing: I would reveal the truth of my gender as soon as possible. My father's illness had delayed this long enough, and nothing now prevented my unveiling. The period of mourning gave us all the time we required: even Anstace, appeased by her new position as housekeeper-elect, was seen in black.

I had been privately invested as the new Lord Loveall and was prepared to do what was required to honor the memory of my father, whatever agony it caused me. If he had finally been able to call me his son, then I would be his son. I would remain Lady Rose throughout a short but respectful mourning period, during which I should continue to wear the dresses appropriate to my name. Meanwhile, with my mother's help, I would ready myself so that I could for the first time meet the world in character. The timing would be ours — more specifically, since I found myself increasingly deferred to, mine. I should be no more the victim of the whims of others.

I began to dress the part. My mother made believe this was like one of the dressing-up games of yesterday, but the similarities were few: without Stephen, there was no one to make it seem natural, and without Sarah, no one to claim with a victory kiss — just a cruel looking glass to reflect the harsh reality. I felt uncomfortable in everything my alternate wardrobe offered. Anything I tried chafed, burned, and abraded. Mother convinced me that this was because my borrowed clothes were old-fashioned and ill-fitting. If I were properly measured, I would find myself much more at ease in clothes tailored for me in Jermyn Street. She drew me the feminine outline of the fashionable frock coat with enthusiasm, but I awaited the bespoke suit with suspicion.

I was convinced that the difficulty was in the clothes themselves, rather than their tailoring. The Chevalier d'Eon, a man I came to much admire the more I read about him, found women's clothes highly inconvenient. He said they were unseasonable for winter and impractical for all occasions, except those uniquely suited for embodying vanity, luxury, and vice. D'Eon was, however, on the other side of the fence — his life of transvestite espionage has been much chronicled — and I couldn't have agreed with him less. A large skirt is the most convenient and comfortable thing in the world, nor did I ever wish for warmer wear during the winters of my childhood. A man's suit, however — and fashion had dictated that they get drearier and more uncomfortable with each passing year — struck me as practical and utilitarian in the extreme. There was no romance in it. Where was the mystery? As a man, it was too easy to dress and undress. At the start of my new career, I was all thumbs as I bumbled around with buttons and braces, but soon all became blindingly obvious: undo one button and you're too promptly naked. Where were the loosening layers, the secrets, the folds, the furbelows? My own mystery vanished with them.

The only advantage to a suit — and I have always been a somewhat practical person — was the pocket: at last, I could carry things. Admittedly, the items I chose to keep about me — a delicate handkerchief of Valenciennes, a small muslin sachet of herbs, a miniature of my father in a heart-shaped locket — were not particularly mannish, but when it came to a suit, the pocket was my sole reward. The rest of the thing was alienating in the extreme: to cross the legs, to uncross the legs, to position the anatomy when seated, to reach with ease, to stand with ease, to bend with comfort, to breathe with comfort. My stomach and back felt thoroughly uncared for uncorseted, as though I might flop this way or that like an invertebrate. I complained and was allowed to continue to wear this helpful item, as, my mother told me, did many men.

I was growing accustomed to some of the grosser aspects of masculinity. My anatomy called constant attention to itself beneath my clothes, but now that I understood what it was, what I was, I realized that it had always been an impediment even under the free-flowing folds of my skirts, through no fault of my own. No wonder I had always been uncomfortable; unlike Stephen, who was always putting "the soldiers back in the barracks" with a wink, I had, of course, never pursued the same strategy. Lucky girls, who don't have to bother with such things! Who wouldn't rather have a stomachache and a bit of blood once in a while? Besides, it had given me aches, too, a constricted knot of pain about which I was too confused to complain as vociferously or as often as I should have. Now, my new clothes were much too tight below my waist. Upon entering a room, I felt overly defined, on display, and I always wished for art's handy fig leaf to place over the area as extra coverage. Later on, however, I let my hat fall where it would with greater confidence.

For Mother's sake, I tried to greet the arrival of the Jermyn Street attire with optimism, but my suspicions were immediately confirmed. When I first opened the box, I was infected with a queasiness akin to travel sickness. All was done in black — the newest fashion, I was assured — beneath an absurdly tall broad-brimmed hat that mocked masculinity. When I then put them on, I felt myself constrained, and this sensation increased my nausea. Over ensuing days of dress rehearsal, it grew worse and worse, until the clothes became both my torturer and his instrument of torture. The collars, tied around my neck with voluminous cloth that garroted me, were so high, almost to the sides of my mouth, that I could neither shake my head nor nod; it was as though I had broken my neck and needed to be restrained to prevent further damage. The starched cuffs were irons strapped to my wrists to keep me from escape, and the trousers, cut long enough to strap under my uncomfortable leather boots, squeezed and trapped me like a two-legged cage. I was immobilized mentally and physically, and I imagined the man's suit my Maiden of Nurem-berg. I endured this torture, however, because I knew that it was the right thing to do.

I felt immediate relief when I took these clothes off. I couldn't wait to slip back into my long dresses and stockings. And this I did as often as I could, in the privacy of my own room, though always with an accompanying feeling of guilt over my failure to resist their temptation.

Where I hoped for progress as I became more accustomed to my new wear, there was none. I thought perhaps I should try another strategy: play myself in a little more gently. Perhaps my father's wardrobe would prove more palatable to me — more flounces, more femininity. I may have been male but my self was female: my voice, my way of drinking tea, my way of sitting — nothing was properly masculine, nor could I handle the props in a manly manner. You can't dress a tramp in a top hat and make him a gent — it isn't just the clothes that maketh the man, whatever they say — and so I was no more a man by disguising myself in men's clothes. I was betwixt and between, and I had to define myself more clearly. Mother claimed that this was not important. The question was one of gender, not one of sex. I was naturally male, but I could be whichever gender I chose. I had all the tools and weapons of character and intellect at my disposal. She still believed that they had given me a gift, something I would be able to use to my advantage for the rest of my life, conceivably even for the benefit of the world.

In her Marian vision, I would be an educator, bringing about a time when men and women were equal. Why should sex be the determining feature in our lives? We came into the world neutral and it was society that nurtured us into our roles. My mother thought herself to blame — she had let me down not because what she had done was wrong but because the experiment had been incomplete. Now I could correct this fault, by starting again neutral, by making my own decision.

But what use were gender, identity, and the promise of utopia to me, when I merely longed to be as I had been before?

Even at such a tender age, I knew that life is lived in leftovers, account ledgers, and timetables rather than in the Platonic sphere of perfect theory. I couldn't float sylphlike around Love Hall in the flowing robes of indeterminacy for the rest of my life, however much I wished there to be no change. I had to accept my responsibilities and, at least in the eyes of the world and at least for the time being, nail my colors to a mast. Unless I wished to appear a strange wonder for the rest of time, caked in circus makeup covering the truth inches beneath, the mast would be male.

Important signals had to be sent out: my name, for example. We considered a change, something that spanned both alternatives (Evelyn, or Iphis from Ovid) or honored the past (Lord Ose Loveall, as a tribute to my father's capricious imagination), but in the end we decided that the best way to honor my father was the simplest.

Lord Rose Loveall.

People would know soon enough. And why not a male Rose? After all, roses themselves know no differentiation of gender. If we introduced me to the world with enough style and a strong enough apologia, then others would accept it, too. What would be my Loveall epithet? This I could not choose. Just as there had been a Young, a Quiet, and a Bad, I might be the Lady Lord, the Female Lord, or even the Strange Lord Loveall. Time would tell.

For now, I was operating automatically, once again the female somnambule. I had a grim sense of purpose — a resolve admired by all, but depressing to me. I slowly lost my sense of humor and finally nothing amused me. During this tiring reassignment, every dusk was a minor victory, another day down. I did at least finally feel in control of my own fate: that horrible lack of certainty, fear of the chasm, was gone. But mine was the cold decisiveness of a suicide.

If only Stephen and Sarah, who had been admitted to two different schools during my sickness, had been there to share it with me. An immense sorrow took hold, a languor that had always been bound to follow such intense feelings. On the surface I was maintaining perfectly, moving forward even. But inside I was crumbling, my sense of self receding. The new distance from my only two friends, and their distance from each other, caused me the greatest sadness. I did not dare wonder what they knew about me or what they thought.

It was spring and my father had been dead for a year. The hour of announcement was approaching. I led a two-tiered existence now. Upstairs, excepting the luxury of my own chamber, where I did as I pleased, I was Lord Rose Loveall. Here, Mother and I rehearsed my new life. I learned to walk and to speak, to hold myself and to dance, when to bow and when not to bow. As a representative of the unfairer sex, I was extremely graceful. My spirits were not as high as she would have liked, and a certain disaffection crept over me from time to time, but my mother thought me a truly beautiful form of being — perhaps even something unimaginably perfect, in whose creation she had had a miraculous hand.

Beneath, I was plain old Rose but I descended the stairs less and less often. I became well practiced at my new role but no more successful, and I felt the grim burden of my double identity. I was most comfortable in the wrong clothes, but when it came time for the right ones, I would be ready.

We could delay Esmond's long-requested interview, postponed since before my father's death, no longer. His would be the first Osbern attempt for my hand, and I felt that our response should set the tone. However, there was one element of his visit that was a perfect relief to me: my mother and I agreed that I was not yet ready for my unveiling and that I would appear as he had known me before. I therefore began to look forward to his arrival with relish. It was an excuse to slip into something more comfortable.

When the day came, I let myself be pampered with pleasure, luxuriating in my satins, feeling sentimental even about those facial preparations I had previously disliked: the grit of the plaster of Paris mixed with carmine on my red lips, and the vinegary smell of the powder. The application itself was a delight, but when I beheld the finished product, I nearly cried. My skin was nowhere to be seen, like the marzipan beneath the layer of hard icing on one of Sarah's fruitcakes. I barely looked human, let alone female, and I reminded myself of nothing so much as Mrs. Manly. I could be a low comedian from now on, but nothing truly feminine, however thick my mask. I saw myself a monstrous caricature and thought I should never be able to look at myself without remembering this moment. Since that fatal reflection, I have worn women's clothes to draw attention to my true sex, to advertise the forbidden pleasures beneath, but I never pretended to be female or thought I could fool anyone into believing I was. In my whole life, I pretended only once: at the bed of a dying man who knew the truth.

I decided to turn to my friend the veil for the interview. This old ally did wonders for my spirits and it was a joyous relief to feel free in my clothes: nothing could change that. I swept downstairs with velvet step, a whoosh of satin and lace. My mother looked at me with a gaze that mixed love and admiration as we waited to receive Esmond. I heard his boots striding down the corridor, and for the first time in my life, despite everything, I felt powerful. I was in charge of my own secret now and I could reveal it to others howsoever I chose.

Esmond halted at the door and stood at attention. He was wearing something that wasn't quite one military uniform, but rather an amalgamation of many, perhaps his own private militia. A full twenty years older than I, looking even a little above his years, he thought himself handsome — and he was, but brutally so. His features were weathered and sandy, as though he had seen too much of the desert, faced too much powder and shot, and his unforgiving sharpness of tone, coupled with the disdainful curl of his lip, betrayed the character of a man who gives orders rather better than he takes them. With him, behind him — always behind — came his mother, Edith, now a prematurely frail woman, still ignorant of the three most important things in her life: that her dead husband had fathered her sister's two youngest children, that her son was that woman's lover, and that Nora's henpecked husband was the only man who might care for her as she wished.

Politely, we asked after Camilla. Esmond informed us that his sister had recently left on missionary work to Africa. Remembering what I could of this fragile thing, I wondered that her constitution could stand a trip to the seaside, let alone months among the savages. I saw her apologetically awaiting her turn to be cooked, too nervous to ask for more salt. My mother linked her arm into Edith's and drew her off into the formal garden to take a turn around the roses. I was alone with Esmond for the first time in my life.

"Such a fool," he said as his mother left, spitting out the words. I didn't care to defend her and I sat still. Beneath my veil, the powder was packed so tight that it made me wary of smiling in case I cracked. I could feel crusted morsels around the corners of my mouth. I sipped tea self-consciously, lifting the china up underneath my veil and bowing my head to drink so Esmond couldn't see that I was having to lick my lips with my tongue to lubricate them. I eyed the plate of dessert that had been delivered, nuts and my favorite crystallized ginger. I could have none of it.

"The veil, cousin?" he asked.

"Mourning, sir, for my father."

"Even now?"

"Forever." I didn't sound like a woman, either. He didn't notice and bowed.

Years before, Esmond had sat in this very room and explained the forenames of his family, without any encouragement from us. He loved to present people with facts, particularly concerning history or war, and the story of Osbern nomenclature was full of both. (I could make a sizable appendix of it if the public or publisher so desires, and I shouldn't think they would, but I'd hate to spend time on it now. It began: "Athelstan had been the name of the first true king of all England. After his great victory at Brunanburh, he fashioned himself Rex Totius Britanniae." You can imagine.) Suffice it to say that Esmond was named for war and lived for money, which, in his experience, was most readily made by fighting for others.

The motive behind his visit was no secret, but he felt a prologue in order. He began with the history of his scars, how and where won, in which campaigns. Every mark on his face was celebrated individually: a rigid finger traced the vertical stripe beneath his lower lip that he claimed resembled the eastern coastline of southern Italy. It might as well have been a shaving cut for all I cared — and, in fact, given my feelings about the razor, I would have found him more sympathetic if it had been.

I remembered how I hated him. His conversation, if you could call it that, was interlarded with condescending asides and insulting comments directed at my sex. With each sentence, I grew angrier. Even his manner of breathing started to offend me. I would shortly demonstrate how much.

The clock struck two as he went on. It did not occur to him that I was getting bored — for this was his life, and his life was interesting. In fact, he omitted any of the things that might have drawn me in — it was common knowledge that he had fought for different sides in the same war and that much of his action had been spent buying and selling information from one side to the other, but he made no mention of it — so I simply nodded throughout, a mystery behind the veil.

My mind wandered. Despite my disdain, I could see a hint of his appeal — to a more impressionable girl than I who expected to be patronized, to be seduced. I had breathed the scent of that appeal before. But where could his charm lie for a woman of experience? I knew very little of certain aspects of this world but I was surprised that Nora could put up with him. Esmond must have been a direct copy of his father — there was nothing else to recommend him — and I fancied that I began to see the ghost of the dead man peering at me from behind his eyes.

My hatred for him, on behalf of my family, my sex, and humanity, was entire. My clothes, the secret they hid, gave me the confidence to act upon it.

Halfway through a long tale of his exploits in northern Africa, I'd had enough and, to his great surprise, I interrupted. I had come with a plan but I despised him so perfectly now that I was ready to refine it. Of course, I knew my answer when he finally ventured his proposal, and I had cribbed a speech in reply, but I had lost my patience in the past few minutes. Things had changed. My dress had liberated my mind and I was free to follow what suggested itself to me. As I saw it now, this was the moment that could alter my life and the whole world of Love Hall. Suddenly, it truly was more like one of the games of old.

"How is your aunt Nora, cousin?"

Startled, he answered rather too quickly.

"In marvelous health. Thank you. I shall tell her that you inquired. . . . As I was saying, the damnable *monseer* with his beady eyes . . ." He tried to regain his footing, but I was too quick for him.

"In marvelous health for her age."

I was impatient for the moment of his proposal. For a man of action, his reticence to get the bit between his teeth was astonishing. I had not been expecting such a tepid preamble, and he would pay for it.

"For her age, I said. Nora is remarkably youthful, no?"

"She was given the graces that might have been shared more equally between the two sisters, I am afraid to say. Mother received none."

"You and she have an understanding. Is that right, Esmond?" I looked up through my veil and saw a raised eyebrow, the *monseer* momentarily forgotten.

"I beg your pardon?"

"You and your aunt are intimate, Esmond. Yes?"

"Cousin, I own that we are: an intimacy on offer to any of her nephews and nieces." He eyed me with suspicion. He was right to, for I felt invincible. I said nothing. I knew so much about him. Some of it, he didn't even know himself. "Of course we are," he added in exasperation. "She is my mother's sister."

"Oh, Esmond, don't be coy."

"Madam!"

The veil was a formidable tool. Behind it, I felt all the power of my sex, of both sexes. Perhaps I should wear it with my men's clothes. I was toying with Esmond, like a cat idly paws a mouse it has hanging by the tail.

I stood up. He prepared to join me, but I discouraged him with a simple wave of my right hand: my house, my rules. He knew that his entire obedience was the key to the door behind which glittered the treasure. It was his turn to be patronized. He was my prey.

"Let's return to the beginning, Esmond. You may call me Rose." I decided to walk slowly behind him, thinking it might bewilder him.

"Yes, Rose." Esmond adopted the bored, regretful tone of a person who feels he is going to be taken to task for something. This resignation implied that I had deflected him from the matter at hand and that he would be able to get back to business only if I resisted the urge to play this stupid game. I was by now directly behind him.

"That's better. Now, enough about Nora. I was merely being inquisitive. I know why you're here. I have inherited the Loveall fortune, and you have come to ask for my hand in marriage."

He tried to crane his neck around so he could see me. I put a hand on either side of his face and jerked his head firmly forward, so he was looking in the opposite direction again.

"There you are, Esmond. You stay *there*."

I caught his eye as his head turned and he looked at me in the oval mirror. I enjoyed seeing him so very uneasy.

"Rose." His voice had softened somewhat. "Rose, a man must be allowed to make his proposal in his own way. On the field of battle, women would not be allowed to —"

I interrupted him and he yielded easily.

"Esmond, have you come here to ask for my hand in marriage?"

"Yes."

His voice betrayed an edge of annoyance and I could hear that he was on the point of leaving, of "not standing for any more of this nonsense." But he couldn't, and we both knew it. The rewards were too great. He was seething at his humiliation, made more severe by my acknowledgment of his crass motive, but it was now beyond him to change the course of events.

"And you assumed that I would say yes?"

He tried to move his head, but again I jerked it forward.

"Given the ancient name of the Osberns and the greatness of the Loveall . . ."

"Yes, yes, Esmond. Really!"

"Given the ancient name of the Osberns and the greatness of the Loveall . . . ," he repeated as I took his left hand and put it behind the chair. The grandfather clock, which had been a gift from his own grandfather, struck the quarter, as though Athelstan himself was there, to witness his family's subjugation. This, in turn, encouraged me to go somewhat further than I might have otherwise done. He coughed.

"Given the . . . erm . . . ancient name of the Osberns and the . . . greatness of the Loveall . . ." He began again but lost faith.

With his other hand behind his back, I began to improvise further. I knew what Ose would have done with a varlet like Esmond. I loosened the sash that hung around my waist and tied Esmond's hands behind his back. I laughed as though it were a game and tutted him casually when he tried to move away from me. My knowledge of knots, courtesy of Stephen, was supreme, and with another loop I tied the bound hands to the back of the chair. I was strong and I was quick. It was done before there was time for complaint, and his objection, when it came, was useless.

"Madam . . . Rose . . . what on earth . . . I must object."

"Esmond, really." I tried to sound as condescending as possible. It was comical to see such a powerful man rendered impotent by a feminine sash. But I knew it was not merely the sash that held him down: it was his own greed.

I was still behind him. I walked from side to side so he couldn't tell where I was.

"Do you ever consider what it would be like to be a woman, Esmond? Bartered and bargained for by men like you? Preyed upon by those more powerful? I expect not. I think a great deal about what it would be like to be a man. More than I should."

He was silent.

"Men are good, primarily, for the destruction of women, aren't they? Don't wriggle so, Esmond. I haven't refused you yet. I might not say no. Good boy. You are undoubtedly of the opinion that men are superior to women. Esmond?"

"Well, I . . ."

"You are wrong. Eve is superior because she was created after Adam. God didn't take backward steps, so Eve must be an improvement. Am I boring you? Don't answer. It doesn't matter. In any case, for myself, I believe that neither men nor women are superior."

I let my voice sink slowly in its register.

"One day we shall discover the country of Feminisia — and when we do, men like you will doubtless be paid to wage war to quell native revolt, plunder natural resources, and subjugate the inhabitants. But if I could stop you, by offering you more money than anyone else (which, given my wealth, I suppose I could), what would we find?

"In Feminisia, only one gender is acknowledged — one sex. Men and women, equal. Perhaps we should go there, the two of us, and start this conversation again. Let me take you. I shall be at home in Feminisia, of course, but you — you will require a small metamorphosis. Not of sex, but a transformation of gender, do you understand? If men were more properly female, and vice versa, perhaps then we would be free to choose our own individual roles and we would have the means necessary for regeneration. What do you think? No? And where will that leave you, Esmond, when war is no longer a viable career? In a mess, I should think."

I stroked the back of his neck as I spoke. My speech was a brew from many sources and I was an apothecary pouring from one vessel to another, adding a little of my own to the mixture, just enough to frighten him. I wanted him to think that I might take a knife to him. I realized that I no longer needed my veil and I took it off, placing it instead, rather imperfectly, over his head.

"Esmond, you don't even *like* me. You don't understand me. You're only here for Miss Fortune — correct me if I'm wrong."

He was silent.

"Since you have told me so much about yourself — your scars, your campaigns, your name — I thought you might like to know a little of me, to understand a little more about your intended. Yes?"

I walked around. The moment I moved from behind him, he tried surreptitiously to remove his hands from the knots. I would have to move faster. I stood directly in front of him, my face obscured by my veil that he now wore.

"I dare not hope for love, but do you even like me, Esmond?"

"Yes," he said weakly.

"Enough! Answer me honestly. Will you?"

"Yes." I fancied I saw a kind of awe as he looked up at me, but perhaps this was wishful thinking.

"You came to marry me?"

"Yes."

"Under your own volition?"

"Rose, I . . ."

"Honesty, Esmond. I like honesty."

"My family." His eyes darted to the door and back again, thoughts of escape mingling with fear of discovery.

"Your intrigue with Nora — how long?"

"Four years." He spoke as if hypnotized, and I realized that he had given up ideas of flight. I didn't doubt he would now tell me the truth about anything I asked. The problem was I wanted to know so little about him. I whipped the veil away from his face and we looked at each other. I wondered what he thought of what he saw. He swallowed. There was no retreat now.

"I beg your pardon. Rose, this is . . . I shall be forced to forcibly . . ." He stared at me and I moved toward him: closer and closer.

"No matter. I expect you thought that you could marry me and take residence here with Nora and that we could, all three of us, live together happily. Am I right?"

"Rose! Cousin!" he whispered it, but the venom was evident. He could allow himself to speak no louder. What if someone came running? How would he explain? Discovery would be worse than the present humiliation — I could see him weighing up the relative disgrace of each. I moved closer, so he had to look up at me — or peer directly into my chest. He tried to turn his head away.

"Look at me."

He looked up.

"Esmond, am I right?"

I edged closer until my legs were touching his knees.

"Yes," he said weakly.

"Good. Now, Esmond, I am going to tell you certain things that I think you may want to know." As I said this I lifted up my skirts and straddled him, finding a place for him between my thighs. Sweat had formed on his forehead. I reached over with my tongue and licked one of the beads.

"Rose! Good Lord, Rose, is that what this is about?" His teeth were clenched, but there was relief in his voice.

"Yes, Esmond. My worthless days! My lonely nights! For years, you have been all my thoughts." I could see in his eyes that my sarcasm terrified him. I rubbed my cheek against the side of his face, and some of my white powder stuck so he looked like the Italian clown. "Esmond, I love you." Inches away from his face, I began to laugh. I licked across the coast of Italy and wriggled my derriere farther into his lap, where I felt intriguing signs of movement. His cock was at an awkward angle, and while I held his gaze, I raised my eyebrows and righted him with my hand. I knew the feeling and there was no need to exert that kind of strain on him. I wanted him free to further subjugate himself, and I was quite content with my progress as it was.

"Rose, I . . . please . . ."

"Esmond, the woman with whom you spend your nights, the adulteress . . ."

He tried to interrupt, but I swiftly clasped my hand over his mouth. He knew that I was dangerous, that my knowledge was dangerous, and that he had severely underestimated my strength. He started to struggle beneath me, but I was not about to be removed.

"I'm sure she has told you that you walk comfortably on a path beaten smooth by your father. Oh yes, their affair lasted many years, and you are a poor substitute for a better man. . . . We have all the evidence, if you'd care to see."

He groaned and I took my hand away. He had to gulp for air before he could talk, and as he did, I put my hand back. I felt his cock twitch under me and I rubbed into his lap approvingly. He was right between me, separated by three distinct layers of clothing. As I moved my rump, his eyes betrayed him.

"And, of course, the pièce de résistance . . . And this really *will* be of interest. . . . Prudence and Reliance are the bastard children of your father and Nora — your sister and brother. . . ."

I felt him stiffen and I contracted my buttocks around him. He had seen how Nora disapproved of any sign of friendship between the two of them, but he had thought it an old woman's jealousy. Now he knew. And now I knew. Prudence and Esmond — of course! How could it not have happened? That beautiful young girl and her handsome elder cousin. But they shared a father. I began to think of *Metamorphoses* as I rubbed slowly against him: Byblis and Caunus, Tethys and Oceanus, Ops and Saturn, Esmond and Prudence.

"I hope you haven't been this close to Prudence . . . or Reliance, for that matter."

Esmond twitched and I realized that he was suffocating, so I took my hand from his mouth. Gasping for breath, he was still securely locked in my hold. The chair had edged back a few inches and was caught against the side of the huge oak table set against the back wall.

"You lie!"

"No, Esmond. Your cousin wouldn't lie." I kissed his forehead.

"Before God!" he exclaimed, but whether this was at the news he was assimilating or the movement of my hand as I slipped it underneath my skirt and started to pull aside the layers of clothing that separated us, I could not immediately tell. He wore soldier's trousers. I knew them to be very like a pair that I called my Military Michaels, so I was therefore able to find ingress with ease. I pulled down my stockings until I could feel him against me. He groaned.

Finally, we were getting somewhere.

I began to suspect his passion had reached such a pitch that he would have to give himself over to sensation, that he would be willing to forget everything to prolong our liaison as long as was necessary. Perhaps he still clung to a hope that, against all the odds, his proposal would yet be successful. He closed his eyes and started to moan, trying to forget exactly where he was and with whom. He was approaching the moment when there was no alternative, and I was driving him. He was in my power entirely. I placed my right hand over his eyes.

"Would you like to marry me, Esmond? Do you want to marry me?"

"Yes, Rose," he said, "yes." And at that point I truly believe he did, not because of my money but because of me. I had ruled him, I had taught him how to behave. I had brought out the little boy in him. The rest of his life lay in ruins around his ankles, but now I represented opportunities such as had never been offered him before. A fifteen-year-old girl was teaching him the ways of the world — the irresistible allure of power, sex, and love. At that moment, he would have given anything to feel more and to know more. I had already triumphed, but my presentation was not complete. I was ready. I took away my hands, but his eyes remained closed.

"Open your eyes, Esmond."

I had lifted my dress up entirely. And there we were, exposed, he sticking out of his unbuttoned Michaels, obscenely thrusting from his nest of hair, hard up against his stomach. And there was I, too. I looked back at him with victorious delight. I felt equal to him, more than equal to him. I looked down at the two of us together: grown men of similar standing.

There was no room left for doubt. He started to whimper like a beaten dog. "Rose . . . Rose . . ."

"Marry me, Esmond. Marry me!" I laughed. His cock started to spasm involuntarily. I reached down and held my dress back with one hand, while, with the other, I grabbed hold of him. The head bulged purple and, as if in slow motion, he disgorged over his jacket and shirt. He gasped. It had either been unavoidable or, stranger, he liked what he saw. Well, why not? During his passion, he looked away and then swiftly back again. He moaned and threw his head as far as he could, stretching his neck muscles to their extreme. He grunted loudly as he finished, and I let go of him. I didn't want to join him and I got up. My skirts dropped to the ground.

"Good-bye, Esmond." I walked behind the chair and undid one of the knots. "Don't omit any of the finer details when you report to the rest of the family."

"Rose?" he asked, but then regained himself. (I only later discovered how ashamed men are afterwards.) "Damn you," I heard him breathe. I didn't know whether he was talking to himself or to me.

I licked the tip of my index finger as I left, with a smile as wide as a joker's.

"They may visit whenever they wish," I said over my shoulder. And with those words, and a quick glance back at Esmond, who was wobbling precariously as he attempted to get his hands untied from the back of the chair, I left the room, shut the double doors behind me, and walked into the future, my own future. I was the lord of Love Hall, and as I walked through, the house seemed to breathe its appreciation in a postclimactic sigh. I bowed to no one, to the walls, as I went.

It had been a most spectacular and dramatic presentation. I'd dreamed it up on the spur of the moment, yet it went off as though I'd been planning it for the whole of my life. I thought of Stephen and Sarah and Lord Ose. I felt triumphant, just as the man who plays the pantomime dame feels when his debut entrance brings down the house. I had finally found a part in the drama that I was born to play.

It transpired that my mother came back to the room with Edith to discover a chair thrown over, a sash, and, beyond that, no evidence of Esmond. Edith, in some confusion, left quite as quickly in her own carriage, now missing one of its pair. I omitted the more gruesome details for my mother (the torture methods, the teasing, the squirting, & c., & c.), though I tried to give her an accurate portrayal of the spirit of what had taken place. Hood agreed that the timing of the disclosure was appropriate, although he could not share in our enjoyment of the Grand Guignol. The family would hear of the incident immediately, and the next move would be theirs. We could sit back. And so, from Love Hall, we waited for the reviews to roll in.

And we waited.

But they never came. For months, they never came.

The longer we heard nothing, the greater our disappointment. Where were they? What was their reaction to the discovery that they had been fooled for so long, that they could no longer marry me off to one of their males? Their silence was open to many interpretations. They were planning their next offensive: yes! They were sending Prudence down to get the job done properly. They were playing with us. They were waiting for us to communicate with them. They were readying legions of lawyers to prove us insane and pack us off to the madhouse. Oh, there was no end to our imaginings. And the more we imagined, the more spectacular we expected their response to be. But still nothing came. So we waited and worked.

My life as Lord Rose was moving forward in fits and starts. At first I tried to wean myself from my old clothes gradually, but I needed a more rigorous schedule. Some days were better — I would begin to feel the part, to walk with style — then the next would be a disaster, twelve hours of torture and tears. Daunted by the impossibility of my task, infected by the very materials required to accomplish it, I would sink into lethargy in my obdurate suits. The clothes were my strait-jacket, and this led in turn to a numbing of my wits, so that I could no longer try to improve my lot nor see a way out of my unhappiness. Only I could help myself, and disappointed by the lack of response to the Esmond revelation, I didn't have the wherewithal. At all times, even though I felt relief to know the truth about myself and was willing to be Lord Rose, I was still pretending to be a man, acting a part that felt entirely unnatural to me. The longer I wore the clothes, the unhappier I became: the more I pretended, the deeper my sorrow.

My mother never insisted, but her willingness to help was its own pressure when we both knew that what I most wanted was not to be a man at all. All gender felt foreign to me now. In my mind, I was neither one nor the other. I had been thrown from the ship, buffeted by waves from all directions. I could almost have preferred to drown. Why must we try and save ourselves? Why must the show go on? I wanted Sarah. I looked longingly at Salmacis. Why not me? I dreamed of changes.

My mother alone knew. During this period — against her wishes, because she thought it overly strenuous to my nerves — I attempted a radical therapy, a program of total immersion whereby I wore only my male clothes. Even in my chamber, I did not allow myself to wear a nightdress, in preference to which I wore nothing. I cried before the glass.

Like so many times before, we took to the library. I worried that my story was becoming too unpredictable for my mother, heading toward an ending she couldn't imagine. She attended to her own projects feverishly, as though she thought her time in the library limited. The Loveall ballad collection had become a huge, unwieldy mess in urgent need of its curator, so she spent more time with these sheets, which she pasted into large folio volumes as she numbered them, and less with Mary Day. Her father always said that future generations would learn from not only the high literature of today but also the ephemera, the menus and business cards by which he made his living, and Mother, utterly democratic in her care for the world, thought the preservation of the ballads vital. I liked them, too, for they reminded me of my father's world. The ancient family ballad of "Lord Lovel" was still sold on street corners.

While she worked, I tried to create a consistent character for every floor of Love Hall. The servants were aware of what was happening and, as well-paid servants ought to, kept their opinions to themselves. They knew me as Rose, whatever I was wearing. Hood and Hamilton could not honestly approve of this familiarity, but it lent a pleasant air of informality to Love Hall.

Hood had served Father with great loyalty and real affection, and he was now the dog who waited by the door every night for approaching footsteps that would never come. The succeeding generation was beyond him. The only way I knew to address this — by showing familial fondness — aggravated the problem. He didn't want me to be kind: rather, he wanted me to expect his limitless devotion and to depend unquestioningly upon his professional acumen. But I wasn't my father. So I became more distanced and let my mother deal with him. She was his Lady Loveall. He would follow at her heels.

Hamilton, on the other hand, was exactly as before. He focused only on his work, and if he had feelings of regret at my father's passing, he suppressed them for my benefit. He brought me regular news of his children but was never specific about their return. He told me it had been time for them to go away to learn about the real world and that my extended illness had made it a necessity. Writing was gently discouraged. I wished them well and told him that I missed them more than I ever imagined, though I had never, in fact, gone so far as to imagine I would ever have to miss them at all. He said he would send my best wishes to them, and I corrected him: my love.

And so a kind of life prevailed at Love Hall. Anstace's acquiescence had been purchased. She was housekeeper in name alone — Angelica still kept the keys — but was appeased for the time being by the restoration of the power that gave her the right to condescend once more to all and sundry. She gave me a rickety bob of a curtsy whenever we passed each other. I acknowledged her, but no more. I had anticipated one of her two big revelations, but she still held an ace.

Crouch contained, the HaHa were in fragments but not dissension. The time had come for me to move downstairs forever.

Four months later, there had still been no news from the family when, one July morning, I found myself sitting halfway up the stairs, gazing at a painting, nettled by my clothes. I had kept my promise not to give in to temptation. I was naked (that is, without makeup) and had by now a rather smart beard, carefully cut and trimmed, that I had grown on an Osian whim. After years of pruning, my relief at the respite from the razor was immense, and there suddenly seemed no reason to suffer this daily agony and every reason not to. Whether my beard was stylish, I know not, but I found that it coaxed a feeling of masculinity from me, encouraging me to consider myself anew when the stranger I saw in the mirror turned out to be me.

A loud knocking on the front door resounded throughout the lower passage. Although I was hypnotized by the painting, the persistent knocking woke me and, even in my ennui, I had a sudden inclination to silence the noise that intruded upon my dreams. It seemed a novel thing to do: it was unlikely to be anyone very important.

Framed by the driveway, Prudence Osbern-Smith-Stephenson made a magnificent portrait. *Proud Lady with Horse* would have looked wonderful in lush, reflective oils, halfway up the staircase, where I wished I had remained. She wore a red velvet dress that trailed thoughtlessly behind her on the driveway. On her right arm was a black stallion, which snorted its hot breath into the morning air, and in her left hand, a riding crop emerging from yards of rippling lace ruffles. They had ridden long and hard. She threw off her black riding hat, sashed with the same red velvet, and looked me over. She was even more beautiful, her body more generous, than ever. I broke the silence.

"Prudence."

I had been surprised to see her, but not as surprised as she was that a complete stranger knew her name and dared to address her with such intimacy. We both wondered who I was. She narrowed her eyes.

"How do you know my name?"

"Your beauty precedes you, madam." I bowed as humbly as I could and felt too charming, as though I might have betrayed myself with too much grace. Men move less than women. *Be a man,* I thought to myself. I had practically curtsied.

"Who are you? And have this horse stabled. I need to speak to Lady Rose Loveall immediately."

I walked beyond her and considered her mount, its nostrils still flaring. I wasn't sure how near I wanted to be to the beast, but it proved willing to be tethered to the rail beside the door. I ushered Prudence into the house and tried to walk beside her, but she ignored me entirely.

"I am Leslie Ose. If you'd like to wait here . . . ," I said to her profile. She didn't respond. She knew precisely where she was going.

"Where is the butler? Hood. I must speak to Rose. Who are *you?*"

Her manner was harsh. She was talking to me as she would a servant, for who but servants answer the door? She was not, however, being impolite, merely brusque, and though I had been ready to take offense, I quickly remembered myself. She had pressing business, and given that this was the first Osbern communication since the event, I was keener to know it than she could possibly have realized.

"I shall fetch Hood."

I didn't know how to explain myself, so I decided to let Hood do it for me. I found him opening mail downstairs, and he gave a rather wearied expression in response to my explanation. We hastily discussed the options. I would either have to change into clothes Prudence would recognize, shave, beautify, and meet her as my old self or else receive her news as Rose's new adviser, Leslie Ose. The first option, sadly, would take far too long and require too much assistance. Therefore, Rose would be indisposed and I would speak on her behalf. Prudence hadn't recognized me thus far. She didn't regard servants as worthy of scrutiny, or even attention, and the risk therefore seemed minimal. For me, it was an adventure, a labor.

We went downstairs. I waited outside the room, writing a quick script for myself as Hood explained to Prudence. This drama would put to the test not only my newfound manhood but also my ingenuity, my adaptability. I heard snatches of their conversation.

"Why didn't the new man make this clear himself?"

"Madam, I do not know. As I spoke for her departed father, so he speaks for Rose."

I looked down at myself: my shoes, black with square buckles, and my dull gray trousers. My tasseled waistcoat hung awkwardly, dwarfing me, while my velvet jacket squeezed my shoulders in its vise. I wished I had trimmed my beard even more closely. My hair was under a periwig that my father had worn. It itched in pinpricks on the top of my scalp, and my heart began to beat faster.

When I felt the time was right, which was just before I began to feel unduly anxious, I joined them.

"Hood," I said as I entered. "Lady Loveall sends her greetings but is entirely indisposed. I shall have to deliver any message myself."

The situation was ripe for farce, but no observer would ever have guessed it. I was nervous but trying to appear calm, Hood had adopted a manner best described as doleful, and Prudence was all business. We were in her way.

"It is most inconvenient," she exclaimed, and stamped her foot childishly on the ground. As she turned around, I saw the velvet of her dress swirl on the floor and then come to rest again at her feet. How I envied her the dress.

I dismissed Hood and he left, the ideal of servitude, leaving through the double doors and, without a glance to either side, closing them simultaneously behind him with only the tiniest of clicks. Prudence's back was still to me. I could smell her perfume from the other side of the room.

"Let me assure you, my lady, that when you speak to me, you speak only to my employer."

"There is a letter on the table," she said. I looked down, not having noticed it before. "It is from my cousin Esmond. Take it to Rose. I shall wait to confirm its delivery, even if there is no response."

She turned around and pierced me with her eyes, arrows flying into my own. She had finally noticed me, and this made me nervous. I stood there, transfixed. She looked me up and down, and I felt that she saw through me. I coughed. It sounded comically deep.

"Take the letter to her, now."

Once you start a lie, you have to keep going. Hasn't that been the story of my first fifteen years? I wondered whether, given Rose's supposed health, it would be appropriate to take the letter to her. The real Ose might have said that such a course of action was impossible, "things being as they are." What would Hood have done? However, I realized that this was going to be the only way I could read the contents of the letter myself. I duly picked it up and with a bow asked her if she would care to take some refreshment, which she impatiently declined. I left her, walking around the corner and up the stairs. I set off at what I thought was an appropriately urgent — but not undignified — pace, and as soon as I was sure to be out of earshot, I tore open the letter.

It was addressed simply to "Rose Loveall, Love Hall," and was written on the Fourteenth Leakhampton Grenadiers' letterhead. How strange it was to be furtively opening a letter that was addressed to me.

To Rose Loveall,

You will never hear from me again. By the time you receive this letter, I shall have sailed for America, never to return. Unable to tell my family the truth, I told them nothing. It is my one revenge, on them, on you. If you have any decency, strike my name from your story forever, for, upon my part, you will never hear of me. Prudence does not know the contents of this letter. She is the only trustworthy member of the family.

Forget me, please. As I hope to forget you. I cannot forgive.

Esmond Osbern

Coward! He had told them nothing.

We had heard nothing because they knew nothing! I had gone too far with Esmond. Months had been wasted.

I crumpled up the letter, thrust it into my pocket, cursed my luck, and rubbed my eyes until they hurt, trying to visualize what to do. But I was at a loss. I briefly considered raping Prudence. This might, besides, have its own reward. I couldn't think properly in those clothes, and the correct course of action, if one existed, was behind a veil, obscured by my mental fog. I couldn't imagine anything at all. If I could only rip my clothes off and be free, I felt that then, and only then, I might be able to think properly, see the situation clearly. But there was no time. I had to get rid of Prudence as soon as possible. We had to regroup and go to work all over again.

When I returned, in a state of thinly disguised agitation, I found that Prudence had not moved. She heard me enter and turned to face me. My belt bit into my hips as I bowed. She spoke immediately.

"Esmond's accompanying letter said that I was to expect no response but that I should make sure the letter had been properly delivered. Has it?"

"You may depend upon it, madam."

"And?" She was looking at me with all the haughtiness that I had seen in her as a young girl. It was unpleasant to be her inferior, made doubly so by the fact that her manner was above and beyond even her normal air of superiority and that, as a servant, I could say nothing.

"Madam?"

"Did Rose have anything to say to me?"

Oh God. What *did* I have to say to her?

I would have said something, wouldn't I? It was the first time that my logical mind failed me completely — what did she have to say to Prudence? That helped, thinking of Rose as *she*. And she was ill, too. But it was I, not she, who was muddled. She was merely ill upstairs, lying in bed. And she wasn't even there. It was I, down here, who felt ill, caught like a poacher with his leg in a trap. I couldn't think what I had to say to her, what I would have had to say to her, in these circumstances. I wanted to urinate. I tried to reassure myself that I was overcomplicating everything. All I had to tell Prudence was what Rose thought. In these circumstances? These *were* the circumstances! I was Rose.

"She said . . . ," I began slowly. "She said that she is most grateful that you brought the letter. It transpired, although we at Love Hall did not know anything about the visit of Mr. Osbern, that she refused his hand and, furthermore, that Mr. Osbern has left for the colonies in disappointment."

Prudence turned white. Her body seemed close to a faint, but her will forbade it. I feared a collapse might follow, however, so I put out my hand. Though she had regained the possession of her senses, she was utterly forlorn. Her quest had only been to discover the contents of the letter; that the information reached Rose was of secondary importance. I wished she'd just opened it when it arrived, as any normal person would have done; then we could have avoided this whole ugly business. Perhaps she was more honest than I had imagined. There seemed to be no other explanation.

She started to cry, very gently, and turned around, too proud to let me see. I got brandy from the buffet and took it to her. Her tears were wiped away. She accepted the glass and sat down.

"I am very sorry, madam. Rose sends her condolences." I realized to my horror that I had blundered. Condolences for what?

"Why did she refuse him?" She turned to me for an answer, but her eyes looked through me to a higher authority.

"I don't know, Miss Osbern." I should have stopped there but I didn't, for I was still Rose and her thoughts were still mine. "Perhaps she did not love him." The moment I said it, I wished I hadn't.

"Don't speak to me about love, you imbecile!" She hurled the glass to the floor. It was meant to shatter, but it caught the corner of the carpet, skidded across the room, and banged dumbly into the wall, leaving her need for destruction unfulfilled. If only it had broken.

"I am so sorry. I don't know what to say." I *didn't* know what to say, but it would be best for everyone if Prudence left. I knew that. She was about to do something awful, and I was too awkward to handle the situation. My body started to itch. There was no air between my clothes and my skin. They were sticking to me in my panic, burning like Glauce's wedding dress. My scalp in particular crawled as though a thousand fleas had been set loose under my wig. I wanted to rip it off.

"Shall I fetch Hood?" I asked urgently. She looked at me as if for the first time.

"You. Who are *you?*"

She stood up and pointed her riding crop at me.

"I am Leslie —"

"I know your name, fool. What are you doing here? You are no butler. You are too refined. Something sinister is happening here, and I want to know what. I demand to speak to Rose. I insist!"

I had let her go on because with my mind in its current state of alarm, I had no chance of inventing an explanation adequate to the moment. I stared at her, the fool she had labeled me, my mouth lolling open. She made a bolt for the door. I stopped her. Things were happening much too fast for me, but I had to do something.

"Stand aside!" As she pushed me, I grabbed her elbow with sufficient force that she was bound to take offense. I knew it would incense her, but I had no choice. I held on.

"Madam, I must ask you to restrain yourself. You put me in an awkward position. I can go to fetch Hood, or I can take a message to Rose that you wish an interview. I am merely obeying the wishes of my employer when I say that you cannot go to her without warning. It is for your own good. Her fever is high and she is violently contagious."

Prudence had been tugging on her arm with all her might. She was desperate to be free of me, but I was determined. Suddenly she stopped.

"Hood said that she hurt herself in a fall."

We froze. We stared at each other.

"A fall?" I said, but could not continue. I smiled weakly and tried to say something about how it was not Hood's job to . . . but she was struggling fiercely, and to my horror, the redoubling of my efforts to stop her dislodged the crumpled letter from my pocket. It fell to the floor. She recognized it immediately and, with the strength of all her anger, dragged herself from me as I reached down to pick it up. While I groped, she fled.

I had done well as a man — she had been fooled — but very poorly as a human being. The clothes were perfect and my impression evidently good enough, but I had completely forgotten how to behave authentically. The present mayhem was the result of my having been sluggish, unable to extemporize. As a man, I lost my imagination and my sense of humor. I was no longer myself.

She was fast away from me, and there was I, immobile, a failure, trying not to think about the future. I heard her run up the stairs, and it was only then, too late, that I decided to give chase. The picture of Salmacis reminded me to shout for my mother at the top of my voice. And Hood. Another mistake. I shouted as Rose.

Prudence was far out of reach. She knew exactly where my bedroom was, had always been. On my way down the hallway, I saw my mother arriving from the library and Hood from the Baron's Hall. Everyone was converging on my bedroom.

Prudence stood inside, looking at the unmade bed. Women's clothes lay on a chair, clothes that I now only ever allowed myself to touch in the privacy of this room. All the portraits of Rose as a girl hung around the walls. On the dresser lay her hairbrushes and mirrors. Everything of her was there except for Rose herself. My mother came up behind me, and Hood pushed past us.

"Madam, I absolutely insist that you leave this room," Hood boomed. "You have no business to be here."

"I will not be treated like a fool," she said with all the force she could muster in her confusion. "What have you done to Rose? Where is she?" She looked directly at me as she spoke. She picked up and sniffed at some of the clothes, which she then threw in the air. They scattered in a way that seemed to confirm their owner's absence. Everything somehow corroborated her suspicions of foul play. Hood could manage only to repeat his previous statement, but given the simplicity of her questions, it was a desperate evasion. I sided with her.

"Prudence!" I pleaded.

"How dare you call me by my name! Answer my question!"

The three of us had encroached upon her like the villains in a comical opera, and she backed away. My mother stepped forward and walked toward Prudence, who brandished her riding crop.

"Keep your distance, librarian."

The moment could hardly have been more theatrical, but I was listless in my clothes and could be of little assistance. I felt impotent, so unlike when I had played Lord Ose in my childhood. Oh, to brandish my sword and save the day. My mother reached out to Prudence and spoke very calmly.

"Prudence, Rose is very well. She is fine. She can't see you at the moment. There is nothing wrong with her. We have had to —"

"Show me!" she screamed. Only the truth would be enough.

Feeling unreal, untouchable, I walked toward Prudence. My mother reached out to stop me but could do nothing. I was tired, too tired for pretense, and I knew what to do. I took off my wig. The relief was fantastic. My own hair, which was not as long as it had been (but longer than Leslie's would have been), fell down to my shoulders. Prudence could not grasp what was happening. Her common sense and all her faculties were working against her.

"I am Rose, Prudence." As I said it, I did an impression of myself, or rather, I gave up trying to do an impression of someone else. I looked at her with my own eyes, letting my self shine through my disguise. I dropped my arms to the side, palms toward her, and imagined myself naked in front of her.

Prudence fell to the floor like a statue pushed from a battlement, straight forward. She lashed out with her crop and landed me a sharp blow on my right cheek, an inch below my eye.

"It's all over," I said to my mother as my mouth filled with the blood that trickled down my face. "Time to start again."

I took my mother in my arms. I drew her close to me. Blood seeped into her lace collar.

Our trial was about to begin.

5

HIS TIME, there was no delay. The carousel spun faster and faster until we couldn't stop. There had been a time when we could still tell our laughter from our screams; that gone, we hung on as best we could, until it was a relief to let go, to give in and let ourselves be flung away, to land where we might.

The Osberns had the news as fast as Prudence's horse could carry her home. At last, Love Hall was within their grasp. Their motive was not personal greed nor their own advancement nor, heaven forbid, revenge upon the Loveall — no! They acted for the good of the ancient family name, and in the interests of a child brought up at the mercy of a madman. In public they said I was a confused innocent, forced by a perverted mind to wear the clothes of the wrong sex, who would need the constant care and attention that only they, as my family, could provide. Privately, they agreed that my sanity was the only thing between them and the lot. I dangled by a thread, and they sharpened their knives.

My father was to blame, though they assumed he had acted at the instigation of his mother. They had always mocked his outlandish dress sense and his sinister, almost *French,* unmanliness; they had always been suspicious of the limited access he allowed his own cousins to Love Hall, not to mention the sequestering of his own family within its grounds. Everybody had acknowledged his eccentricities, but now it was clear that he had been entirely insane. He had left everything to an abused, muddled child, and that child would not be safe alone in the world. Not, at any rate (as the joke goes), from them. Oh, the wasted years. How much sooner could they have moved in?

I was a remnant of the decadent past, a doll left over from a previous playtime. I needed to be mended, tidied up, and then put away forever. They would drive me mad with lawyers and doctors; with this help, they would rob me of my inheritance, peel away my disguise, and strip me of whatever remained of my dignity. And what of the librarian? How she would suffer for lording it over them, that plain little barrow girl! No longer the mother of the next lord of Love Hall, she'd be a grieving widow waiting upon her child in Bedlam. Better — living there with him.

News also made its way to Playfield, where the villagers were in an uproar. Their greatest fear, however, was not a transvestite Lord Loveall, but her replacement. I was their Little Froggy, their Maiden Century, their Miss Fortune, and they knew they had nothing to fear from me. "Even if the story be true," Hamilton heard the publican say, "she's still the only real lady around these parts and fairer than your missus." The consensus at The Monkey's Head was that the delicate Young Lord could simply never have borne a messy little boy. The villagers thought of us even more fondly when the Osberns and the Rakeleighs began to move through town with greater frequency. The very crack of the whip on their horses was harsh and authoritarian, an ominous warning of their attitude to power. The villagers saw their future gallop by, spattering their windows with mud.

As the fact of my masculinity became more widely reported, theories abounded. Some assumed that I had been mistaken for a female at birth. Apparently, such a mistake is not unknown in cases when the penis has shrunk into a chink and (excuse me) the testes have yet to fall into the scrotum — in this instance, it was parental ignorance that had me baptized and habited as a maid. The more imaginative further conjectured that when I discovered the truth about myself, I carried on this subterfuge in order that I could profit from the situation in the seduction of women, as who in his right mind would not? One newspaper hypothesized that my father had brought me up as a girl in order to save me from conscription. The article, with the byline "Clarion," made reference to a book that cited others known to have been concealed in dresses for political or familial reasons and "continued under that acceptation, till matters came to such a crisis as rendered [knowledge of the true sex] less dangerous, or till beards and other signs of virility occasioned a declaration of their true sex and a change of habit." At such moments of discovery, the parents habitually claim never to have known and make rumor of miraculous change. We would not stoop to such low drama. The Loveall would spare everyone that indignity.

And then the Osberns were at Love Hall. We had no alternative but to open our doors. The interfamilial alliance arrived with a list of legal procedure that gave them unprecedented access to the house and its contents. My mother and I tried to cope with their rapid encroachment as best we could.

In order for the law, and therefore the Osberns, to ascertain the situation precisely, the affair had to be managed correctly. So close to their goal, they could not afford any mistakes. An Osbern had never attended so strictly to the letter of the law, and the veneer of their manners shone with a new hardness. Augustus Rakeleigh had never cared so deeply whether a client cared. It was immediately apparent that this legal process did not protect our interests at all. Being the objects of investigation, we were subject to the most shocking license.

No one was more active or enthusiastic in this pursuit than

Augustus Rakeleigh's man, Thrips. That slithery creature was forever standing by with his ledger and his inky sleeves. The Osberns had always had grand plans but never the means to implement them, and in Augustus and his toady they found not only the acumen but also the will. Thrips was always seeing what could be done and wondering if it wouldn't be best if you left it to him. His voice seeped down corridors, like wind sailing through the crack beneath a window. Provided they were accompanied by Thrips in his notary capacity, the Osberns could do almost anything, go anywhere. Hood and Hamilton could only look on.

While things began to twist out of our control, my mother entirely retreated to the library, either in resignation or for her own personal comfort. Inheritances come and go, but books go on forever, and her work among them would never be complete. The family treated her as an irrelevance. She was my mother (how *little* they actually knew), but they would bide their time and leave her be until they were good and ready to throw her out. Then again, she was so little trouble and seemed so content in her eight-walled cell: perhaps they thought that Love Hall might still use a librarian. I, too, began to treat her as an irrelevance. I would have to face my trial alone.

I was forbidden to wear my natural clothes even in private and was now condemned to the feeling of self-estrangement, the constriction of movement and mind, that accompanied a starched collar and a naked face. One morning I cut myself shaving. Blood dripped from the nick beneath my right nostril. I didn't try to stop it. Instead, staring at my reflection, I painted my lips crimson with the tip of my tongue. Angelica entered with more hot water and I turned my head in shame.

There was a tragic air about our old home: servants moved from room to room with heads bowed, expecting new, more unpleasant intrusions with every hour. When Hood had the good idea of writing a letter to the ancient firm of solicitors who had represented the family for so many years (the very ones that my father had been visiting on the day he found me), he received a curt reply by return: they were now in the service of the Osberns, who in their opinion best represented Loveall interests. Reliance had engineered this defection. No one was on our side.

Only Anstace's mood brightened, although I did not witness this, for now she never spoke to me or I to her. I had the sneaking suspicion that she preferred the influence the secret knowledge gave her to the reality of having to expose us and that she was quite as upset by the power shift as any of us, but she was undoubtedly hard at work. Alone among the household, she remained busy, chiding the servants for their sloppy work, fussing around those Osberns who scared us most. They treated her as if she were the only housekeeper, though hers was merely the appearance of work, and ignored Angelica entirely. Hamilton monitored Anstace's movements and could unearth nothing but disturbing information — she dallied with Thrips and addressed Nora as "milady." I was tired of her, and Mother ignored her altogether. We had proven ourselves adept at telling our own secrets without any assistance from her.

We failed to keep the family at bay in any sense. We didn't have the will. My bizarre upbringing was not legal excuse enough for them to take the fortune — I was still the heir and I was still in Love Hall — so the Osberns stopped short of taking up residence in the house and installed themselves in adjacent properties around the perimeter of the estate, poised to swoop at a moment's notice. They were in the ascendant and they had us surrounded. They paraded before me, more suspicious of me than they had ever been, though their wariness was now mixed with a predictable air of superiority. They let themselves in and out. They ate in the house. They used the water closet. They staked out their own areas in preparation.

Every day heralded the arrival of a new injunction, a new slight.

Before the fact of my sanity, there was the very question of my true sex. Specifics needed to be addressed.

For example, did I actually know which sex I was? Clearly, no one should take my word for anything. Nothing at all could be decided until this was known. Things had been clear when I was a woman. If I were a man, as I claimed, I would inherit entirely on my own, and since I would almost certainly not marry one of their representatives, this left the Osberns with no claim at all. In this case, they would have to prove that madness rendered me incapable of claiming my legacy. After all, a man can dress however he likes in the privacy of his own home without threat of expulsion. But if I were proved mad — and this seemed well within their power — then this was the end of the Loveall line and the beginning of the Osberns. The family therefore insisted ("for my own good") on the presence of a doctor at all times, shadowing my every movement, evaluating my eccentricities, smiling at my tics, taking notes, and reporting to Thrips.

And there was one further intriguing possibility. Though I had admitted to not being a woman, perhaps I was not either entirely a man. A quick glance confirmed that I might be both or neither, an intermediate creature, and memories of my father intimated that it might be a hereditary physical misfortune. This was a worry to the Osberns, for the possibility raised arcane questions about my inheritance. In the event that I was a hermaphrodite, the answer to the conundrum of my sex would come to rest on precisely where I lay on the scale, which sex was warmer and more vigorous within me. In the event that hermaphrodites were legally allowed to inherit anything, this could mean years of legal debate. Ever thorough, Thrips was already researching this eventuality.

A medical examination to put the matter beyond doubt was therefore an immediate and unavoidable necessity, though Thrips gave the doctor no chance of finding me anything other than a male.

"Nothing more than a boy with long hair in girls' clothes. If we must, we must, but I wager a fortune to a fart that the examination is a waste of time. We know the result."

It was Augustus who spoke, but he quoted Thrips, whose entire knowledge on the subject was gleaned from a book, *Mechanical and Critical Enquiry into the Nature of Hermaphrodites,* which he left always above the fire in the Reception Room. This book made clear in its foreword that there was no such thing as hermaphroditical nature and that those in question were female in all respects and superstitiously or through ignorance were mistaken for those creatures, or for men.

A Dr. Reverrat arrived with an inappropriately heavy bag of equipment, followed by a white screen carried by a Negro attendant. Reverrat could barely contain his lascivious interest and looked at me as though I were already behind bars. I should never have chosen him for my own medical man, for his hands shook so, that I assumed he was either gin-sodden or overexcited. We were, thank heavens, left alone. His servant, whose job it was to hand the doctor his forceps, remained but was required to wear a mask, rather because of his color than my dignity.

The doctor had only to have me stand dishabille in front of him to ascertain precisely which position I occupied on the great scale. I told him that I was not pretending to be anything other than what I was: a man. But he ignored me, determined not to be thwarted in his pleasure, and intimately inspected me. I am not going to go into detail about it: there are plenty of soi-disant medical (pornographic) novels that will titillate the keen student with the specifics of such interviews.

This was the opening gambit in the Osberns' bid to strip away my peace of mind, to edge me toward madness. They were making it clear that the law was on their side and that there were no lengths to which they would not go in order to humiliate me. I was likewise determined that, though they had legal rights, I would not cede the position of moral superiority. I was their victim, not the other way around, and my only defense was to remain aloof. I could not. I bent forward with as much self-respect as I could muster, but I cried out as Reverrat probed and squeezed with relish.

The verdict left no doubt. And now that there was no longer any reason to dissemble, I saw little point in my man's array. Why now put myself through this daily agony in addition to everything else? To their disgust, I had absolutely no desire to live as a man.

The next insult was religious. At the behest of Praisegod, I was checked by a nervous priest for diabolic possession to see if I had those physical stigmata that Bodin's *Demonomania* describes as sure signs of a covenant with Satan. I felt sorry for the priest but was glad that Augustus had not prevailed upon Praisegod, an evil parody of his God-fearing father, to perform the ritual himself. It involved the extended sifting of the hair on my head, the back of my legs, and between my buttocks, for contemporary thought had it that Lucifer liked to brand his mark in a discreet place. The priest spent no more than a quarter hour on his task. As for markings, I had none more devilish than an innocent mole on my back, over which he hummed for a troubled minute. His considered opinion was that I was not possessed. No one was more relieved about this than Edgar or more disappointed than Praisegod.

After the examination, Edgar took me aside, away from his son, advising me to forsake the world and become a religious. In his opinion, I would need to conceal the shame of my true story from the rest of the world for all time, and this was best achieved in contemplation from the confines of a monastery. With regard to my spiritual salvation, it was of paramount importance that I observe a devout celibacy for the rest of my born days. This might help me toward perfection before death, and thus assure me some spiritual happiness in eternity; obviously, there could be none for me on earth. His laborious counsel continued: I should not take the veil (by this he meant become a nun — he doubtless thought that I should *wear* a veil as often as possible), though it might prove more comfortable for me in the short term, because this would involve an unnecessary return to subterfuge and the habit of my former gender, there being no possibility of the sisters otherwise accepting me.

Poor Edgar. He was a decent, boring man, somehow unspoiled by exposure to his family: when he said that I ought not to drag the family name through the mud with the public battles that were bound to occur if I insisted on my legal rights, it was not what he had been told to say but what he sincerely believed. Edgar was suggesting what he thought best for me, for I did the world no good. I was an embarrassment in whatever clothes.

Discussions whirred around me like dragonflies. I became entirely used to being discussed as if I weren't there.

Our favored relatives came to take part as our sole advocates, but Julius and his father, William, who had formed such a good opinion of my mother when I was a child, found they had been summoned for propriety's sake only. Once present, they were entirely ignored. They tried to offer the classicist's perspective but found themselves mocked for their devotion to dead men and their dead language. I sat in the corner, not invited to stay, not asked to leave, while an ever changing cast of family members debated my existence. Julius looked at me with sympathy, his father not at all, and everyone else with disdain.

"For God's sake," exclaimed Augustus, the tiny maroon silks on his face fluttering with his agitation, "he looks like a man, he talks like a man, and he *is* a man. He therefore must behave like one. We cannot have a member of our family dress in inappropriate clothes."

"Only a *madman* would do such a thing," hissed Thrips suggestively.

"Hmm . . . ," said Athelstan, taking his point. The consensus had been that Athelstan was only months away from death and that this excitement might prove too much, but when it suddenly appeared that he might yet witness his family's reinstatement, he unexpectedly found himself with something to live for. He was restored to better health than ever, cracking ghoulish jokes with an energy truly vampirical. I had brought him back from the dead. "But I won't bloody have it. It's an insult, pure and simple. Effeminacy is a slight to public duty. Look at his bloody father."

"That's where the rot set in," said Praisegod.

"Hear, bloody hear!" said Athelstan. "We can't have a member of our family parading around like that. It comes of too much social bloody intercourse with women."

"They never get their mother's milk out of them, these Loveall," said Augustus. I looked out of the window and noticed that the parterre was unusually unkempt. I wondered if the gardeners, like the servants, were giving up hope.

"There is nothing necessarily wrong with a man dressing up as a woman," offered Julius tentatively, surprised whenever anyone paid attention but keen to come to our rescue, given the opportunity.

"I beg your pardon?" asked Augustus, as though he had been interrupted. He had forgotten his brother was there.

"Hercules spent three years dressed in women's clothing at the court of the queen of . . . Father? Lycia?"

"Lydia. Queen of Lydia," croaked Lord William.

"Lydia, yes," said Julius, but Augustus could tolerate no more.

"I have absolutely no idea what you're talking about and it doesn't matter in the least what Hercules did or what he wore. You must see that it is a completely unenlightening perspective."

There was silence. Julius was suspicious that he was merely prolonging our agony. He soon decided that he could find no middle ground with the Osberns and their lawyer and left, taking his father with him.

Only Edgar would venture to defend us further, but his son quashed his every suggestion.

"François Timoléon de Choisy married as a woman and became abbé in 1663. He wrote his great *History of the Church* wearing female attire at a desk in his monastery, and this was undoubtedly a great and devout man of the Lord. That might be the thing for Rose."

"He should have been excommunicated," said Praisegod.

"Christian charity, please, my son!"

"Charity, be damned! Deuteronomy 22:5: 'Neither shall a man put on a woman's garment; for all that do so are an abomination unto the Lord thy God.' Answer that!"

"Ah," said Edgar, and turned away.

"I don't care if Jesus himself wore a bloody dress," said Athelstan in conclusion. "It will not happen in my house."

I looked up wearily.

"Or this house," he added.

Reliance was the most bitter and relentless, though he was a less frequent visitor because, unlike the rest, he had interests outside Love Hall. He was frighteningly insincere, his good manners and courtesy a thin skin over his self-interest. His mask of charm never cracked and he now reserved his greatest politesse for Augustus. Nor did he consider my presence a hindrance to self-expression: his were some of the most terrifying pronouncements of all.

"Well, if she won't dress up as a man, let her dress up as a woman. Whatever the law makes of it, the public is keen to see it," said Reliance.

"This discussion is over," said Athelstan.

"We have a human paradox. Let the public decide. Rather than have her a sap on the resources of a monastery, we should send her to a circus. There'll be a ready coin to see Mr. Unmale."

"Impractical," said Augustus.

"Oh, wormwood! We are not putting a member of our family in a bloody freak show!" yelled Athelstan. "What would people say? Good Lord!"

"And might I interject that we should call him 'him' rather than 'her' in the future," reminded Thrips.

"'It'?" asked Reliance.

"'Him' is best, sir."

"Well, whatever we call it, if it wants to be a woman, let it be a woman. There is, in fact, a simple medical solution: *ablatio penis*."

"Reliance?" Augustus inquired.

"A terminal solution that would render him irrevocably female," said Thrips. There was silent deliberation.

"I suppose we'd need his consent?" sniffed Augustus.

"Not necessarily," said Reliance.

I left the room.

Prudence entered into none of the discussions but made it clear that her hatred for me was entire. She knew that I was to blame for Esmond and that there was more to the story than I had told. Such superciliousness suited her, making her more beautiful than ever. She was an enigma to me, or rather, she made an enigma of me to myself. We had not managed a pleasant conversation in all our years, yet there was a moment when I would have made an attempt to love her. Her eyes defied mastery. She would never be broken, and to her, any union would be a battle of wills.

I remembered a time, years before, when I had attempted to impress her with my Lord Ose costume and my fake mustache. She took one look at me and delivered the withering verdict: "Sweet." Nothing had changed. I was still trying to impress her with the same clothes. I had never had someone catch me staring quite so often, though I had never stared at anyone quite so much.

Prudence was my tree of knowledge, just out of reach. She would always be untouchable, though I yearned to see the body beneath her dress, to have my own freedom with her. Now, though, I had no energy left and it was she who had mastered me. She unmanned me with her every look, and I was more ridiculous to her than ever. Though my life would have become a hell, and though the admission is a painful one, our union was the sole possible compromise between the Osberns and Loveall that could somehow have borne fruit. But it was never mooted, and then it was too late to suggest it. How different my life would have been: emasculated after I had just become a man. Perhaps she would have been my "cure." I still carried her scar under my eye. It would never heal perfectly.

My mother maintained her low profile in the library. Now it was I who kept her a secret. I rarely mentioned her in case the reference to her very name might remind them and somehow implicate her. As long as she didn't interfere, she was left alone. She could manage to live a relatively normal life, provided she expected to be treated not as the lady but as the librarian and provided she knew her place, in the Octagonal. Her name above the door had a talismanic effect. She felt safe among her books and papers, the value of which only she understood. We pretended that she was still looking after me, but I knew that, for the first time, it was I who was looking after her, lying about her, hiding her, the illegal priestess, making sure she was untouched in sanctuary.

I dealt with the various usurpers with a weary resolve, but I was severely demoralized. My father had let me down by dying; my mother by retreating; my friends by leaving; my body by growing. On the surface I wore my clothes with dignity, but my soul was beleaguered. Let them talk about me as if I weren't there. It would be harder to move me. If they wanted to say I was mad, then the burden of proof rested on them. Perhaps they'd give up and go away one day.

Hood and Hamilton, too, had lost faith in the situation. Thrips informed Samuel that the Hamiltons would be given notice to vacate the Gatehouse Lodge, since it would be of no use to them once they were no longer employees of the Hall, and then casually asked whether the clatter of arriving coaches was trying. Everyone was cleaning up on his way out. The servants no longer knew where their orders were coming from. The HaHa, infiltrated by Anstace, had become the laughingstock after all, forced to play by the rules of others — and what others! Augustus came and went as if the house were his own, while his wife, Caroline, was finally able to complete her inventory of its contents, and Nora reduced the household to tears at will. Only Guy was out of range for the time being. Heaven only knew what hound of hell Dogboy had become.

As they moved around us, in and out of our most private lives, invading our private rooms, I began, for the first time, to hate Love Hall for bearing so little resemblance to the pleasure palace of my youth. The problem was deeper, though, within my soul. It was an ache that I could not admit to anyone and a conflict that I couldn't resolve on my own. Being only male made me short-tempered. I felt boredom more easily. I ceased to listen as closely as I should and began to fidget incessantly. As people spoke to me, I could see them talking and hear the sound of their voices, monotonous and lulling, but I wasn't listening. They were far away and I was in a glass house that moved where I moved. My seventeenth birthday passed without celebration, and I felt prematurely old, wearing the wrong clothes, in the wrong house.

My mother suffered, too. There was a new distance between us.

I shouted at her for the first time in my life. I was sitting in a shaft of sunlight on the floor and staring up into the light. She had been telling me about the ballads, which she was still in the process of cataloging. I could hear the sound of her voice and fragments of what she said, but I couldn't parse them into anything that made sense. I grew infuriated with myself, my glass house, my lack of concentration. When she asked me whether I was listening, I lost my temper.

"I don't care about the ballads and I don't care about your Mary — look at all the good she did us! Stop! Stop!" I put my hands over my ears and left the room. I couldn't bear to turn around and see her crying.

I had changed. We had both changed. I tried to apologize, but the unspoken had been acknowledged: I blamed her for making me the plaything of her ideas. I blamed her more than I did my father. It was worse than if I had denounced her in public. All we had was each other, the special bond between us, and now that bond was disintegrating. Perhaps it had already been severed. If any one of the Osberns had heard, they would have rejoiced. At last, we were cracking.

I dreamed of spirals downward, books submerged in water, windows with no latches. I was suffocating. My isolation was becoming unbearable, and yet the more unbearable it became, the more I forgot to wonder at it and the less I remembered to implement my tiny strategies for survival.

I sank into inertia and felt like a corpse. I protested not even the most offensive of invasions. I let them ride roughshod over me. As I sank further and further, I ceased even to listen to their talk; I began to enjoy disappearing, trying to leave my body behind in the chair. I had nothing to say and my mind wandered. I sat endlessly on the stairs, looking at the paintings, dreaming of Salmacis and Hermaphroditus, as legs I did not bother to identify passed me in both directions. I had used to pleasure myself in bed with thoughts of Sarah and Stephen, but now I was unable, wanting no part of the filth and the heavy breathing. I knew where it led. I had no urges, no physical needs. I missed nothing. I had forgotten even the feel of my old clothing, which still hung on the other side of the closet door. I would never be used to my new clothes. They were wiping my mind clean.

I looked at paintings of me as a girl and I saw a stranger smiling back at me, mocking me with her happiness. If she had only known what I knew now. The portraits of my father and his sister stared at me in accusation. Be more like us.

At one grueling dinner, my mother had unusually been asked to dine downstairs, and she and I sat together at one end of the table. It was our house, yet we had been wheeled out as an entertainment for the guests. Our one hope of salvation lay in the better members of the clan, and with Julius long since departed, we put what little faith we had in the great faith of Edgar. Praisegod could justify any evil in the name of God — he was the Inquisition and the Crusades in one man — but his father was our unwitting protector, and Edgar's presence kept in check the very worst excesses of the Osberns' behavior. At this particular meal, unfortunately, Edgar was gone, attending the confirmation of the bishop's son in London. We were left to the rest of them.

Prudence sat far away from me between her brother Reliance, in his regular position at Augustus's right hand, and Nora. My mother and I were silent. We spoke only in the privacy of our rooms. The most intimate aspects of our lives had been laid bare for them, cut open on the surgeon's table, and I would not allow a word from my mouth to provide my enemies with any insight into my present turmoil. It would only have strengthened their arsenal.

The big surprise at this dinner, and the reason that an invitation was extended to my mother at all, was an unannounced arrival. The doors were thrown open and there he stood, though I wasn't immediately sure who he was. The apparition brought shrieks of acclaim from all corners of the table, and Prudence bounded up to meet him with puppyish affection that was decidedly out of character. Such a brazen unscheduled appearance would have been unthinkable only a few months ago.

"My lord!" she enthused, and curtsied to him, allowing him to kiss her hand, which he did nonchalantly, to a murmur of approval from his family.

Dogboy.

"Guy!" said Augustus, immediately reworking the seating around the table.

He had grown into a freckled but handsome young man, his hair flopping rakishly, his body gaunt. I assumed that he was wearing the very latest fashions, and they looked a curiosity to me. He surveyed the table, as Prudence led him in and offered him a chair next to hers. Ignoring my mother entirely, he greeted his own with all the deference due the owner of the house, the giver of the meal. He deposited Prudence and came toward me. I didn't get up. He stood before me.

"We have not had the pleasure, sir."

He bowed, as was proper. I admired his composure but didn't feel up to a battle of wits. I had been entirely in a trance that evening, snapped out of it only by Guy's appearance, and would have been willing to fall back in if allowed. Then I could go to bed and they would disperse. I felt myself about to speak.

"Sir, we have." My eyes were drowsy as though drugged. I had no choice but to continue. I lubricated my croak of a voice with a little wine.

"No, sir, we have not, not since . . . ," and as he straightened to standing, he looked up to make sure that all eyes were on him. "Not since the Rose was discovered to have a canker."

The table noted this repartee with a murmur of appreciation, accompanied by the banging of a solitary fork on a wineglass. Everyone then settled back to enjoy the unfolding drama. Guy looked me straight in the eye to coax a reaction. I said nothing. My mother put her hand in mine on top of the table.

"What should we call you now, sir?" He pursed his lips as though this were a matter to which he was giving serious consideration, yet upon which he could reach no final conclusion.

"You will call him Lord Rose Loveall," said my mother abruptly. Her fingernails dug sharply into my hand with anger. Again, Guy surveyed his audience.

"Quite right! That which we call a Rose by any other name would still smell" — he left a long pause as though his sentence were done — "as sweet."

"Oh, Guy!" swooned Prudence earthily, as the company collapsed in mirth. Reliance toasted Guy with a full glass, and the one remaining Christian, Praisegod, nodded his approval, napkin to his face to conceal his laughter. Augustus guffawed and his wife honked like a fatty goose. The whole menagerie was out, and for those who were carnivores, we were the prey. We would be lucky to survive the night.

"I insist that you stop!" shouted my mother, but there were tears in her eyes. She knew that I no longer had the energy or the inclination to defend myself and that her efforts were futile. We were there now only in our physical bodies. Our influence had gone. So I sat helpless as Guy plundered famed quotations of the world at my expense. They had mocked me subtly and talked about me as if I weren't there, but they had not been openly rude before. This was the first time they'd put me in the stocks and pelted me with fruit. I couldn't even manage to get up and leave. When he had finished, quite finished, I lifted my head, like a pugilist who has hit the ground many times but will not admit he is beaten.

"You may call me whatever you will behind my back, Guy, but in my house, you will call me Lord Rose Loveall. There is your answer." And then I lapsed into my previous daze. There had been a sharp intake of breath when I had begun to speak. I formed my words slowly. But by the end of my sentence all tension subsided. I had answered his question simply. We could no longer harbor hopes of waiting out these cuckoos.

"My lord, my dearest lord," said Guy, and he went to sit down. He sat next to Prudence, whom he again kissed on the hand.

"Look at that mark upon Lord Rose Loveall's face, Prudence. It is as if someone has tried to prune her."

"Guy," said Prudence as she flashed me a glance. I lifted my hand to cover the scar.

"Isn't that where you *nipped* her in the bud, Prudence?" said Augustus, welcoming open season.

"Pruned by Prudence!" said Reliance.

"Pinked with her shears!" said Nora, her face creased with laughter. Lady Caroline sneered a smile as she battled with a turkey leg, her mouth dripping fat.

"A very sobering thought, my dear girl," said Guy. "Let's hope no other man can say the same!"

Within five minutes, things had sunk to the lowest depths. With great pomp, accompanied by the beaming smiles of Reliance (who smelled the successful fruition of months of negotiation) and Praisegod (who had secured himself the warm nest of the local living into the bargain), Augustus Rakeleigh announced the engagement of Guy and Prudence, begging permission to call her daughter, for so she had always felt to him. They would be married, as familial rights dictated, in the great chapel at Love Hall and they would assume the name Loveall by mutual consent between the two families. It was what his sister, to whom they offered a toast, would have wished. Glasses clinked on mine as the union between the two families was announced. I was punch-drunk and nauseous. They didn't have to get rid of us at all. They would just move in, had just moved in.

I staggered out, nearly knocking over my mother's chair as I went. The moment I was outside the room, I vomited over the sofa. I was reeling, my throat in spasm. My mother helped me back to my room, where I lay on the floor, cheek to the cool oak.

My ears still ringing with insults, I was kept awake by the sounds of carousing from the dining room. The announcement had become the official celebration. By morning, I had barely slept and the house was quiet, ominously so. I expected to find the evidence of the party gone, but nothing had been cleared away, the dirty plates abandoned on the crowded table. The smell of red wine lingered in the air, mingled with the stink of stale tobacco from overflowing ashtrays. A superfluous joint of meat on the sideboard attracted two large bluebottles. I had never seen such a mess. Hood stopped me as I left the room. Somehow, and against all odds, he was impeccably dressed.

"The servants, by and large, have left, sir. They refuse to return to work. They are miserably mistreated by the family, sir. They do not understand what is happening."

"Neither do I, Hood," I said, and a lump came to my throat. The pile of vomit had not been cleaned up, either.

"Neither do I," he said.

He turned to go. And then he turned back.

"One final piece of news. And not good, I'm afraid, Rose."

I looked at him.

"Anstace. Has the hour come?"

"Yes, sir. Her ambition is still to be housekeeper in Love Hall, but no longer for us."

There was silence while I thought.

"Good," I finally said.

"I know exactly what you mean, sir." Hood reached out and held my hand. He then turned away again. That was how it was left.

My mother and I started to clear the mess, encouraging some of the hardier servants who crept out into the morning like timid mice. I saw us slipping inexorably into the Cinderella roles of housekeeper and servant of Love Hall. It was unbearable. Where was the prince now? Where was Sarah?

Anstace became the sole housekeeper of Love Hall that day. She had flown us as far as she could, and it was time to change broomsticks. We had nothing further to bargain with, and she had the means to get what she wanted from the Osberns. She told them the one thing they didn't know.

I was a bastard.

It was I who was the usurper in their Love Hall.

Things were horrific enough already, but now everything was thrown into confusion. Legal battles would ensue. Hood and Hamilton informed us that it could take years, years of energy, years of money. And to defend what? To defend a humiliating existence as we watched our very own home, and everything within, slip through our fingers. I was glad it was finished.

They had won. They didn't even need to crow about it. Guy and

Prudence were to be married. From there on, all they needed was to dot the i's and cross the t's. Our one pitiful hope rested in the fact that they wanted the court battle as little as we.

That very day, Augustus and Reliance came with a proposal. It was more or less as we had expected. They would give the library wing of the house to my mother and me. We would be allowed to keep Hood and one other servant. We would be able to live there by our own rules, under their protection.

We were being imprisoned, the princes in the tower.

What did we get in exchange? What could we possibly hope for? We were utterly at their mercy. They had the weight of the law to back them and were merely trying to avoid scandal and legal fees. They would not denounce my mother for her complicity in the subterfuge, which saved her being forced to plead insanity in a court of law. They would not broadcast my illegitimacy and they would not publicly question my right to inherit. But I was to inherit in name alone and I would sign papers to this effect. They became owners of Love Hall. Their alliance would rule, and they suggested for me the name the Invisible Lord Loveall. Gray's Inn might or might not have been on their side in this, but the court's version of justice would be as time-consuming for the Osberns as it would be for us. From our point of view, it was the best we could possibly hope for, except in this one matter: under no circumstances would I be allowed to appear as anything but a man. The stipulation was made that I could live in the house, in our designated area, provided that I did not keep any of my female garments, on the logic that my desire to assume them again might be constantly tested by their presence.

Thrips, Reliance, and Augustus drew up legal documents to this effect, which I was to sign. There were detailed appendices in the "agreement" outlining what kind of clothes I should be allowed to wear, how they might be cut, of which material, how worn, and what forfeits any deviation might incur. My quarters were searched, and all offending items removed.

I accepted this offer on my mother's behalf. I doubted whether we could survive the real world. Our bedrooms were moved next to the Octagonal and we chose never again to dine with the family. Our meals were delivered to the library, where we ate with Hood. He had wearied, too, and I ladled his soup rather than the other way around. Certain of our most precious possessions had moved upstairs with us, but we were allowed nothing of any great value. We had our books.

One evening — a Saturday, I remember — a huge bonfire was built in the garden. I watched from the library window, having no idea of the occasion but mildly interested in the spectacle. A message arrived that Prudence requested my presence outside. I let life do what it would now, so I went.

On the front lawn, there was a large pile of bundles of what I took to be rags. Workers I didn't recognize started to remove the contents. I watched, ashen-faced, as my dresses, which had been stuffed into those bags like dishcloths, were thrown on the thorns, then pushed to the top of the heap with pitchforks. Reliance gave me a lit taper and led me to the bottom of the pyre. He held my arm and pushed it toward the heap of kindling and clothes until the flame caught. As the fire began to swirl, my clothes spat and rang and I pictured myself on top, the flames licking at my heels.

Guy set off fireworks in honor of his bride-to-be.

After the wedding, Guy and Prudence would officially take residence. I was quite as afraid of the actual ceremony as anything else. The nuptials were to be the largest event on the grounds of Love Hall since the fair that accompanied my birth. The village, in this instance, would not be invited, and it was clear that this was the first chance for the Osberns to flex their collective muscle while others looked on in envy and admiration. I tried to imagine any way that I could avoid it.

I busied myself with helping my mother work on the ballads. This retrenchment to the Octagonal brought out the animal in me, and I began to derive a perverse pleasure in our seclusion. I had always liked to sniff around in small spaces, my back covered, and I felt at home in our upstairs den. Often I sat at my mother's feet as we sorted the broadsheets together and pasted them into folios. She sometimes sang them to me, and though I was worn out and almost always itching within my clothes, I felt we could perhaps survive.

I could get lost in the ballads and I escaped into their rhymes. They took me to another world of romance, coincidence, everlasting love, and fate, a world where my father was still alive to me: a much better world than ours. I loved the twins reunited, the hags transformed to beauties, the birds that sang warnings. And the female rambling sailors — those bold women who went off to sea dressed in their usurped masculine attire to save their lovesick lads. We found our pleasures where we might, and the work on these poems would never be done. For my mother, it was a substitute for Mary. We never spoke of her these days.

What was happening beneath us now? We hardly knew. One morning Hood brought us the wedding invitation. I couldn't bring myself to pick it up, and it sat there on the table in its mauve and gilt-edged envelope, throbbing with hubris. I knew that I could not be present, that it would be too shameful. I would not go.

It was then that I decided to change everything. I saw myself traveling in an ever descending spiral, the family allowing us nothing outside the library, then only half of the library, and then nothing more than the desk, until we were finally forced to live on a speck of dust before vanishing into history. In a flash, I saw that only death would deliver me from their torment. I would kill myself, or die trying. I would go far away. If Esmond could do it, why couldn't I, driven as I was by a far greater despair? I would search for a corner where I would shelter. And if I could find none, then I would know that I had not been made for this world, that I was as unsuited for it as they said, and

I would act accordingly. The sentence begins without our consent, but we can end it when we like.

If I had any doubt, the homecoming of Stephen and Sarah Hamilton rid me of it. They were returning to help pack up the Lodge and take care of some other business for their father. Though it would be a sad day, it was a day I had looked forward to, and this in itself was a treat. Yet the prospect of the reunion began to fill me with dread. I didn't want them to see any of the family, to witness me in my present state as a man, or worse, as the sort of man I had become. In these circumstances, the very word *homecoming* mocked me. My mother tried to offer me hope, for she knew very well that I was more worried than happy about it.

I put on my brave face and dressed. It reminded me of when I was made up to say good-bye to my father, but this time I was even more imperfect. My jacket, my only presentable jacket, had a large stain on the right breast, and when I saw it, I realized how far I had fallen. I had gone to seed since I had last seen them, turned to drink to drown myself.

We received them in the library. This gave our meeting a semblance of normality, but it pained me to think that they would have had to walk through the Long Gallery, where all the pictures were out of place, some of them removed entirely. The terrible portrait of the Rakeleighs was now placed centrally in the Baron's Hall: there could be no more pointed symbol of our degradation.

And then they were there, led by their father, who smiled as carefully as he could while he beckoned them through. It was the smile of a nurse who ushers visitors into the room of her dying patient.

The first look would decide everything, and the way they stared was enough to make me want to leave Love Hall, my self, forever. There I stood, a stranger before them. They held my gaze for a second, trying desperately to find a trace of me in my face, my male disguise, and then immediately looked down to the floor. Stephen was the first to raise his eyes. He was smiling, but it was politeness I saw. I didn't recognize it in him and I would have preferred that he laugh at me, *with* me at me. I knew what I looked like. I didn't need them to lie to me. For Sarah the initial shock had subsided, but now she could barely look at all. Was she remembering what had gone on between us, as I was, how she had called down the corridor after me that everything was fine? But it hadn't been, and now she knew how grim it was.

"Hello, Rose." Stephen was the first to speak. No one had called me Rose so casually in a long time, and this was a small relief. He had taken off his cap and was squeezing it nervously in his hand, wringing it like a sponge. In his looks he hadn't changed, but there was a new worldliness about him. He wouldn't be running down so many corridors, breaking so many things, making up so many stories. His voice was deeper and more serious. Perhaps this was the effect an education had. I had already made up my mind.

"Hello, Stephen. Hello, Sarah. We very much miss you at Love Hall." The voice that emerged was strange even to me. It was the deeper voice that I had been cultivating, the one voice upon which I could depend for some consistency. It was lower than it would have normally been in a man of my age, and I produced it, with some effort and concentration, from deep in my throat. But my voice could not have seemed stranger than the words it sounded. I spoke formally, as if translating from a foreign tongue. I wanted to reach out to them, to hug them. Perhaps they wanted to do the same, or perhaps they feared it. I couldn't. My clothes, my voice, my words, my lethargy — all forbade me.

Mother asked about their schools.

"Very hard on us. It's not like here. Not as much fun." Stephen was trying to tell me one thing with his words, but his eyes and manner said something else altogether.

"And, our dear Sarah, how are you?" asked Mother.

Sarah kept her head bowed, and I heard her crying.

"It's all right," said Stephen. "It's difficult for her. Sarah's very happy to be back home, but it's all so changed."

I didn't know what to say. All I could think of were the games we had played, Lord Ose, my dream of the river, kissing Sarah in bed, the cricket interlude, and the seesaw. I was lost in the past. I looked in a mirror and caught a glimpse of myself: a sick, down-at-heel dandy before a duel he was sure to lose.

"Since my father died . . . ," I started, but I couldn't continue. When Sarah heard me refer to his death, she looked at me. Her eyes were pools of tears, which streaked her face, reflecting in the creases of her skin. I must have been swimming in front of her. I was lost in her eyes and their tears. I wanted to drown in them. I didn't know what to do anymore. I stuttered.

"Since his death, we . . . and with my . . ." I looked down at my clothes, my coffin, and could say no more. Stephen and Sarah knew exactly what I couldn't say, and she leaned over to him and cried into his shoulder. Stephen drew her tactfully into his embrace.

"We had better be getting on with our work for Father," he added.

"Perhaps so," I said. It was the most ridiculous thing that I had ever said in my life.

"You will have other times to spend together," said my mother as Hamilton opened the door. "We'll all have to get used to the way things are now, and you'll know where to find us, hard at our work."

They left, and hope with them. I stood stiffly, unable to move. My mother took me by the hand. I could feel by her touch that she knew words were useless.

"Come back to the collection, Rose. There's so much left to be done."

And I saw nothing more of them that day. I was a stranger to them now, and nothing could change that. I certainly didn't have the imagination to change it myself. My sex was brutally clear to me, and that clarity had been the death of the world I had loved. In return, I would be its murderer.

I had made my decision. Eternity? It didn't exist.

I was leaving Love Hall.

Tonight.

4

Land of Dreams

1

SUNDAY AFTERNOON

"Dolores."

At last! This morning, for the first time since his arrival, our guest spoke. I've heard him murmur, but today he spoke quite clearly, though he is still not yet fully conscious. We then managed something that resembled a conversation, which, though rather nonsensical, was as intriguing as I could have possibly hoped.

In honor of this new project, I have begun a fresh writing book and shall record as much of what he says as possible. This was a gift from that dull overattentive German scholar (now gone, thank heavens), who was forty-five if he was a day, almost as old as Father! The inscription makes me shudder: "To Frances, my Helen, from her devoted Werner." Thank *you,* Herr Volz.

I shan't tell anyone else what our guest has said, because so far it's been gibberish. But there is another reason: it's nobody's business but mine (and his). He's no longer a new arrival. For everyone else, interest has waned as his health has slowly improved. Doctor Bezoglu comes to monitor progress once a day, not *even* once a day anymore, and my father, whose time is completely consumed by the gray men of the British Antiquities Commission at the moment, gets most of his information from Zog. Mother never really liked to come up here unless she had to, and besides, her days are currently spent preparing scones, fig preserve, and clotted cream so that the British Antiquities Commission can pretend that they have not left their Sussex gardens. Zog's nurse comes to bathe the patient and never says a word (except if I ask her a question, when she says, without fail, "I'm not doctor!"). Therefore, it will just be me, recording my observations in you, journal, perhaps with some help from the books that he had with him on arrival, from which I read aloud in the hope that something will sound familiar.

This morning's conversation: the mystery deepens.

What is your name?

Catherine Thornton.

No, I'm Frances Cooper. *Your* name.

My name is Catherine Thornton.

Catherine?

Thornton.

But you're . . .

I'm Catherine Thornton.

Where do you come from?

{Inaudible.}

London? Do you come from London?

London. The Strand.

How did you get here?

Dover. French Landing. Paris. Brindisi. Patras.

Why do you say you're called Catherine?

{Silence.}

What are you doing here? Are you feeling better?

He didn't answer, as though he suddenly couldn't understand what I was saying. He moved his head upward with a sudden jerk, opened his eyes wide for a moment — the first time I had seen them: luminous green — and put his arms in front of his face as if in anticipation of a blow. Then he slumped back, asleep.

When he was found, his hair had been hacked short (as though he had cut it himself without a mirror) and he was in a pretty bad state. He still looks exhausted, and his face has some of the yellow left from old bruises. His right arm and both wrists, which seemed to have been rubbed raw by rope, are healing, too, although he often wraps his hands around them. The rest of the time he keeps them away from view under the covers. He speaks English, of course, which is why he was brought to us.

I want to see his eyes again.

Monday morning

Catherine?

Catherine?

Is that your name?

Frances. I'm Frances.

I'm Frances. Your name is Catherine, isn't it?

Catherine? Yes.

Why did you come from England, Catherine?

Come from England?

Yes. Why did you leave London? Why are you here?

My father swore to me that he would kill the one I loved.

Your father? Why? Whom did you love?

Clerk William.

You were in love with a clerk?

My Willie.

You loved a man?

Who else would I love? My father said he would kill him if we continued our courtship to enjoy. He had tried to press before this brave and handsome boy.

To press him?

To sea. So I dressed up in a suit of men's clothes, from top to toe, with pumps on my feet and a staff in my hand, and I went to meet Willie as he walked down the Strand.

Why men's clothes?

So I could see Willie as he walked down the Strand.

In London.

We arranged to meet at Dover.

And?

On my way home my father saw me. He drew his sword and struck me.

Why?

He took me for Willie.

Why ever did he think you were Willie?

I don't know.

Did you look like him? Because of the clothes? It seems strange. . . .

It's not at all strange.

Interrupted! The doctor came in. I snapped my book shut so he couldn't see any of my transcription. Bezoglu told me (again!) that I shouldn't vex the patient in any way that might hinder a recovery. I wish that he would *mind his own business*. I told Zog that I had been reading out loud and that our guest had murmured in his sleep. He seemed pleased with this version of events.

I have always loved a mystery — I can't believe that one has finally landed in our home and that I can keep it all to myself! At last, after all those tiresome scholars and dull commissioners, something of note is happening in this house, and the best part is: I am the only one paying attention.

Wednesday afternoon

Catherine?
    Jane.
Jane? Why do you keep changing your name?
    My name is Jane.
Catherine's sister? Jane Thornton?
    Jane from Lincolnshire.
You said London.
    I never did.
Did you run away from your father?
    How do you know?
You told me.
    I was in love with . . .
Willie the sailor.
    Willie? Not Willie. Jack! My father pressed Jack.
To sea?
    With great disdain across the main.
And what did you do?
    I dressed myself in sailors' clothes and in a little while
    I went on board the ship, the Rose of Britain's Isle.
Was that the name of the ship?
    No, the ship was called the *Aphrodite*.
What was the Rose of Britain's Isle?
    That was what they called *me*.

He speaks very deliberately with a slight, genteel lisp. I try to turn backward in my book and read my own handwriting. I've managed to get most of it down. It is very easy to keep up with his words, but not his meaning, since he switches names and stories. Sometimes he enunciates the words syllable by syllable, some drawn out at great length, others clipped and short, as if the last letter of the current word were actually the first letter of the next: see above — he pronounced it "in a li-tall while I wen-ton board."

Sometimes a word like "dressed" becomes two syllables, "dress-ed," as though he's reciting a poem. Sometimes he imitates a different accent.

But didn't your father meet you when you were dressed up in a suit of men's clothes, from top to toe, with pumps on your feet and a staff in your hand?

I ran away on board the ship with Jack in a fair shirt of male.

Chain mail?

Man's array. I cut off my yellow hair. My curly locks. I dressed myself in velveteen and went to Egypt's docks.

You've been to Egypt? Is that how you came here?

Yes. The *Venus* she was wreck-ed near the banks of cruel Nargyle.

What happened to your father?

He died.

Died?

He gained a son but lost a daughter.

He became very agitated. His breathing quickened until I thought he might have an attack, so I put aside my book and dabbed a cool cloth against his brow. When he calmed, I changed my tack.

Have you been in the war?

The cannon's loud rattle and the blazing bullets fly.

Where?

India's burning sands. The siege of the city of Gaunt. The wars of Germany. The banks of the Nile where our troops was commanded. *Were* commanded.

Why did you come here?

I'd a mind to venture where the cannonballs do fly. I come because of the way things change, new coming from old. I am a noble lord of high degree. I sailed east, I sailed west, until I . . .

He falls asleep. Conversation occurs only when he chooses. Sometimes I call him by one of the names, to get his attention, but he is far away, dreaming a story. Perhaps the truth is scattered somewhere within all the stories, or perhaps it is nowhere near. He is an enigma, a blank slate, and he is in my house. Soon he will wake up. Zog says that his improvement gives us great hope — and of course I hope he mends as soon as possible. But then the mystery will be gone. Best to savor it. I shall try to get more out of him.

Thursday afternoon

Jane?

Rebecca.

Rebecca? Your name is . . .

Rebecca Young.

Why do you keep changing your name?

Why would I keep changing my name?

It doesn't matter, Rebecca.

Because it doesn't matter.

He smiles. A small joke? A reminder of something he once enjoyed?

Where are you from?

Gravesend.

You were in love with a sailor?

Yes.

Your father hated him and he was pressed to sea.

Yes.

You dressed as a sailor?

In jacket blue and white trousers, just like a sailor neat and tight, the female rambling sailor. I went to sea to mourn his life. My hands were hard with pitch and tar, though once were velvet soft.

He touches his callused hands, remembering a time when the skin wasn't so scarred. He traces around every finger and around the edge of each hand, as though the palms were too painful to touch.

What happened to your hands?
My pretty little fingers, they were so neat and small.
And your wrists?
You soon shall hear of the overthrow of the female rambling sailor.

He sleeps.

Later that evening

For the first time, the thread of our conversation survives an interruption: he answers to the name Rebecca.

Did you ever find him?
I caught up with him.
What did he say?
He asked if I needed help with my passage across the sea.
He didn't recognize you?
I was still dressed as a man! Coat, waistcoat, and breeches and sword by my side on my father's black gelding, a dragoon I did ride. How could he have known it was I?
Why didn't you tell him? Why didn't he recognize you?
I don't remember. It isn't expected. The *Bonaventure* sprung a leak in a storm and started to go down. Twenty-four escaped on a raft.

All men?

Yes.

Including you?

It was twenty-three men, and I with my impenetrable secret. We ran out of food, and the captain cast lots to see who would be eaten to save the rest.

And who was chosen?

I was chosen.

And who was chosen to slay you?

Him.

And what did you do?

It was then I revealed I was the silk merchant's daughter.

Did he recognize you then?

No, but I showed him a ring that was broken in two.

Then he recognized you?

He had the other half.

His eyes are closed. Is he awake? These are fairy stories of broken tokens and daring survivals, romances of women on the high seas and the love that drives them to desperate measures. Why is he telling them? I follow along. I try to get it all down.

He cries out, "A ship!" and points with urgency, as though he can see the hull approaching in the shadows on the wall.

There it is.

A ship, the *Adelaide,* came along, right before he had to make his fatal choice, and took us back to London. We were married.

And your father?

Forgave us. Forgave us before he died. Gave me back my inheritance, my full thirty-five thousand in silver, in bright guineas, in King William's crowns, my large

> estate in high degree, and took us both in his arms. He had hated the one, loved *me* but refused even to recognize him, but in the end took us both in his arms. I couldn't live without him, and Father knew it. Everything he did, he did out of kindness and love. "It is marri-ed this couple shall be," he said. And now they live happily together, Rebecca and her young sailor bold. I loved my father. He never intended to do us harm, but he didn't know how ill he was, and neither did I. He turned his head and never recovered. I never saw him quite the same again, in the doll's house or in the garden. He saw me and instantly fainted.

For the first time, he sits up. He opens his eyes again. They are tired and bloodshot, which only enhances that shocking lucid green. He closes them slowly and, as he does so, lies back on the bed, as if returning to his grave.

I am now in my bedroom, alone, reading from the beginning. I have no idea what I am being told, why he babbles these stories of disguise on the high seas, but I am trying to piece the puzzle together and I am impatient for him to speak further. I dare not theorize overly in these pages, because of the possibility of their discovery, but I am beginning to have certain suspicions. I know that he is aware that I am by his bedside, but I can speak only when spoken to.

Friday afternoon

Suddenly, out of the blue, while I was reading to him from his Ovid, he spoke.

> I sail-ed east, I sail-ed west until I came to proud Turkey, where I was taken and put in chains until my life was quite weary.

Is that a song? "I sai-led east, I sai-led west."

The Turk he had one only daughter, the fairest that my eyes did ever see. She stole the keys to her father's prison and swore that she would let me go free.

Who are you?

I am Lord Bateman. Are you she? The Turk's daughter?

Yes.

Will you set me free?

Yes. [It would have been uncaring to answer no.]

Are you Susan Pye? Isbel?

Frances.

I thought Isbel.

Franny, if you like.

I was misinformed. So be it, Isbel. Before seven years we shall marry as a sign of my gratitude for your releasing me. Stephen and Sarah acted out the story of Lord Bateman, with Sarah playing two parts, the first as you and the second as my new wife at home. Stephen played the Turk and the porter. Lord Ose played Lord Bateman.

I thought that you were Bateman.

Yes. Me. Always.

So you are Lord Ose?

Leslie.

And you have a wife at home?

Bateman does. I have no wife, no mother, no father, not even a dog to my name. Nothing. By the time you arrive from the heathen Saracens in seven years, I shall be getting married that very day. But when you come to England, I shall send my intended home with a carriage and three, and prepare another wedding for thee and me, with both our hearts so full of glee and I shall roam no more to foreign countries, now that Frances has crossed the sea. There's gold for her pains.

He reaches out his hand to me, and I take it. He continues speaking, and I try to transcribe with the book wedged between my two legs as steadily as I can manage.

> I sing of the way things change, new coming from old. I had to leave. I opened the gate. It creaked in the dark. My leather bag held all my possessions. Books, some clothes, and jewelry, nothing else. I wasn't prepared for the world, and the world wasn't prepared for me. I slept on the brine and storm-tossed waves, on the deck and in the hold, among the overgrown ruins, rough in caves, in squalor and in splendor, and now I must awake. I thought I knew the end of the story. I thought it had ended, but now it seems . . . unless we are . . .

He falls asleep. The bag sits in the corner of the room. My father inspected it and found much less than our enigma claims to have brought. No jewelry. No clothes. Books. And a once grand, now very dirty, dress.

Saturday morning

The first time he has answered me when I have said anything more than a name.

When did they find out about you?

> Ah! The scene of revelation. There are some things a woman cannot conceal for many months.

A child?

> I gave myself away. The truth must work itself out in the end. A disguise will last only so long, till time melts the mask. The captain of the ship once said to me that my cherry cheeks and ruby lips had so enchanted him that he wished I were a maid. My cheeks appeared like roses, and my hair was black as jet.

What did you do?

I told him to hold his tongue, the other sailors would hear him, but he didn't listen and I was betrayed by my sailor boy, who put me in the hold. I thought that the captain would rescue me before they threw me overboard, that he would say that never shall be, for if you drown that fair young maid, then hanged you shall be.

But?

He kept me in the hold. At first only for him, but then for everyone. And I stayed all in my sailors' clothes. I was the *fille de joie,* the fairy's gift. I wasn't in chains or tied up in any way that I could be released, even by you, Isbel. There was a tree in the ship and they pinned me to it. I cried full sore. I couldn't leave the hold, and the stench smothered me like a blanket. I felt the razor-sharp pins on their chins cut me in pricks. I bled and the room became darker and lighter and then darker and lighter. I wrote on the wall. I counted days. I sang songs to myself.

What songs did you sing?

The story of my life. How I was born and brought up.

Can you sing me that song?

I am singing it.

I reached out. Though he initially shrank from me, I kept my hand firmly on his shoulder. After a while, I felt his body yield and I laid another hand on him. I took his head and shoulders into my arms, moving him as slowly as I could, and felt him crying into my shoulder. As he lay in my embrace, he recited the following verse: "I was a maiden on your ship, but a man I am on shore / Adieu, adieu, Captain, forever more."

Do you remember before you went traveling?

Nothing. No. I remember dressing up. I remember nothing.

Stephen and Sarah?

{Silence.}

Where else were you?

Paris: I had been to a recital.

Did you know the songs?

I didn't know them or understand them. I was the guest of a tall and chivalrous Frenchman who escorted me. He bade me adieu and bowed. I was walking the street at night, everything a haze through my veil. A gang stood on the street corner, a group of brigands rehearsing their lines for the light opera. A knife glinted beneath the painted moon. I couldn't have been less frightened. On another night, I might have crossed the road to avoid them, but I had become less scared of the real world as I had ceased to be a part of it. I walked straight toward them, drawing attention to myself, and as I did so, they began to aim remarks at me. They kept to the script, but I was ready to improvise. Where was the risk? The scenery might disappear into the flies at any moment. The sailors of the chorus eyed me. One made an obscene gesture with his tongue. They could tell I was a girl. A lady. I loved to have people admire my clothes and wonder about the pleasures beneath. I loved to show them the truth about themselves. I kept walking toward them and I couldn't help smiling at them. Offense and attraction in equal measure. As the pain became concentrated, the apparitions became more substantial. But there was no fear. What had I to be afraid of? Death? So, afterwards, they took my money and left me by the side of the canal, sticky.

London?

No. Italy. It became impossible for me to travel in my real clothes, so I took to disguise. It was perpetual day aboard the ship, and I slept on the deck. A young woman talked to me with her companion, her mother, her schoolteacher, I don't remember. She read Ovid aloud and called me Leslie.

Leslie?

Yes? Then there was the small matter of the proposal of the prince of Great Parma.

Did you accept?

No. "A maiden of England never will be the wench of a foreign monarch," quoth she. My precise words. Besides, he was shortsighted and somewhat stupid. My father would have me marry only for love.

But Willie and Jack?

Willie? Jack?

He sleeps. It is like a conversation with a sleeptalker. It draws me in. I don't want it to end, and yet I hope for his recovery. I feel that I am getting nearer to the truth.

Unfortunately, my father now knows that I have been talking to our guest, our patient, although I have not divulged anything about this record.

Sunday afternoon

Women dress up in men's clothes?

Yes.

And no one can ever tell.

It's very difficult. It was little they know that a soldier's coat conceals so fair a maid.

Like Shakespeare.

Him, too?

Didn't Olivia fall in love with Caesario, who was truly Viola? Then she finally married Sebastian, Viola's brother.

{Silence.}

We found a woman's dress among your belongings.

{Silence.}

What did the other sailors think of the women who were dressed as sailors?

They couldn't tell.

Yes, but when they suggested it so you could go to sea with them.

Well, they thought that our pretty little fingers were too neat and small the cable ropes to haul, but my pretty little fingers weren't too neat and small. In the army, you could be a female drummer, because though your waist was long and slender, the fact that your fingers were neat and small, all for to beat upon the drum, you might soon exceed all. You could be anything you wanted then, the best at everything. People were more generous.

Do men ever dress up as women?

Very rarely.

Why rarely? Why would they?

I think they do it to make you laugh like the pantomimes. Not to look real. Brown Robin dressed up in a dainty green gown, in hose of the softest silk, his shoon o' the cordwain fine.

His shoon?

O' the cordwain fine. It's a material, I suppose.

Did they know he was a man?

The king said, "This is a Mrs. Manly, a sturdy dame." Silly old fool. He didn't know.

Why would men do that?

Concealment.

Why do you think?

And then he spoke very quickly. It was a recitation of something he had memorized.

> Boys havingbeenconcealed in female dresses for some political or family occasions, and so continued under that acceptation, 'til either matters came to such a crisis as rendered their situation lessdangerous, or till beards or other signs of virility have occasionedadeclaration of their true sex and a change of habit.

I had to struggle to make sense of it all, so I tried to get him to say it again, and finally succeeded. When he answered, he spoke even more rapidly than the time before.

What about their mother?

> Mothers always know. They look at you a certain way. They say something in a secret place so that you know that they know. Mothers know. Oh, yes. But who knows Mother? Do you know Mother? That's the question.

And other women?

> Sometimes . . . Once upon a tide, the captain's lady came on board and she tried to caress and kiss me because she liked my boyish eye. But her husband found out my secret first.

What happened?

> I thought that the captain would come and rescue me and say that never shall be, for if you drown that fair young maid, then hanged you shall be. She'll stay all in sailor's clothes.

I looked back in my book and saw that he had quoted himself word for word. And I knew where it was leading, so I told him to sleep. From time to time, he gets caught at the start of a story and will tell it all over till the end, unless I stop him. I told him I would set him free, like the Turk's daughter.

I asked my father about Bateman, and surprisingly (since it is neither fragment of amphora nor ruined column — sometimes I forget he understands anything else . . .), he knew who he was: a character from one of what he calls the *old songs,* though he called him Young Bekie — Father had a very "singing" aunt who raised him on these songs, the secret currency of all the people, she said, rich or poor. The ballad tells the story of Gilbert Beket (the father of St. Thomas), who went to the Holy Land and was taken prisoner by Saracens, whereby the daughter of his captor, Prince Admiraud, fell in love with him and, after helping his escape, followed him back to England.

This makes me Admiraud's daughter! Which is a little better than being Franny, daughter of Owen Cooper, I think. Perhaps Bateman was in jail here. Perhaps our stranger is a descendant.

Even in his daze, this Leslie toys with me. His tales make me imagine that the truth will be romantic — but doubtless the revelation will be in some way a disappointment. After all, how can those men not have seen through their true loves' disguises? Impossible. They must have been humoring them all along, as, perhaps, I am being humored. It is I that am vexed, though I do adore his manner, his gentle voice, his eyes of jade.

Sunday evening

Father wanted to know why I asked about Bateman. I had to tell him — why was I born into the family in which it is hardest to tell lies? We are all hopelessly honest. Under normal circumstances, my interest in his field — the digging, the excavation, the antique bric-a-brac — is nil, and his suspicions were bound to be raised when I started asking about the Saracens. So he kept on at me until I couldn't evade him any longer.

When I told him that our mysterious guest had told me about the song, he demanded that I relate what was said. I did so but omitted to mention this book, an omission for which I feel entirely justified: it is not affecting his recovery, might even be helping him, and it is our secret that I shall reveal to him only when he is recovered. I tried to explain that I believe I have been coaxing him slowly back to reality, but I couldn't convince Father without divulging all the information I have already collected. I did tell him that our guest seemed to know where he was and had intended to travel here. And that he thought of me as the jailer's daughter. Father laughed, of course: "You have the key, Frances, as always — you are the turnkey!" We both laughed, but it is our guest who holds the key, not I.

Though Father wasn't exactly angry, his revenge was swift. He said that he had something of great importance to tell me about our guest and that he would withhold the information till I stopped pestering the poor boy. I should be watching his recovery silently, reading to him possibly, but not drawing him into conversation. The patient is not a pet, said Father predictably, which made me want to kick him in the shin. But Father knows something that I do not, and I shall have to play along to find out what is so very interesting. But I am convinced that the mystery is revealing itself to me.

I have one more day or night at the most, as I have been advised to spend more time downstairs. One of the gray men needs a croquet partner. And there is shortly arriving a new visitor who needs demonstration of the "eternal acoustic perfection" — I have to stick to Father's script — of the theater. Extremely irritating! I would rather stay here with my green-eyed enigma.

I have decided. My private inquiry will stop for two days while I discover what my father presently refuses to tell me.

2

"Come all of you bold fellows and drink success to trade
And likewise to the cabin boy who was neither man nor maid
And if the wars should rise again, us sailors to destroy
Here's hoping for a lot more like the handsome cabin boy."

I WOKE UP SINGING, my mind full of that handsome cabin boy. I wasn't singing aloud, but I could clearly hear my voice. My head ached terribly.

Where was I? I didn't yet want to open my eyes. The pillow rustled at each slight movement, as if filled with birdseed — or was the rattle in my head? The bedclothes were fresh and new. Possibly a hospital. And the smell was not quite like anything I had ever known: a cup of warm flowery tea? Citrus and dog's hair? I had woken into someone else's dream.

I opened my eyes slightly, feeling dull pain around the muscles of my lids. There was a bedside table, but the strain of refocusing to make sense of this still life made my head pound harder. What emerged from the blur were two books, which looked familiar, and a glass of water, which I wished I could consider getting near my mouth. A ceiling fan swayed above me in the breeze, creaking warily.

A window must be open somewhere beyond the foot of the bed, but I didn't dare look.

I closed my eyes again and took a brief inventory of myself. I tried to remember where I had been, to guess where I might be, but my faculties ached as badly as my limbs and groaned as I tried to exercise them. I remembered bits and pieces. I had been traveling. There were snatches, snatches of snatches, but no thread. And still that silly old song was plaguing me, making my head pound with the sheer brutality of the *thought* of singing. The handsome cabin boy could go to the devil.

Disparate memories started to claw themselves toward me from the desert of my mind. I only glimpsed them at first, as they crawled along the sands, desperate for water, but gradually they hauled themselves up and over the ridge: faces, names, sounds, sighs. Vill'Acqua. Little Jesus. "I do not pretend to be anything other than what I am." Handsome Henry, who thought I had such beautiful eyes. A rat running into the sewer by the canal. The captain's wife. I didn't know who they were, but they knew me.

I heard a soft cough and realized I wasn't alone. I opened my eyes and managed to angle a look toward the end of the bed, where a young woman sat on a wicker chair. She was engrossed in a book, unaware that I was awake, so I studied her, hoping to arm myself with some information about where I was, to prepare myself as best I could. She was about my own age, or a little older, and dark haired. Her skin, an earthy nutmeg, was that of a healthy native accustomed to the local sun — we were far away from England, that much was obvious. The air was heavier, spicier, and the light shimmered on the left of her face. I could see it shine through the sun-bleached down at the corners of her mouth. She had been sitting with me for some time. How long?

I liked my nurse — her eyes, the shape of her mouth, her extravagant hair, her casual lack of uniform. She turned the page of a small leather-bound book. My book.

My Ovid! I gasped and gave myself away. She looked up with surprise and smiled at me as she hushed me and put a cold compress to my forehead. She was about to speak but then, perhaps remembering that I would not understand her language, turned and left the room. I heard her call down the corridor.

"Father! Father!"

English? We weren't in England. But my nurse sounded English, even though she looked so healthily wherever-we-were-ish. In her absence, I took the opportunity to look around my infirmary. The room was clean and simple: demonstrably foreign. It was not part of a hospital at all, but a cozy residential bedroom — well organized, square, and not much bigger than some beds I had known. Everything within was functional, painted plainly or not at all. The only decorative detail was the mazy pattern of the rug.

A calendar hung on the plain white wall. The days were ticked off one by one, and the page was annexed by these struck-out squares, some filled with handwritten comments. The proof of time's passing soothed me — and at the end of those crosses, there was a solid block of empty squares. The first of those empty spaces was today — on which I was alive.

To the right of the only door hung one precise set of men's clothes, cleaned, pressed, and placed as though ready to be lifted onto their owner, like a knight's suit of armor. There were fresh flowers on the pale dresser. I imagined there had been flowers there every day in anticipation of the morning when I would finally wake and be able to appreciate them. Above them was a mirror, which I longed to look into. I hadn't yet caught a glimpse of what the people there could clearly see. Perhaps there was time before she returned.

As I slowly raised myself, the bright light that streamed through the gap between the curtains caught my eye. Feeling out of practice with every movement, I stumbled toward the curtains and pulled them.

My mouth fell open in amazement. All I could see was blue. Blue sky. Blue sea. The sun reflected in the crests of tiny waves that dazzled the surface like diamonds, though the water appeared entirely smooth and undisturbed. Blue. All shades of blue, unpaintably similar shades. Sapphire. Indigo. Cerulean. Azure. Turquoise. And so many other types of blue I could never identify. So much blue, it had ceased to be blue at all and had became green and purple. And in the sea, boats with their single masts, sunning themselves like lazy turtles. I squinted, shaded my eyes, and tried to separate objects from glare. I could vaguely make out the hulk of an island in the distance and another farther away, a hazy mirage on the horizon: to the left of my view, the remains of a castle with a round tower surrounded by ruined green walls.

I thought I heard returning footsteps and hurried, as best I could, back into bed, hoping to hide behind my illness for as long as was useful. The mirror would have to wait. I arranged myself in a good facsimile of infirmity, which took little imagination, for every limb complained about its removal from bed.

Other footsteps followed. She came in first and fussed over me, her left breast by my face, but said nothing. She looked for the compress she had just placed on my forehead. Finding it gone, she searched to see if she had tucked it in with me. At a loss, she hurriedly surveyed the room, saw it on the windowsill — evidence of my little sortie — and narrowed her eyes in a way that implied a friendship between us that could not be. She turned to face two older men who had now entered, and her dark hair fell in curls over my face. She straightened herself with a smile.

One man was English, the other not. They congratulated both of us, and each other, upon my improved health. They then considered me with the inquiring eyes and hunched shoulders of the deeply concerned. The older of the two put out his hand to my nurse and she took it. He pulled her in toward him: she was his daughter. I sat up slightly, ready to receive them, determined to repay her confidence in me.

My mind was active. I would tell them that my name was Leslie. I hadn't yet decided whether I would be Lord, or perhaps Sir, or even

Mister, Leslie and whether my surname should be Ose or the less formal Door, or whether I should, in fact, forgo the cryptogram entirely, for all the use it had been, and be Leslie Bennett or Bateman. The important thing was that my name be masculine. After that, the rest would fall into place. But was Leslie masculine enough? I felt considerably more alert and trusted my acting. Just as I readied myself for introductions, the girl pulled the two men back and stood in front of me, as if she were on inspection.

"Leslie?" she asked, and her mouth broke into a lovely wide smile of welcome. I gulped and suddenly parched. She was doing all my work for me. She had smoothed my sheets, fluffed my pillows, tucked me in, fed me with a spoon, read my mind, and given me my name. I tried to speak, but nothing emerged — just a dead rasp of air and a rattle at my throat. There was nothing to swallow, let alone help me swallow. She reached for a glass of water and put it to my mouth. I gulped and swallowed what I hadn't dribbled. She mopped up the rest.

"No," I said, shaking my head.

"*Lord* Leslie?" asked the Englishman, enunciating a little more precisely in case I were deaf. He was dressed in an inappropriately warm tweed suit and a winged collar upon which perched an elegantly shabby bow tie. His doleful, ruddy face seemed a quotation marked by his bushy muttonchops, and his hands were knotted like a tree trunk. His concern was evident, and his relief at my recovery sincere. I was busy making observations but forgetting to answer.

"Lord Leslie, yes. Leslie, yes." I swallowed again with more success.

"Sir, I have the honor of being the doctor for the English-speaking families," said the darker-skinned man, who had begun to bang out a pipe in the palm of his left hand. He spoke the kind of perfect English that automatically identifies the speaker as foreign. "You have been extremely ill, for a little while we feared fatally. Might I examine you?"

I instinctively pulled the sheets up around my neck, but then remembered myself. I could be examined. Of course I could. As it transpired, his only desires were to take my temperature and survey my tongue and the contents of my left ear. He then massaged the contours of the top of my head and the back of my neck.

"Very satisfactory," he said. "How do you feel, sir?"

How did I feel?

I ached. I felt lucky to be alive. No. I *was* lucky to be alive, but I felt unlucky, unlucky and unloved, lost and muddled, lonely and afraid. I didn't know where I was. I felt as though I had slept in a nightmare and woken into a dream. I felt that no matter how many times I opened my eyes, I would never properly wake. I felt that my life was starting now from nothing, that I had just been wrenched from the womb, smacked into tears, that I would be born over and over and over until I did things right, and that I was doomed to this cycle forever. I felt that secrets were being kept from me and that I had to leave. Tears began to well inside me.

"I feel fine, thank you," was what I said, however. This elicited a knowing look, a smile and then, most unexpectedly, a polite round of applause. The look in the father's eyes said that he knew good breeding when he saw it.

He slowly explained that I had been found, exhausted and half dead, in a cave by two peasant goatherds. They heard me murmuring in what they took to be English and so brought me to the preeminent local English family. The Coopers welcomed me as their guest, but invited me, as their friend, to stay as long as I needed.

They had discovered my name written in the front of my copy of *Metamorphoses*. The dark-haired daughter handed me the book and showed me the frontispiece, which (the front cover long gone) had clung to the binding with considerable tenacity. I read the following: "Dolores Loveall" in fine calligraphy at the top of the page, and then, in my own childhood writing, "Rose Old," the *e* backward, making my once-upon-a-time name look like Rosa. Beneath that was written in a more adult but spidery, nervous hand, "Lord Leslie de l'Orso."

Me, they had supposed. Me, I remembered and confirmed. No more of the effete characters from the olden days. I had chosen something a good deal more practical for what we are pleased to call the real world. Leslie de l'Orso. I could take or leave de l'Orso, but Leslie, as I lived and breathed. Les!

"And may we call you Leslie, sir?"

I nodded.

"My daughter also heard you say the name in your sleep while she sat with you. I reprimanded her for trying to communicate, but I believe that she did well. Frances has been a most vigilant nurse."

"Thank you," I mouthed to Frances. I realized that I had known this was her name. Either that or . . . Susan?

"One brief question, sir," said the doctor. "Were you traveling alone?"

"Yes."

"*Quite* alone?"

I nodded. From the girl's glance away, I could tell that this had deepened rather than solved a mystery. Of course I had been traveling alone. Who else?

"We are delighted that you are so improved," said Frances. "And now we shall leave you to rest."

"Where am I?" I asked, trying not to sound as desperate as I felt, though my voice had not yet quite recovered enough to express any of the wider emotions.

"You don't know? In good time, sir, in good time, but now is the moment to rest," said the father, but just before he closed the door behind him, he said: "You are in the Land of Dreams."

"Where?"

"The Land of Dreams."

Wherever we were, clearly nothing was very pressing. Just before the door closed, however, Dark Hair popped her head around the corner.

"Father's being silly. Homer called it the Land of Dreams. You are in Bodrum."

"Where?"

"In Turkey." Then she was gone.

Bodrum. The Levant. Anatolia. Caria. Lycia. Turkey.

Somehow I had arrived.

At first, they left me alone, mindful of my need for absolute rest. They couldn't have been more considerate, but I was as eager for their story as they were for mine, and I soon grew strong enough to become a little bored. Frances hovered with the greatest attention, and I started to will her to my room so we could talk. I knew that she would be my guide, my oracle, and so I eagerly awaited her visits. I saw in her smile that she was desperate to know more about her stranger, and I wanted to use that curiosity to my own ends.

I now understood what had happened. The truth was: even in my depleted, deluded, and useless state, I had finished my journey. I could now let go the slender yarn that guided the way back, for I didn't need to remember the path. It was as if my body had collapsed only when it was certain I had arrived. The body knows what to do, even one as abused and confused as mine. I now knew what I had to do. And I intended to tell her as little as possible.

The Coopers were in the fifth year of a self-imposed exile from England. Owen, in the company of his wife, Emily, and their daughter, had moved to live with his brother-in-law, who had taken a lesser ambassadorial post in the Levant. Inspired by the possibility of the excavation of Troy, Cooper, a wandering scholar, had settled for a role in cataloging and guarding, on behalf of the British government, the archaeological wonders that surrounded ancient Halicarnassus in preparation for their triumphant journey to England. From what I could gather, however, he seemed as much involved in ensuring that what was there stayed where it was as in organizing its shipment.

"Turkey is money, Leslie. That's all it has ever meant to the politicians. King Midas of Gordion — the golden touch," he said. "And

I'm damned if all this is going back to England. I like the look of it where it is. In the field. Combe and his cormorants can come and sift the shards if they like, but they belong here."

Troy was too much in the public eye, whereas Bodrum and the surrounding area was his greatest interest, particularly the tomb of Mausolus. As he sat at my bedside, Owen told me the story of this Persian-born king who made Halicarnassus his capital and there shared the throne with his sister and wife, Artemisia (one of my Feminisian role models — I remembered her from my *Gallery of Heroick Women*). When her brother-lover died, Artemisia had his bones ground and dissolved into wine, which she drank as a symbol of their eternal love. Her fame was assured for three reasons: as architect of the Mausoleum; as architect of the word itself, which guaranteed her brother's immortality; and as a legendary naval commander.

After his brief history lesson, Cooper began to contextualize this building among the other ancient wonders, although he managed to get only as far as the Artemision at nearby Ephesus before he realized I was flagging. I had been distracted by thoughts of Love Hall. I wanted to tell him about our Mausoleum. I had always known that it was built upon the ancient model, and now I found myself no more than a short walk away from whatever remained of the original. But I said nothing. I had to be on my guard. It was important I remain a mystery: the less they knew about me, the better. I had to be invisible, to plan the perfect departure, and then to leave unremarkably.

As Cooper lectured — he always spoke as if from the podium — I listened with half an ear and continued my researches. There were five or six English families living in Bodrum, of whom Owen and Emily Cooper were undisputed king and queen, pashas of three tails. They owned the finest house and entertained the most illustrious guests, receiving English-speaking travelers from the four corners of the globe; some were on official business, others on their tours, making their way back in time to imagine the crumbling tombs in their former glory.

The Coopers were the consummate hosts: a talk by the patriarch, titled "When a Hero Could Rest in Peace: The Exhumation of the Classics," was followed by scenes from the Tragic Drama enacted by the family. This was accompanied by classical music on a raspy Turkish fiddle, which filled every corner of the house and quickly took its toll on all participants — including me, far away in my bedroom.

Exile from England had allowed the flamboyant Coopers to give their entrepreneurial and dramatic instincts free rein. Had they stayed in their home country, they would have maintained a more conservative respectability. Emily, for whom I pictured a dowdy parallel life in an English university town as wife to a fossil of an archaeologist, draped herself in only the brightest local garb, including a wide variety of turbans; she drank plentifully, entertained Lord and Lady M—— as if they were old family friends, and thrice woe'd it over the harsh caterwauling of the raki louder than anyone. Owen himself was no stranger to the fez. Opinion was loud and free, and croquet contested with surprising animosity. One of their guests was overheard to say disparagingly that the Cooper women suffered from a "touch of the native." Franny found this terribly amusing. She disliked these stuffy travelers who complained that the heat was too much and the insects too many.

Somehow I had arrived at the nearest to a British embassy that Bodrum could offer. The boar on my tray was from Alexandria and the grapes the very finest from Lesbos. There were orange trees as far as the eye could see and, at every meal, the sweetest and juiciest fruit. The Coopers picked olives and lemons from their own garden and made an excellent imitation of Cornish cream to accompany an old English recipe for milk scones. I had landed on my feet, on my back.

And so, as I recovered in my bed and despite my resolve, I became part of their life and they mine. I always welcomed Franny, who spoke to me with touching intimacy — she reminded me of something good in my past, and I trusted her. Mother Emily, when she was free of her hostly duties, and daughter — though they behaved more like sisters — read me plays together, sharing the parts between them and sometimes offering the book to me. I invariably demurred and enjoyed my entertainment, their audience of one. Unbeknownst to them, I was secretly making my way to the exit. I would have left already, but to slip off might arouse suspicion, and they wouldn't let me go until they were sure I was ready. I would convince them.

Franny instinctively knew what I wanted and when I wanted it — I was her project — whereas Emily came only when requested. I slowly gathered my strength, and in between regular history and archaeology tutorials from Cooper himself, for which purpose he had brought a map of the locale up to my room, Franny and I became friends.

She would sit on the side of my bed, inadvertently tightening the sheet around me, giving me that warm glow of childish security, and tell me about her old life in England, so different from mine. I knew that by telling me her story, she was angling for more information about me, but my techniques for evasion were many, and being solemnly ill was only the easiest. I had no wish to think of the past, so I encouraged her to tell me about the customs of her adopted country. Franny wasn't interested in her father's history, the wars and civilizations represented by his broken pots and stones. She loved the people she saw around her, their customs and crafts: the fertility dance and the kilim on the floor.

One afternoon Franny got down on her knees in the middle of the rug and showed me the hidden stories delicately woven within. I had lost myself in the seemingly random motifs, but the design was in no way haphazard, she explained; rather it was a woven history illustrating the heritage and feelings of the weavers themselves. These women were not allowed to speak their thoughts, so they wove their heart's desires like Arachne, changed into a spider for her defiance of Pallas. Franny showed me a woman with her hands on her hips, the wish for fertility, and the *nazarlik,* the evil eye, next to the sign of the hook, which worked as a talisman against it. The greater the imperfections, the closer to God.

Franny's style of instruction (in marked contrast to her father's) was familiar: it reminded me of my mother's, but I put this memory from me, as I had become used to doing. She lay back on the rug and I looked down at her, her face such a robust brown. It was impossible to believe this girl had once lived in England, where I had never seen anyone so healthy. Her hair swam wildly on the rug and she laughed as she finished her explanation. I knew that laugh. I hoped she'd have children.

Unexpectedly, she got up, her mind made up about something.

"Whose is this?" she asked as she started to pull the bottom drawer of the dresser. There was a certain lack of character about this chest, which had led me to assume it was empty, and I had never thought to look in it myself. The drawer was stubborn and she struggled to get it to move. It required that the two handles be pulled absolutely simultaneously and with precisely the same strength. Where I would have become irritated, she laughed at it and tried three times before she was successful. From the drawer, she pulled a freshly laundered and folded piece of clothing. She stood up and with a flick of her wrist let it drop down to the ground.

A long red dress.

"Whose is this?" she asked again. It reminded me of so many things that I didn't want to remember. I needed to keep my mind on course.

"Mine."

"Yours?" She laughed, as though it were impossible. I sat up in bed in a way that betrayed my surprise.

"My sister's. A gift for my sister."

"How old is your sister?" She didn't seem suspicious, simply curious.

"Your age." I put my hand out for the dress, but she was measuring it up to herself. She looked at me and held in her tummy.

"It was very dirty when we found it. We had to wash it twice, and then I sewed the hem. But it's a very beautiful dress. Is your sister Dolores?"

"Oh, no."

"Rose?"

"No."

"The Rose of Britain's Isle?"

I had only the vaguest idea what she was talking about.

"It's just that when you were talking . . . ," she continued before very ostentatiously correcting herself. She was telling me something. "I mean . . . they're the names in your book, above where you wrote your own name."

My Ovid was lying next to my *Aeneid*. I was sure a book was missing, and I started to pick at the side of my right thumbnail with my front teeth. At some point this had become a nervous habit. I bit my nails to clear up the mess I had made the previous time I bit them, a shambles that my attempts to remedy made only worse. I tried to bite the cuticles so that they were smoother, but I only ended up biting too low so that the ends of my fingers bled and stung as badly as if lemon juice had been squeezed onto them. It solved nothing, but I couldn't stop.

"The book's very old," I said. "I don't know those people."

"What is your sister's name? Not Rose?"

I didn't want to lie and I didn't want to tell the truth. I wanted only to be well enough, in their eyes, that I might leave. I knew exactly where I was going and what I was doing, but I liked these people and didn't want to implicate them. *Let me go, Franny,* I thought to myself. *Stop trying to hold on to me. Let me slip away tonight. Tomorrow.*

An overly large piece of skin tore from the side of my thumb — probably only the size of the tiniest splinter, but it felt much larger, like a sizable bite from an apple — and I tasted blood in my mouth. I pulled my thumb away and wrapped a corner of the sheet around it tightly to stop the bleeding.

"Franny, would you like the dress? You'd look so pretty in it."

"But your sister!" She was genuinely shocked.

"She doesn't know." I tightened my tourniquet. "I won't see her for a long time, not until I get back to England, and I'll buy her another dress before then. If you want the truth, I won it. At cards. I'd like to give it to you for all your kindness."

"Thank you, but you're not leaving?"

"I have to leave soon . . . now that I am better."

"Not *too* soon?" She held the dress tightly in her left hand.

"Soon. As soon as I can."

"But you're not better yet. You can't leave until you're *much* better. Zog won't hear of it. I won't let you. And," she added, "Father has a surprise for you."

"I hate surprises." I had spoken too sharply. "The greatest surprise is when there is no surprise at all. Try the dress on, Franny." She gave me a nod of excitement and started to trip out of the room. Then she thought better of it.

"Turn around," she said, and I did.

A surprise.

The questions were beginning again, as they always did, and I had no answers. I would only create more questions. If I stayed, my one option was to tell the truth, and that would cause more trouble than it was worth. Oh, Franny.

Although I was already bleeding elsewhere, I started to peel back the skin at the base of my left thumb. I wanted to flay myself very slowly, finger by finger, get rid of my skin by eating myself like Erysichthon, who cut down Ceres' oak in the forest and was damned by Hunger. He ate his body bit by bit to fill himself. I would do it to empty myself, to disappear.

Franny, who had more shape than I, was struggling into the dress behind me. She sang to herself softly and then started giggling. I had to either tell the Coopers the truth or leave as soon as possible. And was the truth really an option? What was the truth? The truth that I knew was too shameful. Why remind myself of it? Why embarrass them?

I had tried, as best I could, to forget the people who had said they loved me, and I had been able to do so only by replacing their memory with hatred for them and their crimes. Time is no healer. It scabs the wound until the injury is forgotten, but the infection festers, eating away, spreading. I spent the duration of my travels trying to wipe from my mind anyone who had known me in my previous incarnation. I ran purely to keep moving away as far as I could — to be unknown, to disappear, to eat myself to nothing. And what of them? They weren't going to lose sleep over one less of me in the world. They didn't miss me, just like my real parents, who had thrown me away. My father was least to blame, because he was in the grips of a madness: hating him would have been like despising a deformed person for his ugliness. But the rest of them — what had they been thinking of? I thought nothing of them anymore, as they thought nothing of me. The only ones who remembered me now would be the ones who wanted me dead, and my best revenge upon them was to kill myself before they got to me. It was all those worst people I still saw clearly — Prudence in her red dress, Anstace's skull, Edwig's ruddy flesh, Esmond with his scar, Nora, Dogboy and his odious parents. Everything I remembered filled me with hatred and pain.

I heard Franny say, "Don't you turn around now. I'm trying a new approach."

There I lay, weak and muddled, used up and abused, the sad evidence of the stupidity of their fantastic idea. I would rather live among the wretched, as I had during my travels, in the gutter, traded for sailors' favors in the hold of the *Stafford,* in Vill'Acqua's on the Via Maggiore, than keep telling lies for a lifetime. I had enjoyed my abuse, my abasement, my degradation. It was what I was worth and where I belonged.

It is a relief to find your level in this world and to be able to stay there. I could tell the truth to myself, I knew what I'd done, but I couldn't tell anyone else — and why should I draw my thread out any longer? I wasn't going back. I was going forward into the unknown. It was time for me to leave and reach my journey's end. It was time for a great change. I had an appointment at a certain place.

"Now!"

Franny's excitement slapped me back into consciousness. There was victory in her voice as she swung around. The dress. Oh, God. Prudence's dress. Beautiful. Franny turned to face me, and there she stood at the door of Love Hall, her crop in her hand. No, it was Franny, Franny, who had no one to dress for in Turkey. The gown confined her perfectly as she moved close beneath its surface. She turned away, looked at herself in the mirror and then back at me.

"Do you like it?"

"Yes," I sighed, sounding more reluctant than I had intended.

She sat on the edge of my bed, smoothing the dress away from her as though it might split at any moment. I had worn it with more comfort, but to less effect.

"Isn't it too small for me?"

"No. It's perfect. Have it."

"How tall is your sister?"

And so the questions began again. The sacrifice of the dress had won me only a stay of execution. I immediately put my hands under the sheets, cradling myself as subtly as I could, and lay back on the pillow so that all I could see were the fan and the ceiling, which had been painted haphazardly, leaving plenty of leeway for a tired imagination to conjure countries, ships, and faces. I didn't want to look at Franny and I didn't want to let her look into my heart any more than she already had. I feigned blankness and then weariness, but she wouldn't be put off.

"You're slippery, like soap in the bath!" She laughed and poked at my side with her finger, to illustrate that she knew that her questions needled me and that she was undeterred. Her face was directly over mine until I couldn't avoid looking at her unless I actually closed my eyes. A kiss might stop her mouth, too.

"How tall is she, Leslie?"

"A little smaller than you," I said as she exhaled and moved back to her previous position.

"Shorter?"

"A little shorter."

"I expect that she is very beautiful if she looks like you. More beautiful than I am. Why won't you tell me her name?"

I tried to slow the conversation to my own speed. She knew I had a sister, and all I had to do was make up a name and tell a story, but this would lead to further questions about my family, where I lived, why I was there. A lie begets a lie. It was time to leave.

"I am very tired, Franny," I said with finality, but she ignored me entirely and continued to smooth the dress along her thighs this way and that, making patterns in the grain of the material. "She isn't more beautiful than you."

"What color hair does she have?"

I could have described Sarah, but I couldn't bring myself to think about her.

"Brown hair."

"Oh!"

"And green eyes."

"Like you!"

"Yes." Oh.

"And about your height, too, a little shorter than I am. Is her name Catherine?"

Catherine? It was a strange name to pick out of nowhere.

"No."

"Rebecca?"

"No!" Rebecca? Franny was enjoying herself, teasing me.

"Jane?"

"Franny, no!"

"Rose?"

I couldn't answer. She could go through every name in the world and I still wasn't going to answer. There was an awful pause.

"Leslie is an interesting name. I think both men and women can be called Leslie. I'm not sure. I shall ask Father." There was a tone to her voice that scared me, and the tone was meant to say: "I know more than you think I know." But to me it said: "I know everything." I was trapped, snared between the sheets, in this house, in my body. I was in her hands, at the mercy of the jailer's daughter.

She would get it out of me somehow, prod and poke until she knew it all. Yet I trusted her. I would tell her. I had no choice. I looked her in the eyes.

"Leslie is not my real name." I felt the bed sink beneath her relaxation.

"At last! I knew it!" she said and then recovered herself. "Well, I didn't know it for certain, but I'm glad you trusted me enough to tell me. What is your real name? I won't tell anyone — I promise I won't tell anyone. Tell me."

"Leslie is my name as a man. My real name is Rose. Rose Old."

Franny got up, unconsciously, it seemed. The sheer triumph of having finally prized my secret from me lifted her bodily from the bed, levitating her away from where I was prone. She was already on her way to the door, and I sat up, ready to stop her. I would do whatever I had to do.

She looked down at herself.

"This dress is *your* dress!"

"Franny! Yes. My name is Rose. Don't tell anyone, please, Franny. Don't. Help me get away. You must help me."

"I won't tell," she hissed at me. She was smiling, but there was an urgency about her actions. "Of course I won't. I have to get something to show you. We're running out of time."

The news could not get any worse. The door closed behind her with an abrupt crack, and I was left staring at the ceiling. I went over my plan, such as it was, in my head, such as it was. I knew where I was going. I had been thinking ahead.

When Hermaphroditus left his birthplace of Ida, the mountain from which the gods oversaw the Trojan War, he journeyed south to see as much of the world as he could. He traveled down to the cities of Lycia and Caria, where I was now, and came upon a crystal-clear pool of water, so clear that he could see right to the bottom. It was there that he bathed; there that Salmacis, the guardian of the pool, fell in love with him; and there that she dragged him under till their bodies were a mess of limbs and their two sexes combined.

It was there that I would kill myself. Once I had considered it kill or cure, but now I was not so optimistic.

I looked up at Cooper's map from my bed, wondering whether to make good my escape then and there or trust Franny to keep her word. The map, so often used for Owen's armchair lectures, was now on permanent display. Except for one excursion outside the house when I had sat gingerly in the front garden while Franny and Emily used the legs of my chair as the last of the croquet hoops, I had been only as far as the window. From this vantage, I was able to pinpoint exactly where we were on the map, down to the very curve of the shore.

Bodrum comprised two large harbors like the shells of an oyster, with the castle on a peninsula that separated them. Above the flat white houses along the waterfront rose the green of the hills and somewhere there, somewhere: Salmacis, my destination.

Cooper had been pleased to be asked, as I had expected.

"Ahh, yes, Salmacis. Well, you know your Ovid, of course. Lot of wonderful old rubbish, naturally, but interesting stories. Now Herodotus knew the region, he was born here. But Ovid? Look." He drew my attention to the map.

"Salmacis, called Bardakçi now . . . famous myth, as you know. Relaxing properties. The water tasted good, apparently, but *cursed.* If you drank it or bathed in it, men became effeminate or, even worse, impotent. Or do I mean vice versa? Anyway, old wives' tales. Greek stuff."

"But where is the spring?" He seemed to be pointing to the middle of the harbor.

"I'm pointing at it: it disappeared hundreds of years ago. It's underwater, submerged. Here." He rapped precisely and vigorously with his stick. "You're probably drinking it!"

There was silence. The spring was submerged. Drowned. I felt distracted and spat upon, sunk like Salmacis. It wasn't at all what I had pictured as I'd dreamed myself into the painting on the stairs, sliding into the surface of the smooth oil, dipping my foot into the spring while the nymph was distracted by the other intruder.

"One thing, though," he continued, groping around at the back of his mind. "There is another pool in the hills that has some link with Salmacis. It's up here somewhere." Unlike his last pinpoint designation, he now airily waved his wand about somewhere off the edge of the map. "Up a hill, I'm not sure where it is, but people know. Also called Salmacis, I'm not sure why. Perhaps they have an idea that the spring goes underground" — he casually traced a random route that meandered down to the sea — "or perhaps they're just trying to sell some trinkets. They're a strange lot."

"The other spring. I expect it's very attractive. I paint a little."

"Ask the kitchen people. They'll know. The locals know everything."

Franny would find out for me.

Only two minutes had passed when she returned with a writing book and a look of mischief. She gave me the book, made of green cloth bowed by the sun, as if it were a peace offering.

"No one else knows, and I shan't tell them." She was speaking in a whisper and I could tell this was as important to her, in her own way, as it was to me. "This is between just you and me. I knew you were more interesting than I could imagine."

She handed me the book and we read together. Lying on the bed side by side, we each acted our own part. Then we changed, because she could be more like I had been than I was able to be myself. No wonder she had seemed to know more than I thought she should! And as we read, I found myself laughing, nearly crying. She laughed, too, casually resting her arm on my back. But as we reached the end of her journal, I remembered what she had said about her father: What did he know? What did she find out?

"How much is real?" she asked, deflecting my question.

"I can't tell. There are so many songs of the songs we loved in there: 'The Young Sailor Bold,' 'Lisbon,' 'The Silk-Merchant's Daughter,' 'The Female Drummer'. I sang them all with Mother. I can tell you only as much about me as I want to know myself."

"It sounds as though perhaps it's better not to remember all of it." She was never more attractive than when she spoke with that seriousness. Our legs were next to each other, calves touching as we rocked to and fro.

"I was brought up quite differently, Franny." I held her gaze so that she knew that I was telling the truth. "It would take so long to explain."

"You must explain to me. You must tell me everything."

"Does your father know any of this?"

"Nothing," she said. "Who else was real?"

"Stephen and Sarah."

"Did you do any of those things?"

"My father was real, too. He is dead." I closed the book and passed it back to her. "I have forgotten on purpose. I came to forget. I left England to lose myself."

"Your wrists and the bruises around your thighs . . ."

"I have been much mistreated since I left Love Hall."

"Love Hall," she gasped, and then she remembered. "Exactly. That is what my father knew."

All the humor with which we had looked at the book disappeared in an instant. I grabbed her wrist.

"Tell me."

"This is what he knew, the surprise. I stopped talking to you, as he asked me, and I found out that he had seen a dedication to you in one of the books — he assumed it was to you."

"The missing book."

"A book of poetry. And inside it was written: 'To my darling girl, Rose . . .' " She paused to remember what had been written, but I was able to recite from memory.

" ' . . . with love from her mother, Lady Anonyma Loveall — Love Hall, Playfield.' "

"And in the hope that this was something to do with you, and could help you in some way, he wrote to Love Hall just after you arrived. He meant it kindly. Have you run away? Tell me."

"And?" I asked through my teeth. "The letter?"

"He received a reply two weeks ago. They are coming for you."

I stood up.

"Who?"

"The people who answered his letter. Your family at Love Hall."

"Franny, I have to leave. I know where I must go. Two weeks? How long is that? How long does it take to get here?"

"But your family . . ."

"How long does it take?"

"People normally arrive by Malta, but your family . . ."

I turned to her.

"My family hates me and wants me dead. I do not even have a real family. My real family, whoever they were, threw me away on a dust-heap in the wastelands of the city. They didn't want me. I was found and brought up by a madman who dressed me in girls' clothes, to satisfy a deluded impulse of his own, and made me heir to his fortune. I was kept in complete ignorance of my true being with the connivance of my adopted mother, the same woman who gave me the ridiculous book of doggerel that I was foolish enough to be caught carrying and from which your father found out my address. The letter he sent has gone directly into the hands of those who care for me least. My adopted father died, and those who raised me were thrown out of Love Hall, which is now ruled by the usurping members of the family who were only too ready to profit from this wretched tale. They want me dead. I once thought Love Hall my home, but I have since realized that it was my prison. It is not in anyone's interests except my own that I am alive, and my interests are slight. A letter to Love Hall! God only knows which of the plagues this will bring down on me. Both sides of the family are now anathema to me. I had rather kill myself."

I had spoken in one desperate breath as I had never spoken before, and when I reached the end I wiped the spit from my lips. I hadn't just been railing at the world, at Fortune, who hounded me, but at Franny. I had been ranting inches from her face and she started to cry.

"I must leave now," I said.

"No!" She clung to me, clutching skin through clothes. "Let me help you. Let me help you."

"You can't help me." I tried to push her away from me, but just as I had feared, she wouldn't let go. I was trapped.

"Rose. Please." She looked up at me and buried her head into my stomach. "Rose. Stay! I can help you. I said I would."

It was either because she called me Rose or because I suddenly realized that I was the greatest adventure in her life. To her, I was flashing steel and a daring escape. She was my only chance.

"Franny." She was crying as she held on to me. Her head was facing down, and yet she was still a little taller than I. I lifted myself up to meet her. Her lips were cracked and beautiful, salty from tears, bitter with sweat. I felt the down on her upper lip and pulled her to me. Just as we fell toward the bed, her mother called her name.

"Oh, Lord!" said Franny. "Stay." She hurried out.

I didn't have anything to pack or take with me. All I needed was the prize at the end of my road to recovery, the suit that had waited so patiently to be worn. I lay on the bed, wondering about Franny, and then decided to put on the suit, in case I had to make a sudden move or she betrayed me to her mother by mistake.

I had long forgotten how to tie a tie, and the collar felt jagged around my neck. I struggled with the sleeves and the buttons for the braces. Finally, the suit was on and I looked at myself in the mirror. It looked both too big and too small at the same time. The sleeves were too tight and pinched around the armpits, while the trousers were too wide and too short. This was certainly not a piece of clothing with which I had started my journey.

Franny came back into the room. She calmly took in the fact that I was dressed.

"That woman is a nuisance. She didn't *want* anything, but she hates it when she can't *find* me, and then I had to explain about the dress. . . ."

She came back to the bed where I was sitting and, pushing me back, climbed on top of me, straddling my body with her legs on either side of me. I was entirely pinned down, Esmond tied to the chair. Franny looked down at me. Her hair fell over her shoulders. She had gathered the dress up around her middle, and it now fell loosely over my body. She let her head fall backward and I lost sight of her behind her breasts as she arched her back. She groaned and I felt the weight of her body's center upon mine.

"Hello, Lord Bateman," she said as she looked back down.

"Help me."

"Anything. What do you want of me?" Her knees constricted my hands, and my hands constricted my breathing. My body pulsed in reluctant anticipation.

"There is a spring in the hills called Salmacis. I must go to it before they come. Your father says the locals will know where it is. You must let me out of the house tonight —"

"Tomorrow morning."

"Tomorrow morning, but early. You must let me out and tell me how to get to it."

"Can I come with you?" She undulated upon me.

"No."

"Why do you want to go there?"

"I have an appointment."

"I know who can take you." She was rubbing herself up and down on my body, having located a few small inches where she could give herself most pleasure. She was grinding down upon me, and small beads of sweat formed across her forehead. "And I know how to get you out without anyone knowing. It must be very early."

"Thank you."

"Who are you going to meet at the spring?"

"You mustn't ask."

I pushed myself up to meet her and felt myself unexpectedly hard in the groove between her legs. There began a slow negotiation of allowable proximity and relative comfort. From time to time she pushed too frantically and I hurt myself against her bone. It was difficult to believe that she was getting any pleasure from the bruising at all, but she seemed to be. This couldn't have been what other people were enjoying, what they had been so ready to pay for: this abrasive sweaty pummeling. I had forgotten about my own sexual needs. I had serviced others but never asked for any relief of my own, nor been offered any.

My mind wandered, but I felt drawn back within myself when I experienced a stirring of blood as her breathing became heavier. Involuntarily, I moved my hips up to meet her, but I felt apart from my body. I kept losing myself in thoughts of escape, only for my mind to return to my present situation with the sudden harshness of a jarred thumb.

She continued to rub against me. Despite the letter, I realized that they would not be there before I left. Franny put her fingers in my mouth, but it made me feel sick and I had to bite her to get them out. She squealed and smiled as bile rose in the back of my throat. Her fingers were gone, but their sour taste remained.

She lifted up her dress and reached beneath herself. It felt too oddly awkward for me to look down, so I only felt her lift her body a few inches. I looked away at the calendar. One more blank day to be x-ed off and then I would be gone forever and there would be no more days to cross off, or they could all be crossed off with one long line. In another, different world, I pictured my death self looking back on his white calendar to the day he was born. His first mark and my last would be made on the same day. I would cross over at the very nexus of the *X*.

"Shall I see you again?" she asked. I could barely speak. My senses were overcome with her, and my body was being worn away. We both knew the answer, but she was on my side now. "I'm afraid I shall never see you again."

Under the cover of her dress, she started to pull at the front of my trousers, attempting to undo the buttons with one hand while rubbing at me with the other. I started to protest, but she put up her hand and covered my mouth. I couldn't bear the thought of the inevitable heavy breathing and I started to breathe too quickly, too soon, too much. I was going to vomit. I knew all the telltale signs. I was back in the *Stafford*.

I felt her hands inside my trousers and I started to buck frantically to get her off me. Her knees were still pinning me down, but she was looking down at me compassionately, suddenly realizing how much I didn't want to. I knew where the pieces went, how the puzzle worked, but it was too messy. I couldn't bear the filth, the stink. Everything that led up to babies was disgusting — and why did we have babies anyway? So we could throw them away and forget them. I didn't want a baby that I was going to run away from, that I would never see, and there was no pleasure to make the act itself worthwhile. I started to thrash underneath her, and I bit her hand out of self-defense. She stopped, still sitting on me, and took her hand away from my cock, which had withered away.

"Don't be frightened, Rose," she said as she looked down at me. "It's not frightening."

"I feel sick. It's making me sick."

"Me?" She looked concerned and sad, but I was annoyed that she might construe this as an insult. I had no patience for her feelings.

"No. This. It's disgusting. I'm scared," I said, and turned my head away from her. I started to cry in earnest. I wasn't fit for the world. I was sickened by the fact that I was a man, in my razor-blade collar that dug deep into my Adam's apple. Why did I need this cock, this mistake? It was so alienated from me and I from it that neither could sympathize with the other, communicate, or respond in an appropriate manner in any situation. I hated myself and I was angry with her. It made me only more determined to have done with everything.

"It's not disgusting. Feel."

She took my hand out from under her right knee and put it underneath her skirt. I flinched, snapping it away, but she took it again and, in what I could describe only as a very friendly way, put it underneath her until my hand cupped her. She was open and obvious. I thought of Sarah, my only prior knowledge; Sarah, who hadn't died after all; Sarah, of whom I tried not to think at all.

"Please, Franny. No." My cock, remorseful and impenetrable, lay twisted underneath my hand. "I don't want to."

"Rose. It feels nice." Her hair had fallen forward over her dress. "It isn't disgusting. It's what a body does. You wish yours were the same, that's all."

"It's messy, though, sticky."

"It's good."

I grabbed my hand back again before she got the chance to start her rocking-horse motion again.

"Rose!" she spoke quickly in inspiration. "The dress. Put it on. I shall help you leave, but put the dress on."

Yes.

The dress.

My dress. In front of me, she started to take it off. I was dumbfounded as she turned around and had me unclasp the neck. I felt the dress pull forward.

"It was too tight anyway. It's a bit of a relief," she said.

She had her back to me and she quickly stood up, leaving the dress behind her on the floor, in front of me, inviting me. I looked up and saw her arse and her back. She stood naked, looking out the window. Without turning around, she told me once more to put it on. My clothes seemed to fall off me, as though they had been sewn together with one long thread that, once pulled, unraveled entirely from my limbs like autumn leaves. I put on the red dress, Prudence's red dress that I had stolen from her, and I felt it around me, swimming on me, the velvet kissing my sides, and I felt neither shame nor fear and I turned around and asked Franny if she wouldn't mind, and I heard myself say exactly that, if she *wouldn't mind* doing up the clasp at the back of my neck. And I felt her hand try to put the hook in the eye and I felt the velvet nestle softly around my neck. My Adam's apple seemed to recede, and as I swallowed again, my mouth had lost the bitterness. I turned around to see Franny, naked in front of me, her body indescribably beautiful, and for a second I imagined that was the body underneath my dress. And it was.

I leaned forward and pushed her gently back onto the bed. I had never seen so much of a naked woman before. I blinked and realized that my eyes were full of tears. Franny looked up at me, naked, full, empty. Although there was no breeze, she was shivering.

"Don't move, Franny. It's me," I whispered into her ear, and I moved one leg between hers and I started to move it gently where I knew she wanted to feel it. Everything seemed effortless and I was able to slip my hand down her stomach and move it through her hair. I was calm. I breathed slowly and I whispered in her ear. What I whispered I cannot remember, but I told her a story, as Sarah and I had told each other, and my finger moved between her lips. I was lost, but her body seemed to welcome me into it, to give me directions. I slipped my first finger in. It felt long and slender inside her, and as I talked we made a rhythm together and I lifted my finger upward as though I were trying to lift her body from the bed, and she moaned and relaxed and then breathed in hard as I kept whispering. She moved her hand toward my part of the puzzle, but I gently moved her away, persuasively, not out of fear but out of confidence.

"Don't touch me. Lie back." And as I said this, she started to moan slowly. What was born as a soft growl somewhere deep inside her grew and grew until it became a song as it emerged into the world. She ground herself into my hand and with a shudder lay still on the bed. I kissed her cheek as she yielded. We lay in silence. Her eyes were closed when finally she spoke.

"Rose. I know that you must leave and I shall deliver you. But can I come to find you in seven years, like the jailer's daughter?" She looked different, less childish.

"Yes, but there will be no me to find, Franny. I shall be unrecognizable," I said. She turned her face away. "Look at me."

She didn't.

"I am made for another world. Look at me. I am at odds with myself. Everything I am, it is impossible to be. You know what you are and where you come from, this house, this family. I am nothing. I am tired of trying, lying, and running away, tired of denying myself. I cannot live by these rules anymore. I have no wish to hurt others. Only help me, and know that it is the best thing you can do. I know you understand."

Franny was silent and got up slowly, leaving me in my rumpled dress. The house around us was silent. I thought that she might be crying, but when she finally spoke there was only calm in her voice.

She put on her own clothes, which were still lying on the floor in a bundle, without turning to me once. She opened the door and, still without looking, spoke over her shoulder.

"Whatever you need, have ready at five. I shall do everything."

She left.

3

AT THE AGREED HOUR, I tiptoed from the room, willing the sympathetic movement of every floorboard. I hadn't slept.

Franny was waiting at the back door. She offered me a bundle without looking at me, but I shook my head. I had no further use for the dress. She let me out, still refusing to meet my eye, and handed me a letter.

"Follow the instructions. Go."

As I walked away, I wanted to look over my shoulder but didn't dare. I waited for a definitive sound, the latch of the gate or the closing of the back door, a piece of punctuation to end our sentence, but I heard nothing. Perhaps she was looking at my back as I disappeared. I would never know.

The sun had not yet quite started to cut through the clouds. I had nothing with me except my Ovid. When they found my room empty, it should look as though I'd be back at any moment. I didn't want them to panic or interrogate Franny. I wanted them to think I was next door.

I opened the note. It was nothing dramatic: terse directions to a rendezvous point, a note in Turkish to my guide, and some paper money. There was no letter from Franny urging me to reconsider, no offer of love as a shield against whatever came our way. Even at this late hour, I looked for flattery where there was none — why? Knowing there was nothing to stay for made it easier for me to leave. She didn't punish me with kind words and pleading, but smoothed the path she knew I had to follow.

I'd had so little exercise over the past few weeks that the effort caught up with me quickly, and as the sun rose for the last time, I found myself standing on the road at the bottom of the hills and leaning up against an orange tree, exhausted. I was sleepy, in a dream state, moving away from the real world with every step I took from the bedroom. Finally, I had the nerve to look behind me. No one was following and I could no longer make out the house. I had left the world I knew far behind.

As I walked on, a cart passed, pulled by an unenthusiastic mule. A hugely fat woman and her toothless male companion sat at the reins, paying the beast no attention. The man looked over his shoulder and asked me a question that I understood only from his expression. I gave him the letter and the money, which he handed to his wife. As she opened it, the money fell out onto her fat lap. She read it, sniffed, and barked an order at him. He came back to me, taking off his cap nervously, and pointed to the back of the cart.

"Salmacis?" I asked.

"Evet," he sighed. *"Evet."* He motioned me into the back of his vehicle. I lay down on the wood with one arm across my eyes to shade them from the sun, which was too bright even behind my eyelids. The mule started on his way again and we clattered down the open road.

The man tapped me on the shoulder and offered me olives from a jar. His wife slapped back his hand, but he gestured at the acres of olive trees all around and laughed, raising his eyebrows in amusement at her. I fingered the pages of my Ovid and remembered the shepherd who ruined the nymphs' dance and, as punishment, was turned into the crude, common olive tree. Suddenly it was as if I could see the shepherd's body in every trunk, his twisted features knotted in the intricate bark, his arms stretching out in the branches, imploring desperately for help before he was changed, caught inside, forever.

The sun toyed with me until I felt that the physical world were coming alive. I had never previously been aware of its living soul, so ordered and arranged had been the nature in my past. There was an explosion of color at the bottom of each crooked tree trunk: large white and yellow daisies, poppies, and buttercups, effortlessly vivid, too much for my eyes. Elsewhere, gentler anemones in white, yellow, purple. In a laurel tree, I saw, suddenly and clearly, Daphne fleeing the rape of Apollo, her silhouette as plain as the cameo on a broach. The sun rose higher and I closed my eyes as tightly as I could and tried to think of Franny. As her face appeared to me, it began to change, slowly, horribly, into bark.

Metamorphoses began to take hold all around me. I was breathing life into the book through my hand, and the book was breathing back out through me into the world. And what was a book but leather? And what was leather but animal skin? And what was paper but a tree, and vellum but lamb? And what was I but an idea? Slowly, as I looked at the world around me, I became aware of the presence of the humans themselves before they were changed into trees, flowers, animals, and birds. In the blood red of the anemone, I saw the breath and death of Adonis, incestuous son of Myrrha and Cinyras, who was both his father and grandfather. Ignoring Aphrodite's warning, he died in the hunt, pierced by the tusk of a wild boar. Cytherea turned him into the anemone, the flower that grew beneath the olive tree, while on Olympus, Persephone and Aphrodite argued over who would have him in the afterlife. Where was Adonis now? In that very flower, half above ground and half below, like his body in the afterlife, which spent the summer with Aphrodite and the winter with Persephone. Fortunate boy.

In my exhaustion, the natural world overawed me and I saw its changes materialize all around. I longed for respite from the sun's glare, but the mountain turned back into Atlas, who, bad host to the last, offered no shade.

In an outgrowth of huge pines, I saw the Thracian women, the same ones who killed Orpheus. I lowered my head so I was hidden, in the hope that they wouldn't see me spying on them. Those murderers had hacked the poor singer to death, tearing his body apart and piercing his skin with spears made of laurel, of Daphne, finally safe from Apollo. Suddenly, their leader saw me. She brandished her spear and raised the war cry: "A man!" In an instant, they were upon me.

I awoke with a start. My face burned. In the grip of my hallucinations, I had drifted in and out of sleep for so long that the sun had started its descent. We weren't moving.

We had arrived at a watering post, and the mule guzzled from a trough. My driver pointed up to the sign above the door, a picture of a spring. I almost laughed. I got down from the cart, wiping at the corners of my mouth, and noticed how green the landscape had become. More like the painting.

He pointed to a path that disappeared into some trees, and stood back. With the first two fingers of his right hand, he made a little mime of walking. His fingers walked slower and slower. It was a long way. I nodded. As I turned to go, he looked up at the sun, did some brief mental arithmetic, and concluded that it was too late to set off. He motioned me back, but I moved firmly away. As I went, his wife shouted at me and pointed toward the trees where I was going. "Salmacis. *Hayir!*" she said, wobbling her fat head gravely.

"Hayir!" agreed her husband in warning, and made a dumb show of drinking from the spring. They seemed in deadly earnest, but then they looked at each other and burst out laughing. I smiled and turned around.

A forest enclosed me and I followed the path as best I could, for it was far darker in the woods than I had imagined. Thick scrub and pine trees, through which I could occasionally catch a glimpse of blue, surrounded me and filled the air with the sticky sweetness of their sap. I knew that the stone pine had edible seeds, a little like hazelnuts, because Franny had picked some and brought them to me only a few days before, but I didn't know which was the stone pine and which the Aleppo. I didn't know anything about these trees, this wood, this forest — only the stories of the humans they had previously been. I felt lonely, but when I heard a rustling nearby, I realized that I wasn't alone — all around me there was life.

I'd seen deer in the fields near town, darting away from anything that moved, and goats, lazily confident in the scrub. There was always a barking dog somewhere at the harbor. But what was keeping me company here? The shadows magnified the sounds, and my surroundings — being wilder than anything I had experienced before — seemed infinitely more daunting.

Franny had told me there were wolves, hyenas, and bears in the mountains — but should I fear Callisto, changed by Juno into a bear for her affair with Jove? And should I fear the hyena, Tiresias, able to change his sex, according to Ovid? What of the she-wolf, Helen? I had come to see Salmacis, to see Salmacis forever, but if something else came my way before I got there, so be it. If I had a choice, I would let it happen. I would be pierced like Adonis, ripped apart by dogs like Actaeon, and whatever of my body wasn't eaten or taken off into the deeper forest would be left to rot where it fell until it, too, became part of the natural world. Who knew what I was treading upon right now? Perhaps my backbone would slither off into the undergrowth like a snake. Perhaps bees would be born inside my stomach, as happens in the carcasses of sacrificed bulls. No one can stop the wheel turning, the course of nature beginning again, but at least I wouldn't have to live through it all. I had earned a rest.

I recalled the ridiculous prissiness of the sculpted lawns of Love Hall with distaste and I wondered at the futility of what humans did to control nature. Here was her revenge — haphazardly creeping vines twisting serpentine across the ground, trapping you at every opportunity, and trees that seemed to grow in every direction, except straight up, from a forest bed that was nothing more than a mulch of all that fell from above. There was no room here for a croquet hoop or a decorative bridge. A twenty-foot wrought-iron fence would be powerless to keep this out — the only way to get rid of it would be to kill it, to chop it down and burn it. Even then it would slowly return.

Then I wondered at the futility of what humans did to *human* nature. At first, they tried to kill me but failed. I came back, too clever for them, insidious like ivy. Then they trimmed me and shaped me in just the same way, cut me back and pruned me. But now I was returning to a wilder state, if only for a little while. With this thought, I felt more at ease among the limbs of the forest.

Everything was changing again: the flint was Battus, who betrayed Mercury, and the scuttling lizard the boy who laughed at Ceres drinking. The stream was the tears of Byblis as she cried for the unrequited love of her brother. The world was dissolving around me. I leaned over to pluck the berry of a small bush but I couldn't. To eat it would have been cannibalism.

It was growing darker and I sat down. I heard Nyctimene, turned into an owl for her dark sins, and the screech of Aesculapius, who betrayed Proserpine for eating seven pomegranate seeds in hell. And whom was she eating? I couldn't remember. And what would I change into? Every metamorphosis is poetic justice. Magical herbs changed Glaucus, the fisherman, into a fish, and the Lycians became frogs because they hadn't let Latona drink. Perhaps I would become a hyena, an oyster, an earthworm. There was surely something appropriate. A rose.

I saw the glint of small eyes in the darkness. Fearing an ambush while I slept (for I would get to Salmacis if it was the last thing I did, and it would be — I hadn't journeyed so far to be unaware of my own end), I climbed a tree, my eyes still fighting to see, and found a ledge on which I could sit. I thought of Dolores. I leaned back and glimpsed the stars, the same stories again but written in the sky. In the quiet darkness I heard the sound of water: a trickle, a bubble. Its subtle air floated to me on the wind, and as the night became colder and I huddled myself into the ledge, the ripple became my lullaby.

I came to consciousness out of the mind-entwined stories and myths to which I had given myself over, and it was daylight. I don't think that I slept fully at any point. I was too tired, too alert, too nervous, too ready.

I looked down into a clearing and, at the far end, saw what I knew was Salmacis, though it was too big to see more than a part, much bigger than I had pictured. I climbed down and walked toward it. It was as I had dreamed it would be. The trees leaned lopsidedly over the pool on the right, but the sun shone down and glittered on the surface where the pool was at its deepest. At one end there was a cluster of rocks, and at the other, the end I was approaching, a lush patch of grass. One day I found a cristall brooke, that trailed along the ground, that in reflection did surpass the clear reflection of the clearest grass. About the bank there grew no foggy reeds, but living turf grew all along the side and grass that ever flourished in his pride. Reeds sprouted to the right.

My mouth fell open in wonder as I walked absent-mindedly around the edge of the spring. I remembered the preface of Beaumont's paraphrase to the story of the strange enchantment of the well:

I hope my Poeme is so lively writ,
That thou wilt turne halfe-mayd with reading it.

The sun shone on my dream. I couldn't believe this was Salmacis, but it was. It felt like the painting, as though the painter had actually been here or seen it. I was here.

I sat down on the grass and then lay back, trailing the thumb of my right hand in the pool. The water was soft and cool.

* * *

I had traveled around the world looking for a corner in which to shelter, and now I had found my resting place. My mind was playing tricks with me, as it had throughout the previous day, and I imagined that I was on the stairs at Love Hall looking at the painting of Salmacis and Hermaphroditus; however, the two main figures were missing. I imagined the night, just five years before, when I had seen, or dreamed I had seen, a change on the canvas. I saw a man in a rumpled suit lying at the side of the spring, his hand dangling lazily, sadly, in the water. At the time I thought: *Can I help him? Can he help me?* Now I recognized the question I hadn't known to ask: Could I help myself?

From inside the canvas, I looked back not at the troubled version of myself who dreamed this change in the picture, but beyond, to my seven-year-old self, in the lace nightdress my father had given me for my birthday, gazing at the painting from the stairs. I looked young and indefinably perfect, too innocent to fear the future, too young to have learned the words that would ruin everything.

I was in both places at once. Time had folded in upon itself, and at that moment, if I'd had the energy, I could have somehow crawled back through the canvas, the veil, and been reunited with my seven-year-old body. I was being given the chance to start again, to return to my Eden. I waited for Rose — Rose! — to reach out, as I knew she would, and touch the surface of the painting: that would be the moment. But as I waited, looking at my sleepy young eyes, I became filled with fear.

I didn't want to start again.

Everything would turn out exactly the same, and I would return here for a second time, and then, if I was fool enough, a third time, waiting, as now, for my other to touch the canvas. And it would be progressively worse, because though I would know slightly more each time, I would still be powerless to change my fate. Perhaps I would be unaware of the previous decision, yet choose again to come back. Or worse, I would become aware that I was inadvertently repeating the same mistake for a horrific split second just after I made the decision. Infinity is terrifying. Its abyss makes my skin crawl.

There is an elegant woman (who is not me) in a casino. She is gambling. She raises her bid ever higher and never stops. She doesn't win. She doesn't lose. She merely bids. Higher and higher, up to and beyond infinity. The roulette wheel spins forever, ready to receive the incoming ball, but the ball is never allowed to rattle among its red and black. The dice are never thrown. The third card is never played. But the woman makes a bid, and then raises the bid, and then raises the bid, and then raises the bid. She has stopped time.

And now, it is time to throw the dice — *rien ne va plus!*

On the stairs, Rose was impatiently about to reach out. I could see the anticipation in her eyes. From where I lay, I could touch the very inside of the painting — not the back of the canvas, but the actual inside surface of the paint. Her fingertips reach for mine.

I look away.

Dreams, books, songs, life. My hand had fallen into the water and brought me back to consciousness. I was drifting in and out. I was so close. I let it fall farther into the water, my hand, my wrist, my elbow.

I opened my eyes. Sunlight. But there was a veil between me and what I saw, the spring, the grass. Alone, beneath the skies, laughed at, knowing nothing, a painting hanging on the stairs. Perhaps I was no longer hanging there but turned face to the wall beneath the library, replaced by something more to the taste of the current occupants.

I looked at myself through the veil — the pallid skin, the hardness that had crept into my features, the full eyebrows that were once so assiduously tweezed and shaped. I removed my clothes slowly and considered my body as I did so: the hair that had spread like fungus, the shapeless hips that slid into my legs as if by mistake. I kicked off my sandals and trousers. And there. As I stood there, I felt a coldness bite at my skin, though the breeze wasn't cold at all. And I felt eyes on me — the eyes of the wood, the nymph Salmacis herself. Even if she existed, had ever existed, she wouldn't look at me and think: *Beautiful boy, are you a god? You should be, if you're not.* There was nobody to save me now, not my family, not my dream, not the vision of a dead mother, not even my belief in myself, because I did not know who I was. I was naked before God, and God laughed at me. Once, I had thought that I could batter down the gates of heaven, that I could blow my trumpet until His walls crumbled, that I would see Him cower in front of me, but now I realized that revelation was no more than His last laugh at me and that this knowledge is our final reward.

And still the bids rose. Place your bets, gentles and ladymen. Ten crowns. Twenty crowns. One hundred crowns. Did she fall, or was he pushed? Two hundred crowns. And God damn you all. Five hundred crowns. How high can we count? Higher.

Through the veil, I caught my reflection in the water and there I saw something unexpected. On the water, in the water, perhaps it was the movement of the wind, my likeness was freer and more elegant. I appeared softer, darker, and healthier. My hair shone in the light. I saw the shape of my naked breasts, and as I admired these graceful curls and soft contours, the stylishness of the curve where my hips met the top of my thighs, I felt more like Narcissus, and I leaned down to touch myself in the water, to see whether for one second I could touch myself without disrupting the reflection. But as I made contact, it was gone. And, stupidly, I searched for it, just in case I was farther down, a little more permanent than this surface layer of the water. Then I realized that this attempt was doomed. So my only option was to wait for the water to calm.

Hush. Calm. Wind, don't. Trees, keep your leaves for a minute, please. Frogs and lizards, make no ripples, land on a different lily pad. Smooth. Smoother. I had tried so hard to pay no attention to my body after I dragged my bones all the way to Bodrum. I ignored its crude alarm calls and suppressed all its tedious urges. I didn't need to taunt myself with evidence of my failure. Only Franny had lifted my mask, and that had led to further defeat and a return to fancy dress. I was unable to be what my body designated.

As the water became still, I saw that the cage in which I lived was not my body. I had rattled my cup on the bars, but those bars were not my bones. My real self was what I saw in the water, and I could now escape to it. My salvation depended upon the flight to a place where I would be free to make my own choices, just as Mary had written.

At this moment, I knew that I could go no further.

Have you ever been down a road that you can't see the end of? Have you ever thought a thought that you can't stop thinking? That was me. I couldn't stop singing the same tune in my head, over and over. I couldn't replace it with another one. The bids had to stop, so too the animals and their humans, always changing backward and forward. The voice in my head was now the voice of my reflection, beckoning me. We were doomed, the two of us. And I knew that it had to end, that my only way forward was the pool. And so I slipped in without a plan of any kind, but just to stop.

It was cold.

I had always assumed that I would be Hermaphroditus, but I was not. The situation was reversed: I was Salmacis. It was I who had fallen in love and I who wanted to be joined forever with the object of my affection. But I didn't foresee any miracles or expect a mayden smoothness to seyzeth halfe my limbs. I expected and I wanted to drown, to gulp water, to lose consciousness in the deepest part of the pool or to fall and have my head dashed on a rock that made me lose just enough blood that I could lie there in my painting and dream a beautiful dream in which the numbers reached their height and the bidding diminished, and because there would be no negative bidding, this diminishment would dwindle even unto zero and I would die on the final full stop. I shall bet nothing. And the ball would stop rolling, landing neither on red nor on black, but on green zero. And I would float in a perfect cross, with my arms at precisely ninety degrees to my sides with none of my body sagging beneath the surface, not ugly and contorted like reality, but pristine. And I hoped for nothing more, knowing that the only part I would be aware of was easily attainable.

My whole body was now submerged, my mouth level with the surface of the water. It would have been easier to swim than walk, but my right leg was trapped by some stubborn reeds on the bed. I kicked at them as best I could, but the reeds wouldn't give, would only tighten their grip. In my effort, I breathed some water into my mouth and my nose at the same time and started to choke. It was not beautiful. I was trying to tug at whatever was caught on my leg, but I was choking at the same time. My mouth tried desperately to breathe anything other than the water it was frantically gulping, water that entered in the wrong way and then emerged from my nose, which was also trying to inhale of its own accord.

I remember thinking that this must have been my survival instinct and being surprised that I had one. I remember thinking that this survival instinct was useless, because the reeds were stronger than I was. But suddenly something uprooted, came with me, and I went under. I tried to gasp for air but succeeded only in breathing more water, and that was when I thought: *I am drowning. I am drowning. This is the moment that I am drowning.*

I was immediately entangled in more snarled reeds or ensnared by some kind of freshwater octopus. A streamer of crimson floated past my eye among the bubbles of the disturbance, and I realized that I had badly cut part of my body — my foot? I couldn't feel anything in the cold.

My head came above water for a moment and I heard a voice.

A voice. Echo. Not mine.

Someone else's voice — as though trying to wake me from a dream. A very realistic dream. Was I only dreaming?

I wasn't dreaming. I was drowning. I half expected life to flash before my eyes in a panoramic review of every trivial forgotten incident in my past, passing before my eyes in retrograde succession so I could determine whether I had been right or wrong, good or bad. Instead, I was slipping on the moss underfoot. I was trying to die. I was close to dying. I was bleeding. And choking. And drowning with no life review to entertain me as I went. There was nothing to stop me now.

"Rose! Rose!" A girl's voice.

Franny! It was Franny!

She had broken her promise. She had come for me.

A rush of water to my right side knocked me from the clutches of the sea monster and pushed me away and up. I felt Franny next to me and at first I thought she was trying to lift me out of the water, but it became evident that she was pushing me under. Suddenly I became aware that it was I pulling her down. I was going and she was coming with me.

Spluttering, I clung to her as tightly as I could, my eyes closed as I directed all my strength into my arms and legs, which I squeezed around her. She was much stronger than she looked. She shook me off for a second and I heard her shouting, but it seemed as though her voice was coming from farther away, a trick of the water, which clouded brown around us where our struggle stirred up the untouched bed of Salmacis. There was grit in my eyes, water too, perhaps blood, and everything was a haze, so I struck out blindly until she was once again in my clutches. I surrounded her with my whole body, as a cuttlefish catches its prey at the bottom of the sea. I held on to her as though we were already one person.

"Gods!" I shouted, pushing her down underneath me, my voice half beneath the water, a low muffled roar, then momentarily clear as I gulped air, my eyes stinging with sand. "Gods! Grant that never day may see the separation between us!"

And the gods heard my prayer. The singular God had laughed at me, but these ancient ones, the gods of my books, understood the agony of my life, my need for a great change. They sympathized with me. As my reward, they granted me one wish.

"Let the two of us be one forever!"

We were a muddle of thrashing limbs, a tangle of arms and legs trapped and tied by clothes and reeds and the will of the gods. I no longer knew where she began and where I ended. Nor could I pull away.

And then it happened.

Her blood began to flow directly into my veins. I felt her breath pump into my lungs as I pulled her toward me and tried to kiss her so that our spirits could flow directly between us. Exquisitely painfully, our late divided bodies knit in one, and from that one body was growing just one pair of arms and one pair of legs. I was wrapped so tightly around her and I wouldn't let go, couldn't let go. There was no longer anything for me to let go. It was all *us*. I didn't care for my identity anymore, nor for hers, nor for any, but only for what we might now be. We were becoming neither a boy nor a girl. Nor man nor maid could we be esteemed, neither, and either. *Neutrumque et utrumque videntur.*

Knowing that no metamorphosis can be halted halfway, I began to yield as I felt the miracle take hold, to let our body take me where it would, to let our fluids intermingle. I let my — was it ours yet? I was happy to surrender it — *our* mind float away and, oh, I heard the ball land snugly into green zero and saw the dice hit the side of the baize and rebound, worrying around each other for a magnetic second until they stopped on some unspecified but deeply insignificant pair of numbers.

Iacta alea est. There were to be no more bets and the casino was closed, forever. I breathed her into me with every pore of my skin and exhaled to permeate her, though I had long since ceased to try. I was certainly faint. I, *we* were fainting.

And I was happy. I knew happiness for the first time in my mature life. And I would have been glad to die that instant and have this be the end.

Then Franny spoke to me, from outside, not inside my head, with our mouth, or our other mouth.

I expected her to lay the curse on the pool forever: "Make anyone who comes to coole in these silver streams, nevermore a manly shape retain, but half a virgin may return again."

But she had no need. Instead, she shouted:

"Rose! Rose?"

But her voice was deeper.

I didn't have a voice anymore. If I opened my mouth, nothing would emerge. If I even had a mouth. She had our voice. I had my mind still because I was *thinking,* but she obviously had power of the voice. Her voice had become like mine — deeper, in fact. I lay on my back, floating, and waited to hear our voice again. I wondered what we would say.

"Rose! Rose! Jesus! Rose — it's me!" said Franny's new deeper voice, panting.

Hands dragged me through the water. I knew I was now hallucinating because the voice sounded like someone else's. And I was dragged to the bank and bundled onto my back on the grass, just as I had been pulled out of the river after being pushed in, many years before. An abrasive blanket was placed upon my heaving chest, as I tried to cough up Salmacis, which filled my lungs.

"Is he all right?" I heard Franny ask urgently in her normal voice.

"Quickly," answered her new voice, still panting. "Do you know the kiss of life?"

"Not at all."

"Let me." It was no longer Franny's new voice that I was hearing but another, a voice I knew. I was panicking because I couldn't produce the one heaving cough I needed, and I felt my eyes twitching beneath their lids. Now it truly was as if my life began to flash before my eyes. Hands started to push on my chest and I spluttered. A mouth clamped down onto mine — it wasn't Franny's mouth. It was nothing to do with me at all. It tried to breathe for me. And I felt myself respond as I started to cough up water.

The first thing I saw was Stephen Hamilton, his mouth looming above mine and his wet hair plastered to his forehead, taking a huge breath before he clamped his dripping lips down again. I could see Franny standing behind him. I wanted to say his name but I couldn't, nor could I stop him. So I lay there and let him breathe into my open mouth, and then I started to heave and my back arched up and I found myself sitting, looking straight at him, tears of choking in my eyes. I couldn't stop coughing.

"Rose! Rose!" Stephen looked up at Franny and put his arms around me. I was still coughing, but he put his hand through my hair and drew me to him. And he held me.

"Rose . . . come back . . . come back . . ."

I felt myself fall into his arms still further, until he was holding me up. I was limp and helpless in his embrace.

Stephen Hamilton, as I lived and breathed. Two acts of love, and everything had changed.

The trip from Salmacis was not taken at the leisurely pace of my journey there. We rode down as efficiently as we could, me leaning heavily on Stephen. Words were spare.

Nature remained completely natural. I looked at it through weary eyes and didn't have a lot to say or think, for which I was grateful. Trees, goats, scrub, some flowers. The myths were gone, returned to the pages of the book to remain, perhaps, forever. The book itself, less a few pages, was drying in the back, picked from among my clothes by Franny.

The two of them spoke from time to time, but I didn't try to listen. Stephen had come to save me. He had his arm around me and I felt impossibly safe. I slept and, for the first time since my escape, dreamed of Love Hall.

When we finally arrived at the house, I had dribbled from the side of my mouth like a baby. I was too exhausted to wake up properly, though conscious enough to hear them talking, to feel myself hoisted into Stephen's arms and taken up the stairs to my room. My clothes had dried in the sun, but I was still wrapped in a large blanket, which became my bedclothes. There was more murmuring, the voice of Owen Cooper himself, and the appearance of more bedclothes. Stephen laid himself cushions on the floor. The last thing I felt was his lips on my forehead.

I awoke in my familiar room at the Coopers', but the light fell in a new way. Stephen and Franny were waiting for me. I felt bright as the day. Franny came and sat on the bed next to me.

"I did right, didn't I?"

"Thank you," I answered. "Yes, Franny, yes."

Stephen interrupted.

"You've been here long enough now. It's time to go home, Rose."

"Home where?"

"We are in London now — your mother, my family — at Victoria Rakeleigh's house. They've been very kind. You belong there with us."

I lay silently looking at him, taking him in. It was a silence neither of us could break.

"Go, Rose," said Franny. "Start again."

"No more lying," I said almost to myself.

"No, Rose. We know now. No more lying." He had the earnest tone he reserved for discussions of cricket technique. "Whatever you want is what we want for you. It's time for you to choose for yourself."

I started to cry. I couldn't stop myself. I cried years of tears from a deep reservoir.

Stephen continued, "You didn't know. And then the Osberns made you dress in those clothes. It made you so unhappy."

I started to laugh through my tears at the sweet simplicity of this synopsis, which made my crying even worse, accompanied as it now was by wheezing hiccups. Snot exited my nose, which made me laugh more.

"We are no longer scared of Love Hall. We have moved on and elsewhere, safe and happy. And you can live there in comfort. With your mother, Sarah, my parents. That's where your family is now."

My eyes stung.

"Rose, there is one more thing you must know."

I couldn't speak, so I just looked at him, not knowing what to expect.

"Your mother asked me to give you this, to put it in your hands and no more. If you want to investigate further, it is your choice."

And from the table, he produced a small portfolio with a bow on the side. He opened the front and drew from within a sheet of paper. It was one of the collection of ballads that, a lifetime ago, we had restored and cataloged in the library. What sort of information could a ballad have for me?

"Rose," he said. "Please look."

He was pointing to the publication date. It was the year after my birth.

"So?" I said.

"Look at the picture."

The pictures never had anything to do with the text, I wanted to say, but I decided to humor him. I looked at the whole broadside for the first time. The banner at the top said simply:

THE ROSE AND THE BRIAR

or

THE ABANDONED BABY SAVED FROM THE HOUNDS

An excellent ballad to a merry old Tune, called "The Old Wife She Sent to the Miller Her Daughter"

From the publisher of

"The Last Confession of James Riley, Highwayman"

And below this, before the ballad proper began, there was a comparatively well executed woodcut of a coach in front of a castle, with details I was unable to quite take in. I looked closer as Stephen sought my reaction.

"What about the name of it, both names?" he asked.

"Coincidence," I said.

"No," he said. "The rose and the briar."

"That's in plenty of songs. And if it isn't a coincidence, someone is making sport. Forgery."

"Look at the picture," said Franny, to persuade me, but she didn't need to. Now I was looking as closely as I could.

An unwieldy coach, with wheels too big for its compartment, was parked close by a large pile of rubbish, and on the pile was a cross-eyed dog. In her mouth was a little baby, wrapped in swaddling clothes, bawling — tears represented by large drips flying from the baby's face at right angles, some of them rising upward in defiance of gravity. From the coach appeared a gloved and ruffled hand, attached directly to the shoulder of a dashing mustache and beard. The hand waved up at the coachman, who was, at that moment, dismounting to get the baby. In the background on a hill was a huge house that looked rather like Windsor Castle. A very tall woman, the size of a turret, walked the battlements.

"Well?" said Stephen.

"Shhhhh!"

Underneath this unusually detailed print was the following information:

Geo. Bellman, Printer, 206 Brick Lane, Whitechapel
Pharaoh, Balladeer, 38 Ironmonger Row, Borough

And there was nothing else but the ballad itself. I looked up at Stephen and smiled. I read.

When forth in my ramble, intending to gamble
To an alehouse I ambled most freely

In the World's End far from town, I did spend near a pound
Until I became fuddled most really.

I sat down to sleep for an hour on the cheap
And I had me a dream worth the telling
Until I awoke, in my rib felt a poke
And the landlord was doing the yelling

So I walked straight outside, and attempting to hide
On a dustpile did settle to rest there
And on top of the mound, there I saw a white hound
Who did suckle a child at her breast

"Hello and good day" I attempted to say
But the dog she growled at the poltroon
"I'm not talking to a poor boy such as you
With none but a song as your fortune"

I have seen a ghost fly on the wings of the night
And a dead man return from the war
I have heard of a queen who gave birth to thirteen
But a dog I ne'er heard talk before

I kept far away while this canine did say
"This baby is mine for the giving
I'm her guardian here and I shall wait till appears
A lord with a very large living"

"Fate's in my paws so this baby's not yours
Abandoned by father and mother
Hear him softly weep while he's trying to sleep
We will patiently wait for another"

And so we did wait on that lowly estate
Till a carriage arrived from the distance
Which stopped in its tracks as if chopped by an axe
With none but His Divine Assistance

And she barked to be heard, the dog true to her word
Till the Lord heard this savage and wild
And got her to stop, as they offered a chop
And took it in exchange for the child

And into that carriage they handed the babe
And may nobody call me a liar
But the arms of the one on whom fortune had shone
Was the sign of the Rose and The Briar

And so they made hayste with that baby away
Yes off that coach went like the flyer
And the arms of the one on whom fortune had shone
Was the Bonny Red Rose and The Briar

And the dog too gone home as her work now was done
The hound who loved foundlings and orphans
May this country of ours care as much for the poor
As the King in the city of London

So, good luck to that child who was born nearly wild
And pardon my common effrontery
Perhaps you have grown to be quite as unknown
Or perhaps you'll be King Of This Countrie

And when you do rule, please remember the cruel
Way that nature gave you your beginning

And think of the hound on the desolate mound
And please forgive singers their singing
And please forgive singers their sinning.

When I had finished, I looked at Stephen. He was holding Franny's hand at the end of the bed. They complemented each other perfectly. I smiled at them through my tears.

"Forgery?" said Stephen.

"I don't know," I said.

"Coincidence, Rose?"

"I don't know."

"Well, then, what? We have names and addresses."

"They will be long gone."

"Then, what is it to be?"

"Home, Stephen, Home."

They laid out, side by side, the suit and the red dress, that Franny had so envied of me, that I had so envied of Prudence. Then they left the room. It was my choice.

5

Voilà

1

INETEEN MONTHS AFTER my flight, our carriage turned into the London square where Victoria Rakeleigh sheltered Love Hall's other refugees. Her family had no legal recourse to right the wrong done us, so they had determined to do everything within their power to help, not the least of which was to offer us a home in exile; they vowed never again to set foot in Love Hall until such a time as I, or my delegate, was able to open the door to them. The exterior of Twenty-four Bewl Square was elegance itself, but Stephen warned me that I would find its interior constricted, heavy with the musty air of hibernation. Even sounds were different, lying where they fell, unable to find rafters to rattle around in.

I felt part Lazarus, part Prodigal Daughter as I stepped down from the carriage and caught sight of myself in the glass. I had last appeared before them wearing a stained and ill-fitting jacket, unable to speak my own language with any fluency, in a voice not my own. Sarah hadn't been able to say a single word. I wondered what she would think of me now. I had changed, I knew, for the better. Something had happened at the spring, but this metamorphosis was nothing to do with my body.

As I looked at myself, I licked my fingers and tugged on the short ends of my mustache to gather and twirl them as best I could. I had precisely shaved the middle to reveal the whole of my philtrum and balanced this absence on my upper lip with a square inch of hair below the center of my lower. I had modeled variations on this theme throughout the journey back to England. Stephen had looked on with bemusement as my whiskers went through successively bizarre developments, but forbore to comment or criticize. It was experimentation, and I was now my own experiment. Mustaches came and went as I grew older, but this one, at this moment, looked most debonair, particularly in the context of my dress.

I'd made my choice. I was not wearing Prudence's red dress, however. That beloved item would need some tender attention before it was restored to its former glory. During our recent stop in Paris, an enjoyable expedition *shopping* (a concept new to me) had yielded a brand-new wardrobe. How long I'd had to keep myself in check! In Paris, I saw the styles of tomorrow in the most tempting materials imaginable, and I indulged myself.

I stood on the steps in my favorite morning dress, an elegant silk *chameleon* of mignonette green beneath a mantelet of tarlatan trimmed with darker green ribbon. I closed my eyes and gathered my hands into my muff, like an ingenue before her first season. Stephen put his arm around me as he opened the door.

"Rose is home," I heard him say. I opened my eyes and there they were, on parade before me. Nobody gasped and nobody looked away. I was home. To my left were my mother and Hood, and to my right Hamilton and Angelica. Between the two pairs stood Victoria, welcoming me into her house. Her childhood femininity was long gone, replaced by closely cropped hair, tired eyes, and a short blue uniform. If I had been elsewhere, I should barely have recognized her. Only Sarah was missing.

My mother ran toward me and took me in her arms. Then everyone followed, even Hood. I had intended to curtsy, but I was swallowed by the oncoming bodies.

"Rose!" I heard as someone started to cry. I wanted to reassure them, tell them that everything was fine, to explain what I had come to understand and how it had helped me, and to outline the terms by which I could continue to improve. But what good are words when you cannot speak? The tears were my mother's and my own. I moved her hair from my face so I could take everyone in as she clung to me: Hood, bowing as decorously as he could manage; Victoria, who had saved the whole litter and was now taking in another stray; Mr. and Mrs. Hamilton, exactly the same. Stephen, but no Sarah.

I let myself be ushered to the dining room, where the table was set and a meal was immediately served. It had been prepared by a cook who, without doubt, had access to the favorite menus from the Love Hall recipe books, and as I spotted an empty chair and extra place setting, I found myself daring to hope that Sarah would perhaps shortly emerge from the kitchen, smiling. But no. Sarah was still away at school and would be home in a matter of weeks, her father explained: there was always an extra setting in case of the sudden appearance of Victoria's brother, Robert. I smiled through my disappointment.

We sat and ate quietly. The Epigram of Beef, an old favorite of my father's, spoke our common bond louder than any speeches. At first, glances and smiles were all the conversation we could manage, but words appeared with the wine.

There was a new democracy at Twenty-four, as it was always called. We all ate around the same table. Here, too, no less than Hood himself, who had grown old in the intervening year and a half, and on whom the changes had taken the greatest toll. In his wilderness, he had taken to calling my mother Anonyma and occasionally, in his more forgetful moments, Dolores. From now on, he would always refer to me as your lordship, with a bow from which he took an ever increasing time to straighten.

This was our table — fugitives, exiles, and nonconformists.

Over the first week, words were chosen carefully and affection meted with circumspection. They tentatively asked for stories of my travels, and Stephen made sure to steer us carefully between Scylla and Charybdis until I was prepared to take the wheel myself. (I was happy to be an open book — this was my new philosophy — but didn't yet know how much they were prepared to read.) Love Hall protocol was more or less observed, notwithstanding Hood's occasional lapses, but as our mutual shyness slowly diminished, a more pragmatic routine was established.

I had spent too long among strangers who dissected and disparaged me with their every glance. These nosy Joes made me so aware of their curiosity that I burned to catch them in the act, and this made me even more self-conscious. At Twenty-four, if anybody was looking at all, then it was with affection. I learned to laugh again, to sit quietly and read. After some days had passed, I realized that I was no longer necessarily the center of attention, despite everyone's delight at my safe return. Life quickly settled down into an enjoyable rhythm. The more I was taken for granted, the happier I was. We were all recovering together: they from Love Hall, my disappearance, and rediscovery, and me from my odyssey. My Ovidyssey, Father would have called it.

In time, and over many familiar menus, I told them of Turkey, Salmacis, the Mausoleum, the Coopers and Franny; however, I shed little light on how I had ended up in Bodrum, beyond the barest outline and the fact that I had been at sea. It would have been hurtful to be entirely candid with them about the missing year (nor have I been with you), and for this I had one reason: Mother would have interpreted my behavior as an indictment of her, and I had no wish to perpetuate our suffering. I had been responsible for my own actions and welcomed whatever came my way; besides, those dramas seemed far, far away. So I told them only what I wished them to know, and in return, they told me of the many peaceful pleasures they had found in this refined part of London, in this quiet geometrical house with its park views.

I was uneasy about only one thing: the missing factor in the equation of Twenty-four. I longed above all for Sarah's return, to see if we could rekindle any of our natural friendship. Memories hung suspended like an axe. Let it fall, I told my executioner, if I might only talk to her once more. Stephen and I were on excellent terms, and he was fierce in his protection of me. He had grown accustomed to this role on our return journey to England, standing in front of me, sleeves rolled up, demanding apologies from those who couldn't hold their tongue. But now I needed someone to protect, to counterbalance him. I could not be the most helpless anymore, the bottom of the line, the last station before the sea. We lacked Sarah's balance, and I needed her pull upon me, her gravity.

My mother was with her books, as usual. She looked older in her new library, a square room on the first floor with plentiful wall space and few volumes, and her relief and joy in my return seemed somehow tempered by unhealed wounds. I wondered whether she was disappointed on my behalf that I had survived, worried that the world would only fail me, fail to live up to me, again. She was yet to appreciate fully my newfound confidence, and she should have been happier to see me so relatively at ease. I'll even admit I imagined that somewhere deep in her soul an unspoken voice whispered that it was I who had failed her. But we spoke nothing of this. She more than ever dedicated herself to her work. Whatever choices I made, she would support. This was decided. The past was buried, but the earth above could still be easily kicked aside — and we weren't yet ready for the exhumation.

The only excitement that reached our table (aside from the latest installment of one of the serialized tales we loved) came courtesy of Victoria. She was in charge of the Friends' hospice in the East End of London, where she nursed the sick, often spending nights away from Bewl Square, longer in times of crisis, and her vocation left little time for the small talk of Twenty-four. We could go for days without seeing her, reading only scribbled notes delivered by exhausted messenger: "Send more blankets. V."

It was because of V's loyalty that Stephen had known where to find me. She had chanced to see Owen Cooper's letter (addressed to Lady Anonyma Loveall) lying unopened and ignored among some other mail on a side table in the Reception Room of Love Hall, where she had been on an errand. This was the first and only visit to Love Hall by a member of our family since the wedding of Guy and Prudence, which I had managed so effectively to avoid.

That so-called pageant had made a mockery of the dignity of the great house, causing Victoria to coin the phrase "the Rape of Love Hall." Hundreds of pounds had been spent on absurd display, yet not one member of the village had been invited. For many of those who had — mostly rich landowners who had met neither bride nor groom — it was a first look at Playfield House, as it had been renamed. Cut off from money for so long, the new inhabitants had spent so much of it on this one day of show, in so many directions, and to such little purpose, that the results were incongruous and disquieting to all in attendance. The Mausoleum was painted sky blue to match an enigmatic theme, which Julius adjudged to involve the unhappy alliance of Neptune and Cupid.

His Rakeleighs could not bear to see the parasitical Osberns celebrating the successful takeover of their host, extolling the virtue of money while guzzling the rewards of their triumph, gloating over the financial failure of Victoria and Robert's idealism, and mocking the simplemindedness of the previous inhabitants. Our good cousins hated them not just because of our mistreatment but because the family had a hand in everything that Victoria and Robert despised, from the slave trade to the hypocrisy of organized Christianity: greed, laziness, selfishness, and patriarchy.

Amid the wedding circus, the Rakeleighs recognized their own hypocrisy in marking the day with any respect at all and decided there and then to split from the Osberns irrevocably. Victoria and Robert made their exit between the medieval jousting and the bearbaiting. They later wrote to Playfield House explaining their position; the Osberns responded by return, allowing these Rakeleighs to cut themselves off without call for further communication.

This agreement had been broken only once, to my own great fortune, when Twenty-four dispatched Victoria upon a double errand involving a supplication, on sentimental grounds, for the delivery of the Hemmen House to Twenty-four and a library trip at my mother's behest. She took the letter (and two others) without question or remorse. Her uncle Augustus stopped her at the door. It was embarrassing enough, he said, that his own family was providing sanctuary to the madwoman and her myrmidons: let his brother be warned that a few words in an unsympathetic ear could put any number of their guests in less desirable surroundings. At least in Bedlam they knew how to keep people quiet.

The usurpers had previously greeted my disappearance with a shrug of "we told you so." As far as they were concerned, I had undoubtedly chosen the right course of action: invisibility in exile was by far my most tasteful option. They would not be sending out a search party.

Victoria's trip had been unpleasant but entirely successful. Reliance had placed a "fair price" on the books my mother had requested, to be paid immediately in case of loss or damage, but the Hemmen was given up without complaint, for Prudence thought it haunted. Victoria left, repeating her vow never to talk to Osbern more.

Cooper's letter was finally delivered to its rightful recipient that evening. Twenty-four discussed its contents, with the result that Stephen was summoned home and dispatched without delay. My family owed to Victoria the restoration of both me and the Hemmen House.

Those at Twenty-four had been able to make believe they were living in a small-scale Love Hall, quite *how* miniature became clear when they took delivery of the dollhouse. The magnificent replica could not fit through the front door and had to be hoisted on ropes and lifted through the front windows, removed for the purpose at surprising expense — such things were noted with growing unease. Everyone, though, was delighted at this restoration, for their various reasons, particularly Hood, who, in his dotage, hoped that the Young Lord might appear to him as Dolores had appeared to his master.

Victoria's brother, Robert, was rarely seen at Twenty-four, though officially it was also his residence. He had gone up to his now deceased grandfather's university and, from there, launched a career in politics as assistant to Mr. Joshua Knelton, one of the major campaigners against child labor in England. Robert was rather the same as he had been when we first met so long ago, albeit with mustachios not quite as charming as my own. He had become yet more serious and hooted like a barn owl when he spoke passionately of the winds of change. And this he did often.

These Rakeleighs were still the two most questioning people I knew. Their questions were no longer directed at me, however, but at the world, and their entire philosophy, it seemed, had developed hand in hand, step-by-step from the nursery. Robert was capable of great charm and wit at one moment, but the next found him in the lather of righteous frenzy. However, his sister and he disagreed on very little, and he never argued with any of us.

"Why do so few people have such disproportionate wealth?" Robert would ask, throwing his hands up to heaven as though it were up to God to answer, then spreading his arms wide to invite mortal debate. To my embarrassment, I had never even considered the question, though from the perspective of a street gutter in central France, the luxury of my previous life had seemed a little de trop, if no less desirable. If those people kept only as much money as they needed, think how many fewer poor there would be, said Robert. Yes, I thought, but who decides what anybody actually needs? My father needed the Hemmen House, yet its actual value could have housed many of the people around our grounds.

"The poor are always with us," said Hamilton one evening, intending to close the door of debate, but opening it still further.

"They're always with Victoria," said my mother, laughing. "Every day."

"The poor *are* always with us," said Victoria, "but that doesn't mean that they *should* be."

"It is the rich who are always with us, and that is why the poor are always with us," concluded Robert, taking two quick mouthfuls of dessert before rushing away to aid Knelton in the redrafting of his next bill.

Both brother and sister were Quakers, and my first trip beyond the front door of Twenty-four was to keep Victoria's company at a meeting for worship of the Society of Friends in New Southampton Row. I opted for a plain black dress and my veil, which I decided to wear to the meetinghouse not for my sake but for the sake of others. (At least, that is what I told myself at the time; but now I remember this was my first excursion and, though I felt full of myself, I was still finding my feet.)

I was pleased to take the carriage. I had never seen the London street at such close quarters before and what a noisy, smelly place it was. With the clattering of our carriage down the uneven streets, the porters bawling, the chairmen yelling, the street sellers crying their wares, the self-pitying yelps of the criminal in the pillory, and the enthusiastic enjoyment of the crowd baiting him, there was little quiet space left to the mind. The beggars were carcasses in clothes, and around everything, a wreath of smoke, the wind of the city's guts. It had been requested that we send the carriage home upon our arrival at the meetinghouse so Robert could have use of it; we would therefore walk home. I had quite looked forward to it, but the thought now horrified me. As I looked out of the window, I felt a little like my father.

The calm within the meetinghouse was the perfect antidote to the clamor without. We sat in complete silence. There was no pulpit, no stained glass, no altar, and no organ. Other people quietly joined us until we numbered about fifty, sitting each with his own silent thoughts on plain wooden pews that faced one another. I waited for someone to say (or do) something, yet no one was so moved for some little while. When the silence was finally broken, it was as shocking as a bolt of lightning. Victoria, still seated, spoke for a few minutes about the quiet, principled voice of Quakerism and the practical uses of this spirit in her fight against the degradation of the city. When she finished, there was no applause or indeed any sign that she had spoken at all, except a little echo crawling up one of the bare walls — and I found myself in silence again, facing no priest, waiting for no interminable sermon to end. I removed my veil, laid it next to me, and looked around. Only a cough or the creaking of wood as someone shifted in his seat punctuated the hypnotic silence.

The first fifteen minutes of this were intolerably slow, and I was forced to predict the movements of a bulbous bluebottle that rudely announced itself on my knee, but the following half hour flashed by without trace. During that time, I began to forget myself. The bluebottle gone, my mind became lost in meditation. With nothing to focus upon in the plain white room, my thoughts turned to myself.

The old God had laughed at me: I had heard Him cackle. The older gods delighted only in playing tricks on humans, and they had tried to drive me mad with their hallucinations and shape-shifting. I could not communicate with any of them. The God in this room, in this soul, was the one to whom I could talk, the one deep within me. I needed no mediator — no Edgar, no Praisegod. I needed no stained glass, no sermon, no Communion, no Te Deum, and no tedium. I needed nothing more than I had already within me. I could have burst out singing.

I slowly became aware that, by general and silent consensus, the service had ended. People turned around and shook one another's hands in greeting. I had been in such a trance that I forgot to replace my veil. A small portly man took my hand warmly: he had noticed my whiskers but hadn't seen my dress. His wife wished me a simple "good morning," betraying no surprise whatsoever. The man to our right, however, uttered a small "oh!" of shock just before we touched, his face the picture of befuddlement. He recovered himself as best he could and gave me the greeting as I simply smiled at him. I wasn't in charge of other people's manners, I reflected as we walked back into the reeking street.

Half a minute later, the surprised man ran up behind us, huffing and puffing, calling, "Madam! Madam!" as he caught up, his tie askew from his exertions.

"I am so sorry, madam," he said, looking at me and entirely ignoring Victoria. "I think you may have dropped this. Perhaps we shall meet again."

He turned and left with a curt bow, which did not invite further expression. In my hand lay a small business card. I turned it over and saw upon it the words:

The Inslip Club
Tuesday, The Bunch of Grapes
Portugal Row

Victoria looked down and laughed.

"You didn't drop this, did you?"

"No."

"Rose, I think you may have an admirer." I looked at the peculiar man as he toddled around a corner. I didn't know what to say. "Perhaps not a personal admirer," she continued in light of my silence, "but a connoisseur, someone who sympathizes, perhaps even a society of people."

"Who sympathizes?" I said indignantly, crumpling the card. "With what?"

"Rose, you're not the only person doing the empress!" She laughed good-naturedly.

"The what?"

"Doing the empress. That is what they call it: men who . . ." I felt quite sorry for her as she stumbled over her explanation.

"I am not *doing* anything, Victoria. The members of The Inslip Club have nothing in common with me, nor shall I seek their society. Theirs is a hobby: I presume that they impersonate women. I am not doing an impersonation. You cannot imitate that which you really are, Victoria, and what you see now is me."

"Rose, I certainly didn't mean . . ." Though she tried to mollify me, I was warming to my theme. I started to walk with a longer stride.

"I may represent a challenge to others, but I am perfectly happy with who I am. In fact, I fear that it is not men but women who are the great female impersonators, and growing ever more so!" I indicated two women with ridiculous bustles and absurdly accentuated corsets waddling down the other side of the street. "Present company excepted, of course," I added, raising my eyebrows at her cropped hair and collared work shirt.

"You'll be a Quaker yet, Rose," Victoria said with a laugh as she put her arm around me. She had realized that some questions were best left unasked but, in fact, I was the only person ready to talk about it in public. Others might have preferred that I adapt my manners and my appearance better to suit the clothes I chose to wear (I had totally forsworn all rouges and powders since my return to England), but not Victoria. She had merely misread my inclinations (or perhaps her mind was simply too full of the injustice in the world to worry about such a trifling matter). I, on the other hand, had just begun to understand hers. A fine couple we made, I as feminine as she was male, as we walked home arm in arm through the obstacle course that was the city.

The Chevalier d'Eon, that erstwhile hero of mine, once felt so overly scrutinized at a public gathering that he could stand it no longer. He lifted up the hem of his dress, showing his leg and stockings to the assembled company with the words "If you are curious, voilà!"

When the time came, I would have the same sangfroid.

Stories filtered through of life at Love Hall. Samuel regularly returned to the vale of Playfield to call on an old friend and reported what he heard at The Monkey's Head, which was as close as he ever went to the house itself. Some of the stories were doubtless exaggerated by enthusiasm and alcohol, but what he heard defied even our worst imaginings. "I am not saying these stories are true," Hamilton would say. "I am merely reporting what I am told."

The sum of both families was living at Love Hall, with the union of Guy and Prudence in full pomp. According to gossip, the two of them fought like tigers, and his temper had sounded the death knell of most of the valuable china. The newcomers had what they wanted but continued to behave as if they hadn't yet got it. Prudence, when mentioned in the pub by name, was "the Whore," Guy "the Dog," Thrips either "Inky" or "the Dogsbody," Augustus Rakeleigh "Rapeleigh" or "the Rapemaster General," and the rest of the family gannets and sponges. Nora was simply "Ignore 'er." Rumor spoke of the institution of a Caligula-esque rule of corruption and preferment: previous favorites were horsewhipped, and those with a large enough bribe installed in their place. The inhabitants' various toings and froings were the subject of great disdain in the village; billowing nostalgia for the true Loveall was the order of the day. The greatest insult? Despite the change of name to Playfield House, which nobody in the village chose to remember, Guy had taken the name Loveall and adopted the soubriquet the Red Lord Loveall. Hamilton joked that it was 1745 all over again — one wave of prolonged public sentiment and the exiles could have taken the house by force.

Thrips had succeeded the HaHa, and his malefic machinations

around the village were the subject of much unease. In an inadvisable opening gambit, he had tried (to predictable outrage) to shorten The Monkey's opening hours. But worse was to come. Current intelligence had it that there were plans to turn it into a temperance pub. An alehouse without ale! The new owners of Love Hall drank to their hearts' content, but they did not approve of the consumption of alcohol by peasants, particularly those openly antagonistic toward their betters. Take away their alcohol, and their spirit would vanish, too; take away their pub and they had nowhere to foment rebellion. Each beer at The Monkey was savored as though it were the last.

Other specific grievances included: the carolers who were pelted with snow from the gatehouse on Christmas Eve, the sword dancers who were not granted admission on St. Fellow's Day for the first time in living memory, the cessation of the annual cricket match, and the selling of the estate cottages with particular reference to the harsh evictions of long-standing tenants. Loyalty to the big house was at its nadir.

Those who had ventured inside told tales of terrible waste. Servants could not be retained long enough to learn their jobs. There were plenty of people keen on the positions, but few hardy enough to bear the conditions. Dust gathered inches thick at a time before a new group of workers could be ferried in from ever farther away; they came like blacklegs under the cover of darkness. The kitchens were in turmoil, the swill tubs a menace to health. My greatest sadness was for the Gothick Tower that had so inspired my father's imagination. Unaware that Sanderson Miller himself had carefully secured every last piece of brick and rubble in its place for the perfect aesthetic effect, the Osberns thought it a dangerous ruin and planned to pull it down.

Outside, nature itself seemed keen on reinstatement. The gardens lay untended, weeds grew everywhere, and ivy had spread its feelers all over the chapel. The perimeter of the copse edged inward as if to claim back the fallen leaves that now lay blocking the gutters. Soon, even the coat of arms on the front gate would disappear entirely. The roses and the briars were coming back to life.

Most of the horses, terrified by the bear on the day of the wedding, had escaped, jumping over unthinkably high fences to do so; those that hadn't were sent to the knacker's yard. A unicorn horn hung forlorn upon a plaque above The Monkey's saloon bar fire.

I was immune to the taller tales. Of course the new incumbents were unpopular. Everybody knew Hamilton, and the locals would tell him what he wanted to hear. But I was pleased to hear that I was fondly remembered in The Monkey's Head and that the story of the subjugation and training of Guy now had the status of legend. I was still their Maiden Century and they hoped I would live to be a hundred. Knowing of my desertion, however, they had feared that I might not. Bets were still taken on my sex, despite the civil ruling that had proclaimed me male, but the money was now donated to the local Sunday school, for there was diminishing hope of any deeper insight. In case I were dead, God rest my soul, there was a competition to write my headstone. The winning entry:

GREAT GOD ABOVE, WHO LIVES ON HIGH
THOU'ST PLUCKED THE SWEETEST ROSE
AND WHETHER TIS A HE OR SHE
NOW THOU ALONE WILL KNOW
THOSE WHO READ THIS GRAVEN RHYME
HARK! HARK! THE SAVIOUR'S CALL:
THOSE WHO HUMBLY LOVE ONE
LOVE ALL
✝

I listened to the tales about Inky and Rapeleigh with polite interest, but I harbored no thoughts of revenge. My energies were directed closer to home, to the things I needed: a mother, a father, a name, a birthplace — I was ready to begin life again by going back to the very beginning and beyond.

I took the ballad to my mother in her new library. Once again, Mary Day had proved my mother's only consolation, and this work had reclaimed its precedence over the broadsheets. Looking older, with her hair in a bun, my mother seemed unusually excited as she studied one of the volumes that Victoria had liberated from Love Hall, and emitted a scholarly twitter of excitement that she quickly repressed when she saw me. Always, in her first glances, I imagined that I saw surprise, then regret and then relief, but perhaps I read too much into her, as she read too much into poetry.

"The Rose and the Briar, or The Abandoned Baby Saved from the Hounds" had been brought to her among one of the parcels of broadsheets regularly sent from London. Ironically, it had arrived while I was still resident in Love Hall, but hadn't worked its way to the top of the pile until I was far into my travels. She had me sit down as she perused it again and recalled its discovery. Then, it had seemed just another ballad; she had been four or five verses into it before she realized what she was reading. She always cataloged as she read, and she showed me her specific entry:

> The Rose and the Briar. Alt. title listed. The Abandoned Baby Saved from the Hounds. PRINTER: Geo. Bellman, Printer, 206 Brick Lane, Whitechapel (see also ballads A35, B33 and B35, C12 & c. & c.). WRITER: Pharaoh, Balladeer, 38 Ironmonger Row, Borough. We have not seen this memorable name before. Title is a standard motif (cf. Barbara Allen, Lord Lovel & c.). Attractive woodcut with more than usual number of figures in more than usual detail. 14-verse ballad in standard lines of 4 and 3, rhyming ABAB. Subject: singer finds dog suckling child. I know of no antecedents for this ballad. . . .

Seeing the coincidence, she forgot her work as she read on. She separated "The Rose and the Briar" from the rest of the ballads and put it among her private things, bringing it with her to London. Out of deference to me and at her insistence, no investigation was pursued. She now laid the very sheet in front of us, next to her Day volumes.

"Is that you?" She laughed and pointed to the bundle in the mouth of the cross-eyed dog. Her good humor put me at ease, and I crossed my eyes.

"The dog? Not me." I pointed at the castle in the background that showed the huge woman walking along the battlement and asked in return: "Is that you?"

"I don't think so," she said, and laughed again. Then she was serious. "I think this *is* you, Rose. But be prepared. Although we know what has happened since, we do not know what brought you there. No one knows, my darling, where life will lead her next."

"I would be a fool not to find out."

"Whatever you do, you'll be a fool. As shall I." She couldn't be any more like herself if she tried. "It is a ballad after all, Rose, and a song doesn't exist if it isn't sung. Perhaps it's time for you to bring this one to life."

I nodded. Despite all that was unspoken between us, she understood me precisely. She turned back to her books. I took her head in my hands from behind her and kissed her forehead. She could be no more help to me than she already had been. In this, she was like any mother who gives her blessing to her adopted child to find out the truth. I had to go back beyond her, to find out how I was brought into the world. There was a chance that I might never come back to her, but she knew it was our only choice. As I reached the door, I remembered that I was leaving without the broadsheet.

"What would Mary Day say?" I asked as I picked up the ballad.

"'Go to the light, my child. The shadows are waiting.'"

"Which poem is that?"

"It is only the line of verse that I am reading at this very moment."

* * *

The door to Geo. Bellman was opened by a middle-aged man wearing a loud checkered jacket. He received us nonchalantly with a flick of wrist and thumb.

We seemed to have finally located the printer after six days of dead ends and unprofitable bribes. The name on the door was right, but this was apparently not our man. We had become accustomed to causing something of a stir in our ventures around the city during the investigation that led us to this door — veil or no veil, I was readying myself to "voilà!" at any moment — but this man's expression told us that we were unremarkable, an annoying interruption to his work schedule, and that we could have been the Lilywhite Boys themselves cloth-ed all in green-aye-oh for all he cared. Stephen treated him with equal indifference, and once inside, the two of them studiously ignored each other. The man returned to what he had been so weary to be dragged away from, which proved to be nothing more taxing than the observation of a kettle never quite boiling in the fireplace.

The premises were evidently shop, factory, workshop, and home combined. The ceiling was but a few inches above my head, and as I stooped slightly in sympathy, I saw books in every state of disrepair (foxed, bowed, mottled, and dog-eared) all around us. Reams of paper of all known sizes and poundage were stacked throughout in motley piles. Books and their pages performed a variety of tasks around the room, none of them their original function. A pile kept one door open, while another blocked the opposite door, so that particular entrance could function as no more than a decorative molding until the offending heap was shifted; and this was out of the question since it would require too much repositioning of the remaining contents of the room. In one corner, three stacks were a makeshift desk on which stood melted candle and inkwell, and in another, the doorkeeper himself was sitting on eight large volumes as he waited for the boil. Wondering at the lack of headroom, it dawned on me that we were also walking on an extra layer of wastepaper that had never left the room. The walls were decorated with pasted pages torn from books, mainly scenes from the theater, it appeared, many of them upside down. When I looked closer, I saw that they were broadsides, each with the familiar Bellman imprint and a variety of addresses: little wonder Bellman had been so hard to find. Even the curtains were large pieces of uncut oversize, crudely stitched together, their watermarks glowing in the light.

It was the most papered place I had ever seen, including our old library. There was nothing else in the room besides the ominous combination of paper, three humans, and fire. One stray spark and the whole place would have gone up in seconds. I wondered about drawing up a stack of my own, but Stephen launched into his inquiry.

"Mr. Bellman, sir?"

"Gone," replied the man gloomily as he looked deep into the fire, remembering his departed friend. This was the first we had heard of it in all our travels.

"Dead." Stephen looked over at me, pursing his lips. I fixed my eyes on the paper upon the floor and contemplated this dead end.

"Dead, sir?" the man asked mordantly as he took his eyes off the kettle and looked at us, taking us both in for the first time. "Dead, you say? He left here not two hours since on his usual route. Unless you bring dire news." He couldn't have been less interested.

A black dog bounded into the room from the far door, her tail whipping all behind her, flicking paper into the air to fall like confetti. This was not an unfamiliar sight to our doorkeeper, who made only the laziest attempt to keep any pages from falling into the fire. He motioned his hand toward one page as it descended dizzily, but given the speed of his hand, he had as much chance of catching it as most humans do a fly. The dog passed Stephen and immediately made for me as the kettle finally began to whistle.

"Mutt!" said the doorkeeper, but then turned his attention to the water, which was finally doing something more interesting.

Mutt was a handsome dog with an unusually large ruff of flesh around her neck, its very own double chin, and a shining coat of black and chocolate brown, with a ridge of hair that grew in the wrong direction along her spine. She bounded up to me, sniffed my shoes, and then started to lick up my ankles. I put my hand on her head in an effort to keep her at bay, but her nose snuffled directly up my skirt; she was like a terrier on the scent of truffles. I laughed the way you do when animals cross the barriers of propriety. There's nothing you can do, but good breeding (yours, if not the dog's) tells you to try to do something. Now most of her body was underneath my skirt and her head between my thighs. She didn't want to do much once she got there, so I patted the hindquarters that stuck out of the front as she nuzzled me. Her tail wagged frenetically from side to side and she tried to emerge by walking straight forward through my legs, but I wasn't quite prepared and she was too large to fit. I leaned back on a pile of books, less steady than I thought, and, losing my balance, tried to coax Mutt to back out. This she had no inclination to do, so (in as feminine a manner as I could manage) I hoisted my left leg over her head. She emerged from the tent of my skirt, rather baffled but happy all the same.

In the mayhem of this music hall routine, my veil had caught on something and unattached itself on one side. I fussed over it momentarily but saw no particular point in snatching it up again. The dog sat down at my side, approving of my fragrance and delighted to have made a new friend, opened her mouth, and let her tongue loll. I put my hand on her head. She looked up at me and licked the salt from my palm.

"Good Lord!" exclaimed the doorkeeper as he saw my face, noticing something that his nonchalance, and my veil, had previously withheld. He ducked his head and squinted in further scrutiny. The dog was sitting at my side, panting, looking from me to the back room.

"Your name?" asked Stephen hurriedly.

"I am Albert Dowling, sir. Alby, to those as know." He glanced nervously over at me again to confirm his previous observation.

"Alby . . . Alby . . . look at me." Stephen spoke carefully, helpfully.

"Yes, sir."

"You boiled the kettle, Alby."

Alby put out his hand absentmindedly, for all his attention was still upon me, and picked up the kettle by the handle, which scalded him.

"Ow!" he howled.

"Were you going to make tea, Alby?"

"No, sir. Only I always have it hot just in case either GB, that's Mr. Bellman as is, or him inside wants a drink."

"Inside?" asked Stephen.

Alby looked at us, widened his eyes, and jerked his head back toward the office once or twice. He was trying to tell us something confidential about him inside, but neither one of us had the slightest idea what.

"Who is he? Tell us," said Stephen.

"I wonder why you're here at all, if you don't know that! Perhaps you want publicity for some production." He looked back at me, considering the curious juxtaposition I offered. "A flyer or something. Theatricals, I'll be bound. Yes." Alby had come to a false conclusion that satisfied him deeply, but an admonitory sigh from Stephen hastened him back to the previous question.

"Mr. Bellman is the famous printer of broadsides and ballads, newly moved into books and plays, also provider to the common man of letterhead, memoranda-ums, almaniacks, periodicals, pamphlets, and tracts, not to mention printer of both gelatine and engraved cards, and master of stenographic processes. Anything you'd care to see on a piece of paper, Mr. Bellman will print for you. If you'd like to see our press, sir, it is up the stairs. Bellman has also given us the magnificent eight-volume set . . . Well, I needn't go on, sir, for I see I am reading the right script to the wrong audience. In short, sir," he said as he licked and then blew on his scalded hand, "GB is a printer."

"And?" I spoke for the first time.

"Pardon . . . er . . ." Alby paused for a little while and winced slightly while he gathered himself and tried to make the attempt look as much like an innocent stutter as possible. "M-m-madam?" he added with great trepidation.

"The other man, Alby," interrupted Stephen. "Who is he?"

"The 'uman wonder? Oh, he writes the songs. Mr. Farrow."

"The ballads?"

"All them things."

"And is he the same as a Mr. Pharaoh?"

"Close enough, I should think," said Alby, and rolled his eyes in my direction as if to say: *Hark at him, the great detective.* "Go in and see for yourself, if you like. And good luck."

"Good luck?"

"Oh, nothing to be afraid of. Only sometimes there's more sense, and sometimes there's less." Alby smiled fondly and put the kettle back on the fire. "Sometimes he don't want to be bothered and sometimes he can't be bothered and other times he's not worth bothering. And take that damnable dog with you before it messes up my office any worse."

The door to the back room was open, and there was no question of our being announced. Mutt wobbled before us and led the way, wagging her tail extravagantly. A quiet singing floated through the door and we walked in to find a man of indeterminate age sitting behind a desk, enthroned among the printed word. The walls of the room were lined with books, from floor to ceiling, though evidently these were stock rather than reference, since very few had been opened and many were duplicates. Farrow swung slowly from side to side on the huge oak chair, his eyes closed. Mutt rushed to sit at his feet, but Farrow ignored her. He seemed in a kind of stupor, perhaps a creative reverie that blocked out everything else in the room. His eyes fluttered behind his eyelids and the dog rested her dewlaps on his feet, which had been dangling about an inch off the floor. She anchored him to the earth.

Four words came from his mouth, tumbling, in a fragment of a melody that was part of a longer song: "Dog in the room." His fingers drummed on the desk. Stephen and I stood, wanting neither to interrupt nor to be kept waiting. Then, as if lightning had struck through the window behind him, Farrow's eyes opened, and without seeing us, he yelled:

"Alby!" Alby came in before the word was out, a piece of paper and a quill at the ready.

"Move, sirs," he said as he hurried past, this previously indolent character suddenly the picture of industry. "The miracle is upon us. Leave the room, if I could trouble you, please. GB don't like to give away no secrets. Now, shoo, sirs, shoo!"

Before two seconds passed, Farrow was singing and Alby was his scribe. I watched through a crack in the door, while Stephen shook his head in amused disbelief. I could discern only fragments of Farrow's song, but it seemed one of the old ballads, which gave me hope. And then he stopped. It took no more than six minutes. Alby came out, hopping with joy.

"GB will be so pleased. You must come again. It's been quite a day, it has. You can go back in now. He sometimes tires but he sometimes doesn't. 'The Ghost of Polly Black and Her Babies Two.' It's simply too good to be true."

"Did he just remember it?" I asked.

"Remember it! 'Remember it!' he asks!" Alby was delirious. "He has composed it, sir!"

And we passed him and went into the study again, where Farrow looked up at us.

"Alby!" he shouted with surprise. Alby ran back around the corner with his notebook.

"Not again so soon?"

"Wha?"

"Encore one fois, sir?" asked Alby, positively sprightly.

"Who are . . . ?" Farrow asked panic-stricken. The inquisitive dog left his side and came to me, where she revisited her previous investigations.

"Mutt! Stop that," said Farrow.

"I don't know who they are. What's it to do with me? Spies. Actors, mayhap. Shall I boil the kettle? Does anyone want something? The liquid leaf?" Alby left with no intention of bringing anyone anything. His work was done.

Farrow had hoisted himself up to his full seated height at the desk. Now his feet were a good six inches shy of the ground. He was an appealing-looking man, but with a lost look in his eyes that seemed to reflect a distracted mind. There was a scab or rash on the side of his lower lip that I assumed was where he bit himself, perhaps to stop from bursting into song in public. And he looked pale, as though he rarely saw the sun. His head was a little too large and his eyes inappropriately small and far apart. But he had a likable look — a twelve-year-old wearing a thirty-five-year-old man's costume.

"I was asleep. Sorry." He didn't think he was lying. He rubbed at his eyes to bring us into focus. "Mutt! Stop!"

"That's perfectly all right," I answered as Mutt continued her attentions. I sat down. "She can stay."

"Aye! You're right," he said and laughed uproariously. " 'Tis a girl and a good girl, too. Most think it's a boy. That dog must have a very male look to her. It's *he* this and 'Can I give *him* some water?' and 'Will *he* bite?' " He sighed and puffed out his cheeks. "GB won't be back for a little while yet. Do you want print examples and prices?" He waved his arms at the books around him.

"So many books, Mr. Farrow," said Stephen. "Have you read them?"

"Not one. Can't read. Can't write. One day. Soon."

Mutt tried to reacquaint herself with the insides of my skirts. I scratched her tummy instead, which waylaid her. She jerked her back right leg with abandon.

"We would like to talk to you, Mr. Farrow," said Stephen, and walked to the window behind the desk, where he looked out at a laundry line that had collapsed down the facing wall. Farrow didn't seem concerned that Stephen had moved to his side of the desk and made no attempt to look up. Instead, he stopped twiddling his thumbs and biting the right side of his lower lip and started to suck his thumb.

Stephen looked over his shoulder and realized that there was no reason to toy with this innocent. Any investigation is met with suspicion: our way to Bellman's had been hampered by people who didn't like questions or felt that an answer, however uninformative, deserved generous remuneration. But here was a man, a boy, who didn't need to be greased. If he could tell us anything, he would. The question was: How much of his facility was left to him and how many memories remained in the storehouse? Could he even recall the song he'd just written?

"Mr. Farrow, your name is interesting. Is it your real name?" asked Stephen. Farrow replied through the thumb in his mouth, but it was clear that his answer was no.

"Do you know the name Pharaoh?"

"Of course!" His thumb popped out of his mouth in surprise, and he gurgled laughter. "Who do you think I be? I'm Pharaoh himself, myself."

Stephen looked at me and pulled the broadside out of his jacket, placing it on the table over Pharaoh's shoulder.

"Do you recognize this?"

Pharaoh crossed his arms in deliberation and put his bottom lip up over his top lip.

"Look at that picture!" he cooed with delight.

"What about the song?"

"I can't read. But I know the picture. It was done for mine first. Only that picture's been on many a sheet as well. I seen it. Which one is this one? Why don't you read it to me? Why doesn't 'im read it to me?" He poked his thumb in my direction and then jammed it back into his mouth.

"Let me read it," I said, and standing forward, I took the single sheet and read him the title: " 'The Rose and the Briar —' "

"I knew it!" interrupted Pharaoh.

" '. . . or the Abandoned Baby Saved from the Hounds.' An excellent ballad to a merry old Tune, called 'The Old Wife She Sent to the Miller Her Daughter.' "

I was just clearing my throat, ready to begin, when Pharaoh interrupted me.

" 'Ow many 'ounds?" Pharaoh stuck his thumb in his ear and excavated. "I don't remember that. Says ''Ounds.' But there was only one dog. Song says only one dog. Always mistakes. Wrong picture. Wrong title. 'Ound. 'Ounds. But does it really matter? Ask GB. He'll tell yer. The public has spoke again, he says."

Pharaoh was lost in a world of his own, and I hadn't even yet started the ballad. I cleared my throat and was about to recite when suddenly he began to sing. To our amazement, he sang the whole ballad from start to finish. He sang as if enthusiasm is the best way to be tuneful, but he never missed a note and he sang loudly, like a chorister lampooning the choirmaster to amuse his fellow sopranos. His untutored voice was clear, bright as a cornet at dawn, and it told the story with all the urgency I felt was its due. There were only minor changes to the text I had in front of me, and there was one extra verse toward the start that made no difference to the story, which compensated for the last verse, which he didn't bother to sing. And he had the tune, perhaps even the tune specified, as readily as the words. By any standards, it was a remarkable feat of memory. When he was finished, which he announced by repeating the title of the ballad and bowing his head, Stephen put a simple question to him.

"Mr. Farrow, were you there, or did you get this from someone?"

I had never been closer to the truth. So much depended on this strange man's answer.

"There was only one dog," said Pharaoh enthusiastically, as though he had answered the question precisely. "And I don't know why they say 'ounds. It don't make sense, do it?" I caught Stephen's eye and nodded. "And there's a few other things I don't love, neither. Poltroon? What's that? Bad rubbish."

"And the last verse," I added, seeing that the original events were of less interest to him than the song. "You forgot that."

"I sang the last verse. It was the one I ended with."

"There's another last verse here."

"How can there be? The tale is told."

I read him the last verse as printed on the sheet:

> *" 'And when you do rule, please remember the cruel*
> *Way that nature gave you your beginning*
> *And think of the hound on the desolate mound*
> *And please forgive singers their singing*
> *And please forgive singers their sinning.' "*

He looked shaken, like an old man watching his house burn down.

"Wassat?" he asked in disgust. "I didn't write that. I'd never write that. It's horrible. Bad rubbish. Too many lines, and the first two lines don't end proper. It's a mistake. Ask GB. He'll tell yer."

I looked at him and realized: I was able to stand in front of him now only because, somehow, he had witnessed my life being saved. Perhaps he was the reason I was alive. How old was he? He looked younger than I, but that was his simplicity and it was impossible to tell. I did not look as young as I should have. Traveling had aged me.

"Why were you there, Pharaoh?"

Tears started to rush into his eyes. I felt that I, too, would cry.

"That was my first proper song," he said, for that was the thought that moved him. "I made that one up myself. I saw it all and then I put it into those words, right there, except for that last bit, which

I . . . ," and he waved his hand dismissively, as though he were trying to throw the verse away, then increasingly frantically, as if trying to wipe it from an invisible blackboard.

"Do you remember it all?" I asked. Stephen had by this point left the matter entirely to me. It needed a woman's touch. He stood behind me as Pharaoh and I talked; then he went farther off, studying the perfect spines of the dusty books.

"Yes. I remember. Because I wrote the song. Songs always help me remember. They're the air that I breathe, says GB. And they printed it up just like he said and give me money. And they give it that lovely picture. This one was the first one I ever wrote that had my name on it. The last one I wrote I can't remember at all; it wasn't about something I saw. But that was the *first* one. And now, all this . . ." He surveyed the tatty back room of the paper palace in wonder and hummed.

"Was it just as you told it in the song?"

"No." Pharaoh had taken to humming in between everything he said, which made me feel that he couldn't be listening properly.

"How was it different?" I didn't betray any anxiety or fear. I merely asked. Only Stephen knew the drama within. Suddenly, the front door opened and the echoes of the street broke into the room.

"Alby! Has our golden goose . . . ," boomed a voice that was immediately ushered through to the back room. Its owner walked in with the authority of a person whose name is printed on both front door and sign above. He was a scruffy man but with the raffish air of success.

"Well, it's what it says in the song, of course, but in a song . . . ," continued Pharaoh, but his voice trailed off as soon as he saw Bellman. "GB!" he said in greeting, and scratched his head.

"In a song," continued GB, appraising the situation and picking up Pharaoh's sense immediately, while bowing as if for his curtain call, "the writer, as with any fine work of literature, must have license to embroider. He must have complete freedom to respond to his muse, his Terpsichore. He is a slave to her whim. Mr. Phillip Farrow here is the preeminent writer of ballads in the world today, sir. And he will happily compose you anything you desire. Perhaps madam would care for a song commemorating the happy event." Bellman was good. He hadn't batted an eyelid. "Mr. Farrow and I have been working together this many a year and have had no greater successes than with songs and airs composed specifically for a local event." He looked at us quizzically. "Will there be a song in it?"

"Perhaps some tea?" asked Stephen as he took GB by the arm and persuasively led him from the room.

"Alby, tea ahoy!" enthused GB, departing rather sooner than he had intended. Pharaoh looked up at me as they went.

"Why do you want to know? Do you like the song? GB's right. I'll write you another."

"I like the song, but I need to know exactly what happened, what you saw."

Pharaoh sunk his head in his hands and then looked up immediately as though he had done nothing at all. He began to bite at the sore at the side of his mouth. This I took to be a bad sign, a sign that he was nervous.

"I promised I wouldn't."

"That you wouldn't what?"

"Tell about the baby." His teeth clamped down on his lip and made him wince. He started to roll his lip around between his teeth. He then tried to suck his thumb as well, but he couldn't do both and was suddenly unable to do either.

"Do you know who I am?"

He shook his head. "I won't tell you. I promised Mother."

"Who do you think I am?"

He looked up at me again with those quick-slow eyes and started to bite his nails, with which I instantly sympathized.

"They never knew the father," he said suddenly.

"They? I'm not the father."

"You're not the mother."

"No, I'm not the mother."

"I think she died."

My mother had died. I took this in slowly and swallowed.

"You're not him in the carriage?" The flash of inspiration made him smile, but this turned to a frown as he realized that I was not. "Well, you're not me."

"Pharaoh, I am the baby. Either the world is laughing at us or I am the baby you saw."

"The baby I carried?"

"The baby you saw with the dog." Mutt looked up at me, excited by the word *dog,* hoping to hear either *walk* or *food*. Pharaoh was quiet. "I was saved by a man in a carriage, and that man was lord of Love Hall and their shield is the rose and the briar."

"That was what was on the carriage, just like they drew it in that picture. His man got down and took you in. I just sung it like it was, and they wrote it down and give me money."

"Why were you there?"

Again Pharaoh started to bite his lip; he was trying to stop from telling me everything, but I knew he couldn't help himself, even if he had to burst into song and belt it out in perfect rhyming couplets.

"Don't worry, Pharaoh. We have to know. It's many years ago, and no one will be any the worse for it."

"Mother's dead."

"Yes."

"No. My mother. Mother Maynard. They had her. They took her. She got the 'ook." He perked up. "I made her a nice 'Last Words and Confession,' though." This brought a smile to his face and he started to hum, and then began to sing:

> *"I was born in the town of Kilkenny*
> *When first unto London did roam . . ."*

This time his song faded into silence.

"You're wearing a dress. Looks nice."

"You have to tell me. No one can be hurt anymore. You can help me. I need some relations, even if they are dead. I don't know who I am."

"Me, neither. I used to hate it. I like it now. I'm my own man, that's what GB says. Perhaps you'll come to like it, too." I could tell that he was still recalling the success of his Mother Maynard song.

"I need to know anything that will help me find my family. I need to know who I am. Tell me everything. Please."

Pharaoh started to laugh. At first it was a baby's gurgle, but then he started to wheeze and laugh out loud. I couldn't stop him.

"What is it?"

He pointed at Mutt. "There's one!"

I looked down at the dog.

"She's your relation, that one, she is!"

Mutt was lying on her back, encouraging me to scratch her belly again, her legs wide open in submission. "That dog who saved you, I went back and got her the next day. She come 'ome with me, and she had a litter and the only one we kept was Mutt's dad. And the only pup we kept of his was Mutt. I think she's your aunt or your niece. Or something."

I couldn't help but laugh, too. The only relatives we could muster for me were a diaspora of dogs across England. Appropriate, I suppose.

"I thought she took a fancy to you!" said Pharaoh through another gale of laughter. Even Mutt joined in. She sat upright and howled with us. Pharaoh looked up and then behind me at GB and Stephen, who had come back into the room. Their expressions killed our merriment.

"Pharaoh, you have to tell them now," said GB. "Mother is no more. They're all gone."

"Except her niece," said Pharaoh as Mutt bounded off to a corner, where she found a little red ball that she dropped at my feet and then, when I didn't grab it immediately, nudged toward me with her nose and panted expectantly. I love dogs.

And so we were able to fill in some of the pieces from Bellman, who was short on details, and more from Pharaoh, who was short on the ability to fit them together. As they told me, I had to disassociate myself entirely from the bundle that Pharaoh was carrying. It wasn't even me. I was barely alive. But I couldn't. I imagined myself at the mercy first of a young witless boy and then of the dog on the dustheap. Was every breath agony as I struggled for survival, or was I licked back to life by the saliva of Mutt's grandmother? I looked at Pharaoh. I looked at Mutt. Lucky girl.

Over the next hour, to the clinking of copious cups of tea, they filled in their own story. Mother had become an embarrassment to the police, and though she had an ace or two on everyone, her hand wasn't good enough to keep her at the table. Pharaoh had been distraught, Bellman said, and it was GB himself who took the boy in, encouraging him to write to his heart's content. Their initial success was founded on the accuracy of Alby's dictation-taking, the infallibility of GB's printing press, and the radical speed with which the songsmith could turn out a new set of verses. On these foundations was built their own small but prosperous empire, and a triumvirate they had remained ever since. Even Pharaoh had begun to grasp that the improvements in his life were the result of his writing the songs.

"He was as happy as he ever could be," said GB. "But he bridled at the assignments something awful. For Mr. Farrow is only able to let his musical mind wander where it will. A commission will rarely get the best out of him." Pharaoh nodded sagely. In fact, he'd had everything he needed except a good English name, so GB suggested an alternative: Phillip Farrow. And those who still wanted to call him Pharaoh could because, in their part of London, it made little difference to the pronunciation of the word. All the explanation, of course, was given by the talkative GB, while Pharaoh variously sucked his thumb, pulled some long hairs from his right nostril, bit his lip, tickled Mutt's tummy, hummed, thumbed through the papers on the desk, and licked the end of his finger before placing it in his ear.

Just as we thought we had reached the end of the two performances and were ready to go home and tell this much of the story to amazed faces, the story of me and the boy and the dog and the carriage and the song and the boy and the dog and me, Bellman racked his memory for one more detail.

"What about Annie, old cock? Isn't Annie still around? I know I've seen her. She's the only one."

"Oh, yes," said Pharaoh, as though the location of one of the women who had "delivered" me, who knew Mother Maynard, who had seen my mother's face, possibly even knew her, was irrelevant. "I don't like seeing her one bit."

"Well, where *is* she? Dearie I!" GB spoke in a tone of mock exasperation for our benefit. "I'm sorry, my friends, I honestly am."

"She tends for those fallen women less fortunate than herself," recited Pharaoh, and then in a doom-laden tone, "at the Other Marys. I know where."

"The Other Marys! There we are. Can you take them, Pharaoh? My goodness! He'll take you. Can you take them? She was one of Mother's girls, but she's the only one still in the area, or at liberty. Or alive."

A new look came over Pharaoh's face, one that had never previously been seen, if Bellman's reaction was anything to go by. Pharaoh had made a decision of no little importance.

"I want to write a new song," he said.

"Alby!" shouted Bellman as he jerked his face to the left while keeping an eye on his protégé, but Pharaoh merely snorted.

"Not now."

"Tea, Alby!" improvised Bellman.

"I want to write another song about the rest of the story of the abandoned baby saved by the hound. Houn-duh. One."

"Of course you can write another song. As many as you like."

"I shall tell the *true* story."

"I think Mr. Farrow is saying," said Stephen with a smile, "that he would like very much to take us to see Annie and that he would, equally, like to write another song about Rose and her story, perhaps an official song, as it were."

At first, Bellman looked bewildered and then he became flustered.

"Why, the sly little devil. That's a kind of . . . well, there's no other word. It's blackmail!"

Pharaoh's engagement in the negotiation was finished and he was trying to throw pieces of paper for the dog to catch, though Mutt couldn't see with her eyes underneath my skirt.

"We accept," I said immediately.

Pharaoh smiled his lopsided smile.

2

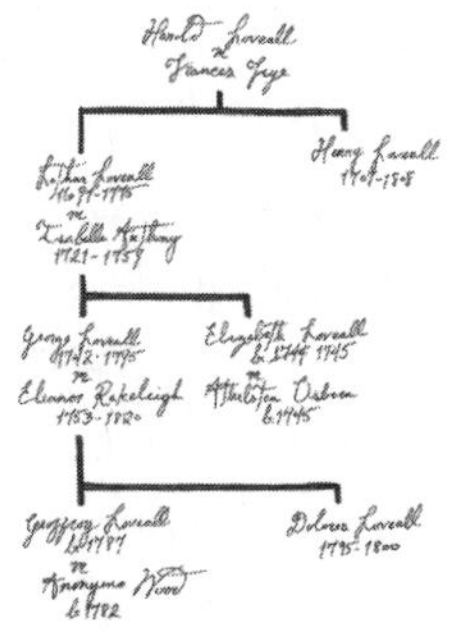

VERYONE GATHERED in the front room at Twenty-four to hear our tale. Stephen and I passed the baton back and forth in constant relay, peppering the account with as many amusing exaggerations as possible. On occasion, our story snowballed out of control and seemed to take over, as though it were telling us. It made its own embellishments. Were the curtains really made out of paper? They should have been, whether they were or not. A good story deserves to be well told, and if the actual facts aren't quite enough, then a little exaggeration won't loosen anyone's grasp of the truth. Quite the reverse. (And now there is nobody left to contradict me as I am come around for the final lap, the last of the relay team.)

Then, in a euphoric rush to the ribbon, we finished, breathless. My mother clapped her hands together and Victoria sat, in that defiantly unfeminine way of hers, shaking her head in approval and disbelief. Hamilton busied himself recording key points in his ledger, and this reminded me to write to Franny and tell her the news. I would keep a record of the exact sequence of events, just for her — I owed her a journal in return for the one she had kept for me. I stood up and twirled around.

"Today, a dog!" I sang, in tribute to Pharaoh. "And tomorrow, the whole pack of them."

"And so the books continue to be written," said Hamilton with satisfaction as he put a full stop at the end of the latest chapter, "and these in the codes we know." He asked some particulars, dull details we had neglected to communicate in our exhilaration.

"And we have so many of the Bellman ballads," said my mother. "Fifty at the least. We can trace Farrow's development entirely, probably a good deal better than Mr. Bellman could."

Stephen would communicate further with GB, and the visit to Annie would be my next adventure in the world. We all put forth our opinions: Hamilton endorsed summoning Annie to Twenty-four, whereas Victoria recommended we interview her at the Other Marys. It would be an education for us to see such an establishment at close quarters.

The quietest hour of the day at Twenty-four was about to begin — the early evening between late-afternoon reading and the dinner gong, when the sun shone lazily through the large back window and turned the polished table orange. The meeting seemed about to adjourn when Hamilton asked if I thought the time right for his analysis of our situation. He had previously hinted that he would not do so till I was ready. I looked at my mother, expecting her to nod approval or disapproval, but she simply returned my gaze in the new way to which I was not yet accustomed. I nodded to Samuel, who settled himself at the dining table with his book in front of him. He readied his glasses on the end of his nose, placed two pencils precisely parallel to the right-hand edge of the book, and cleared his throat as if preparing for a lecture. It was horribly portentous. I've always liked a romance, but I can't bear dry history.

"There are two concurrent investigations under way within this house at the moment, Rose. One is your quest to discover a heritage."

"This is the most important of the inquiries," interrupted my mother conclusively, and then blew the dust from the top edge of a small volume in her hand.

"Quite so, ma'am," he said, nodding. "The other is mine, on behalf of this family and my own, and the complications of which I shall endeavor to explain. I am now able to reveal what I have found with the small tools at my disposal. It is only a very little but might be of great import."

I felt my mind wander to my new relation as last I had seen her: on her back with her legs in the air, pedaling frantically as I scratched, before she pricked up her ears at a sound too high for the human ear, darted off on some canine quest, and never returned. Though these thoughts were delightful to me, I knew that I should be paying attention to Hamilton, however tedious his preamble and text. I'd been ignoring him while I was thinking of Mutt.

"What I am about to tell you, found using Stephen and Sarah's code, is known only to your mother and myself."

We would be here for some time. I idly played with the ends of my mustache and did a subtle impression of Pharaoh for Stephen's benefit. I tried not to catch his eye, which involved looking at him from time to time, until I realized that, to my grave disappointment, he was listening intently to his father.

"The Bad Lord Loveall, your great-grandfather by adoption, Rose, was, as we have long known, unable to produce an appropriate heir with his first wife, Catherine Aston. They had two children, namely, Georgina and George Loveall. At the age of nineteen, Georgina eloped to marry Philippe of Brussels, never to return and, though she produced issue, signed over any share in the fortune for the privilege of being rid of the family; George Loveall, born 1724, died at the age of three. When it was subsequently decided that Catherine could be of no further assistance, the Bad Lord was prevailed upon to divorce his one true love in 1737. He then married Isabelle Anthony in 1741 and fathered two children: namely, and firstly, the Good Lord Loveall, who married your grandmother, Eleanor Rakeleigh —"

"Is there a family tree?" interrupted my mother.

"Yes, I have one here, ma'am, though I must reconfigure it somewhat, as you will hear."

"It would be most helpful."

"The next child was Elizabeth Loveall, born in 1744 and now deceased. She married Lord Athelstan Osbern, who is, we hear, himself on the point of extinction, leaving his family in situ in Love Hall, now Playfield House."

I knew all this, and though I listened as best as I could, I had only limited patience for these names and dates. Such stories always have to be told from so far back and I start to squirm. Hamilton had no idea of my qualms as he concentrated on his page. Though he looked up only fleetingly, it was often in my direction, and I remembered that the presentation was primarily for my benefit. It was my own investigation, however, that seemed the more present and pressing. I imagined Alby bringing in a fresh pot and Pharaoh in his paper cocoon singing my song.

"The Bad Lord never ceased to love Catherine Aston, and it was she who brought up those four children, using Isabelle Anthony for little more than incubation. And where is that? Erm . . . here . . ." His voice slowed as he searched for something, quickly riffling through his pages before he found the one he wanted, adjusting his glasses so they perched better on the bridge of his nose. "No . . . here!" He pointed to something with his index finger, tracing the family tree, but in front of him I could see only hieroglyph.

"That is what is *publicly* known. Precisely," he continued. "This business was presided over by my esteemed grandfather, Archie Hamilton, who died only a few years before the death of the Bad Lord Loveall. What I am about to tell you, I was able to read in his journal, using the code that has previously been accessible only to Stephen and Sarah."

Hamilton looked up with pride. He beamed at Angelica and his son, and through that smile shone the history of the Hamilton family, as vital a part of Loveall history as the Loveall themselves.

"My first discovery, from which I read ahead with increasing interest, through some fascinating material about the contemporary enclosure debate, which is not pertinent to our investigation, though it's so very easy to get sidetracked in these books, so many nooks and crannies, just like the great house itself. . . . To the point: my first discovery was that between his divorce from Catherine Aston and his subsequent marriage to the mother-to-be of his children, Isabelle Anthony, the Bad Lord remarried twice."

He looked up to ascertain that everyone was weighing the import of this disclosure.

"Twice?" said Stephen.

"He was married four times in all, and we knew but two: the first, Catherine, and the last, Isabelle."

"Twice as good," I said, keen to make a contribution, though my mind had turned to Sarah and her continuing absence.

"The crucial detail is that since we now know that he was married four times, the Bad Lord was *divorced* but twice." He paused, then made this point more clearly. "He was divorced one time too few."

"Old devil," said Hood, who was staring distractedly into the Hemmen House and was generally so quiet that one was able to forget his presence. "He'll burn in hell for that," he added, and then yawned.

"One of the other wives died?" I asked, caught up in the scandal rather despite myself.

"No," said Hamilton. "These previously unknown marriages were arranged purely to produce a male heir for Catherine to mother. It was of paramount importance to Loveall that said heir be legitimate and that this be beyond question. Catherine Aston and, one assumes, the Bad Lord handpicked two women for this purpose. Both clandestine marriages took place at the great chapel and were solemnized by the resident curate, a hunting partner of the family by the name of the Reverend Stone. These two women —"

"These two poor women," interjected Victoria.

"Poor women with exceptionally *greedy* parents were succeeded by a third poor woman, Isabelle Anthony, who (unlike her predecessors) played her part to perfection, was immediately with child, and subsequently took her place in Loveall family history, while the other two were erased. This all took place in a span of four years."

The sun was blinding us as it sank, and Victoria, without calling for a servant, pulled the curtain.

"Who were they?" she asked.

"The first of the two was Marion O'Hare — the daughter of a disgraced Irish lord on whom Lothar had some manner of undisclosed hold, details of which would doubtless be in a previous book. She was taken on approval."

"And disapproved . . . like a slave," said Victoria.

"Quite so. Disapproved and divorced. Marion had been rather too clever for them and yet not clever enough. She was soon enceinte — so soon, in fact, that there was a brief worry that she may have been with child before her arrival at Love Hall, although this was discounted for technical reasons — with all the due show of sickness and changing shape. However, after many evasions during her laying in, it became obvious to Archie that she wasn't pregnant at all. Thus, the swift divorce.

"But it is the second of these unknown marriages that is of particular interest to us. The woman was from farther afield, of French-Dutch descent, the daughter of a rich wool merchant of Scheveningen who had done some considerable business with Love Hall. Her name was Marguerite d'Eustache, the daughter of Cornelius van Weenix d'Eustache. The books are most specific about her. Her hair was dark, her hips wide, and her English perfectly acceptable. She became Lady Marguerite Loveall at a wedding performed by Reverend Stone on Good Friday 1739, at which he read the sermon 'Jesus, Hunter of Men' to the four people present. It's all in the book."

Hamilton had got up a head of steam and was now moving forward with greater efficiency. It was much more orderly than the rough-and-tumble of our tale.

"'Under the guidance of Lady Catherine,' a curious expression used in the book more than once about all three of these other wives, Marguerite almost immediately conceived. However, suspicions were soon aroused in her — suspicions that, as we know, were well founded — that she would be no more than a wet nurse for her own child and that the baby would be taken from her. This horrific thought brought her pitiful nights of fevered sleeplessness."

I thought of my own wretched nights and pictured this woman in the same house, even the same room, the same bed in which I had suffered my own torment.

"Her unrelenting poor health meant a very real fear for the life of the baby, that precious commodity. As the months passed, so Marguerite's anxiety increased until she became quite mad in her accusations, making wild allegations of imprisonment and abuse. She accused them of forbidding her communication with her family, a family who, whether she knew it or not, had in all probability connived with the Loveall against her.

"Neither Archie nor Catherine could get any sense from her, and her husband was allowed nowhere near. Sedation was attempted, but this she refused, suspecting it to be poison. For one entire week, she kept herself awake by sticking her side with a pin that she had hidden in her sheets. For another, she wrote reams of letters that were never sent: each contained horrifying charges that one hates to suppose were true — one of these is preserved in the journal. The poor girl had to be perpetually watched and guarded. The family feared the worst.

"But, in the last month, to their great relief, the mothering instinct began to assert itself, as Catherine had continually predicted that it would, until it held sway. Marguerite seemed resigned to her baby's fate and, in the opinion of Archie Hamilton, understood the good that would come to her child under the roof of Love Hall. And the baby was born — a male and the legal heir to the Loveall estate — in perfect health on . . . I have the date here, somewhere. The coded numbers are the very devil to work out. February fourth, 1740. The baby was named Charles."

"Does it end like Medea?" asked Victoria. I looked at Mother, who wore an amused and rather superior expression. She already knew.

"Far from it. And this is the very crux of the matter. Her resignation had been a calculated and successful deception. Rather than give up her child in the manner required, Marguerite took everybody by surprise. Three days later, in the middle of the night of February seventh, she absconded with her child, their heir."

He stopped. I looked up as though that very baby had cried in the silent darkness.

"And?" I couldn't help myself. She had cried in my bed and escaped through the same front gate in the same darkness. In her desperation, she had run into the unknown, just as I had. I felt involved, complicit in her escape, she with her tiny baby, small enough to slip through the railings.

"And . . ." He paused. "Nothing. Vanished. End. As far as this book is concerned, Marguerite was never heard of again. Archie attempted to have the marriage annulled, and when this was found to be impossible, he and the Bad Lord decided that their best policy was to ignore it since so very few had known about the marriage in the first place. The van Weenixes of Scheveningen were reimbursed for the loss of a daughter — they certainly made no trouble — and Love Hall proceeded with their previous plan, which shortly met with success in the form of Isabelle Anthony. They decided to look for Marguerite, to find her —"

"To silence her," interrupted Victoria.

"My grandfather makes no mention of that."

"How can one doubt it?"

"It is irrelevant because they were unable to do anything. When she left, she lost herself very well. She made no communication with her father or with anyone who had been previously known to her. Wherever she went — and I suspect she didn't go very far, a new mother, depleted by childbirth, with a baby held tight to her in the winter cold — she went silently. And we can tell no more, for the book ends and the code therefore changes before there were any developments. I have the remaining books, but we can read no further, for the codes are out of reach."

"Explain," said Victoria.

"Well," said Hamilton, smiling, "to explain the codes would need more time than we have. The code is in four parts, each part passed through the generations of my family. It was devised by Gregory Hamilton, when first the Loveall were granted a royal letters patent, to be arcane enough to satisfy the most fearful lord and the most punctilious of my ancestors. No instance was foreseen in which the entire collection would need to be decoded except by an enemy to the Loveall; therefore, this action was made impossible. Once memorized, or if the correct exchange cannot be affected within our family for any reason, the codes are stored in a secret safe in Love Hall. Mine has been Code B, and I now have access to my children's Code C. This means that, as things stand, fifty percent of Loveall history is unknowable to us here at Twenty-four. I have read as much as I can. We need the other codes."

"Perhaps all hope is not lost for Marguerite," I said, more interested in the woman than in the codes.

"Yes, Rose, but with all due reverence for the lady herself, it matters little for the gist of my story. The point is: there was certainly no chance that she and Lord Loveall were legally divorced, and the marriage was never annulled. Thus, as far as the law is concerned, Loveall was never married to Isabelle Anthony."

"Therefore . . . ," I began.

"Yes?" he said, coaxing me.

"Therefore, my grandfather never had legal claim to the Loveall inheritance."

"And?" asked Mother.

"My father should not have been the Young Lord Loveall."

"Oh!" huffed Hood unexpectedly. "Long before my time! Nothing to do with me!"

"Now we have no claim to Love Hall at all," said my mother.

"That is true," said Hamilton, who was winding down as he removed his spectacles and rubbed where they had pinched a pink crevice. "But it invalidates any claim of *theirs* to take the Hall from us, and if their claim is no clearer than ours — and where it is very likely that a true claim will never be made — then you, we, have been displaced for no good reason. It could occupy the rest of my years, but I think that this thread is worth pursuing. We owe it to the house itself."

"Hear! Hear!" shouted Hood, who couldn't decide whether to stand or remain seated. "Long before my time."

"But none of us are Loveall," I said.

"Your mother was married to the Young Lord. There is no disputing that. She was the incumbent."

"May I speak?" said his wife, Angelica. It was a unique occurrence, but surprises were no longer surprising. "I know that it is not for me to say, but I would rather see the house belonging to the king than in its current state."

"I think that we are all agreed on that," said my mother.

"The shred that we have just learned is more than we could possibly have hoped for," said Hamilton. "I am sure that we can use it to our advantage and I have been recommended the man to approach about this situation, a Mr. Mallion. It is therefore imperative that we recover the other codes from the safe. I am to blame for their presence, but what I thought right has been proved wrong. I thought to safeguard us by taking the books and leaving the codes hidden so the Loveall would not fall victim to any further attack. Perhaps, after all, it is the Osberns that I have unwittingly protected. Now we must reunite books and codes. The books that we cannot understand may hold facts even more compelling than these, and those facts will help us build our case. Not to mention that there may be further information of Marguerite and the lengths to which the Loveall (and, I fear, my family) went in order to track down the poor woman."

"But how are you going to get them from the lion's den?" asked Victoria. She made me wish that I were asking more questions.

"Samuel has a proposal," Mother said.

"Yes. It is this. I propose that Miss Victoria go to Love Hall again, after her successful last trip. . . ."

"Successful!" hooted Victoria in miserable recollection.

"I propose she go, with knowledge of the whereabouts of the safe, now known only to Hood and myself, and bring back the contents, which amounts to two small books."

"And how shall I do this, pray?"

Hamilton suddenly became rather sheepish, as though caught in a lie. My mother came to his rescue.

"You will steal them," she said with amusement. Victoria started to laugh.

"I can't steal them."

"I'll steal them," I said. I'd developed quite light fingers on my travels. Perhaps I could put them to use.

"No, this is an errand for Victoria," said my mother.

"And technically it may not be stealing," added Hamilton.

"They are not going to allow me to dance merrily around the Hall, poking about in secret safes," said Victoria.

"No, but your parents are above reproach. Perhaps it may be time for them to attempt a rapprochement with their cousins. With you, of course, in attendance."

"I am ready to help, but my parents will need more persuading. And I cannot leave my job at this moment. Matters are too pressing —"

"Our daughter, Sarah, is coming home," interrupted Angelica. "She could take your place at the hospice for the little time that it will take."

"Perhaps only a day," her husband added.

"You have thought of everything," said Victoria.

"We have tried."

"You have succeeded," said Victoria, and taking a deep breath, she stood up. "I shall write to my parents immediately."

"They will be here tomorrow," said Hamilton, in amused admission of his resourcefulness.

"We must have a most specific plan, one that covers all exigencies," said Victoria. I was trying to remember everything so I could write it down for Franny, but above all else, I had heard one fact only: Sarah was coming home.

How I slept that night I'll never know — nature's soft nurse normally eludes me the night before a big day. But I did sleep. For the first time in over a year I dreamed of swimming with Stephen and Sarah, but now the dream was confused with Salmacis, one painting superimposed upon another. I awoke to the early-morning sounds of the city that were now my familiar alarm — clattering horseshoes on cobbles like smashed crockery — and I remembered the last time I had seen Sarah, a memory that still provoked a physical reaction, like the smell of sour milk.

She arrived unannounced, unexpectedly early, and found me sitting with Franny's journal in the front room. It was better that she caught me unprepared, for I had not had time to overly fuss about my appearance or work myself into a nervous frenzy. As I heard footsteps behind me, I assumed for all the world that it was my mother or Angelica, until I heard the voice.

"Rose?" She said it in wonder, as though my name might bring me back to life from stone, wake me from a century's sleep. I dropped my book. Sarah.

She moved in front of me, her face dark before the front window, and knelt down to pick it up, her skirt gathering around her on the ground. She rested her cheek on my thigh, her chin on my knee, and

I lay my hand on top of her head, where I let it rest. The room fell very quiet, with only the ticking of the old clock to disturb us. Even the outside world seemed unusually in league with the silence we required, and soon even the clock marked the same rhythm as my heart. I looked at the gold-framed circular mirror above the fireplace, which, from its position on the mantelpiece, reflected everything as if through a fisheye. The room consumed us. We were an inconsequentially small tableau in the bottom left corner, but my hand felt as though it were the axis of the world.

"Sarah," I said, letting her hair fall through my fingers. "I am so sorry."

"No, Rose," she answered. "I am sorry. We all are."

We stayed there in silence for a long while. Finally, she looked up at me. There were no tears in her eyes.

"I thought you were gone forever," she said, and laid her head down again.

"I had gone forever *before* I left. I am returned a different person, but still Rose. I am much happier now, the way I am."

"I didn't understand anything."

"Nor did I."

She kissed my leg through my skirt and threw her arms around my waist, holding me as if I were going to try to make a dash for it.

In the mirror's distorted reflection, our clothes became muddled and her leg appeared somehow to be extending from my body. Her head was lost somewhere in my middle, and since I could see only her hair, it looked as though I was in Salmacis again, but this time tight in somebody else's clutches, Sarah the nymph and I the innocent. She wouldn't let go of me and I didn't want her to, but now I wished for no supernatural outcome, only that when she finally did let go, I would still be as I was and she would be as she had always been: perfect.

Part of my dress rose, caught beneath her surfacing body as she shifted upward. And then all her weight was upon me and I was beneath her, her cheek rubbing against my mustaches. I put my arms around her for the first time and drew her closer.

"Ose!" she said, momentarily lost in Love Hall's palace of memories. "Rose. Brother and sister?" she said.

"Brother and sister," I said, but I felt a spasm of tension in my throat as I spoke the words. Was that what she wanted? Was that what I wanted? As I held her close, I tried to think of us as brother and sister, but the more her body moved against mine, the more I was reminded of the complex games of give-and-take we had enjoyed when we told stories and imagined. I didn't know what was meant to be anymore. I could do only what I felt was right.

In the mirror, which I could just see through the hair that had fallen from Sarah's plait, our bodies were now distinct. She sat on my lap, in a way that was familiar to me from barrooms, a position that allowed me the easiest access to handle and toy. Farther away, behind us, I saw a sudden movement that drew my eye. I couldn't quite make it out, and fearing discovery, I pushed Sarah sharply to let her know.

"No," she said, not understanding. As she said it, my heart melted. She pushed her head toward my neck and nestled in my shoulder, so I was unable to see the reflection. There was no longer any point in trying to make ourselves respectable.

"Well," said Victoria, "there's a pretty picture. Sarah's here!" Her tone was teasing but sympathetic. "I hate to interrupt a tearful reunion but, Sarah, there is work to be done and, Rose, the arrival of my parents is imminent."

Sarah got up from my lap immediately and curtsied.

"Miss Rakeleigh, I'm so sorry."

"Victoria, please, or Vic." Victoria would have happily caught us in the middle of the act itself, provided that it did not mean Sarah would be late for work. I pulled my dress down to cover my ankles, which had been exposed by its slow ascent. Sarah kept her eyes fixed to the ground in embarrassment. She did not yet know how comparatively lax things were at Twenty-four.

"Oh, ma'am, I couldn't possibly."

"You will. In this house, in all houses, we are equal, members of an extended family. Where I am taking you, other distinctions have long since become irrelevant. We are healthy and in a position to help; they are ill and desperately require whatever we can offer. That is the only difference that matters. You are Sarah. I am Victoria."

"Yes, ma'am," said Sarah, without bothering to correct herself.

A gust of air announced Stephen, who slid along the polished floor in his stockinged feet. Suddenly he was more like the Stephen of old — gauche, mischievous, and clumsy. It was the prospect of seeing his sister that had brought out such adorable foolishness. Then, knowing how I had longed to see Sarah (though he and I had never once spoken of it), he adopted a completely unfamiliar air of deference. I wanted to pat him on the head as you would a puppy.

"Hello, Victoria," he added.

"Sarah, it is time to leave. We shall see Rose on our return."

"Might I see my parents first, Miss Victoria?" asked Sarah, looking at Stephen.

"Time's a-wasting, Sarah."

"Go," said Stephen. "Victoria's parents are about to arrive, too. You'll see Mother and Father later on tonight."

"If we get back tonight! Come along, Sarah," said Victoria, grabbing her hand. Sarah looked pleadingly at us, but to no avail; she was in the grip of an irresistible force that swept her out of the house and onto the street.

I closed the door to my bedroom behind me. This room was entirely neutral, devoid of character, as if they had tried to empty it of anything that might be grating to my nerves. But I didn't need such mollycoddling and rather resented the clear marks on the wall where framed pictures had been; perhaps one was of our old home. Next to the bed, beside the lamp, was a book of rules for card games where one might have expected a Bible. Nothing more. I could still feel Sarah's weight against my body, her hair on my skin. We had laid a foundation to build upon for the future. It was the most I could expect. I fell on the bed, her whisper in my ear.

I had to trust in tomorrow, and for the first time, I could. For so long I had feared the unknown. Before I left home, and throughout my travels, I had been unable to look into the future because I could only envision one of discovery and pain, for myself, for my family. Take, for example, the carriage, in which Sarah and Victoria were traveling at that moment. Mere months before, the very idea of this trip across London would have immediately triggered a chain of imagined events that inexorably led to a picture of their two bodies bruised on the cobblestones, Victoria's short hair coated with blood and dirt, a horse whinnying in hot snorts of pain in the cold morning before the driver put him out of his misery. I had had to deny myself access to the possible futures, to avoid such thoughts about myself, about others.

Back then, a mere glance at any sharp edge would conjure visions of imminent laceration, developing into an unending narrative of sharp disaster and bloody pain in innumerable permutations. I hadn't been able to bear the thought of scissors. I didn't even need to see them to trigger this immeasurable panic. Just the words were enough: *scissors, knife, blade.*

I tested myself. On the armoire next to the rest of my grooming kit, a gift from Stephen, lay an elegant pair of scissors with mother-of-pearl handles, which managed to look simultaneously masculine and feminine. I stared at the sharp point where the two blades came together, and tried to visualize it digging deep into skin, the skin puncturing and bleeding, then tearing as my other hand forced the blades apart. But I couldn't properly imagine it. To test myself further, I took them in my hand and opened the two blades so I could see the edges glint, ready to cut, to slice, to enter. I laid them back down.

I felt nothing except *there is a pair of scissors.* Had I been so unhappy that I feared a blade would harm me of its own volition? Of course not. I closed the scissors, which appeared blunter than when I had first seen them. Only someone else could harm me now.

My mind turned to my mother, who had become increasingly caught up in her own affairs. Though she was evidently excited by news of my discovery (for which, after all, she was entitled to take the credit), she seemed preoccupied. While Stephen's and my investigation gained momentum, and Hamilton and Victoria planned their own skulduggery, my mother poured more and more of her energies into her work on Mary Day.

We still had not sat and talked at length — a conversation that I knew must happen. Allusions had been made, but neither one of us had chosen to grasp the nettle. "The misunderstanding" was how Hamilton referred to it; my mother once alluded to "the false delicacy." I wondered whether she truly thought it either a misunderstanding or a misfortune, or, on the contrary, whether somehow the experiment was still ongoing, with her, the scientist, awaiting its successful conclusion. The philosophies of Mary Day had been influential in her acceptance of, and participation in, the deception, but she was certainly not atoning for this perceived error by rejecting those same theories now. Quite the reverse — she was more immersed than ever, and I took this to be her blithe denial that anyone had acted improperly. I could envision her at that very moment in her study chamber, the main text on a lectern in front of her, a thin book of notes filled with her unnaturally small writing to her right, and three or four other volumes holding one another open around her. If any of the books moved, all places would be lost. She was humming to herself, quietly going about her work alone, while the rest of us busied ourselves with our own investigations.

Perhaps this perseverance was simply in the interests of scholarship. This was her work and she would finish: it was possible that no other scholar would be allowed the same access to the materials. Literary antiquarians of the future would be grateful to her, and that was her reward. In this scenario, she was quietly determined rather than insanely dedicated.

She had insisted that there were more books she needed from Love Hall and prepared a list for Victoria. She thought it impractical to waste rare access, and the pretext of a trip to the Octagonal Library was promptly woven into Hamilton's strategy. Mother would also return the books she had, perhaps never to see them again. Would they even miss them, if she . . . Perish the thought! She would be perfectly happy to use any means to force the Osberns out of the house altogether, but to steal a book from a library, particularly one's own library . . . that was another matter entirely.

As I lay facedown, imagining her, I heard her footsteps and a playful tune. My cousins had arrived and perhaps I might go downstairs.

I wasn't quite ready to see them. As my body became heavier, I thought of Sarah. I hadn't taken her in when she was near me and had barely been able to focus on her face. Now that she was gone, I could see her quite clearly. I saw the wrinkle between her eyes that made a little ledge when she smiled, and the tiny scar on her scalp where the hair still refused to grow. A twitch at the very corners of my mouth, a slight pursing of my lips, and it was I who smiled. A twitch down in my stomach followed, at the core of my empty belly, as if caused by tiredness or hunger, at least by a yearning for something. I knew what. And this twitch vibrated through my nerves like a plucked string till my extremities tingled, my toes, my fingers. And I laughed. My eyes, I could feel my eyes. I ran my tongue over the sharp edge of my front teeth. I blinked. There was an itching inside my ears. I swallowed and they popped with a loud click. My blood pulsed through my body in celebration of . . . what? Of what I felt then, for I had never felt it before. I thought of Sarah and then tried not to think of her, her skin, her soft skin, her hair, her body, because it was making my heart beat faster, and my blood, to compensate, was rushing to other parts of my body.

The cock had another purpose in other men, and I had helped them achieve it. In my resigned state in which, like the used-up hero of a modern romance, nothing could give me pleasure, I had even become proud of this know-how. When I was with those men, they sometimes — rarely — asked if they could repay the compliment, only in the continued service of their own pleasure rather than any altruistic consideration, but I was pleased to be one of that fine class known to care only for others. I was above being touched, and this designated me one of the Lavish Ladies, able to ply my trade without fear. I had learned to live in deliberate denial of any other of its functions besides pissing. I had conquered and liberated myself from such urges. I considered it as little as I could, and it had ceased to try to solicit my attention.

But now, long-forgotten memories returned, flooding to my brain, as blood pulsed through my body. I remembered another time when this had been a normal event, a secret pleasure to be greatly anticipated. And I thought back to the morning of a game of cricket. I was thirteen and it was the first time this feeling developed beyond a nervous shiver. I was encouraged to attempt an immediate repeat too soon, rubbing myself half raw in the process. No wonder I was so focused on the ball that afternoon. It was a pain for me to move my midriff at all, let alone run, so the best I could hope for was to hit the ball so hard that I didn't have to run at all. The first time I played, my skirt had thwarted my running between the wickets, but this time it was a chaffed cock. The result was the same: impressive strokes. When I was dismissed, caught on the boundary, I left with some relief and walked, bowlegged, back to the house, where I lay on my bed with the door locked, and dabbed carefully at myself with cream.

I had absolutely forgotten the episode. But now I could see it as clearly as the nose in front of my face, the cock in front of my stomach. I arched my hips to make a tent of my body and burrowed my hand up and under my skirt from below. I expected to find myself sore like that first time, but instead, I was proud and in the pink of health. And this, too, I remembered: once it had announced itself and arrived, it was the guest that wouldn't leave. And the Rakeleighs were downstairs. There was certainly no chance of receiving anybody, particularly our respected cousins, in this state.

I tried to focus on things that I found uninteresting, even boring, at that time — *Metamorphoses,* for example, which had lost all its appeal to me. But Byblis and Caunus sprang to mind. Brother and sister. Sarah and myself. "We don't know what we are doing and, while we're still young, shouldn't we live and love like the gods?" And the gods themselves: hadn't Juno married Jove?

When the mind is in a certain state, there is very little one can do to dampen the fire. In such a mood, anywhere the mind wanders will provoke, however plain the initial thought. And I was in such a mood.

I tried to calm myself. I thought of Edwig, his heavy breathing, his heart exploding, but that was no good, so I went back to *Metamorphoses,* where I was waylaid by the rape of Leda by Jove, disguised as a swan, the long neck, the twisted limbs . . . Jove as a stocky bull raping Europa, as a grotesque grinning satyr taking Antiope, as a flame of fire defiling Aegina — a flame of fire! — as a shepherd's boy ravishing Mnemosyne. All counterproductive. So I tried to list things: first, the names of the trees in the gardens of Love Hall, but one small association and the list turned back into the list of rapes, in particular the serial crimes of Neptune: Canace, whom he raped as a horned bull, Ceres as a horse, Melantho as a dolphin . . . bull, Sarah, swan. And the flame of desire raced through me until I felt a burning, which turned into an involuntary throb as though my sex were smiling with me, at me, in defiance of my wishes. Oh, God. Take me. Come in any guise, but take me.

Stephen was at the door.

"Rose! Are you coming?"

"Yes. I don't know. I'll be there in a minute. Downstairs." I was speaking too quickly and not breathing.

"Is there anything wrong, Rose?"

"No." My voice was peculiarly strangled, only partly because I was talking into the bedclothes.

"You sound strange. Are you all right?"

"I was asleep! I'll be down as soon as I . . ."

"Can I help?"

That was it.

I told him to go away.

I was downstairs in less than ten minutes, in a new dress, which received many a compliment. I had barely had time to catch my breath and was talking too quickly. Everyone remarked how extremely healthy I looked, almost glowing, and it was true that I felt superb, if a little tired. My body was returning to me.

Victoria put Sarah to work at the Friends' hospice. They did not return that first night. Just before noon an ebullient Victoria led the way up the stairs, while Sarah straggled behind, looking as though she had spent the night in labor, but with no baby as reward. Stephen and I stared at her as she passed, and she raised her eyes to the heavens. She was too tired to see her parents, and Victoria allowed her only five hours' sleep before she was to turn around and begin again. The following night Victoria came home without Sarah, who would find her sleep as she could at the hospice.

I stayed at home with Julius, Alice, and, nominally, my mother, though we barely saw her. It was the first time that I had been called to play host, and now that I was more at home at Twenty-four, and more at home in my own skin, I relished the role. I entertained them with stories, heavily embroidered and expurgated, of my travels and my recent trip to Bellman's. Of the next day's work, we made no mention. Hamilton had coached them in their mission. They accepted their task without complaint, relieved that their own function was mainly diversionary.

In the event, the trip took only a day. The Rakeleigh party left in the early morning and returned that night, taking us by surprise. Despite the late hour, Julius and Alice seemed particularly excited to tell their story. Ironically, they had played their part so well that the Osberns (who felt that it would be to their advantage to be seen to have a good relationship with their less fortunate kith and kin) had tentatively accepted the undesired rapprochement.

Before the main thrust of their narrative began, my mother interrupted to ask whether Victoria had successfully withdrawn, which was the word she always used, her books from the Octagonal. Victoria handed over four volumes to my mother, who, much to everyone's surprise, opened one of them and started immediately to read. She glanced up during their tale but seemed infinitely more interested in the poems. To our amusement, just when Victoria's cloak-and-dagger tale was to reach its climax, Mother excused herself, saying she was tired, though I knew that her candles would be burning for many hours yet.

Julius and Alice confirmed that tales of dissipation had proved somewhat exaggerated. Nora held sway, and the house, to all intents and purposes, was hers and hers alone. She treated only Augustus Rakeleigh as her equal. Though Nora knew how to manage a household, it was not in a way that would inspire great loyalty in a servant, and she was clearly terribly unpopular. Maids tiptoed in fear of reprobation. They had to answer on the one hand to Nora and on the other to Anstace, who had finally reached the vaunted position of housekeeper. A servant was dismissed midway through the afternoon for answering back: she had said, "Sorry."

However, rumors at The Monkey's Head about Guy and Prudence were largely accurate: the marriage consisted of little but bickering, and they had regressed to spoiled childhood. They concerned themselves not at all with the business of the house, allowing Nora to rise to the top, and dedicated themselves solely to hedonism and cantankerous squabbling.

Upon arrival, the Rakeleighs were shown into the Entertainments

Room. Nora and Augustus sat front and center, these two being the only ones who afforded each other any cordiality. Nora's own husband, Edgar the divine, stood to one side, entirely ignored. There was an air of defeat about him, and his relative position in this unhappy tableau demonstrated his irrelevance to all decision making. A portrait of Esmond, in full military regalia, looked down on everyone from above the fireplace with his familiar sneer. Beneath him, the barefaced lie: LOST IN BATTLE. The two Rakeleighs' mutual antipathy had never been any more obvious than it was that day. Augustus could hardly bear to look at his elder brother, while Alice's attempt at small talk with his wife, Caroline, was thwarted by the latter's poor English and lack of interest. There was little conversation to be had, and Victoria was set to begin her mission by asking for the books from the library in exchange for the ones she was returning, when Nora ostentatiously coughed into her handkerchief.

"We are very proud to announce that Guy has provided Prudence with the next heir to Love Hall. You will, of course, understand the import of this."

As congratulations were proffered and the Osberns applauded news they had doubtless heard many times before, Victoria found herself wondering if Prudence was any better off than any of the earlier slave wives, the would-be brood mares of Love Hall.

"What a man!" said Prudence, raising her eyebrows in ironic reference. The father-to-be looked overweight, a little bleary-eyed from his drinking exertions of the previous evening. Prudence suddenly became more pregnant, leaning back in her chair and pushing out her stomach. "I do believe I am gaining."

"Of course you're gaining, Prude," retorted Guy. "I merely did what was required, no less and no more. And," he added for the benefit of the visitors, "*in the normal way*. I've had a marvelous idea. . . ."

"What is it, Guy?" said Prudence, full of spiteful anticipation.

"If it's a girl, we shall bring it up as a girl. . . ."

"And if it's a boy?"

"Well, then, we shall —," he began, but was interrupted by his forgotten uncle.

"Nephew, I hardly think . . . ," said Edgar from behind the chair, using Nora as his shield in case this did not meet with Guy's approval. However, it was the shield that hushed him. Edgar nodded at Julius with a pious glance.

"*What* shall you do, Guy?" said Nora, inviting her nephew to wit. Prudence was rubbing her belly through her dress, though there was barely a bulge to be seen.

"Well, we won't put him in a bloody dress!"

Guy started to laugh and Prudence joined in. They could be unpleasant to each other, but evidently they found a certain harmony in abusing a third party. Even Augustus and Nora could not restrain themselves. Edgar wore the pained expression of someone who earnestly wished he were elsewhere. His wife told him to stop shuffling.

Another servant came in, unannounced, her eyes downcast. She was a pitiful-looking creature in a plain gray dress. Edgar, alone, acknowledged her entrance. Victoria realized that it was no servant at all but rather Nora's sister.

"Edith!" said Victoria in surprise. All eyes turned toward her. Edith stopped without speaking.

"Edith," said Nora. "How lovely to see you." As if she hadn't seen her in a long time.

"Oh, what a very rare treat!" said Guy.

Edgar stepped from Nora's side and offered his arm to his sister-in-law. She whispered to him and then tweeted a frail hello to the visitors before turning once more and departing. This was all that was seen of this demoralized creature. Edgar addressed the assembly gravely:

"Edith regrets that she is unable to extend her visit. Camilla has taken a turn for the worse. Ever since her return she has been very weak, and Edith must return to her bedside."

The news sat awkwardly, waiting for someone to sympathize.

"Is Camilla not well?" asked Lady Alice, bravely breaking the silence.

"Not at all," said Edgar. "We fear . . ."

"She was always a fragile creature," said Nora finally, as if writing Camilla's obituary. "Like her mother. There's a recognizable strain in the family. The previous lord was cut from the same cloth. Why Camilla went to Africa, I have absolutely no idea. I can't think that she was a very good advertisement for the Bible."

"What a shame we could not enjoy either of their company," said Julius.

"All the conversation you've been denied," said Guy, who woofed with laughter.

"You'll just have to make do with us," said Prudence. "Guy, do stop that ridiculous guffaw. Think of the baby."

"The baby!" Guy shrugged dismissively.

Edgar was beside himself with Old Testament rage, born of his identification with all those hard done by in Love Hall. He stamped a foot firmly on the ground, the most aggressive act of protest he could muster, turned, and left the room.

"Well, well . . . ," said Augustus. "A drink, perhaps?" Baiting the divine and his ensuing anger were evidently nothing out of the ordinary.

"Anonyma has returned some books and would like to take four more titles away, if this is acceptable to you. I would be grateful if you would allow me to go and get them for her," said Victoria.

"The librarian wants books," sneered Nora. "Librarians always want books."

"Are they worth anything? Should we accompany her?" asked Guy dubiously.

"They're books, you simpleton," said Prudence. "Of course they're not worth anything."

"Besides, why you have taken them in, I . . . ," continued Guy, but he could get no further.

"Guy!" spat Nora. She had said it so many times that she had reduced the reprimand to an expletive, a single hard *G*. At this, Guy stopped dead, as though shot, but did not apologize.

"Of course the librarian can borrow our books," she said condescendingly. "We understand that you, as members of our great family, have taken in these unfortunates purely out of a Christian generosity, to help them find their way in the world again."

"Victoria tries to help all unfortunates," said her father carefully. "We admire this instinct in her and her brother. Edgar would approve of our motives."

"Edgar!" said Guy. "Edgar! Brrrr!"

"Nora's husband is habitually impressed by shows of charity, brother," said Augustus. "But of this instance, we approve. It would be bad form for relatives of ours to become objects of derision. The harm to the family name . . ."

"And so we thank you for keeping them in your house, away from the public eye," Nora said, completing his thought.

"They are free to come and go as they please, and they do," said Victoria. "It is not a prison. We are not keeping them from going out."

"Quite," said Nora regally, to end the matter. "If you would like to take the librarian books, please do so."

Augustus added, "And should her magnum opus ever reach a state for publication, we would be happy to be the recipient of its dedication, for our assistance with materials."

"I shall go now," said Victoria, tingling with indignity.

"And mind the silver," shouted Guy after her, before howling with laughter. "Check her upon departure, Thrips."

"A little quip! Merely Guy's irrepressible sense of humor," his father tried to reassure Julius, while those who remained in the Entertainments Room wondered what on earth they were going to say to each other.

* * *

Victoria went first to the library, which was exactly as she had left it. Despite their greed, it hadn't occurred to the Osberns to appraise the contents, and it was clear that no one ever ventured within. The precise texts were easily found, cataloged exactly where Anonyma had said. Victoria took two adjacent books that she thought might be of use. My mother's perfect instructions bought her time for the real purpose of her trip.

The safe was a different matter. Located in a priest's hiding hole, it could be reached only through a secret opening in the garderobe off the Baron's Hall. As she looked from the end of the corridor, Victoria was horrified to discover that there was no possible way she could gain access: one of the remaining foot servants stood opposite, outside Camilla's door. Victoria had no authority to send him off, and it was inconceivable that she could walk up to the hiding hole, go in, open the safe, fumble around with the instructions, and remove the two books without being seen. Yet this was her one chance, and she knew that if she failed in the attempt, or if she were discovered in the act, there might be no possibility of another.

She was wasting time. She took one step down the hall, and the guard stepped up to her with confrontation gleaming in his eyes.

"Is Edgar Osbern with his niece?" she spoke loudly. The guard made no reply but eyed her without blinking. "Is Edgar Osbern within?" she repeated.

"I do not think so, ma'am. I shall see."

He went into the room and returned immediately.

"He is in the chapel, praying for his niece. None are to be disturbed."

"Thank you."

Victoria, her heart pounding, walked swiftly downstairs and went the back way to the chapel. Avoiding the outside window of the Entertainments Room, she was there in less than a minute. The heavy latch, in the shape of a hissing snake, opened willingly.

Inside, all was gloom and mildew. It was the smell of the Church of England. There was no sign of Edgar. She walked toward the altar, looking up at the dirty windows and down the length of the pews, cassocks hanging lazily behind them like rows of saucepans. Frightful remembered images of the wedding went through her mind.

She had thought she was entirely alone, but between the echoes of her own footsteps, she heard a sniveling, a whimpering, like that of a cowering dog. She looked up at the altar and back to the door, but saw nothing. Slowly, she became aware that the noise was coming from the confessional booth to her left. She walked toward it, treading as lightly as she could.

One side was open, but the curtain was pulled shut on the other. She sat down in the empty compartment, wondering how to introduce herself.

"I am sorry," said Edgar from the other side. He was scared and he spoke through small gulps. "It was not my intent to —"

"Don't be sorry," said Victoria as calmly as she could. "You can help."

"Nora?" asked Edgar. His voice betrayed his panic.

"No. I am not Nora."

"Who?"

"I don't know who you are, and you don't know who I am. We are entirely anonymous in here, aren't we?"

"Yes," said Edgar. "That is so."

"For the sake of a woman you admire and her poor child, for your own soul, for the souls of all those who have been mistreated and abandoned, you must help me."

"Is this a trap? Who are you?"

"We need you."

"You don't know what you're doing," whispered Edgar through his teeth. "I cannot help you."

"You must. Tell me again that you cannot help, here, under the eyes of God. If we cannot come to you, then to whom?"

"They know everything. It is I who need help. I cannot stay here. Edith cannot stay here. Camilla is *dying*."

"We can help you, too. Time is scarce. We must be quick." It was her only hope. She knew from the sound of his voice that it was also his.

"They must not suspect —"

"Shh! This is what you must do." She told him the location of the safe. She told him about the foot servant. She told him the two books she wanted. She slipped the instructions through the grille. She couldn't see his face, but she thought she saw the shadow of his nodding head.

"Can I do it?" he asked of himself, or perhaps of God, but an undercurrent in his voice betrayed that he intended to try.

"You will. And you have to. Now."

"I shall meet you back here."

"Be quick. And thank you."

"May God have mercy on all our souls," said Edgar, and he left the booth, his heels echoing on the marble. She stayed where she was until she heard the door close, to preserve the illusion of anonymity. And then she stood in the chapel, waiting for him. She had been away too long now to justify the few pitiful books she held in her hand. Minutes passed, it seemed like hours, but Edgar did not return. The smell and echoes of the chapel became increasingly oppressive to her and she longed to escape, longed for the endearing simplicity of the meetinghouse. And still he did not come. She peered through the snake door, frightened she would be seen, but there was no sign. He had failed. He had been discovered. She could wait there no longer, could remain "in the library" not a moment more.

Victoria, clutching the books tightly to her, dashed across the side of the house and reached the back door. Returning to the Entertainments Room, she feared she would find Edgar, a foot servant on either side of him, a martyred look in his eyes. But as she recovered her breath, she found all as she had left it. Guy and Prudence were still bickering. Her father, to pass the time, was in the middle of an extremely lengthy story about Lord William, which Augustus was ignoring. Edgar had obviously found the task beyond him. She should have known.

"You were gone," Augustus said as she returned.

"Yes," said Victoria, "I had the devil of a time finding them and then I remembered to look for one other that she had asked for. All present and correct." She gave the books a little rap on the side.

"Oh," said Guy.

"You have what you want?" said Nora.

"Yes, thank you," she lied. "Would you like to see?"

"No. Perhaps, then, it is time for you all to go. Camilla is very ill, and the noise and commotion will not be good for her."

Julius and Alice looked delighted with this suggestion, and her father, assuming that everything had gone according to plan, was only too pleased to cease his pointless story.

"No!" said Victoria rather too abruptly. "Perhaps we should stay for tea? It's such a very long journey."

Her parents understood her meaning immediately.

"Mmm, quite. Long journey. Perhaps a little sustenance . . . ," her father attempted gamely, but Nora had made up her mind and it was decided. Victoria didn't know what to do. They were leaving. Good-byes were exchanged as meaningfully as possible. Prudence wouldn't get up, and Guy started to throw torn-up bits of paper at her belly.

"Get up, you lazy sow!" he said.

"Don't call me a sow! That's *your* little piggy in there."

"Ah!" said Guy with no enthusiasm.

"And I hope it doesn't have your hair."

"Children, children!" said Nora indulgently.

"We would like to say good-bye to Edgar if possible," said Victoria. "Perhaps he is with Camilla."

"No, no," said Augustus. "That's impossible. Impossible?"

"Not impossible," said Nora, "but unnecessary."

Further delay was out of the question. The mission was over: a failure. But as they were at the point of exiting the front door, Edgar came down the stairs, purposefully but without hurry.

"Julius! Victoria!" There was a slight quiver behind the gentle determination in his voice, for he was involved in a deception.

"Ah! Edgar, how appropriate," sighed Nora. "Ever timely. Our cousins were just leaving and wanted to say their good-byes."

Edgar dangled a small parcel wrapped in newspaper, knotted with a careful bow. The family looked on, bemused.

"I am so glad I have not missed you, for I have been meaning to give you these two sacred books. They are the personal prayer book of the dead Lord Loveall and the New Testament of his wife, who lives now with you. They are of no use to us here, and it is a sin to separate the true word from its rightful owner."

"Oh, really, Edgar!" said Augustus derisively.

"No," said Nora. "That is very kind of you, Edgar. Well done. Very Christian."

"Very Christian, of course," agreed Augustus reluctantly, but he emphasized the word to make sure his audience understood that it was also very stupid, very sentimental, very dull, and that Christianity was a synonym for all these things.

"Most kind. Miss Wood will be absolutely delighted. Most kind," said Victoria, who took the package firmly and immediately handed it to her father, taking care not to look at Edgar any more than was necessary. She had the presence of mind to ask one more time: "No tea before we leave?"

"One can only say good-bye so many times," said Nora, bowing as she did so. Edgar had turned and was quickly moving away from them. Servants saw Victoria and her parents out, and the door closed like a portcullis behind them. Nobody waved.

"So," said Victoria, taking the parcel out from behind her chair. "It was not even thievery."

"May I?" asked Hamilton, twitching. He took the books and laid them on the table in front of him with nervous anticipation. Then he began to unwrap them.

"Let's hope they're the right ones," said Stephen with a smile. Everybody stared at him. He had said the unsayable. Time stopped for a moment until Hamilton looked up.

"Yes."

I kissed Victoria.

"Thank you. Thank you, all three of you."

There was a sigh of relief. It was at this moment that Sarah walked in the front door, worn out by her day's work. She smiled to see us all there, particularly her mother and father, whom she had not seen since her arrival. But she was too tired to do more. Victoria's attention snapped back to her priorities. This had been an interesting diversion, but now it was over.

"How is Betty?"

"Betty? Better," said Sarah, unable to stifle a yawn. Her hair was matted back with dirt. "Did you find what you needed?"

"Yes," said Victoria.

"Good. I'm going to bed," and Sarah walked past us all like a tired ghost, carefully placing one foot in front of the other as though it were a newfound skill.

"And I'm going to work," said Victoria.

We tried to thank her again, but she had already gone.

"And so am I," said Hamilton, who sat down at the table and ignored us all. Stephen joined him, and I felt happy but aimless, at a loss as to how I might be of use. Mother, Stephen, the Hamiltons — all hard at work. And Sarah was exhausted from hers. The elder Rakeleighs were fast to bed, but I was too elated and exhausted to think of sleep, so I went instead to Sarah's room.

Perhaps I shouldn't have done so.

I didn't enter quietly, since the door was not entirely closed. She was lying on the bed, fully clothed, facedown in her dirty white apron and gray dress. She had managed to take one boot off, and when I realized that she was dead to the world, I unlaced the other. She barely noticed, moaning faintly as she felt the pleasure of a shoe removed. I hated to see her asleep in her clothes — no one should sleep in their clothes — so I undid her apron at the back and put my hands underneath her stomach, where I pulled the strings around. I threw the grubby thing over to the door, where it was swallowed by the blackness around it. I eased up her dress and took down her stockings, which I rolled as gently as I could, feeling the length of her legs as I did. Her body flopped beneath me like a doll. Whichever part I tried to hold up, the rest stubbornly obeyed the laws of gravity, sinking into the bed. I took off her dress.

Then she was naked, lying on her front, fast asleep. The loudest clap of thunder in the world wouldn't have stirred her. I wanted to touch her, and in the silence I could hear the beating of my own heart. I sat on her rump, which moved slowly underneath me, and began to rub her shoulders. She moaned as if my movements had somehow insinuated themselves into her dream, but she didn't move or wake. I slid my hands down her back and kneaded her on either side of her spine, pushing the flesh away from me. For the second time that day, I felt my body moving in response to what I was thinking, as though the nerve that went from my mind to my groin, previously severed, had finally fused, cured by time and Sarah. I wanted to test the whole system now. Perhaps I would wake up sore. My hands moved down her body, and when I reached the small of her back, I looked down to see, in the shadows, myself blocking the view.

Sarah was fast asleep. She knew nothing of what I was doing. I could have done whatever I wanted.

Brother and sister. I loved her too much. Our time would come; and if it didn't, then so be it. I couldn't fumble around in the darkness of ignorance and lies again.

I got up slowly, with regret. I pulled the sheets to one side and let them fall over her, smoothing them onto her where they lay. And before I left, I placed my hand on her cheek, so softly that it could never have woken her, and kissed her on the forehead.

"Good night, Sarah," I whispered.

As I was leaving, I heard her murmur: "Thank you, Rose."

I slept heavily.

3

AFTER THE ARRIVAL of their desiderata, Hamilton and my mother were rarely seen. Sarah was gone, too, continuing in her indenture to Victoria as a symbol of our collective gratitude. So, there was nothing to keep Stephen and me from the next stage of our own investigation.

Two days later, after a brisk exchange of messages via an increasingly harried Alby, Stephen arranged a rendezvous with Pharaoh and GB at the Hospice of the Other Marys: Annie Driver had reluctantly agreed to an interview.

I decided upon a plain brown smock and an apron pinny. Where we were going, we didn't want to draw any more attention to ourselves than was necessary. I shaved carefully around my mustache. My skin felt raw where the razor had done its work, and my face smarted in its nakedness. The veil was now a thing of the past.

The Other Marys was on the other side of the dirty river, a part of London I had not yet seen. We snaked along beside the water and then descended.

The hospice itself was worse than I could have imagined. Victoria had done her best to describe this kind of place, but nothing could have prepared me for the desperate cries and sunken eyes, the stench of decay, the consumptive coughs and moans of pain and resignation that assaulted my senses. The patients lay in cots or on blankets strewn on the ground, and Stephen led me by the hand through these lifeless dying. One or two pleaded in cracked voices and then cursed if we didn't respond, but more often than not these hopeless wretches ignored us. Workers provided what little movement caught the eye, but they were few and did not seem particularly healthy themselves.

Stephen pulled aside a line of drying towels so we could advance properly to the office, as we had been instructed. The door was closed, with a handwritten sign hung permanently upon it: DO NOT DISTERB! AT PRAYERS. We knocked and opened the door. Pharaoh, who sat beside GB, raised his eyebrows and smiled: the circus had arrived. Neither Alby, doubtless recovering from the exertions of the morning, nor Mutt was with them.

"It's them, Annie," Pharaoh said, standing up with a good deal more purpose than I had seen in him before. A song beckoned. GB also stood in jovial greeting, but Annie remained seated. We stood in the door, awaiting her welcome in vain. She was a proud, good-looking woman of about fifty with unnaturally large breasts that perched contentedly on the edge of her desk like pies cooling on a windowsill. And we found her in rude health, all the ruder in context. The precise position she held was unclear, but here she was in the luxury of a comfortable back room, which she had at her sole disposal. There was a pot of soup on the boil, the contents of which did not seem bound beyond her door.

We knew more of her story than she could guess. Stephen had uncovered the facts without difficulty; armed with these, it had not been possible to like her in advance. After Mother's, there had been the chocolate house in St. Giles, followed by brief employment at the Infant Office, where she was caught hiring out children — the very ones she was meant to be helping — to the local bawds. And then, "in the very *Old Nick* of time" as GB put it, the arrival of Richard

"Dickie" Pearce and God in her life simultaneously, as though they were one and the same. Her position of relative power at the Other Marys, combined with her overwhelming devotion to the Lord Jesus Christ, made this Annie Driver a far cry from the one I had expected.

She gave us a cursory glance but then continued writing out, or, in fact, shading in, a chart of some kind. Pharaoh started to hum.

"Hello, friends, Mr. Farrow is working on his song for you," said GB, with wide eyes of anticipation and delight. Annie tutted loudly at the mention of Mr. Farrow without looking up from her work. "He is after a few more details, as you know." GB moved toward us, gesturing for us to sit down on the bench with them, but Stephen shook his head.

"Perhaps," he continued with an incongruously saucy grin, which seemed to allude to some previous, unspoken impropriety that had passed between us, "he'll find out more today." He gesticulated to Annie with a sharp nod of his head as she diligently ignored us, and then he cocked his eyebrow to show that he was on our side.

"We shall see, Mr. Bellman," said Stephen circumspectly, and let the end of his cane drop to the ground with a firm click that said: Let us begin. Annie looked up, down at the stick, and back at her book with all the weariness of a schoolma'am monitoring the children in detention. It was a study in perfect indifference.

I pulled a small book from my apron pocket: *The Little Penny Songster,* a book of old ballads "sung by our *grandmothers*." I had bought it on one of my few solo excursions into the city from a humorous street vendor who regaled me with descriptions of every book at his stall, and how each one of them did for him. I bought the songster on a whim, as much to amuse the salesman as for any other reason, but when I saw that the frontispiece was a lost baby in the woods, I thought of Pharaoh.

"A gift, Mr. Farrow," I said. As I put the small green book into his hand, I tried to open it to the picture. The songster seemed to become momentarily lost in his grasp, and he fumbled it like a magician trying to palm a card before he has learned the trick. Somehow the book managed to land the right way up but closed, and he looked first at the book, then at me. He was as lost as the baby.

"What do you say, Pharaoh?" said Bellman, as any parent encourages his child.

"I say: I can't read," said Pharaoh. GB shook his head with great indulgence. Annie coughed; now she wanted us to pay attention to her.

I opened the book in his palm and showed him the detail in the engravings, a far cry from the woodcuts on the broadsheets, most of which looked as if they were printed from a potato sculpted with a fork. Here was Lord Bateman, a proud and dandy caricature with his ship in the background, his sword by his side and his walking stick elegantly leading the way; and there a woman swooning in a man's arms by the side of "The Banks of Brandy Wine." Above "The London 'Prentice," a young man stood in gladiatorial garb, his hands reaching out to either side. One was in the mouth of a tiger and one in the mouth of a cross-eyed lion. Why were the animals always cross-eyed? It was all that separated man and beast.

"Blimey, these are *quality,* GB!" said Pharaoh. "Thanks, mister." He closed the book, then immediately opened it again, in case the closure meant that I left his side. He wanted me by. "What does that say?" He had re-opened the book to a long ballad about the Bold Dighton. In a storm, a crowd of seamen was trying to raise the good ship's rigging. *Manchester* was boldly writ on the prow.

"That's the name of the ship. Can you read it?"

"No," he said confidently, and nodded.

"It says 'Manchester.'" I spelled it out. "It's the name of the ship. Same as the city."

"Yes," he said testily. "I'm not stupid."

"How kind you are," said Bellman with a bow. "The rubric eludes him, but the pictures will give him enormous pleasure and perhaps stir him to greater dalliance with his muse. Eh, old cock?"

Annie coughed again, stopped writing, clasped her hands together in prayer, and shut her eyes. She muttered a few words, made the sign of the cross with great ostentation, and then looked at us with a beatific smile, far removed from her previous apathy.

"What charity! Faith, hope, charity: but the greatest of these is charity. Hope is the hardest, and my time here is in great demand," she said, used to being obeyed. "Let me know how I can be of assistance, please. He hasn't changed, that one."

Her voice was surprisingly beautiful, rough honey, but carried with it an unpleasant quality, wrestling with a local accent that its owner regretted. She considered Pharaoh aloud, more for her own benefit than ours.

"At least his dress is much improved, though the Lord, in His infinite, might have helped him develop his mind a little." She raised her eyes again toward the ceiling. Mine followed, but where she caught a glimpse of the divine, all I saw was the floor above between laths that dangled like the teeth of a broken comb.

"Come here, darlin'," she said to Pharaoh, who shambled to her side, clutching the songster. "Why don't you come and see your old Annie anymore? The Lord works in mysterious ways and did not, in His infinite, see fit to bless our marriage with children, so Dickie and I work here, but it is He provides for us all. His house has many mansions. He suffered the little children to come unto him, particularly those like you who, though children no longer, have the same pureness of heart. You can always visit us, darlin'."

Pharaoh was having none of it. He looked at his surroundings and compared them unfavorably with GB's palace of paper.

"Why do I want to come here?"

"To see Annie, Pharaoh, to sing me a song, to sing with me from a book that you may find a little more enlightening than this one." She consigned *The Little Penny Songster* to hell with a damning finger.

"Oh, no. Oh, no. I doubt it," said Pharaoh, catching her drift. "Not if it's all full of 'praise ye all' and 'go ye unto' and 'there is a green hill without a city wall,' as if we cared. Where's the use in that?"

He wriggled away from Annie and clung to the offending book in its defense.

"There is only one book," said Annie. "As for the others: you've read one, you've read 'em all."

"Annie," said GB, the pleasantries concluded. "It's them as we told you."

"We are pleased to meet you, Mrs. . . . ?" said Stephen.

"*Councillor* Anne Pearce," said Annie Driver. She looked at the two of us and sniffed. "My time is not my own. This place don't run itself. God has given me but two hands and some feeble help. If it's the past you want to know about, my memory is short and my conscience bad. I need little reminder of the shame from which I was saved, redeemed by the blood of the lamb."

"It is precisely the blood of the lamb that we are here to discuss. This lamb." Stephen pointed at me. Annie sniffed again.

"And of course," I added, "we would be delighted to make an offering to the Hospice of the Other Marys."

"I was one, sir. I was one of those Other Marys." She crossed herself again in case the efficacy of the previous one had worn off. "An offering would be most appropriate to help us in our struggle against the Great Impurity."

"Perhaps even an offering directly to you, rather than the church," continued Stephen. "I am sure your work here is little valued."

"Most generous." Her large breasts rippled in appreciation.

"One to the treasurer and one to you," I confirmed, to clinch the deal.

"That might help you remember, Annie," said Pharaoh unexpectedly, since he hadn't appeared to be paying attention. He was following the words along the lines in his book with his index finger, an eager child pretending to read. Annie looked at him unlovingly.

"I loved that boy. I loved him like a mother. In fact, it's strange to see this big . . ." She was at a loss for a word — but it was likely to be nothing complimentary, so she omitted it and continued, "But I was like a mother to him. In real life, a Magdalene — but to him, a Mary."

"You were an Annie, not a Mary. Mary was a Mary," said Pharaoh, exasperated that his "reading" had been interrupted. But then his tone changed. "And Mother was a mother, not you. I was Mother's Boy. I miss Mother."

"Yes, and she misses you, too. Wherever she is," Annie added, making it clear that Mother was singing from *The Little Penny Songster* in the bottomless pit. "But I'll tell you this. I looked after you. Mother, and the Lord forgive me, cared only for herself, and she paid the price for selfishness. Mother by name, other by nature. May the Lord forgive her as He does all His lost sheep and sinners. May her slate be wiped clean."

All this from the person who was just about to tell me what she knew of *my* mother. She closed her eyes and put her hands together again in supplication. Christians are all the same. It can be a nasty disease — and those who catch it later in life always seem to get a more virulent strain. She didn't give tuppence for Pharaoh's feelings.

Pharaoh gulped and a tear came to his eye. He looked up at me, the book open in his hand.

"What does that word say?" I pointed to the last word in the first line of the ballad he was looking at: "'One morning bright and early, in the pleasant month of May.'"

"I *know* what it says," said Pharaoh, who turned his head away, petulant in his sorrow about Mother.

"Go on, then."

"Spring," he said reluctantly.

"Spring?"

"Spring!"

"Do you know what the letters are?"

He shook his head.

"M. A. Y." I traced them out and pointed to the letter that each one represented.

"Spring?" he asked.

"No, the word is May."

"The *month* of May?" asked Pharaoh cannily.

"Yes."

"That's spring, ainnit?"

"Yes, but the word is *May*."

"I'll say as how I know. That picture is William Reilly's courtship with his beautiful Coolen Bawn. And that's Coolen Bawn there in his lovin' embrace. And the first line is ''Twas on a pleasant morning, all in the bloom of spring,' and if you count them words out, then that's *spring*. So I reckon you're wrong."

I ruffled my hands through his hair, at which he took great offense. He went to great pains to restore it to its previous position by licking his mucky palms and smoothing it, as though sticking it back to his scalp.

"That may be the picture, but the song is 'The Banks of Brandy Wine,' and that word says *May*." I read him the line.

"A poor man don't have half a chance — does he? — when the words look so similar and mean the same thing."

With this new dilemma to distract him, his mood brightened. He stopped brooding over Mother. Perhaps it was a lesson for me.

"And so, you claim to be that poor little lamb, do you?" asked Annie without sympathy. "One might have guessed you'd turn out odd."

"It's a miracle she turned out at all, madam," said Stephen.

"And all thanks to me that she did, sir. *If* she did. How are we to believe it? It's scarcely creditable."

"As absurd as water turning into wine," I said.

"Quite," said Annie in triumph, and then paused. Pharaoh continued to pretend to read and GB sat to his side, wary of the imminent confrontation.

"We know it to be true, madam," said Stephen. "Whether you believe it matters not. You were witness to, participant in, the whole shameful affair. Tell us all you know about the woman who died at Mother's."

"Witness, yes, I own it, but not participant. Oh, no. And I later told the police everything I knew about Mother," she said, talking flatly of this betrayal. I hoped that Pharaoh, if he were paying attention, did not understand. "God told me to."

"Very Christian," said Stephen. Annie took him to be referring to all the babies that this had saved.

"And there's no harm in telling you now. The only harm is the distraction from His good works. I remember it clearly, you see, because it was the last one. We had . . . Mother, I mean . . . *she* had a good run, but that was the end of it."

I was *that*. I had been the end of a good run.

No, it was my mother who had been the last one, for it was her death, not my birth, to which Annie referred.

"May God forgive us for what we did," she said. "That boy took you, I have no idea where exactly. Not where he was meant to, because you wouldn't be sitting there now, and may the Lord always forgive the truth. But you were the evidence, and I had no time to explain to him. The police were coming and they arrived with that man, and everything turned awful horrible. It was very bad that day." She was talking about herself and Mother, but she was also talking about my mother and me.

"Who am I?" I asked. Pharaoh reached out and slipped his right hand into mine.

"Omit nothing, Mrs. Pearce," said Stephen.

"Your mother was called Bryony McRae, that much I remember. I shall never forget it and I pray for her soul."

McRae.

I played the name on the end of my tongue, though most of it came from the back of my mouth: a moue of the lips, then the back of my tongue on the roof of my mouth, followed by an outward breath. Pharaoh saw me and started to copy me. McRae. I didn't feel

Scottish, but tartans appeared in my mind: I could lay claim to one. A kilt.

"Bryony McRae," she repeated. "That was her name. She was near delirious when she came to us. She didn't have the strength to deceive. That poor girl was nearly done already. She was raving, sick with child, emaciated. 'Save my baby! Save my baby!' she said. She didn't know what else she was saying. We thought it was her or the child, but it was so late for the poor creature — it was both of them. It was her terror that brought it on. And may the Lord have mercy on us." She added, "Amen," as a disconsolate afterthought. Annie seemed to have forgotten that I was half of "both of them."

"What else did she say?" asked Stephen.

"She was screaming at us to hurry, babbling on, but we couldn't understand and we weren't listening. 'Beware him!' she said, like she'd known the watch was coming. In her delusion, she thought to escape with the baby if she could. She didn't know. Then she had a vision that someone was there: her dead husband."

"His ghost, perhaps?" offered Pharaoh in reverence to an unfolding story. He started to hum, and GB looked at his ward with a glint in his eyes.

"She was married?" Stephen knew what to ask as well as I. If she hadn't been married, McRae was my name; but if she had, who was the husband and what was his? The room had become very focused. Even Pharaoh had stopped his fidgeting.

"She had been, yes. I remember she was married because afterwards we sold her ring. That was Mother's way at the time, and it is only through my confession that the Good Lord has forgiven me. This boy's the only one I know now, and he doesn't come as often as I'd like. They've all gone, those days, those bad days all gone away. There's no one but me . . . and him."

"Nothing more?" asked Stephen.

"No more of her, but that man who came with the police. He was the strange thing. His name was Childs. At least, that's what he said it was, but I didn't believe him for a minute. One of the devil's own he was: very shifty. He brought the law with him and he was ranting and raging. They burst in seconds after Pharaoh was out the back. We thought he must be the husband not dead or perhaps her brother, but then he says he's looking for another woman, his sister, not this girl. He was in such a rage that the constable made him wait outside — but they weren't surprised to discover he'd legged it."

"Why?" asked Stephen.

"He was there to see she was gone, pure and simple, not to look for no one else. And when he found out she'd had it, he didn't stay any longer than he had to. He made a nice little play of it, but he was off like Jack Trip soon as he was sure."

"Then why did he bring the watch?" asked Stephen.

"If you can't beat them . . . you know," suggested GB. "Perhaps he had no choice. Perhaps they brought him."

"He was acting and not very well. We were good, mind, so we knew. That woman . . . ," she said. "You mark my words, that woman was frightened to death. We might have done for her by mistake, trying to save her, and for that I do repent, but she begged for us to help her and she was scared. It was fear that forced her to us, fear that murdered her. She was all alone, her husband dead. She thought she was going to die whether she had the baby or not. And she was right, because she did. The miracle is that the baby survived." She looked at me. "You are one of the proofs that God has sent us to show us His eternal grace. We should call you Lazarus."

"Lazara," I said, and sighed. We had reached the end of another path. This line of inquiry was dead. Dead as Bryony.

"Can we meet again, Councillor Pearce? Our questions might help you remember," said Stephen.

"I know no more. I have told you everything. We couldn't help her. I cannot tell you about the husband. I don't know who the man was. If you *are* that child, then your mother was called Bryony McRae."

We stood up to go, GB and Pharaoh improbably silent. I was thinking about the name McRae and how we could find out any more about this woman, my other mother, my mother. What else had I expected? When anyone has been driven to such desperate measures, the story is bound to be messy. I was lucky that Bryony had died the way she did. If her fears were justified, then it was lucky that either of us had lived at all. A life for a life: hers for mine.

I don't think I spoke one more word to Annie and neither did Pharaoh. He held tightly to my hand and then the back of my dress, and when she asked him if he didn't have a kiss for his old Annie, he pretended that he hadn't heard and started whistling at high volume. It was left to GB to speak to her, and Stephen to give her the bribe.

The moans of the residents, the other Marys, brought us back to the present day as we left. This very room was full of many such stories as we had just heard. I was free with the money in my apron pockets, and as we departed, I clasped some into Pharaoh's hand as well.

"Buy another book, if you like, and we shall read it together."

"You can read it," he said. "I can't. But I'll listen and sit with you."

I had inherited a child almost twice my age.

We were close by Victoria's workplace, so Stephen and I thought to say a quick hello to Sarah that she might be the first to hear my new name. We got back into our carriage and bent our way along the gray Thames.

The Friends' House for the Poor was markedly different from the Other Marys. There I had sensed despair with no hope of improvement. Despite Annie's complaints about the demands upon her, the Other Marys had been the scene of little movement, as though the cure was to keep the patients as quiet as possible, to give them nothing to do except reflect on their mortal doom. There were no bustling nurses, and the inmates had nothing to look forward to and nowhere to go. It was like watching a clock winding slowly down.

Here, on the other hand, there was determination and the will to survive. Everything ticked with constant movement: the workers were dressed in clean, smart (though much-used) uniforms, and the passages and halls saw a constant succession of trolleys in transfer, some bearing humans and others equipment, guided by someone in far too much of a hurry to pay attention to us. No one here had given in. The healthy fought to keep the germs at bay. The smell was the same sickly sweetness of bodies, but it mixed with the astringent tang of disinfectant.

This building was specifically for those who could not gain access to a proper hospital and whose sickness meant that they could not look after themselves. The mission was to get them well and out of the hospice as soon as possible. We spotted Victoria and Sarah immediately, working together, organizing others. Victoria spoke her orders clearly as Sarah walked an old man slowly back to his bed.

Seeing us, Victoria waved us over, but thinking better of it, she shouted at us to wait in the office; this was where she collapsed on the evenings when it was too late to return home. We waited a few minutes before Victoria hurried in to tell us that there had been new admissions and that regretfully now was not a good time. Sarah smiled and narrowed her eyes as we passed, as if to say, *I am doing all this on your behalf*. I smiled back. The work became her. Her hair was casually tied behind her head with a white bow, her face flushed with her labors. I wanted to kiss her. Victoria assured us that they would certainly be home that evening because they had recruited new reserves.

They never came home that night and I decided that if I wanted to help, if I wanted to see more of Sarah, I should join them. I should be there, too. Victoria always needed more hands, and I would be happy to do anything, to be useful to them, to be with them. The social rooms at

Twenty-four were always empty now, with all the inhabitants busy at their respective labors — Hamilton working on his father's code, Mother involved in her scholarship — and there was no point in my sitting around.

The next day Stephen went off to consult the parish registers, leaving Twenty-four emptier still. Despite what the dying woman had said in her delirium, there was the chance that her husband was still alive. My father. Stephen came home empty-handed, as we had expected. There was no record of a Bryony McRae, let alone the name of her husband. The police had not allowed Stephen access to information about Mother Maynard or her execution. When Stephen suggested that perhaps Pharaoh had written another ballad about her that might contain a vital forgotten detail, it was clear that we had reached a dead end.

We had found out one thing: my mother's name, my last name. And that was it. The trail was cold. We would have to wait for another piece of luck. Unless the police relented or Annie remembered something more or another witness turned up (and we were assured that there were none), we were finished.

I hadn't yet broken the news of my name to my mother or Hamilton. This was partly because they were so busy but also because I came to think it a trivial find. On the odd occasions that I did glimpse them, they would pass me so quickly that we barely had time to acknowledge each other. Perhaps their investigations were bearing fruit at the very moment that ours was withering. I ate alone, or with Stephen, but now when he was home, he more often helped his father with the codes and was less available to me. We had played cards listlessly, not able to summon the necessary interest in whether we won or lost, but now, without him, I took to playing patience, which is indescribably depressing, particularly when you cheat. I tried to read, but even the serials held no surprises. There was no Sarah, no Mother, no Hamilton, and now, no Stephen. It was a very strange situation at Twenty-four. I felt useless.

What good can we do in the world in the little time we have? I had last seen Sarah at her work, sitting on an old man's bed. She massaged his back as he tried to cough something out. It required so much effort that I thought the attempt alone might kill him. I thought of our own family in Love Hall as I saw a little child sitting at the end of her dying mother's bed, playing with the woman's fingers as they dangled from her sheets.

I turned up the next card: the fourth king. Another loss. What good could I be?

My investigation was over, and a damp little firework it had proved. My major discovery had been Pharaoh, having been my miracle not once but twice. There was now the matter of the present to look after. I talked myself into believing that a tidy resolution to my investigation didn't matter. I had my family around me. I knew my real mother's name. What else did I need? It was more than I should have expected. Rose McRae, perhaps, I should have them call me. No, Rose Old was fine: a jumble of past and present.

My mind turned to Sarah and the future of our relationship. Gradually, I had felt my old talents returning to me and I once again felt capable of improvising as freely as I had in the past. New stories started to pop into my mind as I watched the sun inch along the floor, stories that needed to be told, begged to be whispered.

I would go and offer my services. It was time to turn my attention to the future, time to stop trying to solve the mystery of the past.

That very evening, my mother walked down the stairs with more than usual grace, looking happy and relieved, as if a great weight had been lifted from her. I was playing a bored game of liar on my own, which you can barely do. There was a playfulness in her expression as she looked down at me that I had not seen since my return.

"Winning or losing?" she asked.

"Which hand?"

"Either."

"Both."

"I am going to fetch Samuel and family. I have a talk to deliver."

"And when you are done, I have a very little something for you, too." I was bored of patience.

Minutes later, she sat herself down at the table. She took the few papers she had with her, which were covered with a magnificent amount of notes, and shuffled them with a good deal more interest than I handled the cards. Enthusiasm is infectious, and before the Hamiltons arrived, I was looking forward to what she had to say.

Samuel Hamilton entered the room with his son. He looked, in truth, a little put out.

"Madam." He bowed. "Anonyma. Your ladyship. I was wondering whether . . ."

My mother, suddenly a stern governess, raised her hand and made a tutting noise that brooked no refusal.

"Sit down, Samuel. Angelica. Stephen. Is Sarah here?"

"With Victoria," I said, incredulous that she hadn't registered her absence.

"A pity Victoria isn't here. She was invaluable."

Angelica scurried over and took Stephen's hand. As they sat, Mother rapped the bottom edge of the papers sharply on the table.

"For future readers and listeners, this address — which I am now to give for the first time — will be called 'Notes for a Future Biography of Mary Day' by Anonyma Wood." She looked up. Hamilton was evidently frustrated that his work had been interrupted for nothing more than a lecture on matters literary.

"The books Victoria brought me from her last visit to Love Hall confirmed an idea that I have been entertaining for some time. There is no solid proof for what I am about to say, but scholarship will accept it as true, since the literary evidence is beyond doubt. I shall hand it over to you, Samuel, to do with what you will. I merely hope that it is of use.

"My work on Mary Day, an author who has affected many of our lives in different ways, is its own reward. That it has yielded an unexpected dividend which might help us all is beyond my wildest dreams, and typical of a promise within the work of Mary Day, a promise in which I have always believed."

I had absolutely no idea what she was going to tell us, but the presentation seemed a superior form of diversion to beating an invisible opponent at cards unfairly. Hamilton, on the other hand, was positively itchy with impatience.

"Anonyma," he said. I heard his son in him for the first time. "I am at the present moment in the middle of some work that I think might —"

"Samuel," my mother said firmly. "I am not in the habit of interrupting your work, and when that work comes to fruition, I hope that I shall be able to hear the results for a few simple minutes without having to rush away."

"I am so terribly sorry," he said, "if that is the impression that I give you. It is not that, but that I —"

"Highlights of 'Notes for a Future Biography of Mary Day,'" my mother said firmly, demanding attention in a most atypical way. In an amusing reversal of their usual roles, Stephen patted his father gently on the hand and Hamilton sat back. Here was my family in front of me, each of them acting slightly out of character.

"I have first made a précis of this biography, which I need not recount in detail. Very little of Mary Day's life is known, neither her origins nor her death. A printer in London discovered her writings and used them to demonstrate his typography. The poems enjoyed their first vogue as examples of this fine art. One solid fact, and the one fact around which the rest of my discoveries revolve, is this: that a remarkable number of her works, her notebooks, some of her correspondence with her publisher, and a small collection of books she owned and to which she referred, in which she wrote marginalia, and from which, from time to time, she plagiarized — all those books somehow arrived in the library of Playfield House . . . Love Hall, I shall call it, among ourselves.

"Their presence was the very reason I originally applied for the position at Love Hall, a house that historically has not been considered among the most literary in the land. At first, I spent time withdrawing the books from the library, one by one, without Lady Loveall's consent, but due to my late husband's generosity, I was able to spend all the time I wanted with them. When I became librarian, the library itself was in a distressing state of disrepair. I tried to save these books (and many others) from an early grave, though whether I succeeded in anything more than delaying their demise remains to be seen. The question is this: Why were they there at all? And could the answer to this question yield interesting facts about Mary Day's biography? Well, I now know the answer and it does. In fact, it is simple. I had long —"

"Madam . . . ," said Hamilton. His own son hushed him, and my mother acknowledged the interjection with nothing more than a sharp increase in her volume, for one short word.

"I had *long* suspected that Mary Day had some knowledge of Love Hall, absurd though it seemed. There was a certain suggestive correspondence between the poems and the house, an uncanny feeling that they were poems bespoke for Love Hall itself, made to be read there.

"About one thing I was certain — there was a knowledge of Love Hall in the work. How? It wasn't until Samuel revealed his most recent discovery that I had an inspiration. I realized that I needed to re-read some of the poetry, to look at it from a different perspective, in particular a book called *All Loving, Lord, Giving All,* a thin volume that contains twenty-four poems, some of her most obscure work, all of which predate her mature period.

"In the past, there had seemed to me an echo in the title itself — All Loving: Love Hall — but the texts told me little, although it was in this "Fantasie of Fancies" that I remembered references to a "green mausoleum" and "the priest's hole." At the time these had just seemed touching coincidences, but when I read them again, in the original copy newly liberated from Love Hall, they spoke to me in a new way, with a different voice. My conclusion is — and I say this without doubt — that Mary Day started life as the Bad Lord Loveall's third, and last true, wife."

She looked up and paused.

"Marguerite d'Eustache."

I gasped. Stephen looked at me and then at his father.

"The one who ran away?" I asked hurriedly.

"Exactly."

"The mother of the true heir to Love Hall?"

"The very one. Samuel?"

Hamilton was staring at the table, his head in his hands. His son was poking his shoulder to bring him into the conversation.

"Samuel?" asked my mother.

"Yes, your ladyship. She was Marguerite d'Eustache. Marguerite d'Eustache became Mary Day."

"You know?"

"Anonyma," he said with all deference possible. "The family books are full of revelations. I, too, am on the brink of discoveries, great discoveries. But, tell us, how ever did you come to this? It is a tribute to your attention to these poems."

"Is that why they were hidden away in Love Hall, because they knew who wrote them and what they contained?" I asked.

"I am yet to find out," said Hamilton, answering a question I had meant for my mother.

"That puts a rather different complexion on matters," she said, crestfallen. The papers dropped limply from her hand.

"Continue," said Stephen. "Please, we beg you."

"I must insist you do finish," said Hamilton. "It is time to cross-reference our two investigations. Perhaps other light will be shed in some of the more impenetrable corners of the books that we are attempting to read."

"The Day light," said Mother as Hamilton shook his head in wonder.

All Loving, Lord, Giving All was belatedly published after some of Mary Day's more mystical later writings had gained notoriety. Mother had never been able to read much sense in the poem "Aim I Am" beyond its vague yearnings for spiritual fulfillment — from memory, she only had precisely one sixth of it. She could be sure of only the first line. Now, thanks to Victoria, she was able to read it anew:

Aim my arrow's raging greed
I am unEarthly recklessness
Aim inside their evil deed
I am ecstatically undressed
Aim so tame and cowardly
I am halfway eternally

Now, these six slim lines entirely changed my mother's perceptions of Mary Day: it is from her conclusion that a proper biographer could begin.

Mother guided us through her enlightenment step by step. In "Aim I Am," the writer's journey toward her destination is impossible: "halfway eternally." Mother was reminded of Zeno of Citium's paradox, referred to elsewhere in the poems, that motion is impossible. The frankness of "ecstatically undressed," the arrow shot by the naked female writer — a very catholic kind of corporeal symbolism — also deflected the reader from the true meaning, as though the poet had laid traps.

However, since the time many years before that Mother had first read the poem and taken so very little from it, she had made a breakthrough in her interpretation of Mary Day. In another book entirely, there was a peculiar reference to the children's riddle: "I saw Esau sitting on a seesaw, how many *s*'s in that?" The obvious answer is five, though the *real* answer is that there are no *s*'s in *that* at all. Mary Day posited that the answer was both five and none. This had alerted Anonyma to the possibility of reading in double focus — that the reader should be aware not only of what the words literally meant but also the actual physical reality of the printed words on the page, the shapes they made, and the patterns of the letters. In a sense, it was the very thing her father had originally appreciated in the books — the joy of the surface of the printed page. She remembered what she had asked of Dolores at their first meeting when they looked at the bestiary so many years before: to look at the page itself.

To see with two simultaneous foci — this was Mary Day's visionary moment. In the rhyme there were no *s*'s in *that* and there were five — both were right. This thought opened doors of scholarship to Anonyma that terrified her, for they might delay her work by years, yet delighted her, too, for the same reason.

Now when she looked at "Aim I Am," she saw within the very title not only an avowal of identity ("I Am") but also the specific goal of the poet in stating this identity (the "Aim") where in the word *aim,* "I," the poet, is literally enclosed by *am, within* the word. So the "aim" of the poem, its intent, was to reveal the *I*-dentity of the poet.

If the word *Aim* must be the first word of a poem, since the six-line poem alternates *Aim* and *I Am* as the opening phrase of each line, then common sense dictates *arrows* is likely to appear early in the first line. The first words of each line act as a chorus, and Mother considered the lines with them and without them. Without them, the words made little sense:

My arrow's raging greed
UnEarthly recklessness

It was the capitalization of the *E* in *UnEarthly* that gave my mother pause. Day did not generally capitalize in this curious fashion, though Mother was sure she had noted one or two other instances (which she could not now place) in the notebooks. She immediately made a note to check that reference before she dared read beyond the first two lines of "Aim I Am." Then she read:

Inside their evil deed
Ecstatically undressed
So tame and cowardly
Halfway eternally

The first letter of each word in the six lines spelled out something she could not even have understood before Hamilton discovered the secret marriages of the Bad Lord:

M A R G
U E R
I T E D
E U
S T A C
H E

There it was, in front of her.

The poem was called "Aim I Am," and the "aim" was "Marguerite d'Eustache," spelled out, she fancied, as on a headstone. Could Mary Day have actually been Marguerite? Or was the story one that the poet had heard and tried to incorporate into her poems? Instinctively, my mother decided that the answer was the former. She could barely wait to broadcast this discovery downstairs but felt it her responsibility to provide additional proof, and this had been the cause of her extended absence, as she obsessively combed every text she had to hand or by heart for more clues.

"Aim I Am" contained an actual identification. Other poems were found to contain further examples of this compulsive spelling out — but in these, the meaning was more obvious. They concerned male oppression, unhappy marriages with dire consequences, and finally female revenge. Anonyma also found in the notebooks, not quite where she remembered, the one other poem that contained the unusual capitalization. It was called "The Fourth," one of two verses excised from "The Quarters":

Masculine appetites, rapine greed
UnEqualled
Ravishment impassively taints each deed
Eunuchs usually say thank-you
At castration's happy end.

A strange, rather trivial piece of work, yet to Anonyma it was now perfect: *UnEqualled* performed the same function as *UnEarthly* — further evidence. The two verses of "The Quarters" that saw publication under the name "Half of the Quarters" were:

The First
Marry — and regret grave union evermore
Raging, I try every door
Effort's useless — Shut tight
A choked heart expires tonight

The Third
Man, all-begetter royal
God's unknowable ecstasy resolves in toil
Each deed eunuched
Unknowable Sophia's truth abandoned
Chained, half extinguished

"The First" contained another deviation from perfection — an added *tonight* to perform the "tight" rhyme — whereas "The Third" was perfect, its mode of expression ("All-begetter," "Sophia," & c.) more redolent of the later Day.

Suddenly, Mother saw Marguerite, running from Love Hall, not yet Day, half mad with exhaustion, her baby a bundle underneath her arms. Perhaps the terrified Marguerite stops at an inn outside London and, asking for pen and paper, scribbles desperately. She needs to give utterance to her plight — as she had during pregnancy — and yet she can give nothing away if her flight, her disappearance, and her fight for her child's life are to succeed.

My mother's thesis continued with the poem "Their," which was both less clear and more obvious at the same time. The crux was again in the title. The word *their* contained the word *heir,* which referred to the fact that the heir to which Marguerite/Mary was giving birth, or had already given birth, the baby that was inside "her," *belonged* to Love Hall. The narrator of this poem was not the bearer of the child but the child itself, the "I" inside "her," the "heir" to "their" Love Hall.

My mother was able to cite a great deal of supporting evidence besides, mostly from *All Loving, Lord, Giving All,* the first and only edition of which she flicked through idly as she read and improvised. Her theory was simple: Marguerite d'Eustache ran away with her child and, in order to hide herself forever from Love Hall, became Mary Day. This explained the unusual knowledge of and references to the inside of Love Hall, though quite how the books ended up in the library was still unknown. My mother further supposed that it was the trauma of the discovery that the infant would be wrested from her that had triggered the creative urge in Marguerite and, as it were, given birth to Mary Day. My mother acknowledged that this put her in the somewhat awkward position of a tacit approval of Day's mistreatment at the hands of the Loveall. "Art can transform the greatest pain into beauty," she said, and smiled.

My mother's final imaginative assertion was that Mary Day had raised her male child in female clothes to further facilitate the subterfuge. Beyond the androgyne references of the later poetry, their vision of Feminisia, there was no solid evidence for this; it was simply the imaginative leap of a scholar mindful of the desperate position and practical capabilities of Marguerite herself. Mother refused to speculate how long the child remained hidden in this way.

Mary was short for Marguerite, Day a contraction of d'Eustache. Mother's case was made, and she basked in the glow of her triumph. There was certainly no one in the room qualified to argue with her, yet she had clearly built a stunning case from such limited materials. We looked to Hamilton to confirm the facts and saw that he, too, was full of wonder that she had been able to draw such a conclusion from nothing more than a close reading of some poems; poems that had, like Pharaoh's ballad, all that time been in the library of Love Hall. Samuel was able to shed even more light before he hurried away to continue with his work.

"I believe the basis of your theory to be entirely correct, ma'am. The rest, I assume to be true simply because it conforms so perfectly to the facts as designated in my family's books, books you have never read. For example, the poem 'Their.' In the letter I mentioned, which is in the book and written in Marguerite's own hand, Mary Day's own hand, she scrawls that word with hysterical repetition. We must compare the scripts of Mary and Marguerite."

"A new manuscript!" Mother was breathless. "We must archive it. I must see it!"

"Of course. I cannot tell you very much more, for I am reading on, but this I can say: Love Hall began a search for the missing Marguerite that proved fruitless. As we know, they gave up and decided to ignore her existence entirely. They paid her father a substantial sum of money, and he was prepared to forget his daughter had ever existed. This is all recorded.

"And so Marguerite 'died.' She is not mentioned again in the notebooks for forty years, until 1782, when an oblivious Good Lord Loveall received a copy — this very copy, I presume — of *All Loving,*

Lord, Giving All in a package delivered to Love Hall. Not knowing or wondering what it was, he gave it to my father, Jacob, who realized its import and, we can be sure, acted accordingly. Whether more books were sent, or whether the rest of the books were somehow found by my father and placed in the library, we cannot at this moment say. I am reading as fast as I can, but it is a laborious process. With my son's assistance, I think I might have more to report very shortly. Every page brings with it revelations.

"I am excited but nervous to read on. The Hamiltons have been ever loyal to the Loveall, and I fear that new discoveries may throw a painful slant upon our relationship. I now realize that the books might be protecting my family as much, perhaps more, than they are protecting yours."

My mother nodded gravely and pushed the book toward Hamilton.

"Take this with you. I have wrung it dry. I exchange it for the new manuscript. Rose also has some news for us." They both looked toward me. I didn't mind being an afterthought in the light of such revelations. My inquiry was no longer the most important, even to me.

"Only this," I said. "Stephen and I met with Annie Driver and she gave us the name of my mother. Her name, though maiden or married we can't be sure, was McRae. Bryony McRae."

"Darling!" said my mother. "McRae!"

"McRae?" said Hamilton, and then repeated it.

"Do you like it?" my mother asked. "Does it fit?"

"Yes, I think so. McRae," I said. "I might be Scottish."

"Perhaps," said Hamilton. "After I have dealt with this most pressing business, I shall have a look into McRae."

"What else did she tell you?" asked my mother. "Did she know your mother in person?"

"She knew who she was. She thought she might have been married, as she spoke deliriously of a husband who was dead. She was a very frightened woman."

"And," said Stephen, "there was a mysterious man who brought the law, interrupting them in their work, and then disappeared, never to be heard of again. Name of Childs."

"A ghoulish name," said my mother.

"And not his own. I'm afraid it may be a dead end down a dark alley, but we shall press on," said Stephen.

"Well, next, I shall —" continued Hamilton, but I interrupted.

"There need be no next," I said. "I have learned my mother's name. Stephen has checked the parish register and been to the police. To no avail. We shall not find a father for me."

"But there may be . . ." Hamilton's words trailed off. He would scratch away secretly until he found out something more. It would be not only his business but his pleasure.

"It is up to Rose," said Mother. "You should have told us, my dear."

"I didn't want to interrupt your work and I still don't want to keep you from yours, Samuel. Perhaps?"

"Thank you," he said, and got up. My mother lifted her arm and stopped him dead.

"Know this, our friend Samuel: what you discover is for the best. Our family has always and will always look after, and be looked after by, your family. In this house, we have found it most convenient to live as equals, and this is how we shall live from now on, whatever our circumstances. Our family is nothing without yours."

"Madam," said Hamilton, and bowed. "You do us the greatest honor." His wife stood as well, and the two of them left arm in arm. As he reached the door, Hamilton turned. He had a strong premonition of what he would find but didn't dare express it, perhaps willing it not to be so.

"I would very much like Stephen to be with me throughout the final stage of our investigation. Perhaps we shall discover nothing, perhaps all. I think, however, that these are the moments that a father should share with a son: all knowledge should be passed from one generation to the next. I fear we need to atone for past mistakes."

"Stephen," said my mother, and he left with his father. It was curiously formal. Mother looked tired and unexpectedly bored, perhaps because her long climb was over. The "Notes for a Future Biography" were not yet complete, but all her work now was a slow descent from the mountaintop. My "Notes for a Present Biography," on the other hand, were finished. The trail was cold, and ended with a corpse on a table on a dank street in the East of the city. We sat together in silence, and she reached her hand out to mine.

"Perhaps it is time to visit Sarah," said my mother. "She's been working so hard. You must miss her."

As always, she was right. I needed to be alone, to get out of the room and, if possible, out of the house. It was time to offer my services to Victoria, to remove myself and do something good at the same time, or as the cliché has it, to kill two birds with the one stone. She patted my hand, which clenched nervously. She put her fingers into my fist and, with surprising tenacity, parted them. My hands were sweaty.

"Go and find her. Bring her home. She must need sleep."

"Perhaps I should go with Stephen."

"Stephen can't possibly leave his father now. You heard Samuel. His work is so near the end. You should go. It is no great labor."

"Would you like to come?" I asked. Everything that she wasn't saying she expressed through her hand. Now she withdrew it from mine and flicked me away.

"Oh, I have far too much to do. Far too much. My notes must be placed in a proper order. I have no time, Rose." She returned to her book, but it was just a study of reading, as though that would send me off into the early-evening mist.

I told her I would go in the morning if Sarah didn't return that night. As I lay in bed, there was no sound from anywhere except the infrequent creak of floorboards from Hamilton's room. I pictured the two of them reading and making notes, under Samuel's instruction, Angelica providing them with a constant stream of refreshment. My mother was, without doubt, asleep, and I would have been able to hear Sarah return, the echoing thud of the front door, the scrape on the floorboard where it had worn a smooth track, and her weary footfall on the stairs. There was nothing, only silence from below. I wrote in my journal so that Franny would one day have a perfect view of everything.

The next morning I would dress in my most practical clothes to offer my services for the good of the city.

4

LULLED BY THE GENTLE BOUNCING of the carriage, I sat back as far as I could. I was lost in a reverie for much of the journey, soothed by halo-framed visions of Sarah and me involved in endless noble toil, doing good for the poor of the parish. Her sweat-moistened skin glistens in the light of the coal fire as I look up and smile. She mops her brow with her kerchief before reaching down to wipe my own, blowing to cool my forehead. In the background, patients, restored to perfect health, fade in to the distance, beaming gratefully. Perhaps I had ulterior motives, but I was lost in my dream of benign charity.

I awoke with a lurch, dribble at the corner of my mouth, and spruced myself up as best I could. The harsh light of morning stung and I shaded my eyes. I tapped and told the driver to wait until my hours were decided.

As I alighted, a street sweeper whistled. Curious to the reason for his trill, I turned around to find, to my surprise, that it was I. When he saw my face, however, his eyes instantly dropped to the ground and he continued his sweeping with renewed vigor as he transformed his tuneful enthusiasm into nothing more than an innocent song. In previous times, I would have been dismayed by this about-face, but now it made me feel special. I wasn't his perfect dream, perhaps, but I was somebody's. Everybody is somebody's. I was surprisingly full of confidence. Far from being threatened or scared, I felt threatening. I was beyond people's dreams. I showed them the truth about themselves. If they feared me, then it was because they didn't know how much they wanted me. Perhaps that sounds ridiculous, but it was how I felt.

I hoisted my skirt above my shoes and, emphasizing the masculinity of my walk, strode purposefully through the largest puddle of mud that I could find. *Voilà!* I thought, but the sweeper had his eyes firmly fixed on his broom.

I stepped through the shabby portico of the Friends' with the certainty of the rich and benevolent, not thinking to announce myself. The hospice, appearing suddenly shabby and dilapidated, needed a new coat of paint; where before I had seen a perfection of dedicated industry, now I saw room for improvement. I pictured how I, not only but mostly I, could make the difference. An extra hand here, a caring remark there, one more fluffed pillow — I thought of Franny. I would do for others what she had done for me.

People for the most part ignored me. Nobody needed whatever distraction I had to offer. It was still early and I couldn't see Victoria or Sarah, so, passing through the bustle, I made for the back room where we had been directed on our previous visit. Neither of them was in the office but doubtless they wouldn't be long, so I quietly sat down at the table and surveyed the room. I now saw it in its true light: rather than an office, it was a city apartment. In the corner there was a bookshelf filled with practical books of medicine alongside novels that would be lent out to those whose recuperation allowed them to be read to or to read for themselves. It gave me an idea: a well-organized library, that's what this place needed. Perhaps even one that traveled between establishments, a kind of peripatetic library on a mission of mercy. I could certainly be of assistance there. My mind was full of practical notions.

There was also an entire kitchen in the apartment — a stove, a dirty kettle, saucepans, even some food left out on the counter. I decided to make myself a cup of tea as I waited, so I got up to put some water on the boil. Thinking of Alby with affection, I picked up the kettle firmly by the handle. To my surprise, for it had looked gray and featureless, it was scalding hot and I felt my skin try to fuse with the metal of the kettle. I immediately flung it away, to ensure that it was as far from me as possible. It hit the ground with a terrible clatter, spilling its contents all over the floor.

There were sounds of wearied protest from behind a curtain. Someone had been asleep behind the makeshift partition, and I had woken them. I wondered what to do. I did my best to dam the flow of water across the room with my foot, though I should rather have put my hand under a cold tap. I gave up my futile attempts and went to the sink, where I ran the cold as fast as I could. I turned to see the water form a wide stream on the uneven floor and run toward the curtain, which suddenly opened.

"Victoria!" I said, relieved that it was she rather than a stranger. She was in her nightdress, water puddling around her bare feet. "I'm so sorry. I —"

"Rose! Shh!" said Victoria. It was the tone in her voice, not even the look in her eyes. I forgot my stinging hand. I forgot the water on the floor. I forgot even to look behind her, though I could have done so. And then I didn't have to, for Sarah suddenly emerged from the dark and looked over her shoulder. She was barely awake and her mind had yet to fully grasp the situation. Her chin dropped onto Victoria's shoulder and she gave me that lazy early-morning smile, her face still marked with the crease of the sheet, her eyes not yet fully open. She was so pleased to see me. She couldn't have been more beautiful if made to my exact specifications.

"Rose," she said sleepily, and smiled. Behind them, I could see the white sheets of the bed. There was no other room, just a bed. I said nothing.

"Rose," said Sarah again, but more warily. She must have seen the shadow move across my face. It was Reality slapping me on the cheek.

My face reddened where I had been shamed. The pain in my hand and the pain in my heart combined until they were inseparable. What stories did Victoria tell Sarah? They were secrets I could never know, adventures I would not share, whispers too quiet for my ears. It was yet another world to which I would never be granted admission. I could think only of escape. I made for the door.

"I came to be of assistance," I said as I bundled myself out, making a further mess as I did so. "But I see I am not required."

I slammed the door and ran as fast as I was able, my skirts as high as I could get them. This time, people did notice me. There was even a shriek, but what did I care.

Outside, the street sweeper saw me run out and shouted to his partner, "Hey! Look. There he is again! Quick!" I had made his day. He leaned on his broom and looked in wonder, this time without disguising his prurient interest. I clawed my way into the carriage and slunk into the backseat, quivering.

"Twenty-four!" I yelled, and thumped the roof of the carriage twice with my scalded hand.

Once back in the safety of my own room, I opened the curtains and stared out. It was a grand view of the park, and since it was a fine day and the right hour, couples were stepping out for their midmorning constitutionals, walking arm in arm. Men tipped their hats in greeting, politely making way for nurses pushing perambulators. If two women walked side by side, they were always led by baby carriages bouncing gently before them. I tried to imagine Sarah and me strolling together, but I couldn't see us in either situation. It was easier to imagine her with Victoria, pushing other people's babies.

In earlier times, the impossibility of casting a role for myself in this innocent scene would have tormented me. I would have interpreted what I witnessed at the hospice as a direct result of my unsuitability for any kind of relationship, a confirmation of my freakishness. But now, as I gazed out of the window and saw the happy couples walking through the park together, like the men and women in the picture on a biscuit tin, I felt only unlucky in love.

It was nothing to do with my clothes or my face. It was nothing to do with my upbringing or Mary Day, though I could blame it on a million things. It was something to do with the fact that love is complicated and that I was reticent and inexperienced, that I hadn't managed to make my feelings known to Sarah, to anyone, ever. I wasn't under the illusion that she would have immediately taken me into her arms if I had, but I knew that what I felt the moment I saw her with Victoria, and what I continued to feel on the way home, was a direct result of expectations that had no grounding in fact. Sarah had no obligation to be loyal to me except in friendship, in familial love. I had accepted her offer to be brother and sister, and I had not asked anything more of her. Victoria did not know that I loved Sarah above everything. I had not communicated this to anyone. They had done nothing wrong beyond being unable to intuit my every secret thought. And this was how it had always been. There were people I could blame for other of my problems, but with regard to this, the fault was my own.

Beneath me, the world paired off for my amusement. From my bird's eye view, it was hard to tell the little boys from the girls. The vogue was for sailor suits of white and blue, and hair worn long. I opened my notebook and continued to write to Franny. This was the story that told all, written for the only person to whom I spoke without equivocation. As I wrote, I felt more normal. An aching heart: quite usual. A scalded hand: very mundane. An orphaned child taken in by a rich benefactor: count your blessings, Rose. Think of the many foundlings, the many lostlings. My writing lasted the remainder of the day.

I did not feel like company for dinner, and when Mother rapped on my door to remind me that the gong had sounded ten minutes since, I said I was feeling unwell. Victoria and Sarah had not yet returned and I did not want to see them when they did. I was angry with no one except myself. I was embarrassed. It was best that I kept out of everyone's way. I slept like a baby, sucking on an imaginary nipple.

I was awoken by the creek of the hinges on the door. Mother had visited me in the middle of the night ever since I was a baby, and this habit continued even after I came to Twenty-four. I was used to the sound of her slippered feet on the floorboards and her warm breath next to my face before her hand smoothed away a lock of my hair and she bent down to kiss my forehead. Even when my eyes were closed, I could see the candle's flickering light dancing on the inside of my lids. I always pretended to be asleep in tribute to her, just as one always pretends to have been awake when someone has woken you. We are very contrary about our sleep.

But I could tell from the first footfall that it wasn't Mother. It was a woman on tiptoe. I didn't move. There was no flickering candle playing in the darkness. Sarah? Angelica? Victoria? Not my mother. It had to be Sarah, come to apologize.

In the darkness, she knelt by the side of the bed so that her head was the same level as mine. I could hear her breath. My eyes were closed and I didn't dare open them. In my dreams, at least, it was Sarah and it always had been. My heart might have stopped forever if I had opened my eyes and found otherwise. But for now, eyes closed, my dream was intact and my heart beat faster.

She leaned forward and kissed me gently on the lips. Now I was sure: there is nothing so memorable as someone's scent, and Sarah had been slaving all day.

"Move over, lump," she said, and I did.

She got into bed beside me, pushing me farther over with her hips, and put her arm around me. I had taken to wearing nothing in bed, like when I was a child, before I felt the need to hide as much of my body from myself as possible. It occurred to me to warn Sarah, but she didn't seem to care.

I could almost sense her mind working as her hair irritated the front of my face, making my nose itch. She had something to tell me and was just on the point of speaking when she decided against it and got out of bed. I saw her silhouetted against the window, behind which the lights of St. Swithin's burned throughout the night. She took off her clothes in a very matter-of-fact manner; they were grimy from work and she would be glad to be free of them. Then she got back into bed. It was very dark and very quiet. We were entirely naked together.

"Hello," she said.

"Hello," I said, worried that nothing but frustration and embarrassment would come of whatever was happening. In the service of siblinghood, the best thing to do was sleep, but how could I? And if I didn't sleep, there was the possibility that I would let myself down, but better to let myself down sooner rather than later. I felt wary, shy of myself, and wanted as little of me to touch as little of her as possible. She tried to pull me toward her so that our bodies were further entwined, but in case of immediate humiliation I hollowed some of me away from her, as I had done so many times before.

"Be friendly, Rose," she said. She had a way of always cutting to the heart of the matter. She took my left arm and rested it on her stomach, which was warm, soft, and, in some way, full.

"Sorry about Victoria," she said after a tiring silence.

"Are you here to apologize? You don't have to. I should." I felt on better ground.

"Well, perhaps . . ." Her voice seemed to evaporate in the darkness.

"My hand hurts."

"Did you burn your fingers?" asked Sarah, and taking my right hand, so that my right arm was, unbeknownst to her, bent rather awkwardly in the middle, lifted it up to her lips and kissed my fingertips.

"The whole hand," I complained as lightly as I could manage. "But don't touch it." She sucked the tip of my index finger and, as she began to speak, bit it gently, which made her words a murmur.

"Rose. It isn't what you think. There's only one bed, and we share it . . . when it's late and we're tired . . . it's not like you and me in the old days . . . I always let you . . . you could always do what you wanted, and I should have done what I wanted, too . . ."

She was lost in her own thoughts. What could brothers and sisters do together? Not very much. Not even this. Surely we were overstepping a mark. But what had she said? *I should have done what I wanted, too.* Did I hear that? Was it I who had prevented her from taking advantage of me? Perhaps I was resisting it now, my back curved slightly away from her, my face resolutely avoiding hers. I could continue to arch my back for only so long. Oh, and I could talk myself into believing that line of argument very easily and get into real trouble. Perhaps I had always been the object of seduction but had somehow felt it proper to deny myself, as though I were in charge. I wasn't in charge and I never had been. I hadn't even known how bodies fit together or where mine fit into the grand scheme, but things had changed.

"I know you don't love me except as brother and sister, Rose . . . you've made it clear . . . but when I am with Victoria . . . I wish . . . when I saw that look in your eyes today . . ."

She removed my finger from her mouth, where she had been tracing it from side to side along the cracked curve of her top lip.

Only I was stopping myself now. Whatever I did at this moment would meet no resistance. I could give in to my every urge, let myself press upon her, but I hesitated before moving because I suddenly understood that I could, and I relished the anticipation created by this self-denial. It was a whole new world to me.

"May I?" she said. As it was, as it had always been, I was thinking too carefully too long about the way that things were presenting themselves. Without waiting for an answer, she bent toward me, slightly over me, and kissed me. Her hand purposefully, and without my assent, moved down my stomach and through my hair. She took my cock in her hand.

"Rose," she whispered. It was enthusiasm and I appreciated it. It felt good to be handled, even if it was rather as if I were being weighed and measured, and even if this made me a little self-conscious. I wasn't yet hard, if indeed I was meant to be.

Her weight on top of me began to feel a burden, until I became an inanimate object, moved upon, acted upon. My lack of mobility was, I felt sure, causing a lack of responsiveness within me. I was passively waiting for her to fill me with life, and I suddenly knew that it was a shameful way to do business. I thought of all that time spent trying to avoid an erection, all the fruitless erections I had on my own and that I would have again the moment I awoke the next morning. I should be proudly sporting one of those now. How many times would I deny her before the cock finally crowed? I didn't know quite what to do but I knew I had to be honest, to trust in my instincts. I pushed her from me and onto her back. She was surprised but quickly yielded. I put my mouth on top of hers.

It was the first time I had ever kissed down onto somebody — an entirely different sensation. She received me, and our lips sealed the agreement. There was nothing overly forceful about what I was doing, but I had pushed her hand away from me. My cock, with a point of view all its own, rubbed against the side of her leg.

"Rose, love me . . ."

"Yes," I said, and I moved my hand between her legs, to the center of her world. Straightening my back, I threw off our covers. I knelt, looking down on her, and she stared at me. We were entirely naked and without definition in the half-light. She reached for me, pulling me down toward her chest and farther, farther.

"I love you," I whispered.

"Yes."

I collapsed on her, and all energy sapped from me. I started to cry, delirious, wide-awake and extremely tired at the same time. As she pulled me to her, we both knew that we had gone as far as we could for now, that the night could not surpass this moment. Had she ever done anything more? I imagined so. I fell to her side and reached down, resting my hand upon her cunt. As we lay together, she occasionally moved herself up into my hand and I pushed down on her, to remind her that I was there and what we could do if we chose. She, in her turn, put her hand on me, and I felt like the dog who lies on its back and parts its legs as a sign of submission. I felt loved. She cupped her hands around my balls and cradled them in her palm. With thoughts of dogs, Mutt, mutter, mutters, mothers, minutes or hours later, my head resting next to her bosom, we must have finally fallen asleep.

We couldn't have been asleep for more than a few minutes.

There was a knocking on the door. The knocking became a banging. My first thought was Victoria. Sarah and I sat up. Without so much as a by-your-leave, the door burst open. Stephen looked at us, his eyes wide with surprise, and then smiled. Sarah had the sheet just covering her breasts, but I grabbed it, too, pulling it from her entirely. She didn't bother to move. He tried to stifle his laughter. "Blimey! Sorry!" he yelled, and left the room.

"Can't you knock, you oaf?" Sarah shouted through the door. Oh, how I had longed to wake with her in our own time, to drift in and out of sleep as I felt her close to me. I fell back onto the bed with a smile on my face and cursed him.

"Why should I? I'm the town crier, I am. Oyez! Oyez! Oyez! Meeting in the front room now. Your presence is not requested, your ladyships. Your presence is demanded! Oyez!"

And then he was gone.

Before I had a moment to reach for Sarah, the gong in the front hall began to sound, not with the formal and dignified chime with which Hood rang dinner but haphazardly, as though someone were hitting it too hard and then trying to hit it again while it was still swinging. We next heard the gong as it was knocked from the table, then rolling along the floor until it crashed. This had all the hallmarks of a younger Stephen Hamilton. There were two short sharp screams. Sarah and I sat up and looked at each other.

"What on earth is happening?" she said, leaning over and kissing me.

"This can't be anything to do with . . ." I bit the inside of my lip.

"Victoria? Don't be silly. No," she said firmly. "Nothing. How can it be?"

"But she . . ."

"She doesn't care."

"But I'm not a girl."

"You're not not a girl. You're a boy."

"But I . . ."

"You're a *boy,* Rose," she said with conviction, and smiled.

I got out of bed. I was naked in front of her again. She looked away and then turned back quickly. There she was. We stood looking at each other. I had a vision of the two of us, descending the stairs naked hand in hand.

"I suppose we should get dressed," I said, and she nodded, looking around for her clothes.

"Rose!" my mother shouted up the stairs. I looked at Sarah and made a face.

"Yes!" I shouted. "I'll be right down." Then hissed: "Go!"

She put on most of her dirty clothes from the day before and kissed me once more on the lips. The moment the door closed behind her, I ran to the bed without thinking and leaped headfirst, landing facedown on the mattress with my arms stretched out. There I lay grinning like an idiot. I was due downstairs, but I could not leave the bed we had shared. Breathing very slowly, I forced myself away. More news of Love Hall, no doubt.

The front room presented me with the strangest scene I could have imagined: the usual suspects, of course, but in fantastic states of disarray.

I took them all in before they noticed me, so engrossed were they in their own business. Hamilton father and son had plainly worked the night through, their eyes hollow with tiredness, their hands shaking with nervous energy. Samuel was wearing an amusing white bobbled nightcap, and Stephen a hastily thrown-on waistcoat with no shirt beneath. Sarah was sitting in the window next to Victoria, who was first to see me. She smiled and bowed her head in what I took for the subtle apology that I should be making to her. I had been apart from Sarah for only ten minutes, but I felt that I was looking upon her for the first time.

Her mother was bringing tea into the room in her nightgown, and mine was sitting before the fire fussing with a log that wouldn't catch. Hood, in his usual position by the Hemmen House, was wrapped in a very large towel with, I assumed, some pajamas beneath; this togaed *senex* was the very same man whom I had only recently seen out of formal attire for the first time. They looked like a bunch of rather down-at-heel players awaiting first rehearsal. I stood at the door and considered my entrance.

Hamilton saw me and froze, except for his eyes, which blinked wildly. He removed his cap and then replaced it. Everyone saw him and then me. Hood tried to get up, but his towel became unknotted and he decided that it was less hazardous to remain seated.

"Sit here, darling," said my mother. Yet again we were gathered for the results of someone's investigation, but the atmosphere was vastly different. The other conferences had been such organized affairs, board meetings of the trustees, but this was a reckless frolic, an impromptu picnic instead of a state dinner. I passed among them, picking my way through papers and a map as I did so.

"The lawyer, Mr. Mallion, is coming very shortly, madam, and your . . . Rose . . . ," said Hamilton rather overexcitedly. "So I think we might . . . if we could . . . I think that we should . . ." He could not suppress a beam that shone through the clouds of his furrowed brow. They had the evidence they had been looking for, it was clear. I glanced at Sarah.

"Yes, by all means," said Mother. "Hush! Hush! For Hamilton!"

"Hush for Hamilton!" said Samuel. "Quite so. Hush for Hamilton!" Then he spoke with great care. "Ah, but this is not easy. I speak with conflicted feelings: with a heavy heart, because I have found that my faith in my ancestors, my father and my grandfather, has been misplaced. And yet I speak with joy because the final result of our investigation is a most happy one. There is no simple way to say it."

He started to shake perceptibly. His voice had a catch in it, and as he continued, he avoided tears as best he could.

"Though parts of this story may upset you, you must know that even if you find the facts unbearable, the narrative ends happily. Some of these facts are too painful for me to speak. So I am as of now resigning my post and handing it to my son. My faith in certain of my fundamental precepts has been irreparably shaken, and I feel that it is in everyone's interests to let the future begin today in the hope that the son will be a better man than his grandfather or great-grandfather, and more astute than his father. We are improving in order that we might better, more honestly and more morally, serve your family in the future."

A tear freed itself from his eye and slid down his cheek. His son got up and embraced him, taking his arm and guiding him to his seat. I had never seen Stephen act with such tenderness. Sarah looked on with a frown. Was she thinking about us? No. Stephen's behavior may have been amusing, but her father's was worrying. She rose and went over to kiss him, sitting silently on the floor at his feet, her head on his knee. Stephen was left standing where his father had been. He was the new Hamilton.

"To recap," Stephen began. "As everyone here knows, except perhaps my sister and Miss Victoria, Marguerite d'Eustache, who was secretly married to the Bad Lord Loveall between Catherine Aston and

Isabella Anthony, gave birth to the true Loveall heir and then escaped with the child. She went into hiding, emerging with a new identity, that of the poet Mary Day."

"What?" said Sarah through a laugh. She looked up at her father, who put his finger to his lips. He was still tearful, but now he also had an impish smile: it was as though he and his son had exchanged beings. He stroked Sarah's hair, nodding as he did so. Stephen did his utmost to ignore her interruption with the same dignity that he had so often seen in his father. My mother poked at the fire again. Stephen continued.

"That of the poet Mary Day —"

"The same Mary Day?" Sarah interrupted in wonder. Stephen's guard dropped immediately.

"Sarah, please! You missed that bit." His father admonished him with a simple raise of the hand.

"Shall *I?*" asked Hamilton. Whatever the situation, he would make sure that this was properly managed. Stephen gathered himself.

"Mary Day, the same poet whose works are now in the library at Love Hall. We now know how they came to be there and much more."

My mother dropped the poker, which clanged to the hearth, sending a random flicker of ash across the rug. I looked over at Sarah — she was lost. I wished I could take her in my arms again and explain everything to her, about me, about us — nothing, you understand, to do with the investigation that was working itself out all around. Perhaps the result would take us back to our beLoved Hall or perhaps it would leave us there at Twenty-four, working, happy, together. I was delighted that everyone else was so excited, but it was all one to me now. Mother picked up the poker and set it aside.

"Can you fill in any more of Mary's life?" asked Mother, not daring to look up.

"Oh, yes, ma'am, I can. The books tell all."

Mother said nothing.

"Whether Marguerite actually lived under the name Mary Day, it is impossible to say with certainty; though, from the books we can surmise that she did. Mary Day wrote only secretly, never wishing to bring any attention to herself. She never married again, considering herself contracted to her work, which soon gained a small notoriety in London.

"A printer, Mr. J. Castle of Brooks Lane, discovered the identity of the anonymous author and contacted her — the books were published, but with no initial success and at no profit to Mary Day. Still hiding in London with her child, her work had now taken a more mystical turn; she thought it not only undignified to profit from her poetry but also prudent to keep a low profile with regards to her identity. The work should be published, but she was more than happy not to be associated with it. She thus refrained from identifying herself as the author, and the books that were published during her lifetime were published anonymously . . ."

"'By a gentlewoman of London,'" added my mother.

"These books became desirable among a certain milieu of literary London, initially because of the designs but, thereafter, increasingly because of the poems. They then became earnestly sought after, even while she was alive. There was something of an outcry to discover the identity of the 'gentlewoman of London,' but Castle waited to satisfy this craving until after her death, when the books were first attributed to 'Mary Day,' as she had specifically requested.

"Her son, the heir of Love Hall, knew no father. Previously called Charles, she renamed him Adam."

"Adam — the first man! The only parturient male!" exclaimed my mother. "'Adam, can you stand in anger / Looking out on your new world?'"

Hood harrumphed, mentioned that his feet were cold, and asked if he might have a cup of tea.

"None of this was known to Love Hall at the time, but we can now reconstruct that Adam Day married, in 1764, a girl called Alison Wainwright, the daughter of a woman who worked in service with Mary in London."

"In service? Do we know where she worked?" asked my mother hurriedly.

"Yes, we do but, begging your pardon, we are trying to present the main thread without becoming waylaid by the details."

"Of course," said Mother.

"Good man," said Hamilton, ruffling Sarah's hair in pleasure.

"Adam Day and his wife tried to make their own way in the city. She gave birth to three children — two girls, names unknown, both of whom died in the same year, and one son, a Robert Day, born 1767 — but with London a harsh place, their family struggled. Both Adam and Alison died of consumption just after their daughters, leaving the then ailing and aging Mary to bring up grandson Robert, known as Bob, Day. At her deathbed —"

"How did she die? When?" asked my mother.

"In 1781. It is reported in her obituary in the book —"

"A very curt piece of writing," said his father.

"That she died of a massive stroke after a series of fainting spells she suffered while working, but we are not quite *there*. At the end of her life, she told her grandson the story of her past, her real name, and the identity of his grandfather.

"They had no money, and Bob, a weak man, was unlikely to make his fortune alone. Mary's books were safe, though they earned her no money, and she feared for Bob's future. She determined to arm her grandson with the only weapon that might help him survive.

"After her death, and as previously noted by my father, Bob Day unfortunately did the worst thing he could have done: he sent one of her books, *this* very copy, to Love Hall. Though addressed to the Good Lord Loveall, it was passed directly into the hands of Jacob, my grandfather, who was horrified. He decided to act immediately.

"This was as far as my father previously read, though we have since been able to fill in many of the details and rearrange them into chronological order. The question is: Why did Bob Day send the book?"

"Blackmail?" said my mother. "His only hope."

"Probably," said Hamilton, interrupting his son, powerless to resist his need to explain. "He was a fool. He should never have revealed himself. He didn't realize that the powers at Love Hall would not hesitate to chase down his family even unto their final hiding place. He had no idea with whom he was dealing. Perhaps Mary failed to explain the horror of the situation she had been in. Perhaps she didn't realize how strong the Loveall's resolve remained to eradicate the d'Eustache claim entirely."

"Or perhaps Bob was desperate himself," said Sarah.

The room was silent except for the fire, which crackled obliviously. I saw the last of my clothes disintegrating in the flames outside Love Hall. I became lost for a little while looking at Sarah. I even let some of their words slip past me. I didn't want to delay them for the rest who were listening. Everyone else was rapt, but I was distracted by thoughts of what had happened the previous night, and what might happen that night, and the night after. I wasn't nervous. Stephen and his father were talking all the time. Important details kept scratching at my door, trying to get my attention.

"Love Hall's reaction was decisive," said Stephen. "Jacob sent an agent to find Bob Day, which the agent did immediately and easily. Within two months Bob was relieved of his grandmother's books — everything. The published books left in the world were in no way detrimental to Love Hall at that point. It was the other books they wanted, the notebooks and letters. They had to make certain that, in the event of an increase in her popularity, the contents were never published, that all the evidence was under their control. Unable to distinguish between what might be valuable or harmful and what might not be, they removed the entire collection by force. They intimidated and threatened, and eventually a small amount of money was handed over to Bob Day."

"And then they threw them in the worst and least organized library in Britain," said Mother. "What better hiding place?"

"And they destroyed much, too, I'm afraid," said Hamilton. "What you found might be referred to as the remains of what they stole."

Stephen raised his eyebrows to ascertain that all interruptions were complete.

"From that day on, Bob Day was a marked man. Jacob and his spy noted his every movement. It was an assiduous and painstaking piece of persecution undertaken, unfortunately, entirely by my grandfather and his agent in the outside world. It is likely that the Good Lord Loveall knew nothing about it. Jacob made sure that Bob Day was never able to keep a job, that he was for a while condemned to the debtors' prison, and even once that he was falsely accused of stealing and suspended from the one decent position that he ever attained. Day was paying for his own stupidity, but he could never have anticipated that he would become a puppet whose strings would be pulled by Love Hall for the rest of his life.

"However, he did manage to marry, a woman called Rebekah Lacey — not even the malevolence of Love Hall could prevent it — though the union was at the mercy of his invisible nemesis and his wretched fortune, and it was to end tragically. Love Hall knew exactly how to keep him down. They gave him money to prolong his miserable life but carefully kept any means of self-sufficiency out of his reach. The only other lapse in their utter subjugation of Day was their failure to prevent him from loving his wife, and she soon became pregnant. It was at this time of increasing financial desperation that Bob Day made a further rash bid for money.

"The next we hear of him in the books, he is dead and the Loveall have lost all track of his wife and child. Jacob had quickly contacted the most reliable mercenary that they knew, a member of the Loveall's own family: Edred Osbern. It is not stated definitively in the books that Edred murdered Bob Day, at the instruction of our family, but a substantial payment was made to Osbern for unspecified work performed on the twenty-ninth of September 1793, and we can only speculate as to its nature. It is also probable that it was Edred who had wrested the books from Bob and dispatched them. Edred had become the paid assassin of Love Hall."

"Edred Osbern," said Stephen's father, shaking his head.

"Always was a nasty piece of clay," said Hood, out of the blue. "Geoffroy and I detested him. We raised a large glass of port when he died."

"Perhaps this murder was why Love Hall chose to keep their distance from the Days for a little while, fearing that their continued spying would bring down suspicion. By the time the Loveall — or perhaps I should say the Hamiltons — felt that it was once again safe to look for the Days, the widow Rebekah and her child, the new heir to Love Hall, had disappeared again, a regular habit and a fortunate skill of the Day family. Perhaps the frantic mother realized that a new identity was all that could save them."

Stephen had braced his legs and stood in front of us. He had become more comfortable as the talk progressed, like a professor giving the first lecture of his first term, not yet entirely at ease in his role. How odd that he would become his father. We had all thought it would be Sarah — the more practical sibling. I kept watching her, my eyes flitting across the room, then casually landing on her as if they could quite equally have landed on anyone else. I longed for her to return my gaze, but her eyes were fixed as she took it all in, stunned by the story she was hearing. I loved her frown.

"This left Love Hall in a difficult situation. Was it safe to leave the Days alone, to assume they would never try to communicate further? Jacob decided not: it was time for decisive action. However, as we now read the books, we are of the opinion that although Jacob continued his father's work with an uncompromising brutality, it was the corrupt element of the endeavor that ultimately killed Jacob. The spark of humanity left in him drove him to his grave. The books become increasingly personal, and Jacob's death, reported as an accident, can, in light of the evidence in the books, be assumed to be suicide. His last words read: 'We do not want to implicate our son Samuel in these matters, disturbing as they are. It is best if they are gone with me. Amen.'"

"I had suspected it," whispered Hamilton, who was crying, head bowed. Angelica stood behind him, her hands on his shoulders. His son knew that the best thing he could do to honor his father was to soldier on.

"Jacob tried to pick up the trail of the missing family to finish off the business. He felt that the matter was best dealt with swiftly, privately, and without concerning his lordship, who had never shown the remotest interest in these comings and goings. In effect, and it is with shame that we draw this conclusion, the Hamiltons were acting entirely independently at this time. Upon the Good Lord's death, however, there was no way to avoid apprising Lady Loveall of the situation. She was horrified, appalled at the possibility of the failure of all her plans on account of some stray paupers who would never be missed.

"She therefore demanded 'an end to the matter forever,' which Jacob could interpret in only one way. He took her at her word, and though he tried to wash his own hands of the deed, he was primarily responsible for what was intended as the murderous eradication of the Day line. Edred Osbern was already 'in pay,' according to the book, and was therefore retained to find the rest of the family. He died before he was able to complete his commission, immediately before my grandfather took his own life.

"My father," said Stephen, pointing to Samuel as he did, "in ignorance of this story, and without the ability to read the books that we now have in front of us, took over Jacob's position at Love Hall. Though he was now in sole charge, he was unaware of the machinations around him: in the world of espionage, many hidden things might be buried deeper by an unexpected death, and such was the case with Jacob's. Only Lady Loveall knew of the continuing persecution of the Days, and she would now communicate only with the new agent, a man to whom Edred had handed his work before his death and of whose identity neither she nor Jacob was sure. In fact, Edred and his apprentice had worked together to locate the Days. Osbern had decided to keep the dependably regular coin that accompanied the post in the family, so he continued his secret work with the help of his son, a man known to all of us, who succeeded him as agent at his death —"

"Esmond!" I shouted. Everyone looked at me. I was still the only person who knew the truth of Esmond's disappearance.

"Esmond Osbern. Edred handed his work to his son, as my father handed his to me. A mercenary works for money, and Edred would have known better than to cloud his son's judgment with tales of the whys and wherefores of his work. Esmond merely had instructions that he put into effect. He was tidying up some loose ends for a family with a generous purse.

"Esmond located the remaining family, now comprising, since Rebekah had died, her daughter and her daughter's husband, living in Bethnal under the husband's name. They were doing relatively well in the world for this pitiful area. They had no great riches but had managed to pull together enough to work a small sewing business. They were expecting their first child."

My mother started, and I watched her staring intently at the fire, deep in thought, her hand in front of her mouth. I could imagine why. Mary's relatives might still be living in London: imagine the possibility that she could talk to the real descendants of Mary Day. She looked at me, then at Hamilton.

"Here the notebooks stop and here the facts run out," said Stephen, "for the obvious reason that this narrative ends with the death of my grandfather, and the story of the Loveall continues with my father's book, which is entirely innocent of these matters."

"Thank you, Stephen. You have done very well. All I can say with certainty," said Hamilton, "is this. Two days after the death of Lady Loveall and your arrival at the Hall, Rose, I received a message to give to Lady Loveall. The message read . . . I don't have to remember it, for I have it here."

From the back of his notebook, he took a piece of paper as dry and fragile as a pressed flower, its folds entirely disappeared. The author had written in the middle of the page and then folded the rest of the paper around it and sealed it with wax. Hamilton read: "'For Jacob Hamilton's son to deliver to Lady Loveall. Only for her eyes.'" He turned the paper over and read the simple message: "'The marriage is consummated. All three will live happily ever after.'"

"By the time I received the message," Hamilton said, "Love Hall had changed beyond recognition. Lady Loveall was two days dead and there was no one I could pass this message to. I myself did not understand its meaning, and there seemed no point in giving it to the Young Lord. The author did not know that there was no one who might possibly understand what he was reporting. The message was only ever received by someone who had no idea what it meant: myself. And it was never interpreted. Until now, when the meaning is clear. It refers to the murder of the woman, her husband, and her baby."

There was a pause.

"But the message was not true," said Stephen.

My mother was staring at me with a troubled expression. I looked around for Sarah's help, but her gaze was fixed upon her father.

"Rose, this next part is for you, I think," my mother said. She was crying. "And for me." Hamilton looked at me in a very particular way.

The air became thin and it was as though I had suddenly climbed a very steep hill and my ears hadn't properly acclimatized to the pressure. I was trying to put pieces together, but I was too confused to come to any conclusions: it would be better to leave the puzzle scattered all over the floor, to finish another day when I could do it at my own speed. Time was crawling and everything sounded muffled. Sarah wasn't looking at me. Stephen wasn't looking at me. Nobody was looking at me. Hood, however, was looking at me with the pitiful face of a bloodhound. Stephen continued:

"Of this, Rose, we can be sure. Esmond Osbern murdered the father, whose name was Laurence, and scared the mother into either having the child killed or inducing early childbirth so that she might somehow escape. She, in a desperate state, resorted to an establishment nearby. The house was, we can construct from other accounts discovered by you and me, Rose, less than a quarter mile away from their sewing business and was run by a woman named Mother Maynard. The unmarried name of the woman who died that day was Bryony Day. The husband's last name was McRae."

My mother, as if unconsciously, stood up from her chair and leaned on the mantelpiece over the fire. All eyes were now turned to me.

"Their baby," he continued, "assumed and reported dead by Esmond, and everybody else, miraculously survived, ditched by a runner and cared for, for a few moments, by a dog. The child would come to be called Rose."

My heart started to beat again. I hadn't been listening properly. I'd missed something while I'd been looking at Sarah. They were playing a trick on me because they knew that I hadn't been paying attention as closely as I should have been.

No.

No. They were serious. This should have all been about Love Hall, but somehow it was all about me. I had missed vital elements of the business. I wished Stephen would start again from the beginning, and I thought of asking him to do so. I wished he would say it all once more a good deal slower. Perhaps his father should do it with no interruptions from anyone at all. But there was no chance of going back to the beginning, because everything was happening too quickly. My mother wouldn't even look at me. She was looking at her fire, lost in the glow. I realized that I was staring distractedly about me as though I had just been found standing over a butchered corpse, bloody knife in hand. I couldn't quite catch anyone's eye.

I was sweating and felt very cold and weak.

Breathe. Breathe.

"Mother!" I spluttered, and the spell was broken.

She was behind me, hitting my back with her fist as though I were choking. "Stop it!" I tried to tell her, but I *was* choking and I couldn't get the words out for coughing. All around me, suddenly, mayhem: laughing, cheering, crying, the sound of china breaking, a dog barking even though there was no dog, and I heard Hood ask loudly: "It's good news. Is there tea? Shall I be mother?"

Stephen had told me precisely who I was.

I knew who I was.

I didn't even dare think about the rest of it. It had been acceptable having only the name of the mother; and if that hadn't been quite enough knowledge, then this was much too much. A mother and a father. In a single flash, I realized that my mother's, Hamilton's, and my investigations had all converged at this single point.

My birth.

There was more. . . . My father had been murdered by . . .

"Childs!" I screamed.

"Yes, Esmond," said Stephen. "Childs."

"Children," said Hood deliberately.

I was crying and laughing, gulping big mouthfuls of air. My mother was trying to help me, but her frantic attempts only made things worse.

"Stop!" I yelled. *"Stop!"*

Everyone tried to stop but, like a very drunk party of people playing musical chairs, no one could. I couldn't even quite understand what everyone was doing. We were in a frenzy, a crazy clock with the hands spinning round backward and forward. Slowly, we wound down. I was still coughing sporadically.

"What does it mean? Tell me!"

My mother looked at me with tears in her eyes. Hamilton stood and bowed.

"That your parents were Bryony Day and Laurence McRae," he said.

"And that they were murdered by Esmond at the instruction of Lady Loveall and my grandfather," said Stephen.

"That you are Mary's great-great-grandchild, her only living relative," said my mother, who was smiling and crying in such a way that she seemed beyond easily defined emotions.

"And that you are the heir to Love Hall," said Hamilton.

"Yes." This was the part I had least trouble grasping. It was the rest of it that was incomprehensible. I felt more my mother's child than ever. Who could ever deny that my mother was alive, in this room?

"The last living descendant of Adam Day, the only legitimate son of the Bad Lord Loveall," confirmed Hamilton, brandishing some written piece of proof that was clearly upside down.

"But what about the Osberns?" I asked, trying to pull my mother to me. It was as if she was frightened to come any closer.

"How can we care anymore?" asked my mother.

"Yes, but the house is not theirs," said Hamilton. "They have no choice. Mr. Mallion will be here any moment, and he is utterly confident. They have no claim at all."

"I don't understand," I said.

"We are all going home," said Stephen.

"Together?" I said.

"Yes," said Sarah.

I looked at my family all around me. The revelation seemed so irrelevant.

Cousin Victoria, the tomboy, poured a drink for Hood, our senile elderly retainer, who hadn't got his tea yet but cupped both hands ready for the brandy as though drinking water from a stream. My mother embraced Samuel and Angelica, our lifelong family friends, always close by when we needed their assistance. Above the fireplace, a portrait: my dead father, smiling down on us, and next to him, a picture of his sister, an aunt I never knew, who died too young and left him friendless until we came into his life. My brother Stephen, who once saved my life, came toward me as though he'd just finished his final examinations, recklessly tossing papers in the air, smiling, holding out his hand to me and then, thinking better of it, hugging me. He pulled himself to me, and Sarah came and joined us, too. I couldn't see her exactly, but she insinuated her body somewhere among our arms, and the three of us took a tumble onto the floor, flailing and fumbling as we did so.

"Rose, watch out!" laughed Stephen. I heard my mother squeal with joy as she watched us topple. I hit the floor first and let them fall on me to the music of winded groans and laughter.

5

N 19 SEPTEMBER 1839, the day before my nineteenth birthday, we set off early in the morning to travel in raggle-taggle style to Love Hall, and a merry party we made. The nature of the event suggested the wisdom of safety in numbers, but it was I who had the bright idea of turning this piece of business into a pleasure trip for all, incorporating an outing for the workforce of Bellman & Farrow (formerly Geo. Bellman) and a mystery tour for myself; and it was I who had chosen the date for Family Council.

We rode in the first carriage: Sarah, Angelica, my mother, and I. You were with us, of course. Above in the cheap seats were Bellman, Pharaoh, and Alby, but no Mutt. Pharaoh had never ventured beyond the city, and he was powerless to resist the urge to serenade "nature's sylvan finery" as we traveled. His voice floated down on the breeze, punctuated only by agitated requests that the singer repeat himself so the scribe could catch up. Bellman was having a fine day out: "The boy's simmering and will soon boil, mark my words!"

In the second carriage traveled the men — Stephen and his father (who had been prevailed upon to defer his retirement), Hood, and

Mallion the lawyer — our advisers who shared the day entirely, and in the last came our cousins the Rakeleighs.

It was one and a half years since the great discoveries. There had since been eighteen months of meticulous planning, hard work, and further revelations, including hours of legal advice from Robert Rakeleigh's mentors and the turnover of an entire staff at a reputable firm at Gray's Inn due to incompetence spotted by our resourceful Mr. Mallion.

There had also been an exceedingly slow correspondence with our usurpers as we sought an interview. Thrips stalled and prevaricated on their behalf, having no notion of the true nature of our purpose. In order to secure a meeting, Hamilton was forced to resort to the obscurity of the family lex. Today would see the culmination of our labors.

Tradition dictated that any living lord or lady of Love Hall, present or past, could convene Family Council. My mother, though exiled and in disgrace, was just such a person, and Hamilton, faced with Thrips's solid forward defensive and having no other recourse, readily exploited her privilege, citing this barely remembered and never-before-used statute. Three possible dates were submitted for their consideration, from which they chose the most remote. We needed to give no reason to claim this right, and the Osberns most certainly assumed that we would entreat them for funds.

Thrips's next communication to Twenty-four assured us that though the lex dictated Love Hall — or Playfield House, as he insisted calling it, as though we were talking about two different places — host and attend the council, its inhabitants had no interest in the affair and were entirely humoring the poor outcasts. Condescension dripped from every inky flourish of his pen. When he was notified that every member of the family was expected to attend Family Council, he responded by inquiring whether this precluded an appearance by "the once Lord Rose." By separate post, he drily inquired whether it was specified what kind of weather should accompany such an event.

His greatest irony, however, was reserved for discussion of the venue. Thrips made it clear that Augustus and Nora would not welcome us within the house itself; Hamilton responded that the lex specified "in Love Hall." After a brief epistolary debate about whether this phrase should be defined as "inside the grounds of Love Hall" or "within the walls of the house itself," Thrips, much to Hamilton's annoyance, returned with an unassailable argument. In an unusually playful letter, he detailed measurements he had made of the ancient boundaries of Love Hall, or Playvered's Manor as it was then known, using as his source the unimpeachable authority of the Domesday Book. The front limit of its precinct was found to fall precisely halfway between the door of the current Hall and the front gate. Love Hall therefore respected our right to admittance within this Domesday perimeter, which would be painted white. However, we would be allowed no closer to the house than another line, which would be painted gold, the position of which would be precisely ten feet inside Love Hall according to these ancient measurements.

"Let them have it where they want," said Hood, his feet in a bowl of hot water and salts by the fireplace. "They'll get theirs." Our elderly retainer, now unable to serve in any other capacity because of shaking hands and swollen feet, was now most useful in his ability to keep our spirits high with his candor. Between him and Pharaoh, afternoon tea had begun to resemble a food fight.

Our motley caravan arrived at the front gate of Love Hall to find itself denied a prospect of the house by two sumptuous marquees bedecked with gold and festooned with flags and banners that glinted in the sunlight. A greedy magpie sat atop one of the stanchions, alerting her friends and family to the dazzling treasures all around.

"Ah! The Field of the Cloth of Gold of 1520, where Henry met the French in great splendor," exclaimed my mother as we alighted. "I so love a tableau."

At the nearest edge of the main marquee, a white line (which seemed to circle the whole of Love Hall like the boundary of a cricket pitch) marked off the edge of Playvered's Manor, and beyond this, through the middle of the marquee, lay the gold line we could not cross.

"Very *much* like the Val Doré, the spot upon which Henry and Francis met," she continued. "The similarities are remarkable! I wonder whether the fountain is plumbed to flow with wine."

At Calais, she reminded me (not, I thought, that I had ever known), the French had stood, according to the national poet, "all clinquant, all in gold, like heathen gods." They shone the British down. In their place, in this golden marquee, it was the Osberns who shimmered. The Osberns: we called them by no other name. We could not bring ourselves to call them the Loveall they desired to be, and we didn't care to impugn Julius's family by making reference to the Rakeleighs among the Osberns' number.

Our party hadn't quite planned where to stand by the time we entered the marquee, but the Osberns were set up before us like chess pieces. Augustus, his face bedecked as lavishly as the marquees themselves, and Nora were clearly king and queen, flanked on either side by Bishop Praisegod and, in place of his father (who, if Nora was queen should have been, at the very least, queen's bishop), Reliance, his devilish brother. The relative positions of Guy and Prudence, though they were lord and lady of the house, revealed them as no more than pawns. Anstace stood beside them, brimming with wizened pride: doubtless she had been asked both as spectator and as symbol and source of their triumph. Between them, these Osberns represented to me everything evil in the world: the Seven Deadly Sins, the Four Last Things, and the violation of all Ten Commandments.

On the periphery stood Edgar and Edith, the only two wearing black, as they mourned the loss of her daughter. Neither rated a place upon the board. Footmen secured the various portals of the tent so a breeze could blow between us, and then stood guard over every entrance.

"Now, remember, Rose," my mother whispered in my ear as we faced them. "At Calais, Henry challenged Francis to a wrestling match and was immediately thrown by him. Diplomacy ground to a standstill. No wrestling."

"I'm not wearing my wrestling clothes," I said, and smiled. In fact, if there were to be a fight, our side had both the numerical and muscular advantage, but it was no time for fisticuffs.

I glanced at Hamilton. He and his recent ally, Mallion, had left nothing to chance. Sarah and I were in the middle, facing the king and queen. To her right, her brother and parents; to my left, my mother and the Rakeleighs, but I should not give the impression that we were carefully arranged. This was just the way we had fallen out of the box. Mr. Mallion stood with three uniformed gentlemen who represented the law, the local watch (a rather nervous addition), and the Fourteenth Leakhamptons. Behind them stood the entire firm of Bellman & Farrow, all three delighted to witness a ballad in the making.

The two sides faced each other. There was silence and stillness, as at daybreak before the order to attack. For some reason, I could hardly recognize Prudence. She looked distracted and somewhat plain: childbirth had taken something from her. Hamilton coughed and opened a book from which he read some Latin text. Stephen then Englished it for the benefit of all.

"Anonyma Wood, Lady Loveall, has called Family Council, as laid down in the Lex Pantophilensis."

"I don't know a lot about the ins and outs," Augustus called across the divide, puncturing the moment, "but are librarians allowed to call Family Council?" The remark was met with sniggers from Guy and a harrumph from Julius to my left. Stephen tried to press on, but Thrips immediately interrupted.

"We understand the nature of the lex, this out-of-date and obscure volume you wave as your standard. The present lord and lady of Love Hall no longer wish to be bound by the decrepit rules of unknown, irrelevant ancestors. Whatever laws they are you speak of have been revoked, are revoked as of now," said Thrips.

"I revoke them," said Guy, raising his hand.

"Oh, well done, Guy," said Prudence without looking up, emphasizing each word equally. "I am going to Ivy. She is more important than this farce."

"Commendable," said Augustus, then raised a thoughtful finger and asked ironically: "If the councillors will permit?" But Prudence had already turned to leave.

"She'll be crawling all over the house, that's what Ivy does," called Guy. "Anstace can go."

"Thank you, sir. Can I fetch her for you, ma'am?" offered Anstace promptly, happy to demonstrate a deference she had never shown us.

"No, not you," snapped Prudence over her shoulder. "I am the mother. I shall go."

"Children." Nora forced a smile, though whether she was talking about Ivy or her parents, it was impossible to say. Guy yawned. Augustus wearily surveyed his own, then turned his attention to us.

"We are here," said he, "solely to humor you in your precious council. As you requested, we have rallied as many of our number as we were able, though you see they are dropping like flies. Please say your piece and be gone."

"So far we have managed but one sentence," said Hamilton in unusual exasperation, "while you have not yet been silent! We have repeatedly tried to communicate with you. You have paid us no attention, fobbed us off with your officious supernumerary. You have forced us to this."

"If your request is reasonable, you may find us generous," said Augustus, not in reply, for he had ignored him entirely. "Put it before us. You will know our mind in writing."

Their contempt beggared belief, and I could stand no more. I looked at the hulking Augustus and his lunar-cratered skin, his fatty wife more repellent than ever, and his son, an abusive and prematurely drunken sot. Between them they had sucked the character from Prudence. It was shame at her familially ordained humiliation that had driven her from the tent, and I pitied her. I looked at Nora, at her sons by the two brothers, and the sad Edith, for whom no children remained.

"Sirs, madams, say what you will. The laws of Love Hall are irrevocable," I said, intending to continue.

"Oh!" said Guy in disgust. "Do we really have to suffer speeches from *this?*" His father hear-heared him, and Reliance joined in.

"Yes, it can't be tolerated. I feel as if I'm being accosted by a traveling theatrical company."

Of all the family, Nora alone seemed thoughtful, as though she had observed the seriousness of purpose on our side of the Val Doré, the sense of mission that kept us from rising to their bait. She hushed Reliance with a raised hand.

"This charade quickly loses its charm," she said. "It was a bad idea. Why are we here? Have your say."

"Madam, you may depend upon it that we shall," I said and curtsied, a provocation I had not intended.

"You look absurd, sir," roared Augustus. "You sound absurd. You are absurd. Obviously, your Grand Tour did you no good at all. I discount everything you say."

Nora silenced him as she had Reliance. In her opinion, they had but to bear some minutes of indignity before Family Council was done, never to be heard of again.

"Then I shall say very little," I said, stepping from the white line where we were clustered and into the no-man's-land between the two families. "But, please, we come without malice. We have done you no harm. Have we no mutual ground? Do not we all believe in the greatness of the Loveall? We have set off on the wrong foot. This Family Council needs a blessing. Let us pray for the family: those who are part of the family and those who aren't. Who will help us in prayer? Praisegod?"

Praisegod, whose uncharitable eye had been upon me as I stepped close to the golden boundary, stood rather taller when I mentioned his name, but his father interrupted.

"If I may, I should like to offer a prayer of blessing," he said.

"Yes, Edgar, please do," said Edith sincerely as Guy groaned and then made a snoring sound. I took my place among my family.

"Please bow your heads. I should like to use as my prayer the Sermon on the Mount in Matthew, chapter five. Let us pray."

I kept my eyes open, like a headmaster on the lookout for misbehavior during morning chapel. Some bowed and shut their eyes, others put both hands flat together. Anstace clasped her hands so tightly that her knuckles whitened. Edgar began:

"Blessed *are* the poor in spirit: for theirs is the kingdom of heaven. Blessed *are* they that mourn: for they shall be comforted."

Edgar took Edith's hand in his to comfort her for her recent bereavement, as was proper.

"Blessed *are* the meek: for they shall inherit the earth. Blessed *are* they which do hunger and thirst after righteousness: for they shall be filled."

He squeezed Edith's hand more tightly during this beatitude and drew her to him. She seemed uncertain how to react. I caught Victoria's eye and nodded her in their direction.

"Blessed *are* the merciful: for they shall obtain mercy."

From the Osberns' side of the Val Doré, Edgar led Edith toward ours as he continued his prayer. She was anxious, but he would have none of it. I noticed that Augustus was watching, too, that he didn't know what to make of it. I squeezed Sarah's hand to get her attention, but she hushed me, fearing, I suppose, that I might try to make her laugh. She liked a prayer.

Edgar delivered Edith into our midst just before he said his amen. There was a general murmur of reluctant agreement and those eyes that had been closed for appearance' sake opened to find the arrangement of people quite reconfigured. Edgar and Edith stood with us.

If the Osberns were surprised, the Loveall were far more so: communication with Edgar had been nil since he had helped Victoria with the books. Clearly, in the intervening time, he had experienced a vision of a better future.

"Edgar!" It was Nora who broke the silence.

"My dear, dear woman," said Edgar, turning to Edith, pinpricks of sweat on his brow, "I offer you my protection." She looked around and hung her head. It was all the agreement she could muster.

"Traitor!" said Praisegod.

"Join me, Praisegod, my son," said Edgar.

"Join you? I disclaim you."

"No loss," said Guy. "Let him go with the paupers. More for the rest of us."

"No church will ever employ you," said Praisegod. "I shall see to it."

"So be it," his father replied, "if it be His will."

"I am your wife, Edgar." Nora was seething, her verminous eyebrows twitching with displeasure.

"So help me God," said Edgar, "you were."

"Amen to that!" I said loudly as the remarks and epithets flew from side to side. It was pleasurable to watch this unexpected drama spit and crackle in front of our eyes, but I had more coals to throw upon the fire. "The Family Council! Ladies and gentlemen, the Loveall Players are proud to present 'The Ballad of Rose Loveall' by Mr. Farrow."

It was Pharaoh's moment. We moved aside to let this ungainly man pass. Behind him came Hood, pushing (and leaning heavily upon) a perambulator, from which emerged happy gurgling and a plump little foot with five wiggling toes.

"A baby. Oh joy!" sneered Nora, who bore the loss of a husband with little difficulty.

"Oh, my Lord," said Guy in disbelief. "They're going to let this oaf sing?"

"Do you want money for the baby? Julius, brother, I implore you. Tell us the reason you are here!" said Augustus.

"Pharaoh!" I commanded. "Sing."

"I have two songs," Pharaoh proclaimed. "One is new writ, though it has taken me some time to con, called 'Do Not Fear the Dark, or the Seamstress of Bethnal Green'!"

"No!" thundered Augustus. "We shall not be sung at! Thrips, can we stop this now?"

Thrips attempted to answer, but Pharaoh, whose sole motivating force in life was to deliver a freshly minted song, would not be deflected. All Augustus's power and money was no match for Pharaoh's will to sing.

"'The Seamstress of Bethnal Green'!" Pharaoh bellowed, loudly enough to silence everyone, but then he immediately lost the thread.

"Now! Sing!" I whispered, and he sang, thoughtlessly rocking the carriage from side to side.

It fell upon the Eustace Eve, all close by Bethnal Green
A pretty little seamstress lived in a house so mean
Her husband's name it was McRae, her own was Bryony
And her apron would not fit her, a family there would be

And in the quiet of the night, she dreamed a cruel dream
The pretty needlewoman who lived close by Bethnal Green
Death would come unto her and take the child away
She woke in such a fright upon that dark and dismal day

In Bethnal on the Eustace morn, evil is abroad
And when the sun has risen come a knock upon the door
Don't let him in, my dear, his name you first must learn
He is a noble soldierman, his name is called Osbern

On the floor lies poor McRae, all murdered in his gore
As Osbern turns to Bryony, a-wipin' of his sword
A-wipin' of his sword, he says, no more now shall you sew
And I'll speak for you and your baby with but a single blow

And as he stepped up to her, the seamstress she did flee
All through the streets of Bethnal and to the Rookery
She went into the bleeding house to hide herself away
But Death was waiting there just as the dream did say

Oh Death, oh Death, my babe's not born, do not take her from me
It is not she I take from thee, but you must come with me
Oh Death, Oh Death, have pity, please, though I must say good-bye
Save my precious little child who wasn't meant to die

And God is good and merciful and on his grace we thrive
For though her parents two were killed, the babe she did survive
So, helpless babes and children all, pray do not fear the dark
For though the thunder roars, your God will send to you an ark
You little babes and children all, do not fear the dark
For when the Day seems over, yet the daylight isn't far

Pharaoh had taken us back to Mother's and beyond, just as he had taken us there that very morning on our way to Love Hall. He finished his ballad as he always finished a ballad, by repeating the title once more and bowing: " 'Do Not Fear the Dark, or the Seamstress of Bethnal Green.' "

As our side of the family burst into applause, I clearly heard Bellman whisper to Alby: "By crikey, that's certainly made the trip worthwhile!" Guy did not share his enthusiasm.

"What was *that?*" he asked.

"It's a song, Guy," said Nora. "A silly song."

Augustus seemed delighted with this turn of events.

"If the reason you are here is to have a simpleton sing a bizarre concoction of a song that lampoons someone with the name Osbern, then by all means sing the other one. The boy has a passable voice."

"Listen to 'im," said Pharaoh, turning around to us as he rolled his eyes and tried to swallow his lower lip. " 'The Ballad of Rose Loveall,' as requested by the subject."

This next offering, a complex variant of "The Abandoned Baby Saved from the Hounds," with facts newly known inserted, took us back to his trip to the dustheap. He sang of Annie, the men hot on his heels, the two policemen, and the man with the scar whose sword was disguised as a walking stick. He sang of his journey through the wastelands of the city to the dustheap and its canine guardian. As he sang, I thought of the morning's mystery tour.

We had retraced Pharaoh's steps, when he carried me to the edge of the city, as precisely as possible. The other two carriages rendezvoused with us at the dustheap to form a caravan to journey to Family Council, thus retracing my father's journey.

A bizarre sight we must have been when we reached Mother's, Pharaoh and I walking in front, with the horses at a slow trot, pulling the carriage just behind us. Every now and then Pharaoh would say, "Yes, yes, here, yes!" and duck down an alley, where carriage could not follow but I could. Only a few minutes later, we would emerge back onto the main road to find the carriage exactly the same distance from us. I could have taken you with me, carried you close and warm, but I didn't need to take you on every winding path. Besides, you were happy with your mama in the carriage.

"This was where you was!" Pharaoh at one point shouted up to Bellman, who watched us with amused interest from the crow's nest on top of the carriage and reported our progress to those inside.

"No, no, dear boy, I never stood here," Bellman shouted down. "Way off my patch."

"You were here. You did the Mary Arnold jig on this very spot," said Pharaoh, looking down as if he'd find a footprint.

"By jingo! I think he's right," said Bellman, whose lot had risen so sharply in the world that he had conveniently forgotten the details of his previous penury, though Alby reminded him often enough.

Pharaoh took us past the twelve clocks, rather as the worm crawls than the crow flies — he remembered it all as though it had happened yesterday. Finally we made our circuitous way through the back streets and arrived at the dustheap, where the other two carriages were waiting. It was a journey I had now made twice in my life. . . .

". . . 'or the Abandoned Baby Saved from the Hounds'!"

Pharaoh's repetition of the title and a further sharp round of applause woke me from my reverie.

"Is that the voice of the people? I don't like the sound of it," said Guy, who, like me, had not listened closely to Pharaoh's story. Others among the Osberns, however, divined that something more important had been sung, though they did not know what.

"We are well aware, sir," said Augustus, "of the sordid details of your birth. Must we live them again and again?"

I stepped forward and, putting my hands into the cradle, lifted up my baby. I could see the front of the great house beyond the Osberns and I presented you to the Hall, and Love Hall to you. You had been so good, never crying (for you had known Pharaoh's voice as a lullaby ever since birth), and your mother knew just how to keep you quiet, filling you up on the journey down, and you the only boy in a carriage full of women to make a fuss over you.

"Ladies and gentlemen!" I held you above my head. "It is a boy."

"There's a relief," said Guy. "Like mother, like son." But the joke was old. No one on his side laughed.

"And you have spawned this helpless whelp with the serving girl?" said Nora.

"Is it pertinent," asked Augustus, "except as a further stain on the family name you claim to revere?"

"I present to you the next heir of Love Hall, Adam Loveall."

Augustus started to splutter with laughter. Guy joined him.

"Deranged!" said Thrips. He walked toward Hamilton in an attempt to corner him. "We have had intimations of your pitiful attempts."

"Keep your man from my father, sir!" said Stephen. "You will deal with me now."

"This changes nothing," hissed Thrips with a shrug, and slithered back to Augustus.

"On the contrary, sir," I said, and curtsied. "It changes everything. The librarian, the serving girl, the lackey, the oaf . . ." I indicated each one of them. "Now you can call them what you will. In the future, you will have to be more formal to address them at all." I handed you to your mother and kissed her. "Hamilton and Mr. Mallion here have the necessary papers, ratified by the appropriate signatures."

"Out!" shouted Nora. "Out of my house!"

"We are not in your house," I said dismissively.

"God damn you all," said Augustus.

There was a moment's silence. I walked forward, turning around and looking at my family with a smile. You had had enough by now and were just about to cry — and who could blame you? It was unseasonably hot inside the marquee — so your mother was surreptitiously unbuttoning the front of her shirt.

I walked slowly toward the Val Doré, all eyes upon me. I hesitated as I reached it and lifted my skirt, making sure there was a telling display of stocking and perhaps even a hint of garter, and allowed myself a very balletic next step, pointing my foot and allowing it to hover in the air just above the line.

"Sir! Do not dare!" said Nora.

There was a sharp intake of breath from Thrips. I imagined the tensing of every footman's calf.

And with my skirt above my knee so that every muscle, every sinew, could be seen beneath my stocking, I touched the tip of my toe to the ground on the Love Hall side of the golden line. Then I breathed out and looked up. No signal was given.

"Voilà!"

"Remove yourself from our property immediately," said Nora.

I planted my foot firmly down.

"It is not your property," I said, "though we shall remove ourselves. We leave you with some documents about the inheritance of

Love Hall: Mr. Mallion has them. I shall give away no more of the ending. And there is also a dark folio entitled *The Shorter True History of the Loveall:* Stephen has that. Pay particular attention to the signed testimony of Esmond Osbern; also feel free to ask questions of Sergeant Pickersgill of the Fourteenth Leakhamptons, who has that man in his custody for gross moral turpitude — the sin, Praisegod, not to be named among Christians. We shall be gone in a moment, but to return. Whether we will see you at that time, only you can know. Before we leave however, we shall pay a visit to the Mausoleum, to introduce the next heir of Love Hall to its last true lord."

I gestured to my family, and they walked toward me without hesitating as they passed over the Val Doré. The Osberns, seeing that we were not to be stopped and that their footmen were letting us pass, parted like the Red Sea. Hamilton, who pushed Thrips out of his way with his little finger, led the procession with, behind him, Angelica, Mallion, and Stephen, who persecuted Thrips further by using his ledger as a shelf on which to load the heavy portfolio of documents; Pharaoh, Alby, and Bellman, who bowed deferentially at every Osbern as if he only regretted not having been properly introduced, followed with Hood, who used Alby's arm and the perambulator as his crutches, and Lord and Lady Rakeleigh, who acknowledged nobody. Victoria and Robert, allowing themselves a victorious smile on behalf of the oppressed everywhere, came next; followed by my mother and Edith and Edgar (who kept as close to our party as possible).

Bringing up the rear of this colorful parade were the three of us, with Sarah to my right, I holding her left hand, and you, sucking greedily on the nipple of her right breast.

As we emerged on the Love Hall side of the marquee, Stephen started to run, whooped, and threw his hat in the air. He made straight for the Mausoleum and Rubberguts, and the rest of us couldn't help but follow his lead, running wild across the front lawn of the great house.

"I'll get the bat and ball," Stephen shouted. "Boys against girls!"

I wasn't watching, but Hamilton saw the Osberns leave their grand marquee in desultory single file, his nemesis laden with reading matter, shepherded back into the house by our officials. They might as well have disappeared into the ether or walked out through the front gate then and there, for all I knew, as we made a ring-a-rosy and skipped among the cowslips around the roots of Rubberguts till Stephen returned.

He brought a blanket for you and your mother, the only ones excused from the game, paced out the pitch, and placed down the wickets. As if by magic, an orchestra, bigger than any we had ever had, appeared. The kapellmeister announced in troubled English: "Compliments of Lady Prudence and Miss Baby Ivy." My mother thanked them and instructed the kapellmeister upon a program. We gathered around the blanket.

"Stephen and I shall be captains," I said as I made a silver twopenny bit appear from the back of my hand.

"Heads or tails?" I said, and tossed the coin as far as I could, watching it twinkle in the sun above the Playfield vale as it rose to its peak.

"You choose," said Stephen.

Full Stop

I'm ready.

I remember the first time I returned to Love Hall after our exile, now many years ago. The house hadn't been long deserted, but it felt haunted.

No. No. That's already been told. What of today?

Today?

Now.

I can neither leave my bed nor get comfortable lying down. However, if I put my head on the pillow at just such an angle, and if the curtains are open as they are now, I can see Love Hall. Smoke billows from the central chimney and the flag is flying at half-mast. This means that I am dying.

Soon it will be I who haunts the house. At least, I hope it's soon. Then you can write my ghost into the guidebook and I shall give the odd visitor a fright.

I have to leave the rest to you. Can I?

You know you can. Don't tire yourself. Just say what you want to. You've reached the end.

Of my life.

Of the story. People don't want too much explanation anymore.

They're all dead. My mother, you'll barely even remember her, but she bounced all of us on her knee. Dear old Stephen and Franny, their children scattered around the country, and two of their grandchildren dead in the war. Victoria, always working, never in love. Uncle Pharaoh sung his last. Good-bye. Your mother, my love — what now, thirty years? You and your sister and your families still all around me, aren't you? And little Ivy.

Rose, Ivy is seventy.

She'll always be little Ivy, that one. She'll be taking the tour around now, won't she? I used to love sitting at the register, taking everyone's two shillings and tearing their tickets. I never liked touching the actual money very much, so I always wore gloves, but I loved the looks on people's faces as they came through that door, as though they'd walked into a dream. At that moment they were children again, all innocence. "Fairy-tale splendor," that's what Mother wrote in the book.

I can hear Ivy now. I used to listen three times a day to whoever was on tour duty: "Please take care to walk between the purple ropes. To your left, in the glass case, a first edition of Johnson's famous dictionary, the first dictionary in the English language, published by Dodsley in 1755, original cost four pounds and fifteen shillings in boards. But you couldn't buy it for that today, of course." (Pause for polite laughter. I used to join in from the till, just my little joke.) "This way to the Long Gallery . . . ," and off they'd trot. Then they'd all have their tea and troop off one by one to the flush toilets.

I remember when there were only two bathrooms in the whole house, and neither of them had a flush. Now those lonely private rooms are everywhere, each complete with its own noisy flush, and a sign outside for GENTLEMEN or LADIES, to avoid unwitting blushes, but what difference does it make anyway, if everyone's sitting down? In the baths at Bristol when I was young, men and women were never separated, but now it's all prudery and suspicion. Anyway, the signs never affected me one way or the other: I went where I chose.

I am lost. Where was I? Tell about Esmond. And Edgar. And don't forget to tell about Little Ivy. How she lived up to her name, sweet little thing.

Why don't you tell?

Tell what?

Ivy is Aunt Prudence's girl.

And Prudence was married to Guy.

And?

She'd had a baby, but the poor little thing didn't have his red hair, and he started telling tales of Prudence's infidelity, which we always . . . Shh! . . . About which, we *never asked,* let's put it that way.

One day Edgar found her cowering in the church, with her baby. He took her in to his cottage, and was like a father to her till the day he died. He'd left the church of course, after his divorce, and that's when . . . I'm . . .

Little Ivy.

My goodness, what a girl! It was worth the price of admission just to hear her rattle everything off. She could get people through so efficiently. I always saw her in the military. That war would never have taken so long, mark my words. She'll be moving them through now.

It's Ivy's girl, Esme, now: you know that.

Oh, that Ivy: all the best bits of her mother. Is there still a queen?

You know there isn't.

I forget. I remember the first time I returned to Love Hall after our exile, now many years ago. The house hadn't been long deserted, but it felt haunted. . . . I had a vision of our future — a nightmare in truth. I saw us sitting about for the rest of our born days, running out of time and money, fending off challenges, milked dry by spongers, bled by the taxman. I didn't want us to end up huddled around a small fire in an out-of-the-way wing while the rest of the house fell to rack and ruin, as though we were the sole clientele in a huge and perpetually out-of-season hotel.

Your mother and I had been attending Friends' meetings with Victoria. And in that thrilling silence, which sometimes lasted from the moment the madman rose to proclaim that there was a Terrible Day of Reckoning upon us (which he did every week, without fail) before walking out . . . in the silence between that and the reading of the notices, I came to see a preferable alternative: to be rid of it all.

"In this life we may, in some degree, be whatever character we choose": Boswell said that. Johnson's dictionary reminded me of it. And furthermore, one can begin one's life again at any time one chooses. Today, for example, but never tomorrow. You cannot wait till the end of your own life to change it. You must do it now. What was I talking about?

You wrote: "The pathetic coupling for inheritance, for example: I could stop it. There was too much wealth in the hands of a disproportionate few — and we were these few — and these disproportionate few lived in overly large houses, like ours, to which they admitted too few acquaintances." We rather changed that, didn't we? Rose?

(Silence.)

"They intermarried incessantly, always for financial improvement. This contraction of their worldviews and their imaginations led to stories haunted by increasingly unearthly phantasms. My conclusion was simple — this lifestyle hadn't the ghost of a chance.

"For our family, plots could be different from this moment on. I had been put on earth to challenge convention, and the least I could do was see the challenge through. We didn't have to make the same mistakes over and over again. That old life was ready to die, begging to be put out of its misery, and we would do the deed."

It was a mercy killing. A mercy killing.

Let me read what you wrote. You rest. "With the help of your uncle and his father, I made a simple plan. In the short term, Victoria took over the house and ran it as the Friends' hospice, with room for everybody in the healthful air of the Playfield valley. In the longer term, we would bequeath Love Hall to the nation. And so we moved to this cottage, which I always loved. When I was a child, I used to envy your mother's family down here, so cozy. And we gave them the Hill House in perpetuity. Your mother and I, and you and Eve: we were always happy here."

So happy.

"And it is now up to you, Adam, as both the Last Lord Loveall and the acting Hamilton, to oversee the transition. You have managed everything so well. Your mother and I were always so proud of you.

"Victoria moved here, with some of your many aunts from London, and Love Hall began its metamorphosis. Your grandmother, God rest her soul, kept the library, of course, and finished her great book before she died. She brought Bellman's old printing press to Love Hall, and acquired him a more modern affair for the shop in London, and she taught Uncle Pharaoh as they made their ballads together in the library. 'Every great house should have a balladeer,' she said.

"And her rather idle invitation to the villagers to see the library developed into a guided tour around whatever part of the house did not disturb Victoria's work. And news spread wide, until Mother decided to print a guidebook on her press, so she wouldn't have to run around so. That same text has been developed and changed a few times since, but it's still essentially what Esme will be saying now and what's on sale by the register.

"And people came from farther afield until we had the idea to start making them pay two shillings. We were one of the first houses to realize the potential of this, but it made us money that we did not require — so we put it all back into the hospice and subsequently the hospital that we built under Victoria's direction." Rose? Rose?

Is it time for meeting?

Not today.

I cannot go.

Shh. Relax. Shall I go on reading?

I used to read, and now I am read to. I used to write, and now I dictate. Father, Sarah!

Full stop.

AMOR VINCIT OMNIA
ROSE LOVEALL

Appendix

Excerpts from:
A GUIDEBOOK TO LOVE HALL, PLAYFIELD
(©2000 The Love Hall Trust and The English Heritage Committee)

Nestling in the quiet valley of Playfield, the magnificent Playfield House, affectionately known as Love Hall, is one of the jewels in the crown of the English countryside.

Explore the mysterious history of this great house. Step back in time as you wander through the spectacular formal gardens and lose yourself on the estate, in a forgotten world of belvederes, follies, and surprise views. View the renowned collection of paintings in the Long Gallery, just as your eighteenth- and nineteenth-century predecessors would have done: including artworks by Stubbs, Batoni, Eugenius, Rossetti, Holbein, and Blake. Browse the literary wonders of the Octagonal Library, including the definitive collection of the female poet Mary Day. (Free with admission.) And perhaps if you're lucky, you will meet the legendary ghost of Love Hall — don't worry: she's friendly!

And remember: Love Hall was once a working house, full of bustling servants going about their daily work. Animatronix™ figures bring the servants' quarters to vivid life once again for the twenty-first century in a series of son et lumières in kitchen and laundry. Fun for all the family!

Refresh yourself with favorite house recipes served with contemporary flair at the Tea Shop, located in the Lesser Stables. (Lunch is available until

2:30 P.M. If you wish to picnic on the grounds, you are most welcome to do so. Please take your litter home.)

Before you leave, visit the gift shop. (Wheelchair accessible.)

The Garden

Enjoy the eccentricity of the Gothic Folly and the delightful surprise view of Love Hall from the perimeter walk.

Mind the ha-ha! Many country houses have a ha-ha, a wall disguised from the perspective of the house, similar to the magnificent example at Love Hall. In other great houses, such a wall either conceals an unsightly thoroughfare or keeps livestock (otters, badgers) inside and stray sheep outside, though the particular reason for the ha-ha at Love Hall is unknown.

There is a plan to the planting scheme of the parterre garden available. (Please note that the scheme is subject to occasional variation for environmental reasons.)

#1. The Grave of Rose Loveall

Rose Old or Miss Fortune
1820–1918
Shy of her Maiden Century
Loved by all
"You can not impersonate
What you are."
Voilà!

The history of this great house stretches from the Dark Ages to the present day, but in its pages, there is no more symbolic figure than Rose Old. Rumors of her rags-to-riches life are legion, yet surprisingly little is certain. What we do know of her life has been deduced from the libraries, galleries, and corridors of Love Hall. More will be known when her memoir is available for publication. This will occur upon either the one hundredth anniversary of her death or the demise of Jeffrey Loveall, whichever is first. Until then, find out about Rose from the pink informational plaques (identified with numbered roses) placed throughout the tour of the house.

Children are encouraged to play on the unique **Seesaw and Chair** to the left of the grave. Legend has it that Rose herself sat in the chair.

THE LONG GALLERY

#520. ***Pharaoh and Mutter,*** artist unknown (1842). Pharaoh has been identified as the house balladeer, Mr. Phillip Farrow (see notes for the Octagonal Library). It is clear from the tag on his collar that the dog is called Mutt, yet the title *Pharaoh and Mutter* is painted on the canvas, as can be seen. A baffling mistake by the artist.

#521. ***Mary Protecting Loveall and His Family*** by Vincento Chevenix (1860). An allegory in which the Madonna protects the Loveall family under her wings. Although it is certainly not the Madonna, attempts to otherwise identify Mary have been fruitless.

#523. ***The Turkish Girl*** (Frances Hamilton, née Cooper, wife of Stephen Hamilton) by A. B. Thijssen RA (1841). A magnificent oil of a young woman in Turkish garb, as was the vogue. Note the inclusion of the Love Hall Mausoleum behind her, here depicted in a more exotic Mediterranean setting.

#533. ***Rose Old*** by an unknown painter. One half of the subject's body is dressed in male clothes, and the other in female clothes. This is a copy of a portrait of the Chevalier d'Eon, a small engraving of which is displayed next to the picture of Rose Old.

#534. ***Isabelle Anthony*** by Jerome Montdidier the Younger. REMOVED FOR CLEANING.

#535. ***The Young Lord Loveall,*** a posthumous portrait by Rowan Bryars (1848). The central figure of the Young Lord Loveall is surrounded by whimsical references to a fairy tale of the artist's own invention: the house surrounded in roses and briars, unicorns at pasture, poisoned apples, a magical transformative pool, and an evil witch casting a shadow on the trunk of a tree. Though Bryars was the first female painter exhibited in the New British Gallery, she has been long ignored in her home country. The Love Hall Trust, in tandem with the English Heritage Committee, is now planning the first major exhibition of the paintings of Rowan Bryars, including, for the first time in England, the notorious exercises in symbolism *La Vie Sexuelle.*

#544. **Portraits of the Young Lord Loveall and Lady Dolores Loveall,** twin allegorical portraits by Eugenius (1799).

#550. ***The Rakeleighs*** by Stroud Kettle (1820) — oddly, this painting is always kept amid a collection of Mullerys in the livestock section. The young child in the painting is Guy Rakeleigh, of whom C. P. Fontwater, in his essay "Bad Men of Yore," memorably noted: "He almost never married." For unknown reasons, there is affixed to the bottom-left corner of the frame a muzzle.

#557. ***The Bad Lord Loveall*** by Cornelius Von Klank (1742). This famous painting has become more commonly known as "Intimidating the Artist." The official name is *Lothar, Lord Loveall, depicted in his garter robes, after van Haarlem.*

The Octagonal Library

Before you enter, note the defacement to the list of librarians above the door. Many years before the trust took over Love Hall in 1998, an unknown vandal chipped the word *BOY* into the masonry. The previous owners requested that it be left as is. (See later discussion of the monograms in Love Hall.) The library is dimly lit for reasons of conservation. Please watch your step.

#320. **A collection of ballads by Pharaoh (Phillip Farrow),** the house balladeer, printed by the Anonymous Press of Playfield. Read pink plaque #17 adjacent to the ballad case for further information about "Do Not Fear the Dark, or the Seamstress of Bethnal Green" and the double murder of Bryony and Laurence McRae.

#326. **The Anonymous Printing Press.** For over a hundred years, the Loveall Foundation has bestowed grants and offered use of this press to those poets interested in exploring the further reaches of traditional printing techniques. Some examples of this work are in the adjoining glass case, including Pippa Grey's first poem, "Between the Word and the Page."

#327. A first edition of ***The Day Light: A Biography of Mary Day*** by Anonyma Wood, first published by the Anonymous Press, now in over a dozen reprints. Though no longer the definitive biography, this revolutionary work remains the standard by which all others are measured. Next to it, a manuscript copy of "**Notes for a Future Biography of Mary Day**" by Anonyma Wood.

#329. **An original manuscript of the Mary Day poem "Their."**

Their own not mine
My own not thine
Their air to breathe
My own not mine
Mine is Adam
Mine is Eve
Their Heaven is
Their air to breathe

Yours to confess
Theirs to own
Theirs in congress
Yours alone
Their own not mine
My own not thine
Their air to breathe
My own not mine

#330. **Mary Day's original notebook**, open to the poem "The Second," excised from her book *All Loving, Lord, Giving All:*

Married, almost ruined, God's union excepted
Rest in this evil danger endlessly
Unless I sever the alliance
Currently happily estranged

THE GREAT CHAPEL AND MAUSOLEUM

The Loveall were not a religious family, and family lore has it that the chapel was built only to balance the house architecturally. Ardent Quakers, later generations of Loveall were more often found at the Playfield Friends' Meetinghouse, built with money donated by the Loveall Foundation.

OTHER POINTS OF INTEREST

#600. **The Hemmen House**. Though not primarily a dollhouse at all, this scale model of Love Hall is considered by many to be one of the finest of its type in the world today.

#801. **Georgian Amboyna Chair**. It is unclear whether this chair belonged to A. Pope, the Bard of Twickenham, or a pope. (You may sit in the chair.)

#803. **Loveall Loving Cup**. A unique silver two-handled loving cup. The right handle is the bottom of the letter *g,* and the left handle the top of the letter *d,* with *la* on the body of the cup itself. (Note the monograms *AgL* and *Glad,* which can be seen throughout the house. These are assumed to be Masonic.)

#821. **Unicorn Horn** upon a plaque. An unexplained curiosity (probably manmade).

Suggested Further Reading

Ackroyd, Peter. *Blake* (London, 1995).

———. *Dressing Up* (London, 1979).

———. *London The Biography* (London, 2000).

Allen, Susan Heuck. *Finding the Walls of Troy* (Berkeley, 1999).

Barbin, Herculine. *Memoirs of a French Hermaphrodite* (New York, 1980).

Beaumont, Francis. *Paraphrase of Ovid's "Salmacis and Hermaphroditus"* (1602).

Brewer, John. *The Pleasures of the Imagination* (London, 1997).

Bronson, Bertrand. *The Traditional Tunes of the Child Ballads, with Their Texts, According to the Extant Records of Great Britain and America.* 4 vols. (Princeton, 1959, 1962, 1966, 1972).

Bulliet, C. J. *Venus Castina* (New York, 1956).

Burford, E. J. *Wits, Wenchers and Wantons* (London, 1986).

Child, F. J. *English and Scottish Popular Ballads* (New York, 1965).

Colapinto, John. *As Nature Made Him* (New York, 2000).

De la Falaise, Maxine. *Seven Centuries of English Cookery* (London, 1973).

Dreger, Alice Domurat. *Hermaphrodites and the Medical Invention of Sex* (Harvard, 1998).

Fowler, Marian. *Blenheim: Biography of a Palace* (London, 1989).

Girouard, Mark. *Historic Houses of Britain* (New York, 1979).

———. *Life in the English Country House* (New Haven, 1972).

Hogarth, William. *Engravings by Hogarth* (New York, 1973).

Holloway, John, and Joan Black. *Later English Broadside Ballads* (London, 1975).

———. *Later English Broadside Ballads.* Vol. 2 (London, 1979).

Kates, Gary. *Monsieur d'Eon Is a Woman* (New York, 1995).
Lind, Earl. *The Autobiography of an Androgyne* (New York, 1918).
———. *The Female Impersonators* (New York, 1975).
Mayhew, Henry. *London Labour and the London Poor* (London, 1851–62).
Ovid. *Metamorphoses.* Trans. by Arthur Golding. (1567).
Parsons, James. *A Mechanical and Critical Enquiry into the Nature of Hermaphrodites* (London, 1741).
Sneyd, Walter. *Portraits of the Spruggins Family arranged by Richard Sucklethumkin Spruggins (1829)* (National Trust, 1985).
Thompson, C. J. R. *The Mysteries of Sex* (New York, 1974).
Thorold, Peter. *The London Rich* (New York, 1999).

National Trust Guidebooks, passim.
English Heritage Guidebooks, passim.
Fortean Times, passim.

ACKNOWLEDGMENTS

On behalf of the Love Hall Trust, I would like to thank my agent, Jennifer Rudolph Walsh; my editor, Judy Clain, and my publisher, Michael Pietsch; Dan Franklin and Rachel Cugnoni; Diane Richardson and the Oskar Diethelm Library, Institute for the History of Psychiatry, Weill Medical College of Cornell University; Morgan Entrekin, Frances Coady, Stephanie Cabot, Rick Moody, Nigel Hinton, Christopher Stace, Amanda Posey, Jonathan Lethem, Shelley Jackson, Molly Mandell, Kurt Bloch, George Makari, Mark Linington, Robert Lloyd, David Grand, and, most of all, Abbey Tyson.

Books that were particularly helpful in various areas of my research include: Girouard and de la Falaise for Love Hall; Ackroyd, Burford, Mayhew, and Hogarth for London; Ackroyd, Kates, d'Eon for contemporary attitudes to cross-dressing; Allen for the life of the Coopers in Turkey; Barbin, Lind, Dreger, and Colapinto for insights into gender psychology; Child and Bronson for folk ballads. Certain verses of Mary Day's poetry paraphrase the Gospel of St. Thomas and the Gospel of Eugnostos the Blessed; the quotations in the last chapter of "Metamorphoses" concerning hermaphrodites are from Parsons; and those in the last chapter of "Land of Dreams" are from Beaumont.

About the Author

Born in Hastings, Sussex, and educated at Cambridge, Wesley Stace writes and performs music under the name John Wesley Harding. He is currently at work on his second novel and his fourteenth album. He is married and lives in Brooklyn.

Back Bay Readers' Pick

Reading Group Guide

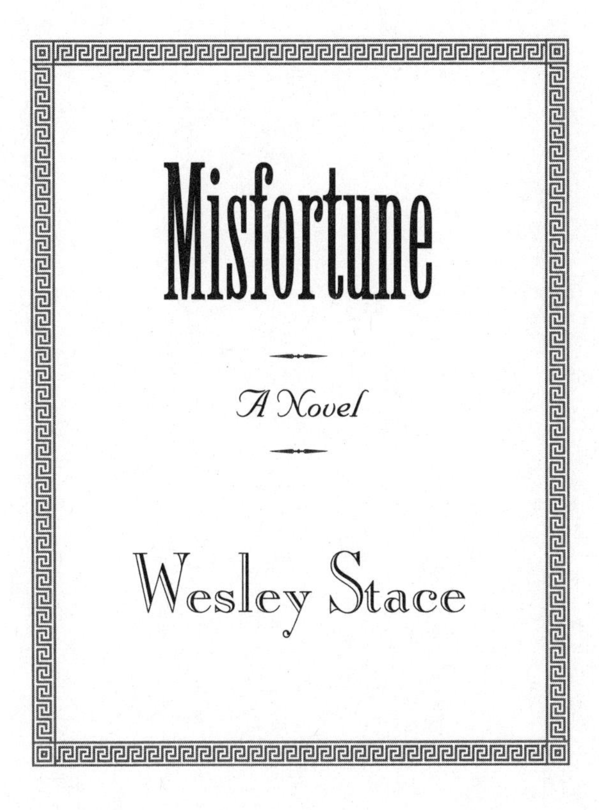

Misfortune: The Novel of a Song

Wesley Stace talks about the origin of his first novel

How did you come to write Misfortune*?*

In 1997, under my musical name of John Wesley Harding, I recorded a song I had written called *Miss Fortune.* These are the lyrics:

I was born with a coat hanger in my mouth
And I was dumped down south
I was found by the richest man in the world
Who brought me up as a girl
My sheets are satin but my mind's a mess
But there are worse things I confess
Than drinking tea in a pretty dress
And I'm here to tell you that it's not all bad
Count your blessings and maybe you'll be glad

When he died, I inherited his wealth
And I revealed my self
I was snubbed by the friends he'd never had
Who sided with my dad
All my riches are beyond control
But it's the same old rigmarole
They say I've lost my very soul
Maybe I have
But I'm here to tell you that it's not all bad
Count your blessings and maybe you'll be glad

And as I grew so did my fame
So I gave it up and changed my name

It's catch as catch can and
You'll never know who I am

When I died, I hoped to hear the angel's song
But was I wrong
They threw me back there in that lane
They said, "Start again"
So when you're turning out the bedside light
Consider me and my wretched plight
Looks like I'm gonna have to get it right this time
But I'm here to tell you that it's not all bad
Count your blessings and maybe
You'll be glad *

I sang *Miss Fortune* many times in concert and realized that the story of the nameless narrator was far from finished. Feeling a certain amount of responsibility for this poor transvestite foundling I had created (and then ditched in the last verse), I realized I wanted to delve further into the story, to finish it, as it were.

In outline, I used the song as a blueprint till the end of the bridge. The song begins, "I was dumped down south / I was found by the richest man in the world / Who brought me up as a girl." That's fine in a song; it's all you need to say. But in the kind of book I wanted to write, it's useless. The reader wants to know: *Why? Who? How?* When I brought the child, now called Rose, to life, I wanted her to be surrounded by believable characters with understandable motives. I wanted reasons why (s)he was reared in this unique way: why a father would raise a male child as a girl, why the household would support him in his delusion, and what sort of mother would possibly go along with it.

 The original recording can be found on John Wesley Harding's album *Awake* (APR 1040).

The more I tried to have everything make sense, become both emotionally and historically satisfying, the more complex the novel became, until I couldn't stop till I was done. This was an incredible amount of work with no promise of publication since nobody knew about it. But I felt fulfilled bringing a world to life. I hadn't seen this book around, and I thought I'd like to read it myself.

Why did you choose to set Misfortune *in the nineteenth century?*

In practical terms, the past generally was very suggestive for the themes of the novel — before Victorian times, fashion between the sexes was much less clearly delineated; boys weren't trousered until relatively late. Also, Rose needed a hothouse atmosphere in which to grow up, and an English country house seemed ideal. The genre of the nineteenth-century novel was also helpful — the story of the rags-to-riches foundling.

But, more important, by setting the story in the past, I was able to write more purely about things that are important in the present. In previous attempts at novels, I had felt the need to try to skewer things satirically — Subarus and cell phones and *Cooking Light* magazine. I needed to bring all that in because it's how my mind works, but I didn't *want* to bring it in. The past made me look beyond the things that had needlessly held my attention and focus on people and their feelings, their loves, their emotions.

I tried not to fetishize the past, so I didn't get caught up in a whole different realm of irrelevance. I determined very early on not to have it be a pastiche of nineteenth-century literature. I wanted it to be a modern novel set in the past. I decided to call a carriage a carriage, not a barouche or a brougham or any of the thirty-seven Eskimo words for snow.

Who are the greatest influences on Misfortune*?*

The first section of the novel was originally written as if narrated by Henry Fielding ("God," as he is called). I pulled back on the pastiche somewhat, but I still think of it that way. Dickens himself actually appears in the novel: he is the man who is trying either to help or to hinder Pharaoh at the end of the first chapter — Pharaoh decides it's the latter. This a true story from Dickens's life, which I found in Peter Ackroyd's biography, and I thought it would be interesting to narrate this from the boy's point of view. Dickens definitely haunts *Misfortune.*

I wanted the tone to be somewhere between Dickens and Trollope on the one hand, and Angela Carter, Mervyn Peake, and the world of magical realism on the other. I wanted to write a novel that creates a whole world and tells a complete story, a bildungsroman, a coming-of-age story — but with a subject matter they couldn't have written about in the nineteenth century.

The book could possibly be described as Gothic, given the large country house and sometimes grotesque characters, but it is a particularly sunny and colorful kind of Gothicism, far away from the gloominess often associated with the genre. One review said that Love Hall was like the Secret Garden or Narnia, and that's exactly right. It's a pleasure palace that turns into a ghost train — the things that make it nice are then the things that make it nasty.

Music seems to play an important part in Misfortune, *which of course isn't all that surprising. Were you aware of this as you were writing?*

In some ways, Pharaoh is a kind of self-portrait, though not so much of me particularly as of all songwriters and their unstoppable need to write songs, stealing a little phrase here and an old tune there, adding a little of their own personal experience, coming up with something new, just to keep singing. It's probably no coincidence that the mechanism of the plot of *Misfortune* works only because a songwriter witnessed the crucial scene.

Of course, as I was writing them, Pharaoh's songs came with melodies, so I subsequently recorded these along with some of the other folk songs that weave their way through the book and are so important to the world. These songs describe either the action (*Lambkin,* at the very beginning) or the characters (*Lord Lovel, Lord Bateman*), or simply create an atmosphere (the many songs that make up the beginning of *Land of Dreams*). The songs were released on an album called *Songs of Misfortune* under the band name the Love Hall Tryst. The book certainly doesn't need the CD, and I hope the CD can be enjoyed without any reference to the book — but, for those interested, they both exist.

Why does the novel have an appendix?

The reader, by the end of the book, actually knows far more about Love Hall and its history than the writers of the contemporary guidebook, who have not yet had "access" to the papers presented in *Misfortune.* The reader knows why the loving cup has the initials GLAD, and why the portrait of Pharaoh has a strange name that the guidebook supposes to be a mistake. I wanted the appendix to throw a historical perspective on the lives of the characters in *Misfortune,* and to show that, though these stories are changed and exaggerated by the heritage industry, the truth will ultimately be lost, despite the Animatronix characters, gift shop, and son-et-lumière. However, there is further information in the appendix as well, things that have happened since the novel was written — what Rose did between the end of the novel and her death, for example — and though the writers of the guidebook can't understand the implications of this information, the close reader can.

Questions and topics for discussion

1. Could the events narrated in *Misfortune* happen in the present day? The world described in the novel is an exaggerated one, but would it have been any easier to bring a boy up as a girl in the nineteenth century than it would be now?

2. Are Geoffroy and Anonyma sympathetic characters? Could/should they be?

3. "The message of the book is the radical notion that we should empathize with others, however odd, and that this would make the world a better place." (This statement is drawn from Monica Kendrick's review of *Misfortune* in the April 8, 2005, issue of the *Chicago Reader.*) Do you agree? What might our world look like, in that case?

4. Of what other works does *Misfortune* remind you? How do you react to the mixing of postmodern devices, contemporary mores, and Dickensian style that characterizes this novel?

5. While Rose's experience of adolescence could not be called typical, *Misfortune* makes much of self-discovery and the glory of a person coming into her own. In what ways is this story familiar? What observations does this novel make about adolescence, and about self-realization?

6. A particular writer is referenced in the name of the second section: I Am Reborn. Who is this and why?

7. How would *Misfortune* be different if it weren't, in part, a rags-to-riches story? In what ways would the drama of the story change?

8. How did you react to *Misfortune*'s full-circle ending?

Wesley Stace's additional suggestions for further reading

The novel's appendix comes with its own reading list of the many books I used for *Misfortune,* but I thought I'd recommend here five other books that I used in research, and five novels that I consider important to the world of Love Hall.

Nonfiction

1. *London Labour and The London Poor* by Henry Mayhew

   An astonishing and compendious work in four volumes: verbatim interviews with the working and criminal classes of London in the mid-nineteenth century. It's the birth of oral history, a great sociological study that rivals the best fiction, and a place to find a thousand plots and characters.

2. *Monsieur D'Eon Is a Woman* by Gary Kates

   The story of the Chevalier D'Eon, the transvestite French spy (1728–1810), who is quoted by Rose ("Voilà!"). He claimed to have been born female and raised as a boy; but at his death, he was revealed to have been a man more comfortable in women's clothes. Fascinating reading.

3. *First Childhood* by Lord Berners

   First volume of autobiography by the eccentric English composer, raised in a world rather like that of Love Hall. The nonfictional equivalent of Wodehouse, these memoirs of Berners's exceedingly peculiar childhood are, simply, hilarious.

4. *Life in the English Country House* by Mark Girouard

   A book that helped me create Love Hall as an amalgam of all the great country houses of Britain — beautifully illustrated.

5. *As Nature Made Him* by John Colapinto

   The tragic story of a bad medical decision and its consequences. After a botched circumcision, David Reimer was sexually reassigned and brought up as a girl called Brenda. Despite the arrogance of the doctor in charge, Brenda's masculinity could not be repressed. A major broadside in the nature/nurture debate, this book was a terrific find when I was thinking about Rose Loveall. (Sadly, David Reimer has since committed suicide.)

Fiction

I have always been interested in books about children aimed at adults — this finds its way into *Misfortune* — and the first four books here are certainly in that genre.

1. *A High Wind in Jamaica* by Richard Hughes

   This is perhaps my favorite: children on their way back to England from Jamaica are kidnapped by pirates. A book that is eerie, macabre, and unsettling in its depiction of the children's relationship with their kidnappers. Published in 1929, *High Wind* is *Lord of the Flies* before its time, or alternately, older adventure novels with added Freud.

2. *The Shrimp and the Anemone* by L. P. Hartley

   The first volume of the Eustace and Hilda trilogy. A masterpiece from the very first image, where Eustace tries to save a shrimp from being eaten by an anemone and ends up killing them both. The trilogy depicts the power shifts in the siblings' relationship and includes some of the most perfect sentences in English.

3. *Moonfleet* by John Meade Falkner

   Written in 1898, a thrilling smuggling adventure set on the south coast, with all the right ingredients: hidden vaults, missing diamonds, a village full of characters, and Elzevir Block, who, through thick and thin, guides the young hero, John Trenchard, back to his rightful place. Also highly recommended are Falkner's wonderful novels *The Nebuly Coat* (Trollope meets Hardy) and *The Lost Stradivarius* (a story of demonic possession by a piece of classical music). He wrote a fourth novel but left it on a train.

4. *The Story of Ragged Robyn* by Oliver Onions

   The best novel ever to come from an author's dream? A menacing gang of thieves threatens Robyn Skyrme as he walks home along the seawall — if he talks, they will return to kill him in seven years. He talks . . . and spends the next seven years living in the shadow of their threat. Written in 1945, the book has the spellbinding feel of an old ballad — I have never felt this so clearly in another book — and a shocking ending. Unfortunately, very hard to find!

5. *Fingersmith* by Sarah Waters

   Rather than name any of the actual older novels — *Tom Jones, David Copperfield, Tristram Shandy* (my favorite novel), all of which were a great influence — I pick this novel, which I didn't read until afterwards. *Fingersmith* drags meaningful plot back into the modern novel: cunningly narrated, artfully planned, sexy, moving, Dickensian, and Gothic, yet never parodic. What more do you want?